RAVENOUS

A Dark Cowboy Romance

BLACKTHORNE RANCH
BOOK I

THEA LAWRENCE

Edited by
BEN BROWNING

Author's Note and Content Notes

While Preacher and Ripley get their HEA, they are extremely twisted and disturbed vigilantes. This book is the darkest thing I've written to date, and deals with deep trauma and EXTREMELY disturbing subject matter, including human trafficking.

You are free to go in blind if you wish, however, I always want readers to feel safe and prepared for what they're about to dive into.

Please use the QR code or click this link to see the full list of content warnings:

For my fellow animal lovers: Preacher has two dogs who are never harmed in this book.

Please take care of yourselves, and read at your discretion.

For every woman who's ever been called wicked.
They haven't seen anything yet.

"Hell is empty, and all the Devils are here."
- William Shakespeare, The Tempest

I Can Live Without It
RIPLEY

JERICHO, ALBERTA CANADA

I should stop stabbing him.

I *really* should stop stabbing him.

He's screaming out for help with a voice that sounds like broken glass— crying out for god, or his mother. I always thought he hated her; seems kind of hypocritical to want her now.

Gabriel grasps my arm and holds on tight as his eyes widen in fear. He looks nothing like his former self: golden-haired and menacing with that awful spray tan and those horrible fucking tattoos. I thought this would be harder, but the memories only make me want to drive the blade further as I keep him pinned to the floor between my thighs.

Now his chest is barely more than ground-hamburger, and everything is red.

A gurgling noise bubbles from his chest as he struggles to take a breath, reminding me of the sound my old fish tank made. His mouth parts, and blood leaks out like honey, sweet and forbidden. I feel a strange compulsion to lean over and lap it up, shuddering as I realize it'd probably be the most intimate thing we've done in years.

Suddenly he lurches up at me, grabbing wildly for my throat as I strain to hold him down. He noticed me hesitating.

"Oh, sweetie no," I bring the knife down again, slicing his forearm right open "You don't get to do that to me anymore."

He lets out another pained howl and I can feel the twisted grin grow across my face.

"I'm gonna kill you," he sputters, flecks of blood flying from his mouth. "I'm gonna fucking kill you!"

"You and I both know that I'm the only one getting out of this alive," I snarl.

I bring the knife down, plunging it into his throat. His body twitches in one final attempt to fight back, but it's far too late. I can feel his grip on my arm slacken as a slow, rattling noise fills my ears.

His final breath.

Out of all the research I did on death, nobody ever wrote about the quiet aftermath, and for a moment I let myself just sit in the eye of the storm. Outside, the birds are chirping, the sun shining through the window and making the room glow a vibrant red. When I look back down at Gabriel, slack jawed and dead-eyed, all bathed in that warm light, I feel...

Euphoric.

But it doesn't last long before the memories return: all the times he slammed my head into a wall, choked me until I blacked out, burned me with cigarettes. All the times he brutalized me.

My body is littered with memories of him.

The permanent kind.

Most people who traffic women and girls aren't the strangers hiding in the shadows. They're not tying shit to your car, or stalking you in the grocery store. Most of the time, it's a partner, or a close friend who wants to 'get you out of a bad situation.'

When I was 17, he promised me a way out of my oppressive home and my overbearing mother, and I said yes without another thought. Of course, I didn't know he would end up dragging me straight into hell.

Our relationship started out as one big party, but over the years I learned that's how they trap you. There were always endless amounts of drugs and booze, anything you could ask for, and slowly but surely I got added to the list. Gabriel offered me up to his friends like a prize, and he made money doing it. Sometimes I was a bargaining chip, others his toy, but after a while I realized I only had one option.

I stare down at him, the blood on his face glistening in the sunlight, like oil sitting on top of a puddle after a rainstorm. My mouth waters, jaw tingling, and I gently glide my fingers through it.

It's still warm.

I find myself leaning forward, like I'm being pulled down by a force I can't control. My lips part, and suddenly my tongue is gliding across that smear of crimson. I hear myself groan as the taste of copper spikes my tongue, and I'm quickly overwhelmed by a horrifying dread.

What am I doing?

What the actual fuck am I doing?!

But just like with the stabbing, I can't seem to stop myself.

Heat rushes through me and I bite down into his lip, hard enough to pierce it with my teeth. That same euphoria I felt earlier comes rushing back, mixing with a morbid curiosity. What would happen if I just... bit it off?

I slam my hands down on the floor beside Gabriel's head and start to yank on the lip until I feel the distinct sensation of ripping flesh, nauseating and fascinating all at once. I spit it out into my palm, staring at it like a science experiment gone wrong. It looks like a little piece of raw chicken glazed in blood and spit.

I look back down at Gabriel, at his glazed eyes, and his rotting teeth staring back at me, newly revealed.

I fucking hate him.

All the horrible names he called me, the horrible things he did, they all come rushing back to the surface. Killing him wasn't enough. I want to destroy him, to ruin him in every way possible, to remove every trace of him.

I bring the piece of flesh to my lips, a shiver running through me as I bite down.

It's a unique kind of rubbery, like a cross between gelatin and a piece of overly-thick gristle, but I can do this. Something inside tells me I have to. Or maybe that's just the post-murder giddiness kicking in? Why the fuck would I do this, does it even make sense?

And then, just as I'm starting to regret the whole thing, a loud bang from outside startles me. Maybe a car backfiring?

I suck in a sharp breath.

I try to breathe, but my airway is completely blocked.

I start to cough but I choke.

Oh god, it's lodged itself right in my windpipe.

I can feel it wiggling around in there like a little slug.

I try to pry it out, but it's lodged so deep I can't reach it anymore.

Shit.

I scan the room, my eyes falling on the dresser covered in cigarette butts and beer cans from a party Gabriel had a couple of days ago.

I jump to my feet and rush over, aiming right for the corner. I slam myself against it so hard, the piece of flesh launches out of my mouth like a cannonball. It bounces off the mirror, leaving a bloody saliva print behind before tumbling down onto the dresser.

I straighten, fresh air rushing into my lungs as my whole body shakes with each step, and I narrowly manage to avoid slipping in the brand new pool of blood. This entire house wants me dead, so it's probably about time I get out of here.

No time to think about what the fuck I just did.

I crouch down next to Gabriel, taking a few moments to rest before fishing his phone out of his pocket and using his thumbprint to bypass the lock. There are 15 Tinder notifications. Maybe at one point I would have scoffed in disbelief, but this is par for the course with him. He wanted a prisoner waiting at home while he got his dick wet somewhere else, and when he got back he'd take all his frustrations out on me.

"How you got all these women, I'll never know," I mutter. "You always had the personality of a big toe."

I scroll through his texts, but they're mostly boring. Sexts to other women, pictures of him shirtless, and more of his little cock. It's surprisingly thin, and crooked like a witch's finger. I shudder just thinking about it.

No time for that now, I'm looking for something very, very particular.

"Did you delete it, Gabe? Oh, sorry, I guess you hated it when people called you Gabe." I lean over him. "Gabe, Gabe fuckin' Gabe! Fuck you, Gabe!"

I keep scrolling and scrolling until, finally, I find what I'm looking for.

ADONIS

Were the fuk r those 20gs you owe me?

Adonis Murphy, one of the meanest motherfuckers in Jericho and the President of the Disciples, a motorcycle club that has territory all the way into Saskatchewan. Adonis isn't even his real name, it's actually Billy, but he rebranded, thinking of himself as a God.

I don't think a God would have frosted tips and breath that could knock a buzzard off a shit wagon, but that's just me.

He and Gabriel started out as friends— in fact they were such good friends that I was offered to Adonis at a party. He got whiskey dick and decided that hitting me was a better use of his time.

ADONIS

don;t ignore me

ADONIS

$$$

ADONIS

u pay me or I take that woman of urs

Gabriel started out as a Prospect, doing low-level errands for the gang, but quickly worked his way up the ranks. By the end he was mostly running drugs and recruiting girls, but things fell apart when he started taking a cut of the cash he was supposed to be giving to Adonis.

He always wanted more power, and even more access, so he started stepping on toes and breaking rank... all the shit you don't do in a motorcycle club if you want to stay alive.

I scroll through more texts, my brain trying to process the information as fast as possible while I listen for sirens outside. Someone had to have heard him screaming.

GABRIEL

ull get her and the cash. I just need time to get it bro and ill be gone

"Making a deal, huh?" I shove his lifeless body. "You disgusting son of a bitch."

The timestamps show months going by without a message between them, until one final text, sent last night.

ADONIS:

i gave u a chance bitch

ADONIS:

> Im gonna cut out ur fuxing tung and take
> whats mine

"Jesus Christ, it's t-o-n-g-u-e, you dipshit. How hard is that?"

I toss Gabe's phone onto his body and pick up my knife, heading into the bathroom as adrenaline continues to crawl through my body. I need a shower, but first I need to leave some evidence behind.

I place my hand on the counter, spreading my fingers. If I want this to look believable to the cops, I have to leave a piece of myself for them to find.

I catch my reflection in the mirror as I'm preparing, a little startled at what I see staring back: my usually chestnut hair soaked in blood. There are streaks smeared on my face as well, only slightly obscuring the healing bruises from where Gabriel took his rage out on me over and over again. If I hadn't known better, I could have sworn I'd bathed in it. But as I stare at the new me, reborn in all this blood, I can't help but notice my cobalt-blue eyes have some of their old brightness back. I feel more alive than I have in years.

Hopefully that'll make this next part at least a little bit easier.

I glance back down at my hand, letting out a breath as I try to decide which finger is getting the chop.

"The pinky should be okay. I can live without it."

I suck in a sharp breath, like I'm about to dip beneath the surface of the ocean before bringing the knife down hard on my finger. The sickening crunch of bone makes me spew vomit all over the mirror, and I let out a gurgling cry. It's not enough. I bring it up, and down again and again and again, heaving through the pain until finally my pinky sits in its own little pool of blood on the countertop.

"Breathe," I whisper. "Just breathe."

The pain is overwhelming, and I drop to my knees, nearly vomiting again before I manage to rally. I grab some gauze, ready and waiting in the medicine cabinet, putting pressure on the wound as I gingerly lower myself onto the edge of the tub. It takes quite a while for the bleeding to stop, my head spinning the whole time as I strain, listening for distant sirens in a silent panic.

But it looks like nobody's coming.

If it had been the other way around, and it was me on that floor in a pool of blood, nobody would care. They might even never know.

I check the wound, maintaining pressure as I clean it and wrap it up tight, then strip down to nothing and start the shower. The water is practically scalding, melting the tension in my muscles. All of that fear and anxiety, everything that was coursing through me for the last 24 hours of planning is washed down the drain, along with Gabriel's blood.

It's only now that I notice the deep cuts on my forearms. Defensive wounds from when we were both struggling for the knife. Little flashes of it all come back as I try to scrub myself clean.

I pounced on him from behind the door when he came out of the shower.

That was the entire plan, no technique or skill to it.

His skin, slick and warm.

The smell of soap.

Droplets of water from his hair landed on my face as we whirled around the bedroom, me hanging off of him like a fucking koala.

At one point he managed to throw me off, his feet squeaking against the hardwood. He slammed me into a wall, pried the knife from my hand, and for a second I was sure he was going to kill me. All it would have taken was one good stab to the gut.

But he hesitated.

"You never could commit."

The Seventh Circle

PREACHER

BABYLON, SASKATCHEWAN

There's no bigger thrill than watching the light leave someone's eyes, breathing in their terror and knowing that I'll be the totality of their final moments.

I like to think of myself as a fixer of sorts. When the law fails, as it usually does, that's when I step in. It's what I've been doing since I shot my daddy. He was a hard-drinking, hard-living man who did unholy things to my mama.

Maybe a little ironic for a minister, but by the time I was finished with him, his little slice of God's house looked like the seventh circle of hell.

Blood drips onto the concrete floor, and I glance up at my current project. There's a kind of angelic quality to Joshua's pose, his head dipped to the side, his arms relaxed, and his feet barely touching the floor as he dangles off of the meathook. If someone walked in right now, they might even think he was floating.

I stride over to my knife roll, carefully laid out across a big steel table. A layman might call it a peculiar sort of leather, with dark faded markings scattered across it. My fingers glide over a large blue cross. That one was my father's favorite.

After we buried what was left of him, I changed my name and dedicated myself to a brand new purpose: ridding the world of men like him. Each one of them that I gut and process gets me a little closer to my own kind of twisted salvation.

But it would be a lie to say he didn't leave anything positive for me to remember him by. Even the cord that binds the knife roll together, so soft to the touch, and looking like a piece of toughened string to the untrained eye... I made it from his stomach lining.

"You like music Josh?"

The man groans as he watches me pick up a small, curved knife, twirl it in the air and catch it. Normally this would be careful work, but the client needs these cuts by tomorrow. I promised them someone athletic, someone violent.

Someone who hurt women.

After reviewing several 'applications' in the form of court documents, I decided that Joshua was the best candidate for the position: a twice-convicted rapist and serial abuser. Corrections Canada let him walk out the fuckin' door... and right into my tender, lovin' arms.

I grab my phone off the table and scroll through my playlists until I see one that makes me snort with laughter.

"Yeah, this is it."

Weird Science by Oingo Boingo blares through the speakers I installed in the far corners of the barn. I do my best work when the music is so loud it pushes every other thought out of my mind. And the best part? Anyone driving by will think I'm just having a party.

Sweat drips down Joshua's face, his skin starting to turn a sickly shade of grey. From the way his chest is shuddering, I can tell I've collapsed one of his lungs. I start to trail my knife down his chest, then his stomach, pressing down a little harder when I reach his limp pecker. As if on cue, his eyes spring open, and he lets out a bloodcurdling scream that's entirely consumed by the music.

I feel like a kid in a candy store.

"Scream all you want, pretty boy. All the way out here, you're mine."

"Somebody help!" He howls. "Please!"

"I'm gonna start by skinning you." I move around behind him, kicking his clothes aside. "Now, this is gonna hurt like a bitch, but I want you to stay in the moment. Really feel that fear. The more terrified you are, the better you're gonna taste."

"You're a fucking psycho!"

"Guilty as charged."

I listen for the change in his voice that I know is coming. I've heard a lot of last confessions, and even more apologies over the years I've been doing this. They're always good for a laugh.

"Please!" He begs through heavy breaths. "Please, you don't have to do this!"

His voice is getting weaker. I think he's going into shock, which means he might not feel some of this, and that's a damn shame.

"I'm gonna start by cutting your achilles." I grab his foot, holding it firmly in place as he struggles to pull away from me. "Then I'm gonna work my way up your leg, and it's really gonna hurt."

I slash at his ankle, slicing the tendon clean in two. The longer half snaps up, balling beneath his skin like an elastic band as his screams ring through the barn. They remind me of the old church bells that used to echo across Babylon when I was a boy.

Blackthorne Ranch used to provide the entire town with pristine and beautiful cuts of beef. Mama, my brother, and myself butchered while my daddy ran the local church.

We practically owned this town.

But now the ranch is nothing but a funeral home, and my brother and I are all that's left of the family.

"You've got more spunk in you than I thought, Joshy boy," I chuckle. "It's funny, with a cow, you gut 'em and then you skin 'em. It's just the proper order of things, y'know? But with you? I'm *really* enjoying listening to you sing for me."

I move slowly, sliding my knife underneath his skin and working upward, all while his howls vanish into the pounding synth. I don't mind it, it adds to the ambience of this place. Dark, ominous, and covered in shadow. A little on the nose for a serial killer? Sure, probably. But sometimes it's fun to play into the clichés.

In contrast, I keep my house on the other side of the property: pristine, modern and well-decorated. You read about some of these serial killers, and they live in fucking cesspools. Blood everywhere, bodies in the bathtub, body parts just laying around for the cops to find. It's barbaric. Me? I do my best to separate these two worlds. In this barn, I'm a monster. At home, I'm just 'Preacher.' I've got my dogs, my books, and my records, everything I could ever need.

"I'll mention this to the client— all that fight you've got in you. They'll like that, it gives the meat an extra kick after all. I think they said they wanna make short ribs for their wedding anniversary."

I hear a garbled noise, and then Josh's screams go quiet.

His body goes limp.

All that fight he had suddenly snuffed out.

Holy Mary, Mother of God, pray for us sinners now, and at the hour of our death.

I work with the music, skinning the rest of him with ease, but taking care as I peel it off in a few large pieces.

Usually, I just wind up incinerating the skin.

But I guess I *do* need a new wallet.

I LEAN BACK IN MY CHAIR, SIPPING ON SOME WHISKEY AS I SAVOR A WELL-earned pan-seared steak, courtesy of Joshua, fried up with some caramelized mushrooms and a few sprigs of asparagus. I usually keep a few cuts for myself once I get everything packed up for a client, and with how exhausting rush jobs like this can be, well... call it a perk of the industry.

Joshua's driver's license sits on the table next to me, the words *short ribs* and *porter house* scrawled on the back. It'll go into my little box in the cellar, along with all the rest.

I hear growling from beneath the table and lean over, spotting Hades and Charon playing tug-of-war for Joshua's femur. I give them bones to chew on after kills, but they know to keep them indoors. The last thing I need is them dropping a human fibula on the ground outside and abandoning it. What if some nosey passerby saw? That could lead to cops, which leads to questions, which leads to dead cops, which leads to, well, more cops. Circle of life.

Luckily, Babylon's never had the most robust local law enforcement. It's located right on the highway, but most of the town was abandoned when the auto plant closed down. All that remains are a few gas stations and a couple of convenience stores for folks who are passing through on their way to somewhere better.

I'd like to say I used to know all the locals, but that ain't true at all. My daddy's cruel and malicious ways meant that my brother and I didn't get to socialize much. We were homeschooled, went to church on Sundays, ate dinner every night at 5:00pm, and had Bible study what felt like every single night. If we ever stepped out of line, we were beaten within an inch of our lives. He really took that whole *spare the rod and spoil the child* shit to heart.

I stare out the window into the darkness, drawing in a deep breath as Charon rests his head on my thigh. I reach down and scratch him behind his ears. I found him and his brother in the barn one freezing cold morning in the middle of winter, two little baby rottweilers, barely alive.

I bottle fed them as pups, keeping them in my jacket pockets to make sure they stayed warm as I went about my day to day. It feels crazy that they'll already be two next month.

Charon licks his chops and I chuckle.

"You already ate. Both of you."

Just as I'm considering giving in, and heading to the cupboard to get him a Milkbone, my phone rings, the only contact I have saved flashing on the screen.

I'm obligated to answer. He's family, after all.

"I'll be there in ten minutes."

Raphael's voice is permanently raspy, like he's spent his whole life smoking cigarettes.

"What, no hello for your favorite brother?"

"How many boxes?"

I can already hear the annoyance creeping into his voice on the other end of the line, and I decide not to poke the bear any further.

"Two. Cash will be in an envelope on top of the box as usual."

Without another word the line goes dead, and I slip the phone back into my pocket.

At 36, Raphael is the brains of the operation. He's got the tech and the skills to hunt down anyone without laying a finger on them. I'd be in prison without him stepping in and helping me funnel my homicidal tendencies into something more productive. To be honest, I felt lost before we started this business venture.

Once the town dried up and most people fled, I sold a lot of the cattle we had to try and stay afloat, but the stress was getting to me. I needed some kind of outlet, and we needed to make money, because I refused to dig my daddy up so that someone could buy our family home. He's buried out back near a patch of trees on the edge of the ranch. Most people think he ran out on us and left with everyone else, and that's the way I like to keep it.

So then, Raphael came to me with an idea.

He's always liked to lurk in the darkest and most grimy corners of the internet. I'm not really sure why, maybe it makes him feel morally superior, but he stumbled upon this group of people with a twisted vice and seemingly bottomless pockets. He got himself connected with them, some of society's sickest, wealthiest motherfuckers, all who were willing to pay a shockingly good price for 'exotic meats'.

And there it was, a business of our very own:

We bring them the flesh of sinners, and the clients make us rich.

I'm judge, jury, executioner, and the Devil himself.

When it comes to the business, Raphael's more organized than I am, and a hell of a lot more meticulous. He has some kind of complicated vetting process, makes sure that everyone involved isn't going to cause any trouble down the line, but a lot of our clients are powerful people, at least powerful enough to have some skeletons in their closets. One of them snitches and he's got a nuclear option that blows all of us to smithereens— Metaphorically speaking, of course.

Mutually assured destruction does wonders for a relationship.

But me? I like the way we do things, and I have no interest in controlling his side of the business. After all, I'm just the beast he keeps on a leash.

I finish the rest of my meal, pour myself another drink, and start on the dishes while I wait for my brother, but it's not long before Hades and Charon are barking at the sound of tires rolling on gravel.

I glance out the window in time to see him hop out of his truck, striding quickly toward the front door. He's a few inches shorter than me, with dark blond hair that contrasts my own brown, but both of us have that Black-thorne jaw, square and slightly flared, just like our daddy's.

I open the door, and the two of us begin loading boxes into the back of his truck without a word. When we're done he stuffs the envelope of cash into his pocket: ten thousand to be paid to our runner, who may have the most dangerous job of all despite the protection we can offer. He transports the meat along with some race horses that Raph sells for legitimacy.

"Clients want another round of orders."

He hands me a small note, folded up like he's passing it to a crush in class.

It's funny how something as consequential as a death sentence can be delivered on something so plain.

We never use anything that can be easily traced in regard to clients or orders, nothing electronic, no texts or e-mails, just in case the cops happen to intercept one of us for something unrelated, and confiscate our phones. Or I fuckin' lose track of mine, which I do more frequently than I'd care to admit.

When it comes to murder, and everything involved, I prefer analog.

As for the note, I only see two names scrawled down, all in slanted capital letters along with some key details.

Chad Brooks - Rape, domestic violence, drug trafficking.
William Lane - Four counts of child molestation.

The clients put in very specific orders. They like to know the crimes these people committed so they can feel some kind of justification for their own sins. Because you can't be that rich and still be a good person, but they sure try their hardest to pretend.

That's usually where Raph's research comes in. He can dig up anything on anyone, he just needs a Red Bull and a couple of hours of peace and quiet. And as for these two? I don't give a fuck about the drugs, but the other charges are enough motivation for me.

"I'll need a few days."

"Seems a little long for you to wait," he scoffs. "Was that last one too much for you or something?"

I roll my eyes. While he first started researching our prey, I looked into what *not* to do when it comes to Serial Murder 101.

"A longer cooling off period is gonna make sure the cops don't show up. You should know this stuff, Raph, try reading a fuckin' book sometime."

He flicks his head toward the house, completely ignoring my jab.

"Blue looks nice."

I turn around, smiling at the new sky-blue trim that frames the windows. It was mama's favorite color.

"Did it last week."

It looks like he might have something more to say, but the ringing of his phone cuts things short.

"I gotta go. Have to meet a man about a horse."

"That real, or do you just wanna leave?"

"Kinda both?"

He re-adjusts his baseball cap, shooting me a quick nod before hopping back into his truck and peeling down the driveway, leaving a big cloud of dust behind him.

I sigh as I watch him go, glancing up at the sky just in time to see it start to turn that gorgeous golden color I know so well, with a few streaks of pink strewn across it like paint. Nothin' beats a sunset on the prairies.

I need a hot bath after a kill. It's always nice to relax those aching muscles after a workout, but this kind of thing needs a little preparation. Hades and Charon are still battling over Josh's femur in the hall as I make a beeline for the living room.

"You boys be good," I call. "I don't wanna hear any ruckus out here."

I fix myself a glass of bourbon and thumb through my mama's records, pulling out a Connie Francis album.

She loved Connie Francis, and every time I put one on, it's like there's a little bit of her in the house again. If I close my eyes, I can almost smell the chocolate chip cookies she used to bake on Sundays.

There's not much that beats that warm and inviting sound you can only get from vinyl, and with *Who's Sorry Now* crackling through the speakers, I make my way to the bathroom, leaving the door open just a crack. I strip my clothes off, staring at myself in the mirror: all the muscle I've built over the years, all of my scar tissue cloaked in tattoos. My favorite is the one on my throat. A giant African swallowtail butterfly. They're so poisonous that they have no natural predators. It seemed fitting for my line of work.

I've covered almost every inch of my body in ink, making sure it stretches all the way up my neck, hiding a lot of mostly self-inflicted damage. Before I embraced what I am, I used to try and cut the evil out of myself. I carved crosses and holy symbols into my skin as though God himself could protect me from my urges.

Now? I decide who lives, who dies, and whose sins are meant to be forgiven.

I may as well have become Him.

Finder's Keepers
RIPLEY

SOMEWHERE ALONG THE ALBERTA-SASKATCHEWAN BORDER

It's pitch-black. I can't see shit out here.

Normally I could use my phone for light, but of course I didn't bring a phone, because phones ping cell towers, and pinging cell towers means someone can track your location.

I found a road map in Gabriel's car, but it turns out I can't read the damn thing. All those lines and numbers? I don't have the patience for that bullshit. All I need to find is a bed to sleep in, and that's it.

Well, after I bury the body.

Right now though? I've been busy picking out a name for myself.

Christine Annabelle Winter died yesterday in that bedroom.

Ripley is my fresh start, a brand new me, and all I know is that she's heading straight toward Saskatchewan.

I don't know why I picked that direction, I just wanted to get as far away from Jericho as possible, but it might not be so bad. Maybe I could sling drinks in an old cowboy bar, really lean into the whole being on the run thing. I could come up with a fake backstory, something sad to get men to fawn all over me.

And then I take them back to a hotel and tear them to pieces.

Jill the Ripper.

I kind of like the sound of that. Derivative? Sure, but every killer has to start somewhere. Or is it a faux-pas to give yourself a nickname, like George Costanza calling himself T-Bone?

I smile at my reflection in the rearview, gripping the steering wheel as I belt out the chorus to *Kokomo* into the night. You've got to listen to The Beach Boys after you decapitate your ex-boyfriend and stash his tongue in your getaway bag. It's the rule.

That's not weird, by the way. Plenty of killers keep trophies: heads, clothing, driver's licenses, jewelry— Hell, Alexander Pichushkin made a mental chessboard, with each victim occupying a square. His goal was to kill 64 people, the number of squares on the board.

He only made it to 60.

So, a tongue? Not the weirdest thing you could take from a crime scene.

Maybe if I start making a habit of this it'll become my signature. Men talk an *awful* lot, it's about time a hero came along and shut them the fuck up.

I stare down at my bandaged hand, feeling it throb as I grip the wheel. I managed to get the bleeding to stop by heating up a knife and cauterizing the wound all at once. It hurt like a son of a bitch, but I wasn't planning on passing out on the highway for some dumbass cop to find me and take me in.

I left my finger on the bathroom counter, and probably more importantly: Gabriel's head sitting on the bookshelf. The goal is to make it look like Adonis broke in, slaughtered the two of us, and left a warning behind. My DNA being all over the house is irrelevant, or maybe even a positive. The cops are going to take one look at those text messages and know exactly who was responsible.

And they'll know I was just collateral damage.

I press down a little harder on the gas, relishing my newfound freedom.

I've already got a new name, which means maybe I'll get a new look once these bruises heal. I've always felt more like fractured pieces of a human being, glued together through careful observation and rehearsal of social norms, so the idea of becoming someone completely different doesn't really phase me. It could be due to my upbringing and the trauma I endured at the hands of my father, or it could be the way my brain is wired, but I think I've always been fucked up. At the very least, I've been fantasizing about picking up a knife for quite a long time.

But with all that weight on my shoulders, everyone still expects me to be a pretty little thing and smile. Wanna know how? How to smile like you're a normal fucking person? The trick is to squint a little, just the tiniest bit.

Makes people think you've got that light behind your eyes, just like them.

I glance up at myself again in the rearview, flashing my perfectly curated smile just long enough to feel accomplished before everything becomes flooded with red and blue lights.

"You've got to be fucking kidding me."

I whip my head around to see a fucking cop *right* on my ass and my stomach drops, my heart thumping so hard it feels like it's going to explode. Psychopaths aren't supposed to feel fear, that's what the textbooks say, but that has to be wrong because I'm pretty sure I'm shitting myself right now.

Or maybe I'm just not the class of killer I thought I was.

I pull over to the side of the road, my hands shaking on the wheel as the police car rolls to a lazy stop behind me, lights still bathing everything in that rotating red and blue.

There's a duffel bag filled with clothes, cash, a few wigs and zip ties in the trunk, incriminating enough on their own even without mentioning the headless fucking corpse jammed in there.

Of course, the pig is going to make me sweat it out. He's gotta be running the plates, probably going to figure out the car is stolen, and then he's *definitely* going to haul my ass off to jail. So now I'm caught in a debate with myself over stepping on the gas, and right into a high speed chase, or crawling into the back to get my knife.

Suicide by cop could be pretty gnarly, and either option guarantees going out in a blaze of glory. The media could weave together a brutal but heart-wrenching tragedy. I can see it now: A beautiful, young woman caught up in the world of drug lords and crime, corrupted by the devil and taken from us far too soon. So long as they made me look good, I wouldn't even mind being the subject of a Fifth Estate piece.

That's some high calibre shit.

After a minute or two that felt like they stretched into hours, I finally see a flashlight bobbing toward the car, and I can feel my body immediately coil up like a spring: jaw tight, gritted teeth, and my heart thumping in my throat. Even through the closed window I can hear his boots grind into the pavement, and all too suddenly there's a bright light shining in my face.

I let out a hiss as I avert my gaze, quickly rolling down the window.

"License and registration."

He's young, maybe mid-twenties with slicked back blond hair and green eyes. I spot the big RCMP badge on his shoulder, the emblem of a federal agent shining like a beacon. He's kind of cute, and I have to admit the aftermath of all of this has left me... well, let's just say I may even be horny enough to fuck a cop.

But only if I get to kill him afterward.

God, can you imagine the kind of power you'd feel?

Am I crazy?

Wait, maybe I can plead NCRMD.

Not Criminally Responsible Due to Mental Disorder, a lawyer's favourite loophole.

But then we'd have to prove that I didn't know what I was doing, because the actus reus—

"Ma'am?" The officer snaps, yanking me back to reality. "Did you hear what I said?"

"Wh— oh, yeah. Sorry."

I reach for my purse, cursing myself for not slamming my foot on the gas and gunning it while I had the chance.

"Have you been drinking tonight, ma'am?"

"No, sir. Sober as a judge."

Oh, God. I'm going to fucking jail.

I flash him an awkward smile over my shoulder as I search for my wallet. It seems to make him a little more suspicious, but there's an uncertainty in his eyes that screams *rookie* to me. My bet is he got put on late-night traffic duty until he works his way up the ranks to be a *respectable* officer— whatever the fuck that means. All these sons of bitches are just as corrupt as the gang banger in my trunk.

"Having trouble?" He asks, tapping his finger on the doorframe.

"Uh, no. Sorry, it's just... it's in here."

He turns the flashlight slightly, leaning in a little closer toward the car.

"Hey, what happened to your face, sweetheart?"

I swallow as he examines the bruises from Gabriel's last attack, the light making my eyes water as I continue digging through my purse.

"I, uh..." I blink furiously before glancing back over my shoulder. "I fell."

He gives me a blank stare in return.

"You fell."

"Yeah."

He sighs.

"You sure that's what you're going with?"

I bristle, feeling the hairs on my neck start to stand up. It might be time for that blaze of glory after all.

"Look, am I in some kind of trouble, officer?"

"Not yet, but I still need to see that license and registration."

There's only so long you can stall with a cop on the side of the road, and there's no way in hell I'm giving him I.D. that directly links me to a less than 24 hour old crime scene.

"Alright officer, I—"

A car blasts past us, nearly clipping the cop and making me jump in my seat as it careens down the highway .

"Jesus Christ!"

He drops his flashlight, and I hear it clatter against the asphalt as he practically vanishes into thin air. A door slams, sirens wailing angrily as tires squeal; the smell of burning rubber floods my nostrils as I watch him speed off into the night.

I sit, dumbfounded, staring straight ahead, my hand clutching the knife still half-buried in my bag.

I can't possibly be this lucky.

Terror gives way to relief and I start to laugh, tears are streaming down my face as I open the car door and take a look up and down the highway, one last precaution in case he had called for backup.

But the only thing on the road is that big, shiny black flashlight.

"Finders keepers, officer fuckwit."

Murder Really Limits Your Options

RIPLEY

SOMEWHERE IN SASKATCHEWAN

I'm dripping with sweat, illuminated by the headlights of what used to be Gabriel's car. He won it off Adonis in a game of poker long before I took it in our little game of death, so its plates couldn't have been exactly clean.

I wonder if the cop figured out who it belonged to.

Reality is starting to sink in as I dig in silence, the stars the only witness to the brand new life I'm about to embark on, out in the middle of nowhere. My guts wrench every time the shovel hits dirt. I just killed a man in cold blood and I don't have a plan beyond *bury the body and fucking drive.*

"Maybe I should have just left you in the fucking house," I snarl at the corpse.

It might have been smarter, but I also know there's potential evidence on his body that doesn't point to Adonis being his killer. If he's six feet under, at least all of that might dissolve into the earth before the cops manage to dig him up.

I heave a sigh, my stomach churning as my head swims with anxiety. Am I sure I can live a life on the run? How do people deal with the cold hand of dread on their shoulder the whole time? Who do you trust? Do you trust anyone? I wanted the blood and the action, but the consequences?

That shit's always sucked.

"Alright, that's enough philosophizing," I mutter to myself.

I have to stay in the present. Bury Gabriel and keep fucking driving until I find a shitty motel where they won't ask questions, and that takes cash. From there, I don't really know what the fuck I'm going to do. I'll need a few days to think, that's for sure, but eventually I'm going to need money. The little bit I managed to scrounge up isn't going to go far, but for now…

My stomach growls.

It'll put a shitty roof over my head and food in my belly.

"Focus, Ripley," I mutter to myself. "One crisis at a time."

I keep digging, sweating, and pushing only toward my end goal: to make this hole as deep as I can, but after about twenty more minutes I can feel my muscles shaking as my vision greys at the edges. I've gone about as far as I can go.

I really should have pulled into a gas station and at least gotten a granola bar or *something*. How embarrassing would it be if I passed out right next to a shallow grave with Gabriel's body sitting in the trunk? I'd be on that *World's Dumbest Criminals* show for sure.

I toss the shovel into the dirt and lumber toward the car, getting ready to lift a corpse with all the strength I have left. I should have done more push-ups while I was locked in that godforsaken house but instead, I was busting my ass making meals, doing laundry, cleaning, and trying not to get my ass beat— on top of coming up with an escape plan.

"I swear, you make things harder on purpose," I snarl. "Fucking dickhead, even from the grave."

The logistics of the whole thing are much more annoying than I expected, and it takes a few minutes just to angle him correctly before I can actually begin. The black trash bag he's wrapped in is slippery on my sweaty hands, making it impossible to keep a hold as I'm hauling the body out.

His shoulders slip right out of my grip and I drop him, taking a step back in surprise before nearly falling into the grave I've dug, but managing to catch myself at the last second.

I take a moment to reset, sitting on my haunches and gulping down humid air as sweat pours down my back, and I stare at a corpse in a bag.

"I can't wait to dump you in this shitty hole and never think of you again."

I know how crazy it sounds, but I kind of wish he'd say something. Then

I'd have a reason to knock his teeth in all over again. Unfortunately, his head's back at home.

Well, not home anymore.

Just one more step: all I have to do is put the body in the grave and I'm free.

"You can do this, Ripley. Just gotta shove him in."

I drag the body the rest of the way to his makeshift grave, and a final few kicks are all it takes for him to topple in with a dull thud. My shoulders sag with relief. The hardest part is over, and all things considered, it wasn't as bad as I thought it might be.

"Okay, now we just gotta fill the hole back in and—"

That's when I notice the trail of blood illuminated by the headlights, leading all the way back to the car. I pick up the flashlight I stole from that cop and, sure enough, there's a giant red stain right on the rear bumper.

"Goddammit, Gabriel!"

I stumble forward, shining the light into the trunk.

Blood's already seeped into the fabric. I can't take this to a body shop, unless I manage to run into the Russian mafia on the prairies.

I let out a pained sigh.

Murder really limits your options.

I pick up the shovel and start piling dirt onto the body, running on autopilot and humming *Kokomo* as I work. That son of a bitch needs to be buried in the ground before I turn the page to the next chapter of my life.

I'm pretty sure my brain is shutting down after everything it's been through tonight... but something's shifting and I start to feel oddly zen, like coming home to a hot bath after a long day's work. I'm sweating, bloodied, bruised, and battered, but I don't think I've ever felt more refreshed.

I could spend the rest of my life chasing this kind of euphoria, leaving men scattered across highways like leaves. I'd be so prolific it'd be impossible to ignore, but they'd never be able to catch me, and then when I finally decided my bloodlust had been quenched, I'd vanish without a trace.

Nothing but a ghost story.

Back in reality, I sling the final clump of dirt onto Gabriel's grave, patting it down and shining the flashlight over the whole thing to make extra-sure he's fully submerged. Then, content with the result, I start the rest of the cleanup.

I grab an old t-shirt out of my bag to wipe away the blood on the bumper, inspecting every inch of the exterior of the car with as much rigor as my exhausted eyes can muster. The last thing I need is someone spotting a bloodied hand print at a gas station.

Content as I can be in a situation like this, I change into a pair of black jeans and a matching tank top, and shove my filthy clothes into a plastic bag in the back of the trunk.

And now, sitting behind the wheel again, with all the slip-ups considered and dealt with, all the speed-bumps to this barely handled disaster...

I think I just got away with murder.

Time to Take a Walk
PREACHER

SASKATOON, SASKATCHEWAN

The music in this place is horse shit.

Pounding bass. Repetitive, mindless lyrics. And yet, people are eating it up, flailing and grinding against each other on the dance floor. The last thing I want to be is stuffed into this sticky booth that smells like cheap vodka and grapefruit juice, but I'm working tonight.

My brother managed to track down the target to a shitty, overpriced nightclub in Saskatoon, and I drum my fingers on the table as I scan the bar, checking my phone one last time to make sure I have the right picture seared into my brain. The shit stain is so ugly his mom probably had to tie a pork chop around his neck to get the dog to play with him. And to add the name *Chad* on top of that? That's gotta be some kind of lawsuit waiting to happen.

I've seen a lot of shady shit in this bar over the course of the evening: guys who wouldn't take no for an answer, trying to convince girls they always need just one more drink, and the guys who are looking for prey... just like me.

I've been watching him for a while now as he lingers at the bar, shooting his shot with any woman who even breathes in his direction. I just wanted to make damn sure I had the right person. Being a predator is all about reading human behavior, and you learn how to spot your own.

Christ, he looks like one of those dickless wonders who can't get a girl, so he spends all of his free time online complaining. He's dressed in a tight polo shirt that shows off a body he spent years carving out in the gym, but not for any sense of self-improvement. More likely just because he got bullied for that fuckass haircut. It's even worse in person.

He's on his third strike, still trying to talk to a woman who's not at all interested in him. He keeps inserting himself between her and her friend, no matter how many times she turns her body away. Finally, he grasps her shoulder, but she fully rejects him, shoving his hand away.

It's at that moment that I see his mask slip, his mouth twitching, his fists clenched, and he takes a *deep* breath as she continues chatting with her girlfriend, completely oblivious to Chad's internal temper tantrum. Me though? I can hear him screaming inside.

Her drink sits behind her on the bar, and he glances around to make sure nobody's watching before making his move. I look down, making sure he can't tell I'm watching, but keeping him in my periphery as he pulls something out of his pocket.

I grab the needle I've been concealing in my coat, slipping out of the booth and striding toward him. It's filled with Midazolam, and a subcutaneous injection will work within a few seconds. To him, it'll feel like a night of alcohol hit him all at once, and to the rest of the club it'll look like I'm just walking a friend out of here.

Looks like we both came prepared.

Just as he reaches for one of the drinks, a couple of big cowboys approach the girls... and he has to back off.

Chad looks *pissed*, and it's hard not to laugh.

The cowboys motion to the dance floor and the girls follow without even the slightest resistance, taking their drinks with them and leaving Chad in the dust. He looks pathetic, swiping a hand through his hair as he abandons his drink and heads for the back of the bar.

Straight for the bathroom.

"Perfect."

I'd prefer not to make a scene in public, because it turns everything into a big event and that makes me memorable. When it comes to my occupation, that ain't something I wanna be.

I slip through the crowd of sweaty college students and head down a long, narrow hallway to the bathrooms. It's dark and surprisingly empty. Usually in a situation like this, there's some drunk I have to dodge.

I wait at the door for a count of ten before slipping in to find my target taking a piss, whistling to himself as he sways from side to side. Most of these guys need to get plastered before they indulge in their darkness. People always think Bundy was clean-cut and put together when he hunted, but the truth? That guy was a raging alcoholic narcissist, and booze was the only way he could kill what was left of his conscience.

Being born too late to get a shot at Bundy was one of my great regrets. I'd love to have that fucker hanging from a hook in my barn, squealing like a newborn pig.

I reach behind me and flip the lock. I've got to get Chad out of here and into my truck out back without drawing too much attention to myself. Raph already cased the place, and I've memorized where the security cameras are located. All I've gotta do is keep my hat pulled down and stay out of their line of sight.

I pop the cap off the needle, ready to move in, but the clatter of plastic on the floor makes Chad turn his head. I lunge for him before the gears in his brain manage a single rotation, covering his mouth with one hand and holding the needle to his neck with the other. It's a little more careless than I like to operate, but it'll have to do.

"Scream, and you're dead. Nod your head if you understand me."

I can feel his heavy, inebriated breathing quicken as he nods, only a confused groan escaping his lips. He reeks of liquor and piss. I'm pretty sure I can hear it spattering on the ground as we speak.

Nice touch.

"That's right, there's nowhere to run, princess, now take those drugs out of your pocket."

His muscles stiffen and I chuckle.

"Thought you were real smooth, didn't you? I'm actually shocked you haven't been caught before now."

With a shaking hand, he reaches into his pants and pulls out a little eyedropper.

"GHB?"

He nods.

"Good boy," I chuckle. "Now, I'm going to take my hand away from your mouth, and you're gonna swallow all of that. If you make a sound, you'll be dead before you hit the floor."

I graze his skin with the needle, a little reminder of my imminent threat, and he lets out a whimper as he trembles in my arms. He's terrified, so much so that I can hear his stomach gurgling as the sweat pours down his face. God, this shit makes me feel giddy. I'd like to play with him some more, but we don't have time.

"Wh– why are you d– doing this?"

"It's simple, Chad, I don't like men who hurt women."

"How do you— I don't—"

"You and I both know what you are," I snarl. "Two counts of rape, domestic violence charges—"

"That wasn't me!"

I squeeze his throat, feeling his blood pumping beneath my grip. I can't tell you the amount of freaks who have told me their criminal records never belonged to them.

You've got the wrong guy, I swear!

It's not my fault!

I've heard it all.

"Take it or I'll fucking kill you."

"There are people outside—"

"You're right, but we both know not a single one of them gives a *shit* about you."

His hand shakes like a leaf as he brings the eye dropper to his lips, hesitating just before the plunge.

"Be a good boy, Chad."

I glide the needle up and down his neck, relishing the sense of control. Someone could rattle that door handle any minute, and my prey could call out to them, ruin this entire thing, but somehow I'm completely calm. Focused. I've made mistakes in the past, letting prey slip through my fingers in a moment of pique.

I always caught them in the end, but not without serious risk.

Chad breathes deeply, looking at me with pleading eyes a final time before giving in and draining every drop. It won't be long now.

"See, that wasn't so bad, was it? Now we're just gonna sit in here like friends for a little bit. Let's call it bonding."

It takes around ten minutes for GHB to fully kick in, but he took a much bigger dose than normal, so my guess is we'll need about half of that.

I lean up against the wall and check my phone, keeping one eye on my prey as I do.

RAPH

Got him?

I chuckle.

Chad's leaning over the sink, sticking his mouth under the tap in a desperate attempt to... I don't know, flush the drugs out of his system?

Not gonna happen.

ME

Yep. Just waiting now.

RAPH

Let me know when I need to come by.

ME

Always do.

It doesn't take long for Chad to start getting woozy. He stumbles, trying to grab the wall for stability, but he nearly slips and hits his head right on the damn urinal.

"Alright," I grunt, slipping my phone back into my pocket. "Time to take a walk."

This part's always a pain in the ass. If I had my way, I'd sit out in my truck with a tranquilizer gun and shoot them while they walked up to the front door. It'd be so much easier than this whole dog and pony show, but we have a procedure for a reason, I suppose.

I stick my head into the hallway, making sure the coast is clear before I walk Chad to the back exit, pulling my hat down over my face just before we pass under the final camera. Outside, the summer heat wastes no time assaulting me, and I do my best to ignore the moisture that's already gathering on my forehead as I toss Chad into the passenger seat.

The first thing I do after slamming the door is turn on the police band radio. Mostly, I listen to make sure I'm not driving into any traffic stops, but sometimes it can get a little more serious.

"We're going to need units on standby for a tornado warning near Fox Valley, all the way up to Babylon."
"Shit."

There Goes Plan A
RIPLEY

LOST IN SASKATCHEWAN

You'd think after all my years of growing up in the area, I'd learn not to drive through a place called *Tornado Alley*, but here I am, smack dab in the middle of it.

"A warning has been issued for Fox Valley and the surrounding areas. We advise that all residents take shelter immediately and do not make unnecessary journeys."

Aside from the radio, all I can hear is the rain and hail pounding against the roof of my car like a barrage of bullets. It's all I can do to grip the steering wheel, struggling to keep calm as I careen through the night.

Out of the corner of my eye I catch a bolt of lightning illuminating the sky.

"Well, that's not good..."

Suddenly, a chunk of hail the size of a baseball smacks against the glass, shattering it. Oh God. I'm in the middle of fucking nowhere with the wind howling around me, and I *swear* the hail is getting bigger every minute. I'm gonna die out here.

I wrench the wheel to the right, pull the car over to the side of the road and kill the engine. Another bolt of lightning strikes, brightening the sky just enough to give me a distressingly good look at the funnel cloud looming in the distance.

Significantly less of a distance than the last time.

I have to find shelter. Now.

I grab the flashlight and climb out of the car, picking a random direction and start to run. I don't even know enough about the area to make an educated guess, but someone *has* to live out here.

Right?

The wind howls as rocks of hail beat mercilessly against my body. I keep trying to hold my arms up to protect my face, but dropping them again every time I realize I need to be able to fucking *see*.

Suddenly, a sharp, searing pain slices right above my brow, and my vision immediately goes red in one eye.

Thunder roars like a lion, nearly shaking the earth and I'm struck in the head by another massive chunk of hail. This time the hit is so hard I can feel my legs give out, and I land face first in the mud as my flashlight flies from my grip. I can see it glowing in the muck while the rain and hail get even more intense, coming down in sheets.

"Fuck!"

I crawl toward the light, grunting and straining as the storm pelts my back.

My first day of freedom, and I'm gonna to die here?

Just outside a shithole town I never even meant to be in?

As I struggle to pick the flashlight up with slippery, trembling hands, another flash of lightning crashes through the clouds, drawing my gaze just in time to see a distant farmhouse illuminated in the night.

I've always considered myself an atheist, given everything I've been through, but I'll be goddamned if this isn't a sign from the big man himself.

I struggle through the field, using every last bit of strength in my body to make it across the long stretches of land and up to the front door, pounding on it for what feels like forever.

"Please..."

My voice is raspy and broken as I sink to my knees.

"Somebody—"

I barely manage to squeak the word out when I hear the roaring wind pick up close by, and I turn to see a funnel cloud brushing the ground like the finger of God, fully illuminated in the patchy moonlight. It's surreal watching it swallow up everything in its path, almost beautiful in a way.

Until I see something recognizable get pulled into the air...

Something that looks a hell of a lot like my fucking car.

I scramble to my feet and start to pound on the door all over again.

"Help!" I scream. "Somebody! Please!"

But the only new sound I hear are dogs barking from inside, as the wind continues to roar like its own vicious beast.

Debris starts to pick up as the funnel gets closer, and I stumble down the steps, running around for the side of the house, desperate to try and find another way in. There's got to be a window I can smash.

Something.

Anything.

I scan my surroundings, aiming the flashlight anywhere and everywhere, landing on nothing after nothing after nothing.

And then...

My heart nearly stops: a fucking storm cellar.

I rush for it, wrenching at the double-doors, but a padlock holds the two handles together with a link of chain. I yank on the lock itself in vain desperation, but to my surprise the damn thing clicks open almost immediately.

"There's no fucking way..."

My doubt is dragged off into the sky as a plank of wood whips up off the ground, nearly clipping me as it flies straight past my head.

I pull the lock from the chains and unspool them from the door, throwing myself inside and tumbling down a small flight of stairs. Sharp pain ricochets throughout my battered body, and all the air is sucked from my lungs as I land at the bottom, flat on my back. It takes me a few moments to gather myself, every breath I take like someone stabbing a dagger into... well, everything.

I can hear the doors of the cellar slamming over and over, open and shut. I don't have the strength to climb up those stairs again, let alone to close them. All I can do is drag myself into the far-corner and stare, begging the tornado not to touch down on the house, hoping beyond hope that it won't reach me down here.

I slump against something cool and metal, my vision blurring from the head wounds as rain and hail continue to pound relentlessly outside.

I just need to close my eyes for a second.

Either way, this will all be over.

Whether I wake up or not.

Blue and red lights flood the room.

"We have the property surrounded!"

No.

The cellar doors shake, and I struggle to get to my feet, stumbling over something and falling back to the floor as they try to get in.

As my vision adjusts, I see the blood on my hands.

And Gabriel's headless, mutilated corpse at my feet.

No. I buried him. I got away.

They can't do this to me.

I can hear the cellar doors explode inward, and I lurch up from the floor with a jolt, gasping for air and looking around the empty room.

It's dead quiet.

No cops.

No lights.

Just me, and this fucking headache.

I reach up, feeling dried blood on my face and blindly pawing around to find the wound. It's tender, but the cut isn't as big as I thought.

It's always the small ones that bleed the most.

I breathe through the pain as my body hums and throbs; the ache is so deep I swear I can feel it in my goddamn toenails. It feels like my senses are cranked up to eleven, making me acutely aware of everything: My jeans digging into my waist, the tag on the back of my shirt like fingernails grazing my skin, and my puckered little raisin toes in my waterlogged shoes.

I try to stand, but the combination of the head-rush and the vicious pain causes me to immediately vomit. Everything twists and rips my nerve endings until I'm nothing but a collection of fraying, crackling wires.

At least I'm alive, even if I don't deserve to be.

I manage to get to my feet, slowly this time, trying to plan my next move. This is a temporary shelter, but whoever owns this property is probably going to be back soon, unless I hallucinated the sound of those dogs. I need to find a way to patch myself up, maybe change the bandage on my hand, and get the hell out of dodge.

I glance around, my eyes still struggling to adjust to the light, or maybe my potential concussion. This place is chock full of tools, and enough self-labeled canned food for a small army. I pick through the cans of beans, soup, and even some chilli, not a store-bought brand in the pack.

"Maybe I'll come back for you."

I find some old tools caked in something rusty, parts for farm equipment, spooled-up barbed wire, and a little wooden box on a shelf off on its own.

"Well well well, what're you hiding in here?"

I flip the lid, my brows knitting together as I rifle through it, hoping to find some money, but all that's there are a pile of old IDs and some keys lining the bottom.

I pull out one of the cards: an old Saskatchewan driver's license with some of the typeface worn off the front, making the man's name nearly impossible to read. Maybe a Zack, or a Mack? It'd be hard enough to tell in normal circumstances, and my eyesight is still extra-dogshit thanks to that goddamn hail.

I turn it over in my hand, frowning at the scrawled text on the back.

SIRLOIN

CHUCK

FILLET MIGNON

BOTTOM ROUND ROAST

I snatch up more IDs, checking them one by one.

They're all men, and they all have that stuff written on them.

Types of meat?

I glance around the room again, eyes landing on a metal door I hadn't noticed before. It looks like one of those walk-in refrigerators... with another giant fucking padlock on it.

Okay. Alright.

Nobody would leave this place abandoned, not with this shit lying around.

I have to get out of here.

Maybe there's a car I can hot wire outside...

I spent months preparing to murder Gabriel. Reading, researching, and trying to commit everything I could to memory. The fantasy became all-consuming as I went over *every* detail, not wanting to leave any evidence that could implicate me. My job was to be the perfect victim, all so that I could transform into something greater.

I snatch the flashlight, hobbling back to the rickety wooden staircase that leads to the open cellar doors. I slowly make my way up, stair by stair, until I can feel the rain dripping down onto me from the wood above.

I can't have been out that long, even through the crack in the cellar doors I can tell it's still dark. I hesitate for a moment, a palpable sense of dread washing over me as I reach for the door, but I crush it back down and shove my way into the dark of the night. It seems like I was worried for nothing, though, because the clouds have cleared, no funnel or lightning in sight.

I can even see the stars scattered all the way across the sky.

I start to shiver, wandering around the property, my flashlight trembling in my hand as I look for something to hotwire. Just my luck though, no cars, only debris the storm had kicked up. Pieces of wood, branches, and scattered leaves from a patch of forest around the back of the house.

"There goes plan A," I mutter.

I spot a massive dilapidated barn at the edge of the property and limp toward it, wincing with every step. Mud squishes beneath my sneakers and I mutter curses under my breath. Why didn't I check the fucking weather before I drove through this godforsaken province?

The barn doors are chained shut with a lock firmly in place, making that three for three.

"Shit."

Maybe the safest thing for me to do is wait it out in the cellar for someone to come back. Best case scenario is they head inside the house to check for damage, or on their dogs, and I can slip out and take whatever they arrived in. Worst case... Well, at least there's shit down there that I could use as a weapon.

All my plans are replaced with terror, however, as I spot distant headlights cutting through the darkness, floating straight for the house.

My stomach sinks and I can feel the sweat start to drip down the back of my neck. There's no way for me to get back to the storm cellar without seriously risking getting caught, it's all the way on the other side of the property. I quickly shut the flashlight off and limp as fast as I can toward the back of the barn, trying to make myself as invisible as possible as I crouch down and peer around the corner.

It's less than a minute before the headlights slide into view again, and the large truck pulls to a stop. I watch in silence as a man steps out into the cool air, the night seeming to swallow up every other sound save for the gravel grinding like teeth beneath his boots. All I can see is his silhouette in the moonlight, but I can tell he's got a sturdy frame, large and imposing, topped off with a wide-brimmed hat.

He walks around the truck, wrenching the passenger door open, and something large falls to the ground, wiggling like a worm in the dirt.

The big man puts his foot on the thing, and it lets out a whine.

"Please..."

Oh Jesus, it's alive.

"I thought I told you to shut up."

He picks up the man with ease, hauling him right over his shoulder and heading straight for the barn. I'm mesmerized by the fluidity of the movements; the body he's carrying is seemingly weightless, like a prized kill slung over his shoulder.

But of course, he's still heading straight for the barn.

Straight for me.

I try to make myself even smaller, pressing my body down into the mud and dirt, but still desperate to see what happens next. You know the curious idiot who hears a weird noise in a horror movie and goes to investigate?

Turns out that's my role.

The big man unlocks the barn door and steps inside, the wood making a loud thunk that cuts through the eerie night as it closes.

This might be my best opportunity, but I'm frozen in place.

If I run now, he might hear me, but if I stay, who knows how long before I slip out of consciousness again.

It's actually a pretty easy choice, when you put it like that.

I make a break for it, pushing through the pain and what are probably broken bones until I reach the truck, blindly fumbling around the cab for the keys, and finding a hell of a lot of nothing save for an empty Tim Horton's cup.

In a moment of weakness, I press my head against the cool window, breathing hard as I keep myself from slipping away.

I have to come up with a plan.

And I think it's gonna involve at least one more corpse.

Blink and You'll Miss It
PREACHER

BABYLON, SASKATCHEWAN

The music is pounding, and my heart sings along with its sweet melody.

Dissection is meditative, and oddly soothing. It calms the most restless parts of my mind, so where many killers find corpse disposal to be the most stressful part of murder, I actually enjoy it.

I strip off the pieces of meat the clients asked for, and carve out his heart, placing both into vacuum sealed bags that will be kept on ice until we're ready to make the delivery. I never ship one thing at a time, it's always in bulk.

Butchering a human isn't that much different than an animal. I just needed to brush up on my anatomy before I started killing. A few textbooks will tell you everything you need to know. The head comes off first, and then each limb. You want to get everything broken down into manageable pieces. It's less stressful that way.

I work with a bone saw, which ensures all my cuts are clean. Good clean cuts make a world of difference, after all. That was one of the few things my daddy actually taught me.

I wrap Chad's right leg up in plastic, setting it off to the side while I work on severing the other at the hip joint, working back and forth and taking extra care not to tear up the meat.

Some of this is going to be mine. I might make a stew out of these cuts and freeze it for the winter, but what I don't keep, I have to incinerate. Luckily, it didn't take long in this business for me to realize that once the hide is tanned, human skin doesn't look a hell of a lot different from leather. These days I make wallets, belts, and even collars for the dogs.

Very little goes to waste.

That's another thing the old man taught me about butchering: you have to respect the animal, and use as much of it as you can.

With one final slice his bone snaps, and I'm able to pull the leg away; I can't help but whistle at the quality of the cut.

"That is *pristine*, Chadwick! I feel like we're close enough that I can call you Chadwick, right?"

I poke his plastic-wrapped head with the tip of my knife, lazily knocking it on its side.

"No comment? I'd have thought you'd have better manners than this. A guest in another man's barn and you're giving him the silent treatment?"

I slice off a few key pieces of flesh, marking them as my own before I load the rest up and get to wiping things down. Tomorrow this place'll get a deep clean, all the prep necessary for the next victim, but for now, a little sponge bath will be just fine.

It's dawn by the time I make it out of the barn, and I find myself stopped dead in my tracks mid-way to the house, gazing up at the golden skies that stretch out as far as the eye can see. After a few moments I glance down at Chad's severed head in the plastic bag.

"You know bud, you're really quite lucky... if you blink, you really do miss the good shit."

If you only looked at the sky, it'd be hard to believe that just a few hours ago a tornado was tearing through the fields, threatening to unearth all of my dirty little secrets. The moment your eyes touch the ground, however, things become a lot clearer. There's little bits of debris and damage all over the place, things where they shouldn't be, and things missing where they should. Hell, it feels like half the trees got knocked over, one of them right onto my goddamn fence.

Honestly though, I don't mind. Checking the property for damage might be busywork, but it reminds me of the days when this place actually functioned as more than a black market slaughterhouse.

I walk the length of the property, looking for broken windows or other major damage that would need to be dealt with quickly, but luckily the search reveals nothing worth worrying about. That's what's running through my head, at least, until I see it a few feet from the storm cellar: the very conspicuous padlock, sitting open on the ground.

I bristle, the hairs on the back of my neck standing on end as I reach into my jeans and pull out my pistol.

When I was driving up to the ranch, I spotted a car in the ditch.

I figured the twister had just tossed it aside like an abandoned toy, but maybe...

I open the doors, slowly aiming my gun down into the darkness, half expecting someone to come racing toward me, but after a few heartbeats I'm only met with silence. Maybe staying up all night has made me paranoid. Maybe I left it unlocked before I left for Saskatoon.

Or maybe someone's in my fucking cellar.

Slowly, I start the descent, but really that's being a bit dramatic. It's only a few steps into the abyss before I reach the bottom, and by then I can smell it: the clear stench of a body.

A live one.

You're Allergic to Friends
PREACHER

The first swing is ferocious, the way they always have to be if you're hoping to make it out of a place like this alive. I manage to step to the side just in time, dropping the bag of mismatched Chad-parts on the floor, but the crowbar still half-connects with my head, pain crashing into me like last night's storm. I lurch back, trying my best to ready myself as another swing comes in, this one smashing into my outstretched arm. It's just as vicious as the first, but I know it's coming, letting me move with the strike and get right up next to my attacker.

There's fear in their eyes.

Her eyes.

Fear, along with a frantic, murderous intent that may as well be all she's got out here, in the middle of nowhere.

In a killer's cellar.

My cellar.

I slam her against the wall and the two of us grapple for her makeshift weapon.

She got me good twice, but I don't want to kill her, just subdue her; you can't interrogate a corpse, no matter how good a listener one might be. Problem is, she's got a surprising amount of strength for someone I have at least a whole foot of height on.

She jams her elbow hard into my ribs, managing to break away and swinging the crowbar again, forcing me backward. There was a moment or two where I was worried, especially after that first hit, but without the element of surprise, every moment that goes by tips things further into my favor.

Because as powerful as her attacks are, she's also panicked.

Afraid.

And that means mistakes.

She lunges at me again taking her biggest swing yet, but she's tired, not used to this kind of thing, and her weapon slips ever so slightly. I pivot, snatching her wrist and twisting it back until I feel something start to tear. She cries out in pain, crumpling forward as the thick piece of steel tumbles from her grip.

And for a second, everything is calm again.

That is, until she starts kicking behind her, trying to take out my goddamn knees.

"I'm gonna rip your heart out, you psycho!" She roars.

It's a battle cry that sends a jolt of lightning shooting through me, excitement I haven't felt in quite a long while, but now that she's seen me, there's no way in hell I can let her go.

I get her in a headlock, squeezing just hard enough to cut off the blood flow to her brain. It won't do permanent damage, she just needs to pass out so I can get a fucking moment to think.

It takes nearly 30 seconds of thrashing and cursing before she finally slows down, but only another 10 before she's limp like a ragdoll in my arms. I ease her onto the ground, slowly, carefully. She looks so peaceful– hell, even beautiful, despite the blood on her face.

Maybe because of it.

I let my eyes dance up and down her body as I figure out what to do next. She's got a hell of a figure, and the t-shirt she's wearing does little to hide her curves.

I can't let my mind wander too far, she could be anyone.

I head over to a small crate in the corner, grabbing a long chain with an ankle cuff on the end. When I first started killing, I tried to make it into a little game for myself. I'd chain these assholes down here and leave the key right at the very edge of reach, just to give them some hope. If they managed to dislocate their arm or something, got out and made a run for the road, I'd be waiting on the porch with a shotgun. My brother said it was cruel, and maybe he was right, but I didn't care.

I was having the time of my life.

I close the shackle around her ankle, securing the chain to a big steel loop next to her, and this time I double-check to make sure the padlock clicks shut.

"Raph's gonna blow a gasket when he finds out about you," I mutter.

I already know what he's going to say.

Kill her. Fuck, kill her yesterday!

But I can't, not just for self-preservation.

No women, no kids. That's the line I'm not willing to cross.

I step back and fully take her in for the first time. She's covered in mud, battered and bruised with clotted blood in her hairline. I crouch down to get a better look at the wound on her forehead, nasty and in need of stitches too. I could do it myself, but she's not going to be out forever, and I doubt she'll let me anywhere near her without trying to take another swing.

As I continue my exploration I notice the bloodied gauze wrapped around one of her hands, and a little wretched stump where her pinky used to be. Jesus, that's going to need to be cleaned and re-bandaged. Suppose I can do that, too.

"How did you end up here, little rabbit?"

That car in the ditch has got to be hers.

If she's reported missing, there's a damn good chance her vehicle can be traced back here, and there's no way in hell I'm having a shootout with the RCMP.

I double-check her shackles before getting to my feet, tossing the bag of body parts into the freezer before heading outside and leaving her in the dark. How the hell she got here I'll never know, but she's here now.

I pull my cigarettes out of my pocket, slipping one between my lips. My brother says these things are gonna kill me one day, and he's probably right, but that asshole drinks Diet Coke like it's water. I bet his insides look like they've been preserved in formaldehyde.

Ten feet from the door to the house and my boys are already barking up a storm, pulling me from my thoughts.

"Hey, hey!" I chuckle, greeted by wagging tails and a hell of a lot of slobber. "Daddy's home, don't you worry. You want some breakfast?"

They're always so well behaved until someone gets close enough, then they go absolutely ballistic, the results varying depending on how much they like whoever's slipped past their little bubble. For now though, they both bolt toward the kitchen, waiting expectantly while I grab their kibble, and top it with a little bit of Robert-brand jerky. I did such a damn good job dehydrating that one, you wouldn't even know the difference between human and beef.

I set the food down in front of the boys, and they stare at me, practically buzzing as they foam at the mouth for their meal.

"Wait..."

Both of them have their eyes fixed on their respective bowls and I chuckle.

"Wait..."

Charon almost lunges, but holds himself back at the last second and I smile, snapping my fingers.

"Go."

The sound of claws on hardwood takes over the room as the two of them crash into each other, each one desperate to be the first to get to their bowls. They've been like this since the day I found them, everything's always a competition.

I fix myself a cup of coffee as the boys gobble up their food, taking a minute to pull up Raph's contact in my phone. I could put this off a little longer, but it'll only make things harder in the end, so I take a couple deep breaths and hit call.

My brother's got that quiet kind of anger, the type you swallow for *years* until one day, seemingly out of nowhere, it finally explodes. He's punched me in the face for shit I've done decades ago, in the blink of an eye, and without a word.

Me? I prefer to deal with things more direct.

"Yeah?"

It felt like an eternity before he picked up, but I suddenly wish it had been longer.

"The fuck were you doin'?" I ask, starting strong with some pointless antagonism. "Too good to pick up when your brother calls?"

"Making sure the packages got to their destinations," he grunts. *"How's the Devil's work?"*

"A hoot and a half as always." I grab a bottle of whiskey and pour some into my mug. "I gotta talk to you about something."

"You're quitting murder to become a priest, I knew it."

Sometimes this motherfucker is actually funny, and it's made all the better by the driest delivery you've ever heard.

"Nothing so noble," I chuckle. "Actually I came home today and discovered that the ranch has an... unexpected guest."

It's only a single beat of silence, but I find myself nearly choking on it.

"Guest? The fuck are you talking about? You're allergic to friends."

The edge in my brother's voice would normally make me grin, it means I'm getting a rise out of him. Today, though? I'm defensive. Nervous, even.

"Found her in the storm cellar when I went down there this morning—"

"Her? Who the fuck is she?"

"Relax. She's tied up, and she's not going anywhere."

"And you're sure about that? Sounds like she got in there easy enough."

I stare out the window as panic pulses through me. He's not gonna like it.

"Preacher, **how** *did she get into the cellar?"*

I'm not afraid of my brother, but I am afraid of what he'll do to the girl if he deems her a threat. I could tell him no a hundred times, and he'd just slip in while I was gone and get the job done. He'd do whatever it takes to keep this thing running smooth.

"No idea. Maybe the storm tore the door off. That, or I left it unlocked."

I hear a loud bang followed quickly by a steady stream of curses. Sometimes, when my brother gets angry, he reminds me of our dad, and that's a bit of a tough thing to reconcile. Over the years, when we've let things come to blows, I swear I could see the old man in him.

"I'm coming over."

"Why?"

"Because when I get there, you're gonna do your job, and then I can help clean up this mess."

I don't give a shit what Raphael says or what he wants, I ain't doing it. Besides, there's something about her that's piqued my curiosity.

"I've told you before, I have rules."

"This is a liability," he snaps back, as if he anticipated exactly what I'd say.

"I'm pretty sure I saw her car in the ditch, I was gonna—"

"Alright, head over to it. I've pinged your location so I'll meet you there."

"Raph—"

The line goes dead before I can finish my sentence, and I lean up against the counter, sipping my newly-spiked coffee and ignoring the low growl of my stomach. I grab my keys, my hat, and my jacket, before hopping in the truck and heading down the long driveway toward the main road. I need to fix this first, and *then* I can eat.

The tires jump, kicking over rocks and debris the storm left behind, and I make a left turn toward what's left of Babylon, passing by the old abandoned church my daddy used to preach in. It's condemned now, with most of the aging stained glass windows boarded up in an effort to save them from storms over the years.

It's another five minutes or so of swerving around random stuff the tornado left behind, but eventually I spot the car: a brown sedan with the bumper and tail lights halfway torn off.

"I sure hope this is yours, little rabbit."

Windows punched out, shattered glass strewn all over the sidewalk… looks like she was luckier than I thought. I pull up beside the car, in time to spot Raphael's big black pickup approaching, heavy metal blasting from the speakers. I don't know how he listens to that shit. Feels like half the songs don't even have lyrics, it's just screaming.

Raph pulls over to the side of the road and kills the engine, climbing out with a deep scowl already etched onto his face. He's in a maroon Henley with faded blue jeans and cowboy boots, his usual black ball cap turned backwards, with long dark blond hair peeking out from underneath it. He's always been the more boyish looking one out of the two of us, but he balances that out with his death-stares.

"Where is she?" He asks. More of demand, really.

"Good morning to you too."

His piercing green eyes turn icy the moment they meet mine.

"Don't fuck around with me, Preacher. Where is she?"

"I told you, she's out cold, chained up in the storm cellar. You feelin' okay, pal?"

Usually his memory's not this shitty, unless of course he spent the whole drive so pissed that he practically forgot our entire conversation.

"I'm fine," he grinds out before flicking his head toward the ditch. "You wanna play fuckin' detective or something? How do you even know this is her car?"

Actually, that sounds about right.

"Took an educated guess," I shrug. "Not too many people live around here, and by now I know all their vehicles by heart. Sure, maybe it's some other passerby, but if it is... where the fuck are they? Storm's been gone for hours."

Raphael clicks his tongue, glancing around cautiously before he heads around the back and lifts the loose trunk open. I immediately spot a large black duffel bag tucked in the back, conspicuous enough for being all on its own. Raph and I go for it at the same time, but I'm faster, managing to shove him away. He mutters more curses under his breath as I open it up.

"Wigs, some clothes, zip ties... Jesus, duct tape, and some plastic bags." I sigh. "Well, she's definitely running from something. That, or someone was running from her."

I rifle through the rest of the bag until I find an ID stuffed into an inside-pocket.

"Pleasure to meet you, Christine Annabelle Winter."

Even in a black and white photo her eyes are startling; pretty, but there's something empty about them. It's that dead eyed psychopathic stare I've only seen a couple times before.

Hollow.

A thrill runs through me.

No, my luck can't possibly be that good.

"Aww, that's sweet," Raphael hums. "You get to know her full name for when you're slicing and dicing."

"I told you, I'm not killing—"

I stop mid-sentence, my fingers wrapping around something soft and squishy at the bottom of the bag, pulling it out from under a bundle of clothes.

"Well that's... something."

I blink, still not quite sure if I'm seeing straight.

"Jeeeesus Christ!" Raphael groans. "You've gotta be shittin' me!"

I let out a bemused chuckle, slowly unwrapping what looks to be a human tongue from some plastic. I should probably be more worried, a little more eager to get back home and check on our would-be psychopath, but the only urge I feel is to take a look at her handiwork— if it's even hers. It's a hack job, no pun intended. Looks like it was done in a hurry, and by someone wholly inexperienced with butchering. Well, at least one kind. The cuts are jagged, almost like she sawed it out. That takes energy. Rage.

Or maybe....

"What are we thinking?" Raph asks. "Contract killer? Passionate hobbyist?"

I run my thumb over the velvety flesh.

"Maybe."

Trophies are specific, and very personal to each killer. I've heard of some that take eyes because they view them as the windows to the soul. Others take jewelry, body parts, lingerie, locks of hair— hell, even makeup. I chose skin, in part because it's practical and easy to hide once it's been worked on, but I'd be lying if I said wearing a dirty little secret wasn't exciting.

What are the odds that *this* woman would stumble into *my* storm cellar? And what are the odds that she's just like me? Right now? I'd say pretty damn high.

I need to talk to her, figure out what the hell's going on.

"You want my advice?" Raph plucks Christine's ID from my hand. "Move the car, just in case the cops pass through. Hide it somewhere they're not gonna find it and come snooping, and..."

"And?"

"And kill her, before she causes any more goddamn problems."

His boots crunch over the gravel as he trudges back to his truck.

"Where are you going?" I ask, my eyes still fixed on the severed tongue.

"Research. And I wanna get the fuck outta here before you whip your dick out or somethin'. Just remember what I said: you need to deal with her. Also, not for nothing, but we could sell her for some serious cash if we found the right people. Either way, she needs to get gone."

That's all he's concerned with at this point. He doesn't care about my rules, and he doesn't appreciate the artistry of what I do.

But maybe *she* will.

Murder By Apathy

RIPLEY

It feels like I got run over by a truck. Twice. You know, just in case the first time didn't take. At this point, all of my pain has melded together and it feels like my whole body is on the verge of breaking down completely. I don't even have the strength to push myself up off the floor; the second I try, my arms give out, and my chin collides with the ground.

"Fuuuuuck."

Every time I try to breathe, it feels like I'm being stabbed in the lungs by a hot poker, but I still manage to hear something buzzing above me. Electricity? A bug? It's hard to identify because my ears are ringing so loud that any noise makes me want to vomit.

I force my eyes open, coming face to face with a pair of black cowboy boots with shiny brass toes, and finding myself recoiling involuntarily.

Something metal drags along the concrete.

And it's attached to my ankle.

"Been waitin' for you to wake up, rabbit."

If his voice weren't so bone chilling, he'd sound kind of sexy, like he's been locked in a dark room, forced to smoke cigarettes and eat gravel his whole life.

I manage to find the strength to lift my head, looking up at the shadowy figure, and trying to take in as much information as quickly as I can: broad shoulders, bulging forearms, and he smells like sweat, cigarettes, and leather.

Then everything comes screaming back to me.

The bag of body parts.

The crowbar.

The fight...

I'm going to die here, aren't I?

I glance down, getting a good look at the thick metal cuff around my ankle, attached to a big, rusted chain.

Yep, I'm definitely dying down here.

My eyes dart around the room, fear's long fingers wrapping around my throat and squeezing tight as I struggle to find something, anything to help me. But it's no use, even the crowbar I tried to hit him with is long gone. It's just me, my brand new ankle accessory, and this... *dude.*

"Let me guess, you're gonna kill me."

I practically spit the words out at him, my voice sounding like I've been swallowing broken glass, trapped somewhere between violent and deeply desperate. I expect him to start a monologue or some shit, but he just ignores my question, sucking on a cigarette before blowing a cloud of smoke right into my face. I try my best not to give him the satisfaction of reacting, despite all the fear that's pumping through my veins right now.

When the smoke clears I finally get a good look at him: dark hair, olive eyes, and a long straight nose that's slightly bruised, possibly in our little tussle. Very little out of the ordinary, but the thing I find myself focused on is the intricate tattoo splayed across his throat. I trace as many of the lines as I can with my eyes before my vision starts to blur again, but it's enough to recognize the shape of a butterfly.

"How'd you get here?" He growls.

My brain is rushed into panic mode:

Be a good girl.

Play nice.

Submit.

And then, when I get my chance, I'll tear into his chest with my bare hands and eat his fucking heart. He might have me chained to the floor, but he doesn't know what kind of animal I am.

"I used my legs, dipshit."

He sighs.

"I meant how'd you get into this cellar, specifically."

I look up at him, a little smirk tugging at the corners of my mouth in spite of all my better judgement.

"Well, people usually attach their locks to their doors before they leave for the day."

Just as I feel like I'm making the tiniest bit of headway in our little battle of wits, the nauseating smell from his cigarette spikes my senses, and the room starts to spin again. I can feel my body lurch forward, completely out of my control, and I double over as I gag, trying a little too late to cover my mouth.

The man lets out another deep and heavy sigh.

"Jesus tit-fuckin' Christ, you're a mess."

I'm on all fours, heaving like a cat struggling to puke up a hairball.

What an attractive image, maybe he'll take pity on me.

"I need a doc—" I hiccup, trying to wipe away the spittle that's running down my chin. "A fucking doctor."

"No. You don't."

Tears rush down my face, but it's not from fear. I'm angry. So overwhelmingly angry. It wasn't supposed to be like this. I was supposed to start a brand new life.

"Fuck, just let me go!"

I can feel the veins pulse in my neck as I struggle to regain my composure, and he takes the opportunity to crouch down in front of me. I spot a pointed silver canine that sends a chill down my spine. There's an intensity to his stare that leaves me both unsettled and...

Aroused?

Okay, how hard did I hit my head?

I know how this game goes: I should look away, or smile, at least answer his question politely— submissive gestures that I know all too well. In most primates, eye contact is a silent signal of a threat or aggression, but I refuse to take my eyes off of him. I'm fucking bored of submission. When I plunged that knife into Gabriel's chest, I swore I'd never be a victim again, so if this Dollarama Lone Ranger is going to kill me, he's gonna end up learning just how crazy I really am.

"I know what you did," I rasp. "I saw you drag that guy into your barn, you fucking freak."

The man pulls something out of his pocket and drops it on the floor, but

I refuse to look. I'm not playing into whatever sick, twisted game he's got planned for me.

"Well good for you, seems like you have two functioning eyes after all. But I think what's more important is I know what *you* did to wind up here." His eyes flick down to the ground. "Look at it."

When I refuse to follow his command, he grabs me by the hair, shoving my face down until I'm forced to confront my recent-past, still wrapped in plastic.

"Found that in your car, along with a bunch of other little goodies. You've been busy, haven't you, little rabbit?"

"You don't know a goddamn thing."

"I know you were drivin' around with that tongue packed up safe like a trophy. Why don't you tell me where you got it?"

Is he mafia or some shit? Hell's Angels? Just curious? Regardless, I'm not telling him anything.

"That's not mine—"

"Obviously," he laughs. "You've still got one flapping around in that mouth of yours. Now, tell me the truth."

I take a breath, tilting my head with a cocky grin. Deny, deny, deny, that's the first rule of doing anything wrong. I've cultivated the skill over the years; learned to lie my way out of everything. Some people are born with a silver tongue, I used alchemy for mine.

"What will you give me if I do?"

I'm not really in a position to be bargaining with anyone, let alone a man who's already got me chained up, but at this point I'll try anything.

"You need to be patched up, clothed, and fed. I can do that, but only if you cooperate."

"So I'm a prisoner, then?"

He doesn't answer, pushing himself to his feet instead, and my eyes slip down to the big brass toes on his cowboy boots, a bull skull engraved on each of them.

"Did you like how it felt?"

I frown.

"What are you, a shrink or something?"

He snorts.

"You tell me."

"Well, if we're being honest with each other, I think you look like you stole a cowboy costume from Party City," I snarl. "But anything's possible. You could be a cop for all I know."

This whole thing could be some kind of elaborate ruse to get me to confess. Maybe the cops in Jericho found Gabriel's body faster than I thought. I have every reason to be paranoid, and every reason not to trust this asshole.

"Okay, you wanna play shrink?" His tone is mocking and dripping with malice. "You had a bad childhood. Bad father, maybe?"

"Jesus Christ, is that the best you've got?"

He snickers, cocking his head to one side. I'm about two seconds away from slapping that smirk right off his face.

"Yeah, definitely a bad father. The older you got, the angrier you got, but you kept quiet because you didn't want things to get worse. When you were finally able to get the fuck outta there, you picked someone exactly like your daddy—"

"I'm not being psycho-analyzed by some hillbilly motherfucker who looks like he takes Deliverance as gospel," I growl.

"Ohh, she's *feisty*," he purrs. "What are you gonna do chained to that floor?"

A pit forms in my stomach, but I can't tell if it's rage or fear.

"That's what I thought. So, did you enjoy it?" His gaze is hardened, but I see a glimmer of curiosity behind it all. "Was it as rewarding as you thought it would be?"

The chain around my ankle grows heavier, and I'm getting pretty certain that I've seen this movie before: just as I learn to fly, a man clips my wings and stuffs me in another goddamn cage.

He stands back up, drawing himself up to his full height after a few moments of my silence, all power and confidence. He's exuding a dominant energy that keeps my eyes glued to each and every one of his movements.

"Alright, so let's start again. You were about to tell me why you've got a human tongue in your car, along with a mess of other shit that makes you look *real* damn guilty. Deal hasn't changed: you tell me the truth, I'll patch you up. Hell, I might even bring you into the house."

"Oh, goody. I can't wait to see your fine collection of human lampshades and skin curtains. Are you gonna make me crawl around like a fucking dog, too?"

He clicks his tongue, running a hand through his hair.

"Alright, you wanna be like that? It'll be about three days before you're so dehydrated your organs start to shut down— actually, it might only be two given how beat up you are."

"So what's stopping you from just killing me?" I ask, trying to ignore the growing pain in my skull. "You seem like the kind of guy who doesn't take kindly to witnesses."

He stares me down, his eyes glittering with a practiced malice. He reminds me of a lion, calm and powerful, only striking when he deems fit. I can't help but wonder how fast his heart is beating, because mine hasn't stopped its chaotic rhythm since I woke up.

"I don't generally tell my deepest darkest secrets to men I know nothing about."

He smiles.

"I'm the man in charge of your fate, little rabbit."

I scoff, rolling my eyes. That nickname is really starting to grate on my nerves.

"Just tell me your *name*, you drama queen. The least you can do is give me that."

He arches a brow. I know I'm not getting anywhere calling him names, but after everything Gabriel put me through, whatever he could do to me would probably be a blessing. Besides, I think it's working.

"You think I have to give you anything in this exchange? The medical attention is generosity on my part, but if you just want to sit down here—"

"But you're curious, aren't you?" I grin, cutting him off. "About me? About what you found in that car?"

He lets out an irritated grunt, tongueing at his silver canine.

"Your name is Christine Annabelle Winter. Your birthday is October 15, 1996, which makes you 29 years old, you have an Alberta ID— oh, and you're probably wanted for murder. Sound about right?"

I *knew* I should have cut that damn card up.

"Fuck you."

The man only smiles, back in the saddle again.

"Well Christine, you've put me in a real shit position, because now I have to decide if I'm going to strip the meat off your bones, or if I need a little... pet."

Pet?

Did he just call me a fucking *pet?*

"I'd rather die."

He draws in another long breath, a contemplative look on his face for a couple moments before he shrugs, scoops up the tongue, and gets to his feet.

"If that's your choice. It'll be slow and it'll be painful; not the way I'd want to go out, but I won't stand in the way."

He strides up toward the exit, the wooden steps whining beneath his massive frame. As he pushes the door open a beam of sunlight shines through, carving him out like a macabre and terrifying statue for just a moment before it slams shut, leaving me cold, and in the dark.

So I guess that's it.

Murder by apathy.

Demonic Delights
PREACHER

Maybe I should be pissed off that she's interrupted my quiet existence, seen a bit too much of what's going on behind the curtain, but I'm not.

I'm curious.

Curiosity, though, without answers, is just frustration.

Interrogation didn't work, so I've decided to try a softer approach. She has no reason to trust me, but I have no reason to keep her alive outside of the dozens of questions rattling around in my brain.

Well, it's not just questions.

Underneath all those bruises and all that rage, there's beauty, and it's lying down in that cellar like a goddamn Christmas present, my name written in big, bold lettering on the tag.

I can't wait to unwrap it.

Her.

The plan is to move her from the cellar into my mama's old room, and I've been busy playing records and scrubbing everything down in preparation. The only thing I've replaced is the mattress, but other than that, it's stayed exactly the way it was since the day she died those seven years ago.

Christine needs stitches, food, a shower, and then...

I'm not really sure. I'll figure it out as I go.

Because after everything she's seen, I can't just let her walk away.

The closets are still filled with mom's long floral patterned dresses, sewing kits, and piled-up sketchbooks. She made all of our clothes growing up, and even taught me a thing or two about working with hide. How to skin it, tan it, and shape it into something beautiful. Something new.

Mama was a seamstress before she met my daddy, always said she wanted to be one of those big, fancy New York designers, and see her creations strutting down a runway. Unfortunately, she lived and died in Babylon, just like the rest of us.

At least after we put daddy in the ground, this room became her sanctuary. Sometimes when I walk past it at night, I swear I can still hear her humming a Connie Francis song on the other side of the door. I always picture her with a smile on her face, perched in her rocking chair by the window while she knits and looks out over his grave.

I've never mourned that motherfucker. He was evil and cruel, even became a preacher just so that he could have power and influence over this town and everyone in it. Thing is, it worked. He was well-respected and revered in Babylon, but what people didn't know were the things he did to us at home.

I can still feel his hands on me, all over— where they had no damn business being.

If you make a sound, I'll gut you like a fish, boy.

I shake off the thought, taking a drag off of my cigarette before wiping down the rest of the grime off of the windows.

The world is a damn sight better off without men like him.

It's early afternoon by the time I've cleaned the floors, wiped the baseboards, and put fresh sheets and blankets on the bed. I even replaced the musty lace curtains that were beginning to yellow from years of neglect.

But as I continue the work, my mind keeps wandering back to Christine.

I want to know what she did, how she did it, and most importantly, who the fuck he was. I want to know how she justifies taking a life, if her reasons and mine are one and the same.

Back in the cellar, I found my focus slipping, my mind pitching into thoughts of those blood-stained lips wrapped around me, about how pretty she'd look while I fucked her throat.

I squeeze my eyes shut and let out a soft groan as my cock strains against my jeans.

She knows what I am.

At least part of me.

That thought alone would normally be enough to make me want to crawl out of my skin, but this is different. I'm curious. The way she looked at that severed tongue, it was like she was reliving the scenario, reveling in the memories. I swear I saw the same light in her eyes, the same spark, one I only experienced once.

My first kill.

I put mama's trinkets into boxes, fold up her clothes and tuck them away as I try to shift my focus back to the tasks at hand, but it's not doing much good.

I wonder what she looks like under all those clothes. I bet she's soft; I bet her skin feels like fucking silk.

I wonder if she likes it rough.

One hand around her throat, carefully slicing my name into her skin with my hunting knife in the other. I want her on top of me, those perky little tits bouncing while she screams like an animal. Or on her back, writhing on my bed all bathed in crimson.

Fuck, she'd be so dirty, staining my pristine white sheets.

A sinner, chanting my name like a prayer.

My little demonic delight.

"Fuck this."

There's no use trying to crush these primal urges.

I shove one of the boxes aside and sit down on the bed. My cock is a demanding son of a bitch sometimes, always distracting me at the worst possible moments. I unzip my jeans, running my finger over the Jacob's Ladder that runs up the underside of my shaft: three thick barbells that give it some extra weight. I saw a guy in a porno with the piercing and thought it looked badass, but more importantly, he kept saying how good it felt and...

Shit, he wasn't wrong.

I spit in my palm and squeeze the shaft, letting out a soft hiss as the studs glide along my skin. My cock got more sensitive after the piercing, and I've had to build up some extra endurance over the years.

"Fuck..."

My thoughts start to dip into the darker corners of my mind, flashes of a chase through those woods in the pitch-black. Maybe once she's recovered, I'll leave the door unlocked one night while I lurk in the darkness.

It's always better when they think they have a chance. It lets you smell their fear.

Their desperation.

I want to see how a new predator survives as prey.

My strokes get faster, and I pull my hand away for a split second to coat my palm in more saliva. It's been years since I've wanted a woman this badly. I think the last time I fucked someone was...

"Ten years?"

Christ, it's embarrassing to hear it out loud.

I don't even remember her name; not sure if she ever gave it to me. To be honest, I didn't really care at the time. I met her at a nightclub after a failed hunt. One of the early ones. She was just my type: brunette, soft smile, and one hell of a wicked tongue.

I do like the mouthy ones.

But Christine? She might take the cake.

"Jesus Christ, little rabbit."

Heat spreads through me and I start to shake, but keep a steady pace as the heel of my hand bumps against my balls. It's a little painful, but addicting.

A soft grunt escapes my lips, and I squeeze my eyes shut until ropes of hot cum rush over my fist like a river, shivering and twitching as bliss courses through my whole body. I have to breathe in deep, slow and steady to calm my racing heart, but as I come back to earth, all I can think about is how I'm going to make that woman *mine*.

I take a breath, shoving my cock back into my jeans and zipping them up before heading into the ensuite bathroom to wash up. It's only a moment or two before I find myself staring into the mirror, into those cold olive eyes that are exactly like my father's. I've always hated that I look so much like him. It's why I got the tattoos. Daddy always said they were sinful, *the Devil's mark* he called them. But no matter how much muscle I build, or how many marks I add, I can't escape those eyes.

I run my hand under some cool water before pressing it to the back of my neck. It's sweltering outside, and with all the work I've been doing, I've been sweating like a fuckin' pig.

Suddenly, my phone lights up, buzzing on the bathroom counter.

RAPHAEL CALLING...

"Perfect timing," I chuckle, bringing it up to my ear. "I was about to call you."

"She dead yet?"

"Nope."

He sighs.

"I found a client willing to pay a small fortune for her."

I grit my teeth, trying to keep the snarl out of my voice. The last thing I need to do is piss my brother off right now.

"Not happening. She's staying with me."

"Goddammit, Preacher. She probably already knows what you are, wait much longer and she might find out about—"

"You know, I feel like we've had this conversation before, and it was just as boring back then." I lean up against the dresser, doing my level-best to cut the snark from my tone. "She needs clothes."

"Yeah? So what, you gonna go to La Senza and pick her out a cute new outfit?"

"You know I'd love to, but turns out you're the one with access to the bank accounts. Get her something comfortable, nothing too tight. I'm pretty sure she's got a broken rib or two."

"Fuck it, you know what? I've got some of Wren's old shit packed in boxes. I'll bring it over. Don't say I never do anything nice for you."

"Never have, never will. See you soon."

Looks like she gets to live another day.

Can't Stay High and Mighty Forever
PREACHER

I watch as he hurls my mama across the room like she's a fucking ragdoll. She hits the wall with a stomach-churning thud, rattling the house and knocking down our family portrait.

"Please, Elijah," she weeps as she sinks to the floor.

Her face is bloodied and bruised, her jaw and eyes so swollen she's barely recognizable.

How could he do this to her?

He said he'd love her in sickness and in health, and here he is, beating her until she's on the verge of death.

My rage becomes an inferno in my chest and I glance over at Raph, who's clutching his gun so tightly his hands are bone-white. We were always taught that killing is a sin, but then again, so are a lot of things daddy's been doing since we were kids.

My mother lets out another piercing scream as my father moves to grab her by the hair one final time, and I give Raphael a nod. The two of us raise our rifles, with his trembling in his hands as I'm calmer than I've ever been.

"Get the fuck away from her," I snarl.

He stops, straightening up. He's still in his Sunday fuckin' best.

I remember, in that moment, I saw the entire thing play out in my mind before it happened:

Elijah Blackthorne will take two shots to the torso, blood will splatter all over the *fireplace that he built with his own hands. It'll seep into the floor, into the roots of our home, and then that's all that'll be left of him. Nothing but long-dried blood.*

And a recurring nightmare.

I wake up with a start in mama's room to the sound of the dogs barking downstairs, followed by the familiar buzz of my phone. I lean over to read my brother's name on the call display.

Missed texts, too.

> RAPH
>
> Let me in.
>
> RAPH
>
> Hey, fuckass. LET ME IN.

Shit, how long was I out?

> RAPH
>
> I'll kick the door down.

"Hades! Charon!" I shout, running down the stairs double-time. "Heel!"

Both dogs fall silent, sitting back on their haunches as I step between them, finding my brother with his phone in hand on the other side of the door.

"What the fuck, man? Where were you?"

"Asleep," I grumble. "Thanks for pissing the dogs off though."

He just snorts, pushing right past me.

"Sure, yeah, come on in."

"What am I, a goddamn vampire? I'm your brother, I don't need a fuckin' invitation."

He tosses a duffel bag onto the coffee table, beaten brown leather, and I spot one of daddy's faint tattoos on the side. I made a matching set; gave one to him for Christmas the year after we did the deed as a joke. He said it was the most disgusting gift he'd ever received, but that didn't stop him from using it.

Practical to a fault.

"Go on, take a look." He slides his phone back into his pocket as the dogs sniff away at his legs. "I wanted to make sure everything was to your satisfaction, *Yer Majesty.*"

I rifle through the bag, finding a few pairs of jeans, some shorts, leggings, and a sweater or two, all of it mostly black and nondescript.

Good, I follow the same rule: simple clothes, simple colors, and no logos. A criminal who sticks out like a sore thumb is more than useless, after all.

Raph's mentioned a few times that the tattoos don't do me any favors in that area, but I don't give a shit. Skulls, crosses, demons, and poisonous flowers... I spent so much time enduring a monster during my childhood that now... well, let's just say I enjoy looking the part myself.

"So? What the fuck are you gonna do with her? Keep her as your own personal blow up doll?" Raph asks, wandering over to the little bar in the corner of the living room and picking out a glass.

"Just because your marriage went into the fuckin' gutter doesn't mean you have to take that out on me," I reply, folding the clothes back up and stuffing them back into the bag. "Thanks for this, by the way."

"I needed to get that shit out of the house, anyway," he murmurs, pouring himself a drink. "I don't wanna see it anymore."

I know *that's* a damn lie.

He's still sensitive about Wren walking out on him, and I don't think he's been with another woman since. We don't really talk about that kind of shit, though, so I guess I can't be sure. Our relationship is mostly business, sandwiched in between snipes and punches.

"You never answered my question, by the way."

"She'll work on the ranch. Helping out with the animals, cleaning, repairs—"

"What, like she's your wife?" He chuckles. "You and I both know you ain't the marrying type."

I cock a brow.

"You really want to keep treading ice this thin, baby brother? Because we could get *real* personal *real* quick."

I've got a laundry list of criticisms that would make him blow a gasket... and get me punched in the jaw, but I'll give him a chance to defend himself.

"You might as well have heart-eyes for her," he chuckles. "Fuckin' soft."

Okay, maybe I *will* hit him.

"She killed someone, Raph. And I wanna know who."

"There it is," he shakes his head. "So she's a project."

I want to tell him he's wrong, but I can't. I could mold her into an expert hunter, watch her lure unsuspecting men in like a spider, only to sink her fangs into them at the perfect moment.

And then I'd fuck her in a river of blood to celebrate.

Just the image of her taking my cock is starting to send me over the edge. She's on all fours, eyes rolled back, nails digging into the wood floor while I pound into that sweet little ass.

We could be incredible together.

"I ran her ID and the plates on the car, by the way. Found some breadcrumbs."

My stomach jumps.

"And?"

"Car's stolen, no surprise there. But it seems like she was with some dude named Gabriel Young. He was a member of a biker gang called The Disciples, over in Jericho— anyway, he's got a record as long as my cock."

I roll my eyes as he squeezes his crotch.

"You're fuckin' hilarious."

"Thanks." He grins, clearly proud of himself. "Anyway, looked through some police records, and the cops were called multiple times for domestic disturbances, but nothing ever came of it. He probably threatened her, made her sweet-talk them into dropping the charges."

"Sounds familiar."

When we were kids, we tried reporting our daddy to the police. What we got was a visit from an RCMP officer where he was on his best behavior, perfect gentleman, and faithful servant of the Lord. Then we got the beating of our lives once that car disappeared down the road.

Seems like Christine may have just been trying to protect herself. Maybe she's not a real predator after all.

"Preacher, you know someone's gonna come looking for her."

I've considered that as a possibility, but it's not like I couldn't take care of a few looky-loos on my own. Besides, Hades and Charon could use a new chew toy.

"She cut his tongue out, Raph. She's not just some pathetic charity case."

"Yeah, well I wonder what else she cut off," he chuckles. "You've got yourself a little psycho. Maybe she can match your freakazoid ass."

He struts toward me, handing me his nearly-full glass of bourbon.

"Be a doll and finish that for me, will ya? Can't be weaving back and forth over that center line, the pigs might pull me over and find a bag made of human skin or something. Wouldn't that be a hoot and a half?"

He dumps the clothes out on the sofa, looking up at me with a little twinkle in his eye.

"Have fun with your new cellar-girlfriend, and good luck not getting your dick cut off. Actually, does she take requests? Maybe she could do your tongue too."

"Fuck you," I chuckle.

"Ah, there's that classic Preacher wit." He ambles toward the door, taking one last look at me as he grasps the handle. "Don't call me, I'll call you!"

I shake my head as the door slams behind him, trudging back to the pile of clothes on the couch. I'm compelled to fold them, and so I do. Everything in this house has its place, and my brother knows damn well I can't stand to see a mess. One more little dig to get under my skin.

We've always fought like this, sometimes with fists and others with words, but at the end of the day, he and my mom might be the only things I've ever really loved. The problem is, I don't even know if that's true. I'm not even sure what that shit's supposed to feel like, after all.

Not to say I feel nothing. Most people get that wrong about psychopaths, they think we're pretty much robots, designed only to hurt and to kill. It's not like that, though. I definitely *feel,* the real problem is that most of those feelings are kind of superficial.

That is, except for anger.

And then there's lust.

Once all of the clothes are carefully laid out in their neat little piles, I gently scoop them up and take them upstairs to the sky blue dresser that my momma loved so much. It still smells like her rose-scented perfume, and if I close my eyes, I can practically see her in front of me in her pink apron, her dark hair pulled back into a long braid.

My daddy would yank on it when he'd bend her over the kitchen table in front of us. Said he was teaching us how to break in a woman.

My stomach lurches and I swallow bile.

My memories of her are tainted, stained with the torment he inflicted for so many years. The cuts and bruises, the brutal assaults, the broken bones. She endured all of his rage because she thought it would protect us. Of course, it didn't, but that doesn't mean she didn't try.

Out of the corner of my eye, I spot Charon wandering in, his claws clicking gently on the hardwood as he approaches.

"Daddy's having a friend over," I tell him, crouching down and letting him lick my face. "That means you and your brother are gonna be on your *best* behavior, you understand me? No biting, no barking, and *no* begging for food."

He butts my chin and I wrap my arms around him, kissing the top of his head.

"You're a good boy." I get to my feet and let out a breath. "I suppose it's time to bring the princess up to her tower."

I considered bringing the tranquilizer with me, but I figure the threat of a gun should make her cooperative enough, stuffing it into the back of my jeans before I head out to the storm cellar.

The moment I hit the outside air, I start to sweat. I've lived here my entire life and I've still never gotten used to this kind of humidity, the type that sinks right into your skin and weighs on your bones. Makes me wish I left a fan down there.

I unlock the cellar and slowly pull open the door, greeted by darkness, and a heavy silence both expected and a little worrying at the same time. God, I hope she's not dead. I've done too much work for it to end up all wasted.

When I reach the bottom of the stairs I find her curled up on the floor, and I'm more relieved than I should be to see that she's shivering, covered in sweat with her head tucked between her knees. I can't tell if she's sleeping with all that dark hair obscuring her face, but she's in no condition to fight back either way.

I approach her with caution, my hand resting carefully on my pistol, but when she looks up at me, all I'm met with is a mixture of exhaustion and despair.

"Just kill me," she rasps, her voice torn and shredded. "Get it over with."

"You need to be patched up."

I crouch down in front of her, brandishing my gun, matte black, with a gold bull skull engraved into the handle. It's the most precious thing I own aside from the land, and those two gorgeous beasts in my house.

"But I need you to know you're not escaping, no matter what. Understand?"

I take a risk, reaching out and brushing a few strands of hair away from her face.

She doesn't even flinch.

"Eyes up, little rabbit."

She obeys, another raggedy breath escaping through parted lips.

"I'm going to take you out of here, and if you so much as even *think* about trying to run or do anything clever, my little friend will make damn sure you don't get away."

Suddenly her exhaustion seems to fade a little, and her eyes blaze with a newfound anger. I can tell she's been threatened like this before, but I want to see what that rage can do when it's honed, and sharpened like a knife.

"Do you understand me, Christine?"

I keep my voice calm and measured as she sizes me, up eyes dancing across my face.

"My name is Ripley."

"Did you hit your head or somethin'? I know your name's—"

"I know what the I.D. says, you fucking donkey. I don't want to be Christine anymore. It's Ripley or it's nothing, take your pick."

I ignore the insult as a thrill rushes through me. My birth name is Michael, after the Archangel, but I threw it away the day I killed my daddy.

"Alright. Ripley it is, then."

Maybe we really are the same.

Folie à Deux

RIPLEY

He carries me up the stairs and into a quiet little bedroom at the end of the hall. It smells like bleach, and that Sunlight dish-washing liquid my mom used to use when I was a kid. I'm in so much pain that even the sight of a bed is a blessing. I just need to sit on something soft because every bone in my body feels like it's about to turn to dust.

The man sets me down, and I glance around at the soft lace curtains, the little doilies on the dresser, and the pale blue wallpaper with little flowers on it. For a guy who dresses all in black, and threatened to shoot me at least a couple times in one day, his choice in decor is oddly... tranquil?

I watch helplessly as he rifles through a large brown leather bag, setting his gun down beside it as he digs in a little deeper. I think about rushing him, but that thought is quickly replaced by a pain so sharp I'm forced onto my side.

"You've got broken ribs, a concussion, and you're heavily dehydrated. Now, I've got the medical supplies and the know-how to help you, and all *you* need to do is answer some questions for me."

"Why?" I ask. "You keep asking shit about me, why do you even care?"

He's quiet, like he's weighing his options, but before long his plush lips curl into a little half smile.

"Folie à deux. Do you know what that means?"

God, he's smug, staring at me like he thinks he's so much better. He probably thinks I'm some dumb little girl who wandered into murder. He'd shit himself if he knew how much planning it took.

"Bonnie and Clyde Syndrome. First discovered by Charles Lasègue and Jules Falret," I reply flatly. "Two people who share the same delusion— in a psychiatric sense, at least."

"And in a metaphorical sense?" The man asks.

I did a lot of reading while Gabriel was out running drugs and fucking other women. I found one of his old burner phones, kept it charged, hidden under a floorboard, and used it as my gateway to the outside world. I spent countless hours reading and researching: True crime books and old textbooks, in every field from sociology to criminology to psychiatry. I've read so much I probably know as much as some of those suckers who spent years getting their doctorates.

Then, the morning of the murder, I wiped that phone clean.

Nothing like a good ol' factory reset.

"It's two people who bring out the worst in each other," I sigh.

God, if he's looking for the Bonnie to his Clyde, he's going to have to do a lot better than chaining me up like a dog.

He sets the bag down at my feet. The stitching is slightly crude, like it was done by hand, and then I see the markings on it. Faded blue and black ink that bleeds into the textured material.

I stare at him, my heart rate picking up as he looms over me.

"Are you really gonna be able to help me? You said I'd be dead in a few days."

"Maybe you already are." He crouches down in front of me, those deep olive eyes striking in the morning sun. "Maybe I'm the Devil coming to take you home."

"You think rather highly of yourself, don't you?"

He roots around in his bag, chuckling as he pulls out a stethoscope, a bottle of alcohol, some wipes, and some bandages. Something in me is oddly proud I was able to make him laugh.

"Are you a doctor?"

"Not even close. Just read a lot of books."

He leans over me, getting a little too close as he presses the bell of the stethoscope against my back, but strangely, I don't mind it. It helps that he smells good, like a campfire mixed with motor oil and leather.

Silence stretches out between us as he moves the bell around, pressing it in different places while staring straight ahead. My body creaks like an old house as I shift, and I can feel the rattling in my lungs get worse the deeper I breathe. Maybe I caught the fucking plague down in that storm cellar.

He gestures to my hand.

"You're missing a finger."

I glance down at it, my breath hitching a little. I've been in so much pain I somehow forgot what I did back at the house. It's probably still sitting on the bathroom counter.

"Yeah, guess I am."

"Who did that to you?" He asks.

"I did."

He frowns.

"Why?"

"Are you gonna patch me up or not, hillbilly?"

The man snorts before crouching back down, and gently unwraps the bandages while I suck in a breath through gritted teeth. My body shakes from the adrenaline as flashes of pain pulse like a dull electrical current.

Jesus, it looks bad.

"You're lucky you didn't get gangrene," he tells me, beginning to clean the wound.

It hurts like a son of a bitch.

"I was gonna go to a clinic."

"Yeah?" The man snorts. "And tell them what?"

"Man, why do you even care?"

He secures a new bandage with some medical tape before moving on to clean the wounds on my face.

"I already told you, folie à deux."

"That's not a real answer to my question."

"But it's *an* answer."

Nothing worse than a deranged motherfucker who thinks he's a comedian.

"Okay, fine. Tit for tat, what's your name?"

He lets out a soft, contemplative hum, like he's trying to judge if telling me his name would be too dangerous or not. Or maybe he's just not used to people asking.

"It's Preacher."

"Wow, that's a... *really* dumb name."

His jaw ticks, and I wonder if I hit a sensitive spot. Maybe he's already sick of me.

"I gave myself that name after I shot my daddy and buried him out back."

He presses a cotton ball onto the bridge of my nose, and a sharp stinging sensation shoots through face.

"So, why did you take the tongue?"

The things Gabriel would say while he hit me, while he held me down and... it's all stuck on a loop in my head.

Worthless cunt.

Nobody could ever love you the way that I do.

It was the cruelest part of him, so I took it.

"I don't know," I whisper. "Are you going to let me go?"

Preacher studies me for a moment, his eyes gleaming.

"You saw what was in the cellar, and maybe more... You think you're gonna walk away from all this?"

"Fine. Then what are you planning on doing with me?"

He lets out a sigh, standing up and tossing the bloodied cotton balls into the trash.

"You'll stay here with me. I can teach you how to be better."

Preacher reaches into the bag once more and pulls out a black collar. He grabs me by the hair and slips it around my neck, tightening it enough that it's snug against my skin.

"What the fuck are you doing?"

"This has a tracking device in it. It's connected to my phone, and if you wander off the property, I'll know." He grins. "You're in my playground now, little rabbit. Whether you like it or not."

It's dark, soft leather, firm but almost buttery beneath my fingers. In the center is a small black circle that I assume is a tracking sensor.

"C'mon, you need a bath. You're gettin' mud all over those nice clean sheets."

He's surprisingly gentle, placing one arm on my lower back, and guiding me toward the bathroom just a few steps away. It's a classically pretty room with a large clawfoot tub and soft lighting. On the counter are a pair of leggings and a sweatshirt, neatly folded next to a set of towels.

"Be honest, do those belong to a dead person?" I ask.

"I sure hope not. Got 'em from a friend."

He strides toward the tub, and the tap squeals as hot water begins to flow.

Christ, the very *idea* of a bath is making my muscles ache. I can't wait to sink into that water, and—

"What the fuck are you doing?!" I squawk.

He's pulled a knife out from the holster on his belt, the blade pointed right at me.

"I'm cutting those filthy fuckin' clothes off you."

I clench my fists, my body coiled like a spring and ready to strike.

"You're not seeing me naked!"

He rolls his eyes.

"You've got broken ribs and a fucked up hand. You think you can lift those arms above your head?"

What a joke, of course I can. I know I can. I'm standing in front of him in the worst pain I've ever been in my fucking life, but if he thinks I can't lift—

"Ow, mother*fucker!*" I scream, my arms barely halfway up before the pain makes me double over.

Preacher catches me, barely keeping me from hitting the floor at the last second, and before I realize it I'm staring into his eyes.

They're softer than I expected. Maybe even warm?

"I want to make a deal."

"What kind of deal?"

He smiles.

"You like role play?"

"You're a sick fuck," I snarl.

"Takes one to know one." He cuts through the rest of my shirt. "How about this, we'll play teacher and student. I have a hell of a lot of knowledge to share... and you *were* planning on killing again, weren't you?"

I let out a hiss, my heart pounding as the tip of his blade gently nicks my skin.

"Oops." Preacher grins again. "I guess my hand slipped."

"Bullshit."

He guides the blade upwards and cuts my shirt open, revealing the black sports bra I put on this morning. I fold my arms over my chest, feeling totally exposed.

"Can you turn around while I get undressed at least?"

"You tried to beat me to death with a crowbar, and you think I'm gonna turn my back on you?" He scoffs. "You must have hit your head pretty damn hard. Get in the tub."

"Are you seriously going to watch me bathe?"

He isn't ashamed about letting his eyes wander, and I feel goosebumps rise on my skin. I'm a little surprised by how much I like the way it makes me feel. Wanted. Desired. More importantly, it's something I can use to my advantage.

"Fine," I sigh.

"Atta girl. I'll even do you the courtesy of keeping my eyes on the floor."

He averts his gaze, and I slowly pull down my jeans, wincing slightly as they take off some dried blood and leg hair along the way.

That's when I realize...

I didn't pack any panties.

You always forget something on a trip, don't you?

My movements are slow, partially because of the pain, but partially because I want to see if he'll sneak a peek. It feels like we're both testing each other.

"Get in the damn tub, Ripley," he growls.

I quickly peel off my bra before walking over, glancing up at him as he continues to stare at the floor. I kind of feel like I'm standing in front of one of those guards outside of Buckingham Palace. When I was a kid, my sister told me they were trained to kill. I think that's bullshit, but I never bothered to google it.

My muscles begin to melt the second I step into the tub, and finally, for the first time in days, I can feel all the tension start to fade. Preacher lifts himself up onto the bathroom counter, still dutifully keeping his eyes fixed on the floor. I stare at the dark tattoos that decorate his arms, tracing the lines all the way up to the butterfly on his neck.

I swear I can feel him soften as I stare, the crease in his brows practically disappearing in moments.

"So, why didn't you kill me?" I ask. "You can't have been on this whole Bonnie and Clyde thing from the start."

"It's really simple, I have a code: no women and no kids."

I smirk.

"Oh god, you're a psycho with a moral compass?"

Preacher doesn't say a word, but I catch his lip curling into that same small grin I've seen a couple times before as I start lathering myself up. When I reach up for my shoulder, the pain shoots through my ribs all over again, and I drop the soap into the water with a loud splash.

"You need help?" He asks, still careful not to let his eyes wander.

"I'm fine."

I reach into the tub with my uninjured hand, but the soap slips from my grip.

Once.

Twice.

Three times...

"You have got to be kidding—"

There's a sudden thud and he's right next to me, grabbing a washcloth and reaching into the tub to get the soap.

His fingers graze my thigh.

My breath catches in my chest and I bite my lip.

"I can—"

He lifts it out and scowls, his eyes locking with mine.

"Just let me help."

My body goes rigid as he glides the bar along my back, but he's careful, not going any lower than my shoulder blades and taking care to keep his eyes locked on mine.

Is it wrong to want him to keep touching me? I can't remember the last time a man was kind, or even neutral toward me. I have to admit, it feels good to be taken care of like this.

But then my stomach growls, loudly, making this already embarrassing situation that much worse.

"Hungry?"

"I already ate."

Actually I was running on nothing but Diet Coke and homicidal rage when I got here.

Fuck that tornado.

"You're gonna need to learn to lie better than that, little rabbit," he chuckles.

"Why do you call me that, you think it's funny or something?"

"It's because you have big, beautiful eyes. Like a scared little bunny."

I've been told my stare is intense, almost unsettling. My eyes are a bright and cool blue color, just like my mother's. My father said they made him nervous. Used to make me close them when...

Well.

Preacher dips the washcloth into the water, his knuckles brushing up against my thigh, and I get another electric thrill rocketing through me as he rinses away the suds.

Once he's finished, he holds out the washcloth and the bar of soap.

"You can do the rest on your own."

I wonder if he felt the same excitement that I did.

Communion With the Devil
RIPLEY

To my surprise, Preacher's been letting me wander around the house— all under his watchful eye, of course. He was quick to show me the tracking software on his phone.

I'm just a little red dot.

I peruse his living room, trying to ignore the tightness around my neck from the collar as his eyes follow me from the kitchen door. There's a bar cart packed with expensive booze and fancy glassware, sketches of horses, and some abstract paintings, but what really draws my attention are the books that are lining his shelves.

Poetry, Shakespeare, Jane Austen, anatomy, and even legal textbooks.

I guess if you're going to break the law, you might as well study it.

He's also clean— almost *too* clean. The house feels like a museum, and I'm here standing behind some imaginary velvet rope.

"Were you in the military?" I ask, dragging my finger along the bookshelf.

Not a speck of dirt.

"No," Preacher chuckles, glancing back to the stove. "Why do you ask?"

He's sipping a drink, eyes gleaming as that sizzling sound from the pan grows more intense.

"Because you're a neat freak. Most military dudes are neat freaks. They also kill a lot of people."

"No military, just a strict religious prick of a father."

I snort. We have something else in common.

"How long have you owned this house?"

"Inherited it after my mama died."

"You got siblings?" I ask.

"Yep. A brother. You?"

"I've got a sister."

"Younger?"

I nod.

Gabriel was my first ticket out of that fucking house, and I didn't look back.

I pull one of his books off the shelf, flipping through it until my eye lands on a poem called *The Drowned Lover* by Percy Shelley.

Oh! dark lowered the clouds on that horrible eve,

And the moon dimly gleamed through the tempested air;

Oh! how could fond visions such softness deceive?

Oh! how could false hope rend, a bosom so fair?

Thy love's pallid corse the wild surges are laving—

"That's one of my favorite collections."

The book tumbles from my hand in surprise, but he catches it, grinning at me.

"Jesus, warn a gal, would you?"

Preacher's smile grows wider as he slides the book back onto the shelf. There's a fine dusting of flour on his hands, a bit of it messing up his otherwise pristine shirt.

"Come and eat. I made pasta and meatballs."

The table is fully set, with wine glasses, shiny plates, and cutlery, all accented by a crimson tablecloth, with his two rottweilers guarding the meal like gargoyles. I'm a little nervous, not quite sure how they feel about me, but as we approach, one of them takes a step forward and gives me the opportunity to hold out my hand to him.

"Charon," Preacher warns. "You be gentle."

Charon sniffs at my fingers before gently licking them. I like dogs. I always have. They're loyal and protective. Easy to trust.

"How do you tell them apart?"

"If you look carefully you can see Charon has a smudge on his nose, and Hades... well, he's just an asshole."

"I mean, you know what they say. Some dogs take after their owners."

Out of the corner of my eye, I swear I see him grin. But then his hand wraps around my waist and he pulls me in close, lips pressed right up to my ear as warm breath fans against my skin.

"Don't forget who saved you, little rabbit." He releases me just as quickly as he grabbed me, pulling out a chair. "Sit."

Charon lets me give him one little scratch on the top of his head and I slide into the chair, looking down at a beautiful plate of pasta with a single large meatball resting on top. My mouth waters and it's a struggle to stop myself from grabbing my fork and digging in immediately.

This is all so strangely civil for a man who has a collection of missing person's IDs. I really can't figure him out. He's rugged, dangerous, and certainly deadly, and yet this meal looks like something you'd find on a curated Pinterest board.

"Here." He pulls a small green pill bottle fom his pocket and taps out two white tablets, dropping them right next to my fork. "Take those."

"Ooh, is it cyanide! You really shouldn't have."

"It's Percocet, you smartass. You need something for the pain, right?"

I look down at the pills, shining like little gems against the blood red cloth.

"How do I know you're telling the truth?"

Preacher stares at me before tapping out a pill and popping it into his mouth, following it up with a big sip of wine before showing me his tongue.

"Satisfied?"

Maybe he really *does* want to help.

I snatch up the pills, staring at them for a moment.

"You'd better not be bullshitting me."

I wash them down with some wine, grimacing at that obnoxious phantom-feeling, like the pills are still lodged in my throat despite knowing they're long gone.

"Atta girl. Now, eat up."

I go right for the meatball, choosing to ignore the way the *atta girl* made my cheeks warm. I need to be on my toes, and that shit isn't helping. A little bit of the juice seeps onto pasta sauce when I cut into it, and my mouth waters involuntarily. The groan that leaves my body along with the first bite probably sounds inhuman.

It's a struggle to eat like a civilized human being when this is the first *real* food you've had in months. Suddenly, another meatball is dropped onto my plate and I look up at Preacher.

"What's this for?"

"You're obviously starving, just eat it."

I stare at my plate, suddenly flooded with shame. Gabriel starved me on purpose, forcing me to exist on nothing but saltines and peanut butter half the time, so this feels positively decadent.

"Where'd you learn to cook?" I ask, tentatively slicing into the second meatball.

I keep expecting him to cruelly yank the plate away, or worse, throw it at me like Gabriel did. I was hoping that fuckwit wouldn't have such an iron grip on my mind after he lost his head, but here we are.

"Well, my mama taught me everything she knew before she passed." He tops up our wine glasses before digging into his own food. "She always said the way to a woman's heart is to cook her a good meal. Hasn't really worked for me before, but—"

"I mean, you've got your own unique 'chain her to your floor' method, so there's that."

I expect him to get angry, but all he does is grin, giving me another good look at that silver canine.

"Let's just call that plan B."

Preacher's demeanor reminds me of an animal's, his energy bordering on playful yet... aggressive. It's like he could flip on a dime, and there's something very compelling about that specific kind of danger.

"So, let's get this out of the way: you kill people, right? Lots of people? That's why all the ID's were down in the cellar."

His throat bobs as he takes a bite of pasta, chewing for a moment in contemplation.

"It's not quite that simple, but you're not wrong."

Finally, we're getting somewhere.

"Alright, so what kind of people do you kill? You said no women and children, any other rules?"

"I kill... bad men."

"But what kind of bad men? Am I gonna find out you're gutting dudes that run red lights, or are we talking more biblical here?"

"Well, the guy I was working on before I found you was charged with rape and domestic violence." He takes another bite of his food, his eyes gleaming with pride. "That bad enough for you?"

I'm starting to figure out our dynamic a little more. He shares, I share, and then there's some trust. But where does that little bit of trust lead us? He still has me collared, so of course he feels comfortable enough to start revealing some truths. There aren't any real consequences if he says too much.

"What do you do with them after you kill them? You bury the bodies out here?"

He chuckles.

"Did you ever take communion? The blood and body of Christ?"

"When I was a kid, yeah."

It's hard not to be enchanted by his smile, soft and boyish with a devilish charm that makes it nearly impossible to tear your eyes away. I kind of hate how attractive he is, it makes this whole being a prisoner thing a little bit harder to handle.

"Well, I have clients who are willing to pay good money for exotic meats. Let's just call it communion with the devil."

It's so quiet, you could hear a pin drop. I glance down at my food, suddenly *very* aware of the texture in my mouth.

"Exotic..."

"Don't worry, I wouldn't feed you something like that without askin'."

I swallow what's still in my mouth before dabbing at my cracked lip with a napkin. I don't know if I believe him, but it's not like I can do anything about it at this point.

"Okay, so what you're telling me is... you sell human meat?"

He cocks his head just a bit, leaning back confidently in his chair as he observes me.

"That's right."

The room starts spinning, or maybe it's been spinning for a while now. I can't tell if it's the wine, the percs, or the confession I just heard.

Probably all three.

"I— Oh god, do *you* eat it?"

"Chef's gotta taste his own cooking, doesn't he?" He tilts his head the other way, a little playfully. "Does that bother you?"

"Jesus, why not just become a hitman or something? Did you wake up one day and think 'wow, it sure would be a cool idea to traffic human meat'?"

"I sort of am a hitman, actually. Turns out the money's just better on this side of the business."

My nausea slowly gives way to curiosity. I want to dig deeper, but I'm also afraid of what I'll find when I do. However, it only takes a few more bites of food and sips of wine before the list of questions in my head begin to pile up.

How does he choose his victims? How does he hunt them? How does he kill them?

And where the fuck do you store a whole human body?

But instead I ask...

"How much do you make?"

"More than enough. I keep what sustains me, and this house, and give the rest of it away. Usually my partner funnels it into different charity organizations and shit like that."

I'm pretty certain that's money laundering, but then again, I *used to think* it was when you put your money in the washing machine to clean off that invisible tracking ink, so what the fuck do I know?

"What kind of charity?"

"Women's and animal shelters, food banks, things that help people."

I frown.

"I have to admit, I've never heard of an altruistic serial killer before."

"Well, I get something out of it, too." Preacher leans forward, his piercing eyes locked on mine. "But I have a feeling you and I share the same darkness. I have something to offer you, a proposal really, but first, I need you to lay all your cards out on the table. So tell me, little rabbit, is the truth something you're willing to trade?"

This man has an undeniably powerful presence, and even seated in his chair, it feels like he's looming over me.

"I... need to know what I'd be getting in return."

And there's that smile again.

"How about salvation?"

Already Mine
PREACHER

"And what does this salvation look like?" She asks.

Ripley's been in fight or flight her whole life, I can see it carved into her skin like a brand. When you come crawling out of that kind of hell, you start to smell it on other people like a sickness. I want the truth as she knows it, to swallow every last morsel until I truly understand her.

"Anything you want. Money, power, and a constant flow of bloody chaos to satisfy that beast inside of you."

I reach up to brush away a wave of damp curly hair, and to my surprise, she leans into my touch. There's no denying the fact that she's beautiful, even with the bruises and the split lip. It's those eyes that kill me, though. That bright blue that both unsettles, and takes my breath away.

"All you have to do is tell me what you did."

She breathes deep, scrutinizing me as I listen to her heavy heartbeats. I take in every bruise, every freckle, and every line on her face. The longer I stare, the more captivating she becomes.

"I killed him," she snorts. "Obviously."

"How?" I lick my chops like one of the dogs under the table, hungry for any morsel of information she can give me. "Why?"

"Why? He kept me prisoner in that house. Starved me, beat me, tortured me!"

My anger rips through me like a bullet as I see my own past reflected on the woman in front of me.

"How long were you with him?"

"Almost 10 years. Funny part is I ran away to be with him, dropped out of school and everything."

All that time, all that wasted potential.

"I thought he saved me at first." She scoffs. "What a fucking joke."

"Saved you from what?"

She bristles a little, draining the rest of her wine.

"Let's just say a different kind of monster."

I nod, grabbing the bottle and pouring her another glass.

"Alright, so how'd you kill the boyfriend?"

"I stabbed him until he looked like ground beef." Her face changes, her eyes gleaming as she licks the last of the wine from her lips. "And then I cut off his head, and took his tongue."

The hairs on the back of my arms stand straight up.

Fuck.

I swear I've never listened more intently to someone in my life. These days, it's always just my brother yammering in my ear about how we have to be careful or what the client wants.

It's rare that I get to talk about the intricacies of a kill like this.

Ripley's chest heaves and she takes another swig of wine, almost like she's trying to distract herself, or keep herself from saying something she shouldn't.

But I can't let her relax; I want to hear it all, all of the grimy, sinful details.

"What'd you do with the head?"

"I put it on a bookshelf facing the bedroom door."

She lets a giggle slip out, the cracks in her mask beginning to show me her true face.

"That's a hell of a nice touch."

"Thanks."

She's me, but not really me, sadistic in her own way, while being less curated and controlled. The problem is she's still too focused on this one man. At least for now.

"Gabriel was in deep shit with this guy named Adonis, from the Disciples? Not sure if you've heard of them. Anyway, Adonis told him he was coming to take his head, along with me and the rest of his stuff. Guess I did half the job for him."

"And how, exactly, did you do it?"

I'm starving for the details.

"Found a saw in the basement. Used that for the head and a big-ass knife for the tongue. I was kinda surprised by how hard it was."

I let out a soft exhale, slumping back into my seat and she frowns.

"What's wrong?"

It's impossible to ignore her pointedly raised brow, almost like she's challenging me.

"Nothing," I laugh. "I was just thinking that explains why your cuts are so sloppy."

"Oh, I'm sorry. Should I have given you a call? Asked for some tips?"

She's funny. Maybe a little annoying sometimes, but funny.

"I can teach you how to do it properly. There's a much smaller knife for that kind of detail work."

And if she sticks with me, I'll teach her everything else as well. It seems like we both like to let our demons out to play.

Ripley's shoulders start to shake, and at first I think she's crying, but then she lets out a hyena-like cackle that makes both dogs get to their feet. I quietly hold my hand out, letting them know to stay put. She's not a threat.

"What's so funny?"

She doubles over, the sound of her fork clanging against the plate like a gunshot, howling with laughter as she ignores everything else around her. That's when I realize the booze and pills must have finally hit her, all at once.

"I stuck him like a fucking pig!" Little wheezes eek out in between gasping breaths. "He begged me to stop."

I'm feeling that giddiness all over again.

"And the blood, what about the blood?"

This is *exactly* the kind of crazy I was hoping to get from her.

"There was so much. So much fucking blood, all over everything."

The moonlight drips through the little crack in the curtains, making her look even more grotesquely beautiful, her corpse-like skin and the mottled bruising around her eyes reminding me of the body parts I keep in my freezer.

"Did you feel guilty?" I ask, keeping my voice as calm and gentle as I can manage.

"No," she snorts, a big stupid smile eclipsing her face as she finally begins to catch her breath. "It was fucking beautiful."

She suddenly looks a hell of a lot more relaxed, like a weight's been lifted off her shoulders. That's a good sign; the more free she feels around me, the easier it'll be to gain her trust. In time, I may even be able to take that tracking collar off.

"I remember when I shot my daddy," I murmur, the words leaving my lips before I even realize they're coming. "Seeing all that blood, it felt like seeing the ocean for the first time... Or at least I assume. Never been before."

Ripley stares at me, her eyes half lidded as she gnaws on her lip.

This might be the most intimate I've ever been with someone, at least if you don't count the intimacy that comes with drawn-out torture. Sex is just a reflex, a short and simple blissful moment between two people that you both forget eventually.

But this? Breaking bread and confessing our sins?

This is a bond.

We sit for a while, a long silence working its way in between us, and I find myself feeling strangely vulnerable, ready to tell her almost anything.

And then Ripley starts snickering again.

"What's funny now, little rabbit?"

"I choked on his goddamn lip."

"You what?"

She lets out another wild cackle.

Oh, fuck. She really is high as a goddamn kite.

"I don't know what the fuck I was thinking! I just... tore it off."

Sometimes I miss that rush that comes along with not *quite* knowing what you're doing. Over the years you become more confident, more controlled. You start to pick up skills and add them to your bag of tricks, making everything so much easier. Removing the friction.

It's a necessity, really, staying ahead of the curve. After all, every serial killer who stops killing does so for two reasons: they die, or they get caught.

Still, I've lost a lot of that manic whimsy over the years. Now, everything I do is calculated, right down to the way I skin my victims. No room to improvise. Ripley, on the other hand, seems like the type to make things up on the fly.

I can work with that... to an extent.

"Did you clean up afterward?" I ask.

She shakes her head, lifting her bandaged hand and gesturing with it.

"Had to make them think I was dead too, right?"

"Clever rabbit."

Her mouth twitches, *just* short of curling into a seductive little smirk before she pulls it back to neutral.

"So, who's your main target?" She asks. "Like, what do you look for specifically?"

This is more of a Raph question, but can't rope him in just yet. Not until I know who and what I'm really dealing with.

"It's pretty broad, actually. Men who rape, men who hurt kids, men who beat or kill women... People the system lets slip through the cracks." I clear my throat. "We have clients and those clients put in specific orders, and that's where my partner comes in. He starts hunting through court records, arrest documents, and police databases. He aims for the guys who think they've gotten away with it, anyone not currently being seriously investigated anymore, and then that list of names is delivered straight to my doorstep. The market for sinners is small, but some people are willing to pay a hell of a lot for what the Devil has to offer."

"Nice metaphor, Shakespeare."

"Well well, was that a compliment?"

"I have no fuckin' idea." She frowns, like she's just realized something for the first time, and leans forward. "Okay, so what's your modus operandi?"

"Mm, so clinical."

She stammers a little before clearing her throat, clearly embarrassed.

"I, uh, I read a lot about people like us. Modus Operandi means—"

"Your method, your tools, your victimology." I grin. "You really think I'm just some dumb hick, don't you?"

She looks mortified, but I reach out before she can turn away, sliding my fingers beneath her chin and tilting her head to face me.

"You know what your little trophy told me about you?"

I release her as she swallows, steadying her breathing.

"Enlighten me."

Her voice is smooth and sharp, teetering right on the edge of control. She's not angry, but she is challenging me with her gaze, asking me to share.

"Your beast is vicious—"

"Thank you."

I grin.

"But you're also timid."

She frowns, obviously annoyed with my reading.

"How so?"

"Years of social conditioning. Being told to sit down and shut up, being called a 'good girl' for blending into a crowded room, for being a wallflower. It's made you afraid to step into your own power."

"Were you afraid?" She asks, leaning in closer. "Before the first time?"

"I was angry."

"I wasn't angry when I cut out Gabriel's tongue," she whispers. "And I wasn't afraid, I was…"

She trails off, like she's struggling to find the words for this darkness we share, one that envelops you like an old friend.

"Tell me."

She glances over her shoulder, like she's afraid the cops are gonna bust through that door and take her away at any moment.

"It felt like I was possessed."

Every new detail draws me in deeper. If she can be trained, if I can break her down and rebuild her again… she could be perfect.

"Tell me more."

"It was like something overtook me, holding all of my anger, all of my grief… All of the things I wasn't allowed to feel. But then all of a sudden, that shit was gone, all at once with that first clumsy thrust of the knife." Her eyelids flutter, and she absentmindedly licks her lips. "It was fucking orgasmic."

Her whole face changes and I see it clearly: she's opened a door she can't close, straight to the woman I want.

"Orgasmic," I rasp. "That's an interesting word choice."

She's malicious, vile, and cold-hearted, everything reflected infinitely between us.

"What would you call it?"

I grin, confidently studying her once more as I cock my head to the side.

"Total freedom."

"That's oddly poetic for a cowboy."

I snicker, and we settle back into our comfortable silence, each of us cleaning our plates. It's not until she leans over to let the dogs lick her fork that I notice she's starting to nod off, her head drooping ever so slightly. I push my chair back and quickly pluck the utensil from her hand to keep her from accidentally poking one of them in the eye.

"Ripley?"

She rolls her head to the side, staring up at me, eyes half closed with a big, stoned smile on her face.

"Hmm?"

"You need to rest."

She barely makes a fuss at all as I scoop her up in my arms and carry her all the way upstairs, kicking the bedroom door open and laying her down on the bed. She must have been further gone than I thought.

"Get some sleep," I mutter. "I'll check on you a little later on, to make sure everything's alright."

She watches me as I head across the room, laying in silence as I switch off the lights and lock the door behind me. I half expected more resistance, for her to try something at the last second, to rush for the door, but no.

She doesn't know it yet, but she's already mine.

Don't Think, Just Eat It

RIPLEY

The second it hits me, I'm scrambling to cover my face. It feels like barbed wire being pulled too tightly around my nerve endings, making them burst. I'm curled up like a sad little piece of cocktail shrimp, clutching the duvet for dear life; is there anything fucking *worse* than the sun waking you up at the asscrack of dawn?

"Goddammit."

Slowly, very slowly, my body starts to unfurl, begrudgingly rolling over onto the side of the bed. That's when I spy a glass of water waiting for me on the nightstand, along with a conspicuous green bottle.

I don't remember much from last night, other than sitting at his table, cackling gleefully while I recounted how I killed Gabriel.

Orgasmic.

Why did I say that? I could have said anything else.

It was all that weird, murdery sexual tension he's created. Standing too close to me, grabbing my waist, watching me bathe... It got me riled up.

I grab the glass of water and scan the green bottle on the nightstand.

"Hydrocodone," I murmur. "What the fuck is that?"

I skim the label, spotting the brand name.

VICODIN.

"Nice work, cowboy."

There are only two pills left, which is probably intentional; makes sure I can't swallow the whole bottle as an easy-out.

"Maybe he actually gives a shit about me," I mumble, tossing the pills back. "Hope this doesn't bite me in the ass."

The clock on the wall reads 7:00am. I don't know when I went to sleep, but now that I'm awake, I feel strangely refreshed despite the soreness. I take another sip of water, pausing to listen to the birds singing outside; it's a chipper little melody that kind of makes me feel like Cinderella, even if just for a moment.

Even if I'm locked up in a psychopath's house.

Gabriel used to have me on edge the moment I woke up in the morning — demanding breakfast, demanding I clean, demanding sex...

I was his prisoner.

"Hades, cut it out!" Preacher barks.

God, of course he's already up and about. I guess cowboys wake up early to feed... pigs and shit? You'd think I'd know more about the farm lifestyle, considering I grew up around them, but I lived in Edmonton, which means a whole lot of gunshots, but not many cowboys.

I make my way to the window, cautiously parting the curtain as I take another sip of water, and what I see almost makes me drop my glass.

Preacher is shirtless, sweating as he drives post after post into the ground. His jeans hang low on his hips and I can see his muscles rippling as he slams his sledgehammer down again and again.

"Fuck me," I murmur, tracking his movements as he walks toward the big pile of posts, his arms flexing a little as he drags another one into place.

Last night as I was getting dressed for dinner, I couldn't shake the thought of his other reason for keeping me alive, besides his moral code.

What did he see in me outside of the severed tongue and the kill kit in my car? More importantly, does he see me as a protégé or potential competition? Is that why he wants to teach me everything, so he can keep tabs on me?

I don't need a fucking babysitter, or worse, another warden, that's for damn sure. He was right about one thing though, I was sloppy. I left some serious carnage behind in Jericho.

Every so often I think about that cop on the road, and a familiar shock of terror rushes down my spine. Did he have time to run the plates, and even if he didn't, is there a chance he'll remember me enough to pick up the trail?

Should I tell Preacher, or is the knowledge I might be a risk to him gonna get me killed? Even with his code, I can't imagine he'd keep me around if me just being here was threatening his entire operation.

I watch intently as he places the newest post, centering it carefully before leaning down to grab his hammer, his jeans slip just a *little* lower than before, giving me a damn good look at the defined dents in his hips.

Before I notice it I'm fogging up the window, my nose practically smashed up against the glass like fucking a dog who just heard her owner coming up the driveway. It's kind of pathetic, but...

"I wonder how big he is."

Jesus, back the fun-bus the fuck up, Ripley. I've gone from telling this man he looks like he robbed a Party City to wondering about the size of his dick overnight.

Like I said... pathetic.

But I can't deny the heavy, pulsing heat between my thighs.

Preacher glances up, catching my eye for a moment before I'm able to fully take a step back. I hope he didn't notice how intently I was staring. To my surprise, he only smiles, giving me a polite nod before driving his post all the way into that newly dug hole in one swing.

My stomach growls, and I'm grateful for an excuse to switch gears from crushing on my captor to more immediate concerns. I need to figure out a way to let him know I'm starving, and step one in that process is definitely *don't be almost completely naked when you try to get his attention,* but when I turn toward the dresser, a large silver platter catches my eye.

How did I not notice that before? Oh, right, I got busy looking at the hot psycho outside before I actually did anything to explore my surroundings. Well, it looks like he already anticipated my grumbling stomach.

I crane my neck, tentatively taking a few steps forward while trying to see exactly what's in the bowl; hopefully it's not his special brand of meat, I'm not sure I'm ready for that kind of initiation first thing in the morning.

As I get closer, a small nondescript jar resting on the platter beside the bowl catches my eye. At first I think it might be honey, or maybe jam of some kind with the lid wrapped in that traditional red and white checkered cloth, but no.

I can clearly see Gabriel's tongue floating in formaldehyde.

My heart skips several beats and I rush forward, plucking it off of the dresser and gazing gleefully through the glass. The tongue bobs like a buoy as I gently turn the gift in my hand, looking at it from every angle.

It's a strange offering, but somehow makes me feel...

Appreciated?

Wanted?

I admire it for a few more moments before my stomach starts to growl all over again, begrudgingly putting it back down and turning my attention to what's in the bowl.

"Oatmeal?! Fuck, why don't you just give me a big bowl of congealed jizz?"

Okay, maybe that was a bit much.

It actually doesn't smell too terrible, and while it looks like little chunks of slime in between the berries, there's some honey and a small bowl of fruit to go with it, which will make choking it all down a little easier.

I draw in a breath, like I'm bracing myself to jump off of a cliff.

The berries are tart, and the honey gives it a good sweetness, but it's still a nightmare to swallow, slick and slimy as it slides down my throat.

Don't think, just eat it.

I'm hunched over like an animal, practically forcing the food down, which is probably why I don't hear the footsteps coming up the stairs. I barely have time to react before the door swings open, and Preacher steps inside, fully clothed this time.

Shame.

He stares at me, sweat still glistening on his brow, his cowboy hat tipped up just right to perfectly frame his cool, dark eyes. The oatmeal slides off my spoon, plopping into the bowl as he glances around the room.

"You find your medication?"

I clear my throat, straightening up and wiping some slop off my chin.

"Yes, uh..." I stammer, not sure exactly what to say. "I guess I should thank you?"

He lets out a soft grunt, ignoring my question as he flicks his head toward the jar.

"Didn't want to waste your first trophy, hope you don't mind."

I glance back over my shoulder, biting my lip to keep from smiling too wide. I'm not certain if this is the grossest thing someone's ever done for me, but it might just be the sweetest.

"It's nice. I like it."

What a horrifying thought.

Preacher takes off his hat, using it to gesture toward the door.

"You're gonna see the barn and the incinerator this afternoon."

"That's pretty short for a tour, what's so special about those two spots?"

"That, my dear, is where the magic happens. I told you that I can train you, shape you into something better, but to tell you the truth, having some help with this side of the business'll make things a little easier on me."

He's practically beaming, clearly excited to start this whole process, whatever it is.

"You want me to work for you?" I ask, the incredulity already slipping back out from behind my lips.

"We'll see if you've got what it takes. First off, I need to teach you what I know, about killing these sons of bitches and everything that comes after."

"And then what?"

"Then, there's the hunt."

"Does that mean I get to—"

"It ain't what you think, rabbit. You gotta see things from both ends before you'll really understand."

I bristle, my hands balling into tight little fists. I'm nobody's goddamn prey.

"You want to train me to be a killer, but you're gonna chase me around your fucking farm like a psycho? What the hell does that accomplish?"

"The goal is to see how well you do as the *hunted*, before you get to play the *hunter*. I want to see your animal instincts, your adaptability, how resourceful you are, and how well you fight back."

There's a malicious gleam in his eyes as he lets his gaze wander up and down my body, but I don't shrink, or turn away. I haven't forgotten about the sizzling chemistry we had when I was in the tub. I was convinced he was going to take what he wanted then and there, just like every man I've ever met, but he didn't.

Maybe now I know why.

"You can't be a good hunter without experiencing how the other half lives... and dies. Learning how your victims operate is the most important thing you can ever know in this vocation."

Vocation.

He sees it as a calling, like some higher cause.

Oh god, Preacher. He fucking named himself *Preacher*.

"I want to get a taste of your instincts. How well you can run, if you can outsmart me. After all, if you can't understand how they hide, how in the hell do you think you could ever seek?"

I wonder how long he's been dreaming of this moment.

"Alright, so when does this test start?"

"After the training, when I say you're good and ready for it."

A part of me craves approval, desperate to do what I've wanted since I was 14; back when I found my first corpse, just lying in the bushes... Since I pictured my father lying in a stranger's place. I've had years to simmer in this rage, in the unfairness of everything that made up my life. If I kill enough of them, maybe I'll manage to kill the source of this pain.

Either way, I'll be doing the world a favor.

"Now, are you ready for your first lesson?"

I nod.

"Then finish up, and meet me downstairs."

Ain't Afraid of the Reaper

RIPLEY

Preacher's waiting by the door, watching as I limp my way down the last few steps. I thought sleep was supposed to be the body's main method of repairing itself, but apparently mine didn't get the memo. The longer I rest, the more shit hurts.

"Put those on," he grunts. "It's muddy outside."

I stare, dumbfounded at a pair of black leather cowboy boots with gold stitching, just small enough to fit me.

"How did you know my size?"

"Didn't. These were my mama's, and they'll do for now. Can't have you walkin' around here barefoot."

"Oh thank god, I can scratch 'is he a foot fetishist?' off the list."

The joke doesn't land. Most of my jokes don't, but that's fine.

He's not that funny either.

Preacher lets out a grunt as he pushes the squeaky screen door open, the dogs following closely on his heels with their tails wagging along the way. He doesn't give a shit about people, but it's clear he treats his animals well.

A psychopath with a soft side.

And I mean, everyone's got layers, right?

I learned that much from Shrek.

As I make my way outside I'm surprised to see most of the debris from the other night has already been cleaned up, and even the sky itself is clear from any indication of the storm, a beautiful cerulean blue with great big fluffy white clouds floating past. Now that I think of it, this is the first time I've seen the place in daylight, and it's... pretty much normal.

My mind begins to wander, and I find myself wondering what happened to my car. Preacher's probably had it towed, or even destroyed at this point — maybe had his partner do it for him. He probably doesn't like to keep missing vehicles on or around his property. That shit's bound to attract cops.

A sharp whistle slices through the air, and I find Preacher leaned up against the barn, a cigarette dangling lazily from his lips.

"You know those things'll kill you, right?"

"Sweetheart, I ain't afraid of the reaper, he's afraid of me."

"You sound like a redneck Bond villain."

He grins as he exhales a big cloud of white smoke, and I get another glimpse at that solitary silver tooth. I wonder how he lost the real one.

"You know what? I'd watch that movie in a heartbeat."

He winks, heading toward the barn and ushering me inside. The first thing that hits me is the smell of bleach, but there's a musty undercurrent as well, maybe from rotting wood? The building is definitely old enough for that to be the case, virtually barren with the only source of light flickering from a couple buzzing bulbs above our heads.

My sister used to say she could feel energy in places, and while I know I don't believe in any of that hippy dippy bullshit, 10 seconds inside this place and I'm already feeling something in the air.

"How many have you killed?" I ask, staring up at a big rusted hook hanging from the ceiling.

"Dunno." He glances down at me, those cold eyes practically glowing beneath the dark brim of his hat. "Probably hundreds by now."

"Hundreds..."

So there's no question anymore: this is his slaughterhouse, and I can tell by the look on his face it's his pride and joy.

He heads straight for a metal table in a corner, cutting into the dirt floor as he drags it back toward me like a coffin. Soon enough I'm staring down at a knife roll, like the kind those fancy TV chefs use. It's made of a tawny colored leather, and I spot scattered marks on it that look like...

Tattoos?

It's hard to tell, but I'm finding it harder and harder to shake the thought.

"What's this made of?"

Preacher takes my hand, bringing it gently down toward the leather and guiding me as I trace the small faded markings and crude stitching.

"My first kill."

Wait— didn't he say the first person he killed was his father? That's why he changed his name, that's why he—

"Oh Jesus..."

He skinned his father and turned him into a *fucking knife roll*.

"I didn't get to listen to him scream before I peeled his skin off." He sighs. "You win some, you lose some."

He looks euphoric as he reminisces. Almost makes me wish I'd turned on my family long before I killed Gabriel.

"Alright, but you only have so many *evil* family members, so how do you find victims?" I ask, trying to keep things as light as possible given the subject matter. "You said you had a partner?"

"That's something you'll find out about soon enough, little rabbit."

I hate these bullshit non-answers. Someone's paying him, which means even if he's got an equal partner, he has bosses too. I just want to know how many people are in on this fucked up little business venture.

"You use all of these?" I ask, unraveling the roll and running my fingers over the blades.

"Sure do."

My jaw tingles at the feeling of cold steel against my fingertips, something that's been happening since I was a little girl; whenever I was angry or when I felt too much, and then later whenever there was something dark I knew I couldn't share, not with anyone. It starts in the back near the molars, sharp and intense, similar to the feeling you'd get if you bit down on a lemon, or a piece of particularly sour candy. Sometimes, if I let the dark thoughts stray a little bit too far, I end up with my whole mouth filled with saliva. It's kind of become a reflex to my homicidal urges.

I'm yanked back down to earth by the vaguest dull ache, and the sight of blood smeared on one of the blades.

"Shit."

I must have run my finger a little too hard along one of the knives, but I don't feel anything.

"Wow," I mumble, wrapping my lips around the wound. "Vicodin really works."

I'm not sure if it's the taste of copper or the shock, but the sensation in my jaw is mildly satiated. I glance up to see Preacher leering back down at me, his hungry gaze catching me off guard. I can't tell if he wants to eat me or fuck me.

Or both?

It might be both.

"Each one serves a specific purpose, little rabbit." He picks up a large knife with a razor sharp blade, and a curved tip with some light serration at the edge. "For example, this one. Have you ever gutted an animal?"

I shake my head and his eyes immediately light up, just like before.

"I was a city girl."

He flips the knife in his hand, pointing it at me.

"You wanna learn?"

I should be afraid, it makes complete sense to be afraid, alone on an isolated farm with a killer. Considering the fact that I just escaped one monster and ran into the hands of another, it would be the sanest thing in the world.

But this one isn't like Gabriel, and I'm not feeling even an ounce of fear.

"Teach me."

He studies me for a moment, like he's trying to assess whether or not I'm cut out for this life.

"You think you can handle it?"

"You doubt me after what you found in my car?"

His tongue darts out like a snake's, but he stays silent as it slides across his lips, merely taking a knife and pressing it right up against my belly. I'm not afraid. The only thing that concerns me now is how willingly I've taken the Devil's hand.

"I don't doubt your enthusiasm, rabbit. It's just some folks? They're a hell of a lot of talk and very little action. If you're gonna work with me, I need you to be vicious. Bring that same energy you did when you slaughtered that little boy-toy of yours."

I swear I can feel the sweat on my skin ignite, sparks popping off of me like little fireworks.

"I can be vicious." I pause, shaking my head. "I *am* vicious."

He grins, gliding the very tip of the knife up my body, just barely grazing the fabric.

"It's similar to guttin' a deer, or any other animal really. You wanna make a nice clean slit right up the belly... So all the good shit comes spillin' out."

I feel the sweat start to run down the back of my neck as I keep my eyes on the blade, watching as he stops just below my breasts. His voice is making my skin prickle, low and gravelly as it grinds its way into my every thought.

"Now, it might seem tough, but a good knife like this? Well, it'll slice through all that muscle tissue easy. You just gotta know how to use it."

Warm breath fans against my cheek as he gazes down at me, massive and imposing. My body doesn't know whether it wants to fight, flee, or fuck.

"The first strike has to be deep," he practically purrs, gliding the knife back down until the tip hovers just above my crotch.

This is a dance, and he's challenging me to show I know the steps.

"And if you get that first cut right? You should be able to tear someone open with your bare hands."

His voice is gentle, but his eyes are blazing, like he's reliving every kill he's ever had all within the span of a few seconds. What he has seems so much deeper than revenge on a repulsive ex-boyfriend. I want to know what it's like to have that kind of body count; to be the one who doles out punishment.

My whole life has been building to this moment.

"Teach me."

I'll say it over and over, as many times as it takes for him to turn me into what I'm supposed to be.

"Soon, rabbit," he smiles. "But first, you're gonna tell me everything."

You Got a Death Wish, Cowboy?

PREACHER

I watch as her breathing gets heavy, everything she's been carrying weighing heavily on her shoulders. There's still an obvious hesitation in her eyes, but there's no hiding around here, not from me.

"Tell me."

She and I are cut from the same bloodstained cloth.

"The night before I did it, he beat me," she mutters.

It's half-hearted, like she's grudgingly going along with my request, but I want more.

"Let me guess, you said something he didn't agree with?"

"I was always saying stuff that pissed him off." She studies the knife in her hand, her eyes tracing the blade all the way to the tip. "Or I didn't have dinner on the table when he came home from fucking another woman, or I looked at him the wrong way."

Ripley clenches her jaw tight, tipping the knife to the side as it glimmers like a star calling a lost traveler home. She's clearly spent years bottling up these feelings, so it's only fair that someone teaches her how to let them out.

"Tell me what you did, step by step."

She sighs, still playing with the blade absentmindedly as she recounts the events.

"I had it all planned out: I'd wait for him to shower, grab the knife I'd hidden under the mattress, and wait quietly behind the door. It felt like forever. I was *covered* in sweat, and my heart was beating so fast I was terrified he'd hear it somehow." She squeezes her eyes shut. "I heard the tap squeak and for a second and everything went quiet; the wait was so painful I almost didn't go through with it, but then this bird– I think it was a robin? It landed right on a tree outside the bedroom window."

I stay quiet, silently watching as I leave her space to get her bearings. It's an old police interrogation technique I picked up early on, and it's surprisingly effective. Eventually, the truth always comes out.

"I remember thinking I wanted to be as free as that bird. That I *had* to be."

I want to reach out and touch her, but I stop myself short. Judging by the way her voice is shaking, this is still raw for her, so I've gotta be gentle here for once in my life.

"And then?"

"Then the bathroom door opened. I jumped on his back, and started stabbing." She breathes in deep, like she's centering herself or some shit. "He threw me off of him, but I managed to get back up before he could grab me... that's when I stabbed him in the gut the first time."

"Show me." I lift up my shirt. "Here."

Ripley's mouth curls into a salacious little grin as she focuses on the patch of bare skin I've revealed to her.

"You got a death wish, cowboy?"

I can't tell if she wants to hit me or fuck me, but I'm not going to pretend like I haven't seen the furtive glances, or the way she gawked at me from the window this morning.

"That depends."

"On what?"

"Your skill."

Ripley takes a step forward, pushing the blade up against my belly, and I can feel the tip begin to dig into my skin as she puts on the pressure.

"We started fighting for the knife," she purrs. "I think we were up against the wall? Some of it's a blur, but he wasn't as strong as I thought he'd be. That's when I..."

With a flick of her wrist, she twists the blade, nicking me in the same place that I got her the night she took her bath.

"Keep talking," I growl, my cock starting to stir, slowly thickening in my jeans.

I watch that darkness take over, those pretty blue eyes turning a violent and stormy shade of grey as she continues her story with a newfound glee.

"He screamed like a fucking pig. Before I knew it I had him on the floor, and I just kept stabbing him, over and over in the chest."

She begins to slowly drag the knife up my body.

"How many times?"

"I don't know." Her low, smoky laugh sends shivers across my body. "There was so much blood, the bedroom floor looked like a disaster..."

I can see her changing right in front of me, her spine straighter, her head held a little higher. It's a kind of confidence I doubt even she's ever seen in herself before.

I want to bring it all out of her, mold her into the perfect predator— an equal. All those nights I wished for someone to share this with... it could be her.

Maybe God does answer the Devil's prayers.

After all, even the Devil was an angel once upon a time.

"I want to show you a better way, a more efficient way. All that stabbing you did? All the fighting? It takes energy. You must have been exhausted by the end."

I pry the weapon away and slip behind her, gently placing one hand on her waist. She's so warm, yet I can still feel her shiver beneath my touch.

"This is a tool, and you need to learn how to use it properly."

I hold it to her throat, letting my free hand slide around her stomach, fingers gently teasing the waistband of her leggings. I fan my breath against her ear and Ripley lets out a sinister chuckle.

"Are you gonna show me, or are you gonna dry hump me like a fucking frat boy?"

Ripley's no wilting flower, she's as sharp and as ready as the blade in my hand. All she needs is a little nudge in the right direction. She plays the fearless femme fatale pretty well, but I think she's getting off on this as much as I am.

"What's the matter?" I roll my hips, nipping at her ear just to make her jump. "You don't like foreplay?"

"Just show me," she chokes out. "How you would have done it."

I know this knife as well as I know myself by this point, including exactly how much pressure I'd need to slice right through her neck, but I leave my hand where it is, the blade still tucked against her skin just firmly enough not to leave a mark.

"Once you're behind him like this, all you need to do is sever his vocal cords; cut right through his windpipe... if you use enough force, you might even be able to decapitate someone."

I can see the goosebumps prickling on her neck, heat radiating off of her.

"Does that turn you on, rabbit?" I slide my hand a little deeper into her leggings, only to find she's not wearing panties. "Tell me to stop."

She moans as I play with her soft little hairs.

"Don't you dare."

It would be so easy to just pull these leggings down and take what I need, but I'm gonna wait until she's good and ready for my cock. I want to hunt her like a fucking animal and rip her to pieces, to rebuild her into someone who will never let *anyone* hurt her again.

Except for me.

She unzips her hoodie, letting it fall open to reveal her soft, perky tits and bruised skin, moaning as I put careful pressure on her clit.

She's so close to perfect.

All she needs is someone to show her how to take her power back.

I pick up the speed of my finger, playing her sweet little cunt like an instrument.

"You're twisted, aren't you, little rabbit?" She's getting wetter, her breathing more erratic. "How long's it been since you've been touched like this?"

I let the knife loose from her neck, dragging it down her bare torso before lightly grazing her nipple.

"I don't remember."

I can tell she's getting close, and the anticipation of her juices soaking my fingers is almost too much for me to bear.

"That's a damn shame."

She's just like me, reveling in that space where pain and pleasure meet. The rush you get, the power you feel when agony turns over into bliss... It's like nothing else.

She grinds her ass against my cock, her breath ragged and heavy as her voice begins to break.

"Fuck, baby! More!"

Baby.

I'm harder than goddamn granite right now.

"Tease your nipples for me."

She does as she's told, twisting and tugging on them, moaning louder as I continue to guide her toward the cliff's edge. The pain seems to be turning her on, mixed up in the danger of it all; her body is so hot it feels like she's running on pure electricity.

And then a loud horn blares outside, making us both freeze.

You've got to be fucking kidding me.

"Is that—"

I slide my hand out of her pants and stuff my fingers between her lips.

"Suck on these, and shut the fuck up," I hiss.

It could be a fucking cop. I don't know if someone followed her. Maybe someone saw her car and reported it before we got there.

"Preacher! Where the fuck are you?!"

Or maybe it's my loudmouth fucking brother.

What the hell is he doing here anyway? He usually calls first, and... That's when I remember I left my phone in the goddamn bedroom.

"Son of a bitch." I pull my fingers out of her mouth, setting the knife down carefully on the table. "Fun's over, sweet thing."

But before I make it more than two steps away I feel her yank hard on my shirt, pulling me right back into a sharp and painful slap across my face that nearly knocks my damn hat off my head.

"What the fuck—"

She's fuming, staring at me like a woman possessed, and for a split second I think she might pick up that knife back up and put it right through my heart.

"I was *this* close, asshole!"

Hell hath no fury, I guess.

"You wanna go back down to the cellar? Keep up the attitude."

"It would have taken you two more seconds."

She's seething, rasping through clenched teeth like an animal. I can't help but think she probably fucks like one, too.

"Then do it *yourself*," I growl. "Stick your hand down your pants and come on your own greedy fucking fingers."

"I hate you."

I know my shit-eating grin is only making her angrier. She's cute when she's mad.

"We'll have to work on your lying, too. Come out when you're ready, you can meet my partner."

"Preacher!" Raph barks from outside. "I can hear you in there, stop wasting my damn time!"

I turn on the ball of my foot, leaving her desperate as I head out the barn doors, straight into my brother's scowling face.

"The fuck's the matter with you?" He slips his sunglasses into his shirt, shifting irritably on the spot. "I called you a thousand goddamn times."

"Good morning to you too, Princess."

He opens his mouth to say something snarky, but stops when he notices Ripley walking up behind me.

"Jesus, lady, you look like shit." His eyes bounce back to me. "So, is this your new little pet?"

"Raph, this is Ripley," I grin, putting my hand on her shoulder as I watch the anger flare in her eyes again. "Ripley, say hello to my shithead brother."

Pixie Dust
RIPLEY

I've always had trouble getting to know people. It really just comes down to one little thing, call it a personality defect: every time a man is rude to me, I can't help but want him dead.

Take Preacher's brother, for example. He ruins my orgasm, insults my appearance— which I *can't* help, by the way. Oh, and the icing on the cake? Calling me Preacher's *pet*? I have half a mind to march back into that barn and grab one of those big-ass knives. He won't be so snarky when it's jammed down his throat.

It's sweltering as we approach Raphael's big black pickup, the kind you have to be lifted into like a fucking toddler because it's so high up off the ground. I take a step back, watching as he wrenches open the driver-side door and pulls out a big bag, shoving it into Preacher's arms.

"The fuck is this?"

"Consider it an early birthday gift."

"You don't even know when my birthday is."

"That's insulting, considering we grew up in the same house and you had it *every year*. It's... uh..."

Raphael looks up at the sky, tapping his finger against his chin.

"October..."

"Fuck you." Preacher chuckles, opening up the bag and pulling out a brick of white powder. "And this would be?"

"I think those are called drugs," I mutter, just loud enough for them to hear me.

A smile tugs at the corner of Raphael's mouth, but he manages to pull it back into a scowl.

"New shit that's going around. Biker gangs are big on it. It's called Pixie Dust."

Preacher's face falls, looking like someone just stole his parking space right out from under his nose.

"Pixie... dust?"

"Look, I know the name is—"

"Is this some kind of joke?" Preacher demands, a deep scowl etched on his face as he stares his brother down.

Usually, when people get mad at something as dumb as a goofy name, it's a sign of a deeper issue. If I were to venture a guess, I think that a certain broody cowboy might be grumpy that our sexy little knife session was cut short.

"It's better than the Midazolam you were using, and you don't run as much of a risk of accidentally dosing yourself. This stuff is brand new, and it's powerful."

"What are the side effects?"

"At the right dose, it renders the victim totally compliant and suggestible, like a truth serum. You can tell them they're in fuckin' Disney-land and they'll believe it. Works on the prefrontal cortex, does stuff to glutamate levels, and lots more shit you'd never know if I was just making up."

Preacher grumbles under his breath, turning the brick over in his hands.

"I don't give a good goddamn what nerdy bullshit this works on, it's called fuckin' Pixie Dust! Makes us sound like we're five years old!"

It's hysterical to see a man like him *so incensed* about something as simple as a name. Good to know he can be just as petty as I can.

"What's so damn funny?" Preacher snarls at me.

He's got a deep crease between his brows that looks like it was permanently etched there, and I do my best to keep a straight face.

"You know, if you keep frowning like that, your face is gonna stay that way."

"Preacher, listen to me, okay?" Raphael takes him by the shoulder, turning him to the side. "You don't have to call it that. You can call it murder juice, or whatever you damn well please. but I promise you, it's easier to use. Besides, you'll get a hell of a lot more variety out of it."

"What do you mean?"

"Well, the guy who sold it to me said he put it in breath spray."

"God, what was so wrong with a simple needle?" Preacher groans. "It's elegant."

Is he... *whining*? About his choice of drugging method?

"I mean, besides the time you stuck yourself in the middle of a job?" Raphael asks, tilting his head knowingly.

Preacher sighs.

"Alright, who gave it to you? The Reapers?"

"Who are the—"

"Nobody you need to know about," Raphael snaps, handing Preacher a piece of paper. "And I can fill you in on that later. For now, we got some requests. A hundred grand. *Each*."

Preacher blows out a breath, shaking his head as he looks down the list.

"Three in a month is a big risk."

His brother claps him on the shoulder.

"What are you so worried about? You're a heavy hitter! Hell, you're *the* heavy hitter in these parts. You know what you're doing!"

Preacher didn't tell me he made absolute fucking *bank* doing this. Granted, I don't actually know that much about him, save for his occasional indulgence in human flesh, the fact he shot his dad in cold blood, and that he still owes me an orgasm.

"Fine, I'll think about it. No promises though."

"Great, I'll be back for the product! Be careful not to snort too much of that tempting pixie dust."

"Go to hell."

Raphael reaches over to knock his brother's hat off, but he gets his wrist snatched up at the last second.

"Try that again and you're gonna lose this arm."

I don't know why, but something about the whole interaction is oddly endearing. It reminds me of when my sister and I would fight as kids. Some days, I'd just stand in her doorway and smile at her. It was enough to piss her off, and I got a big kick out seeing her get all bent out of shape.

I was always testing her limits.

Raphael hops in his truck and the engine roars to life, peeling down the driveway as Creed starts blasting through the speakers.

Of course this dipshit listens to Creed.

"Is he always this much of an asshole?" I ask, the two of us watching the big cloud of dust trailing into the air.

"This is him in a good mood, actually," Preacher grunts. "Come on. I got one more place to show you."

"Oh my, is it your bedroom?"

He snorts, shaking his head as he leads me back around the house, all the way to the storm cellar.

"Look, I don't want to sound ungrateful," I mumble. "But I actually became pretty acquainted last time I was down there."

I can't overstate how much I *don't* want to see this place ever again.

"There's a hell of a lot more to it than you think."

He crouches down, flipping open the padlock and motioning for me to follow, the short trip far less intimidating during the day. When we reach the bottom, I spy my bloody handprints staining the concrete where he found me.

"This way," he grumbles, striding toward the large metal door I noted when I was first down here.

Preacher glances over his shoulder, smirking at me.

"You ready?"

I nod.

Really, I have no fucking idea, but it's not like I have a choice. He wants to teach me how to do this, and I want to learn.

He opens the door, and a foggy mist immediately starts to roll out across the floor like a goddamn horror movie. The first thing I notice as he leads me inside is the dim blue light that gives everything this particularly eerie glow. But besides that, it really is just an ordinary walk-in freezer... Or it would be in not for the wall of body parts at the back, all stacked on top of each other and carefully wrapped in thick plastic.

Instantly, I'm covered in goosebumps.

Everything is neatly arranged, a testament to his meticulous organizational skills. His entire operation is so much less chaotic than many of the serial killers I've read about, piling bodies in bathtubs, keeping boxes full of bones, or worse— storing everything in their fridge.

"You like it?"

"It's…"

I'm looking for the perfect word: grotesque? Psychotic? Abhorrent?

No.

"Inspirational."

I pick up an arm, the blue marbling of the skin making it look fake, like something you'd find in one of those Hollywood prop shops. That is, until I start to take in the details: the creases in the palm, the torn skin around the fingernails, and the fine hairs on the forearm.

I notice a sticker on the plastic, piquing my curiosity even further.

JONATHAN HOWSER

It's handwritten, all in sharpie, but it's clearly not rushed. Every letter is carefully measured and spaced.

RAPE, *HOMICIDE*, *DOMESTIC VIOLENCE*

"You write their sins on the bag…"

"That's right," Preacher replies, the sound of his feet on the cold floor giving me chills as he comes up behind me. "It's a little reassurance for the clients, so they know they're getting what they pay for."

I'm mesmerized, brimming with excitement. I *want* this. I want to be able to see my trophies on this shelf, and show someone everything I've accomplished.

"This is amazing," I murmur, glancing over at him. "And so organized, I never would have guessed from looking at you."

Preacher looks oddly proud, puffing his chest out just a little.

"The cleaner I keep it, the easier it is to hide from the cops."

I spend the next couple minutes looking around the rest of the room, touching more bags, drinking in the intoxicating atmosphere as I read the little details on all the ziplocked sinners.

"There's only torsos and limbs in here," I murmur. "Where are heads?"

"Incinerated. Teeth and dental records are one of the easiest ways to identify people. I burn the heads, and any teeth that are left behind are smashed."

"Do you ever burn other body parts?" I ask, trying my best not to sound like too much of a keener.

"I will, if the meat's past its prime, but I prefer to keep 'em on ice just in case the client wants more. There's always something leftover, no matter the volume of the order, so sometimes I just eat 'em myself."

"And... when do I get to try?"

I have to admit, I've been curious ever since he first brought it up. Does it all feel as rubbery and rough as Gabriel's lip? Is this the kind of thing where if it's prepared right, you couldn't tell the difference between a person's bicep and a piece of beef? I read somewhere that people kind of taste like pork, but I always thought that was some kind of dumb internet myth which just managed to stick around somehow.

"Once you pass the final test, little rabbit. Then we'll feast." He reaches out, brushing a strand of hair away from my face. "After what I'm gonna put you through, you're gonna need it."

The test again, the one he's being so goddamn mysterious about.

"What happens during this final test, then? Besides me being the prey of course."

"Pretty simple. You run and you hide. I follow and find you."

"You're awfully confident for a man who barely knows me."

"I know you well enough by now to know you won't escape."

"Sticking your hand down my pants doesn't mean you know me."

He traces small circles on my thigh that make my skin light up.

"I know what you want..." Plastic crinkles as he presses me up against a wall of body parts, reaching between my legs and gliding his finger along the seam of my leggings. "And *you* know what you want."

What I *want* is safety and warmth, but I crave depravity. I don't understand how those two things can co-exist, but here they are, biting deep into my chest with monstrous teeth.

"Tell me more about the test."

His breath is warm, and his tongue darts out like a snake's, flicking my neck. I smell spice and cigarettes as he runs his lips along my jawline.

"There's a patch of forest out back," he growls. "Behind the barn. I'm going to hunt you in the dark, and when I find you, I'm gonna make sure you feel *everything*... pleasure... pain. And do you know why?"

A whimper spills from the depths of my throat as he pulls down my leggings and pushes two thick fingers inside of me, but there's a surprising tenderness to his touch that makes my chest feel tight. He's focused on *me*, not on himself.

"Enlighten me," I manage to choke out.

"Because I'm going to break you down, and free you."

"From what?"

"From all of it, everything that inhibits you. I'm going to take it all away, and then—"

I'm already so fucking close I can practically taste it— sharp and bitter and beautiful on the back of my tongue, like the first sip of coffee in the morning after a deliciously long sleep.

My spine arches, my body pressed into him in offering.

Take me.

Fucking *take me*.

But he just keeps stroking that spot, steady and unrelenting as leans in and whispers in my ear.

"Then you'll be ready to take everything back."

Pressure builds and builds until I'm gasping for air, but Preacher doesn't let up. On the contrary, his strokes are even more merciless, bringing me right to the edge and holding me there until I'm a quivering mess of nerves.

"Let me come," I moan as he starts to guide me toward my peak. "Oh, fuck, let me come."

"Beg for it, rabbit. It'll be good practice for your test."

His purr is so rich I can feel its texture on my skin, heavy with all of his sins.

"Please," I whimper.

Preacher's free hand wraps around my throat and my vision begins to get fuzzy at the edges, lost in a haze.

"You can do better than that."

And then it occurs to me, my life has never been about what I want.

"I don't... know how."

Preacher pulls his fingers out, presenting them to me as they glisten in the fluorescent light.

"Then we'll do this again and again. I'll bring you right to the edge and deny you, until you learn."

He slides his fingers into his mouth, sucking them clean while refusing to break eye contact. I should kick him in the balls for what he just did, but I'm rooted in place, pinned against the body bags by the daggers in his eyes alone.

"Fine," I grind out through clenched teeth. "I'll just fix the problem myself."

"Of course you can, but your fingers won't be nearly as good as my cock."

He dips his head, nipping at my lip.

"And you know it."

Serial Killer Soup

RIPLEY

I was so close. *So* fucking close and he just... ripped it away.

I've been doing my best to be normal, trying to be good, but mostly I've been walking around feeling like a frayed wire. I tried using my own fingers, but for some reason I couldn't push myself over the edge.

Preacher said he wanted me to learn how everything works on Blackthorne Ranch, including meals. So, I'm chopping up tomatoes for a beef stew while I watch him out of the corner of my eye. He moves with ease around the kitchen, expertly dicing up a big hunk of meat before tossing it into the pot. It's been a whole day, but I've still spent the evening silently hoping he'll bend me over the counter and fuck me.

"I told you, you had enough," Preacher grumbles at Hades, pushing away the dog who's been pawing at his thigh.

Despite his firm tone, it isn't long before he's tossing a few extra scraps on the floor.

"I never pegged you as such a softie."

"Yeah, well, other than my brother, there ain't many people who understand me." He shrugs. "But the dogs do... on some level, at least."

I can't help but wonder if life has been as lonely for him as it's been for me.

"Strange to find a serial killer who doesn't hurt animals."

"Well, I slaughter the cows," Preacher replies. "But it's humane. I knock 'em out first and the kill is quick. They don't feel a thing."

"Did you ever hit your head as a kid?"

He flashes me an incredulous look followed by a huff that *almost* sounds like a laugh.

"Sweetheart, I work on a goddamn ranch and my daddy was a tyrant. 'Course I hit my head... why you askin'?"

"I, uh, did a lot of reading, and there's an interesting correlation between serial killers and head injuries. Skull fractures, concussions, car accidents..."

"Did *you* ever get a concussion?"

I flash him a deadpan stare and he nods.

"Right, I get it. Stupid question."

Preacher hands me a bundle of carrots and some celery that he's been growing out back in one of the gardens. One of the biggest surprises over the rest of the tour was finding out the ranch was so full of life. The biggest was realizing I've already started to think of this place like home.

"So, how much do you know about what you are?" He asks. "What I mean is, anything clinical? Doctor diagnosis, something like that?"

What I know is in 9th grade we got to dissect frogs, and I'd *never* paid so much attention to science in my fucking life. I pictured my father in the creature's place as I slit open its soft little belly.

I dreamt about it.

"Well, like I said, I did a lot of reading." I begin cutting up the carrots into bite sized chunks, one at a time. "At first, I was trying to prove I *wasn't* predisposed to go down this sort of road, but..."

"You can't escape destiny."

I'm realizing that despite Preacher's tendency to be a gruff and arrogant asshole, I feel surprisingly safe with him. There's no anxiety, no walking on eggshells, no plates or knives being hurled at me. Sure, I'm here against my will, and sure, maybe he'll decide to gut me for a decent meal, but I'd say in terms of captors, I kind of won the lottery.

I still have to wear this stupid tracking collar, and he locks my door every night to make sure I don't escape, but right now? I'm content.

"So... did you always know?" I ask.

"To an extent," he replies, soaping up his hands in preparation.

I love the way the water cascades over them, highlighting the large veins that pop out when he scrubs between his fingers. He washes like a surgeon, precise and clinical, and I have to keep pushing away some incredibly sinful thoughts or I'm going to cut *another* fucking finger off.

"And you kill for money, maybe bloodlust too, but what else? There's got to be a deeper reason."

"Does there?"

"I don't think you're that shallow."

He grins.

"I think that's the nicest thing you've said about me."

I roll my eyes, choosing not to indulge his little quip.

"You could have made a small fortune in a few kills and gotten out of the game. Why go on for so long? Why not just let the cops handle the scumbags?"

Preacher flicks some of the water off his hands before grabbing a dish towel.

"How many times did the cops show up at your door when you called them?" He asks. "How many times did they get sweet-talked by that manipulative shitbag boyfriend, only for them to get in their cars and drive away?"

A pit forms in my stomach.

I don't know how many calls I made at first. I don't know how many men in blue saw my bloodied and bruised face. Maybe they separated us for a night here and there, but Gabriel had me so isolated that I had no other choice but to crawl right back to him.

That was the point.

"That's why," he murmurs, taking the meaning in my silence. "Because the cops don't give a shit, and too many of these animals slip through the cracks. One less scumbag off the streets means someone like you or my mama sleeps safer at night."

He's doing something virtuous with his bloodlust. Me? Well, I'm not even sure I can control mine, but his confession makes me want to open up. Is this that empathy thing therapists are always yapping about?

"When I was a kid, I always felt like an alien. I never really had anyone who understood me, or what was going on in my house."

"What was going on?"

"My, uh... my dad was, um—" I clear my throat.

I barely talked about it, never even with my mother, but I always wondered if she knew. The one person I told was Gabriel, and he used that fact to his advantage every time I'd try to leave.

You gonna crawl back to your daddy? I bet you like it, you sick little bitch.

I breathe out, trying to control my rage.

"He would come into my room at night when everyone else was asleep and…"

Suddenly, my eyes well with tears and I'm just that scared little girl. It's funny how saying it out loud makes it real all over again. It means it really happened to me, and it wasn't just a dream. I have goosebumps just thinking about those nights, about the shame that poisoned me until it rotted out my core.

"He would, uh… put his hand— I mean, it started with just his hand. I remember the shadow—"

"Under the door," Preacher murmurs, his voice closer this time. So close.

Before I can even consider turning my head, he's gently sliding his fingers beneath my chin, forcing me to look at him.

"My daddy did it to me too."

I wonder if his father was a violent drunk like mine, doling out punishment for the slightest offense.

"Did he hit you?"

"More than that." His breath shudders. "He was nasty and cruel. I remember he'd stick our heads into hot bathwater and wait until we couldn't hold our breath anymore. And when we were right on the verge of death, he'd pull us out and perform CPR. Raph and I had burn marks on our faces and inside of our mouths. I learned what torture was long before I started doing this."

The tone of his voice makes this all sound so distant, but the pain in his eyes is loud, and unbearably close to the surface.

"So that's why you did it," I whisper. "What did it feel like?"

Preacher smiles.

"It felt like justice. He couldn't hurt us anymore, and our mama lived out the rest of her days here in comfort. She passed away in her favorite rocking chair looking out over the ranch."

His tenderness surprises me.

"I'm sorry."

"Death's just part of the cycle." He shrugs, and that pain and vulnerability in his eyes vanishes as quickly as it appeared. "So, did you kill your daddy?"

"No."

"Would you like to?"

I feel a thrill crackling in the air like an oncoming storm.

"Nobody's ever asked me that before."

"Well, I'm askin' now."

In my dreams, I was the one making him hurt. I felt truly powerful in those moments, only to crash back down to a brutal reality the next morning.

"Tell me his name."

"Edgar Winter," I frown. "Wait, why do you want to know?"

"Where's he at?"

"Last I heard, prison. Don't know for how long or how much longer."

"I'll keep that in mind."

Preacher wraps his arm around my waist, pulling me close to him. It's probably the most tender moment we've shared since he patched me up in my room. I'm not sure *what* the two of us are meant to be at this point, but at least this is a far cry from me on my hands and knees in the cellar, begging him to kill me.

"Are you afraid of getting caught?" I ask. "In general, I mean."

"If anything happens, we all go down. Me, the clients, Raph..."

"Me?"

"Sorry, little rabbit," he murmurs. "But that's just the way it's gotta be. If it makes you feel any better though, we probably wouldn't be going to jail."

I guess that's the risk I'm taking, getting roped into all of this, but he's been doing it for this long with no issues. It's gotta be more than luck.

Preacher returns to the stew, throwing in some herbs and spices while I finish chopping the rest of the vegetables. It's actually a bit frustrating, taking a lot longer than I expected on account of the fact that I'm missing a goddamn finger. Who knew you actually needed your pinky for this shit?

"When's the first time you realized you wanted to kill someone?" Preacher asks without looking up, pouring some red wine into the pot. "Was it your daddy?"

"Maybe? I don't really know. I was abused, isolated, bullied in school... I'm not saying those were the causes, but every killer has different ingredients to their specific soup, right?"

He turns to me, brow cocked.

"Their... soup?"

"Yeah, I don't know, that's how I always thought about it. You have the vegetables, the meat, the broth, the seasonings... Separately, they don't do much, but when you put them together?" I bring my fingers to my lips. "Chef's kiss."

"Never heard the soup analogy before."

There's something about Preacher that makes me want to tell him all of my secrets. I wonder if his victims feel the same way; how many sins get confessed before a final, haggard breath?

"I do remember the first time I saw a dead body."

I watch as he perks up.

"Oh do you now?"

"I was walking back to school after free period and I saw this foot, just sticking right out of the bushes. It was white, covered in frost..." The memory is so vivid in my head, playing out like a movie. "I thought it was fake. I remember I looked around to make sure I was alone before I crawled into that bush, and then I... I just stared at it. Him. My heart was pounding, I was sweating... and my jaw was tingling."

"Your jaw was... tingling?"

He pours two glasses of red wine, walking over and setting one down in front of me, encouraging me to continue. The smell of bright berries and pepper floods my nostrils.

"I don't know why it happens. I think it's a reflex of some kind. I see blood, or I feel angry, or trapped, and... that's when it starts."

"So what happened after you crawled into the bush?"

My body is brimming with excitement, jaw tingling at the memory of staring at that beautifully marbled skin.

"He was nearly the same color as the snow, face down, and he had these blue veins that stuck out, clawing at the back of his neck, almost like they were trying to pull him underground. It was grotesque and beautiful all at once. I wasn't scared or anything like that, but I, uh... I did have a pocket knife."

Preacher licks his chops like a starving dog, desperate for more and more morsels of information.

"I thought maybe I'd take a piece of him. It was fucked up, and I *knew* it was fucked up, but I did it anyway. I opened him up, but there was no blood. It wasn't pumping anymore, it had all pooled at the bottom of his body."

Lividity is the second stage of death, invisible to the human eye until the person has been dead for at least three hours. I didn't know that at the time, but it wasn't long before I was devouring every little bit of information I could find.

"Can I ask you a personal question?" Preacher asks, snapping me out of my walk down memory lane.

I already told him my deepest, darkest secrets. I don't know what could be more personal than that.

"Ask away."

He pushes himself off the counter, taking a couple steps toward me until our bodies are so close I'm sure he can hear my heart pounding. He's got that look in his eyes, the same one he had in the barn.

"When you fuck, do you think about it?" He asks, his voice husky yet soft at the same time. "Killing, I mean."

I swallow hard. For a while it was the only way I could get off, picturing oceans of blood... It took time, but my fantasies escalated, and now my old standby is riding a man's cock while I tear into his heart like a pomegranate.

"Yes."

Okay, maybe it escalated more than a little.

Preacher grins, reaching out to brush a strand of hair away from my face. His eyes are stormy and his touch is electric.

"Do you want to know a secret?"

"You're full of them today," I breathe.

The sound he makes is something you'd hear from a ravenous animal, and suddenly I'm pressed against a wall of solid muscle, the warmth from his body making the hairs on the back of my neck stand straight up.

"These days, the only way I get off is thinking about gutting someone." His eyes flash with a terrifying, violent sharpness. "Memories of people I've already killed, fantasies of someone new, it doesn't matter."

I whimper, sliding my hands beneath his t-shirt, but stops me.

"Not until you learn to beg, remember?"

Perfect Fit
PREACHER

She's a stain on my subconscious, and I hate how much I want her. I was dead serious when I told her I wouldn't give her what she wanted until she begged, but after a few more days even my ironclad will is starting to bend.

As her body starts to heal, she grows more confident in her appearance. Lately she's ditched her baggy sweatshirts and leggings for tank tops and a pair of tiny jean shorts. It's hard not to stare at her ass when they fit her like a goddamn glove. Some mornings, I wake up to memories of her raspy moans and my hand is already wrapped tightly around my cock.

It's pure masochism, and I think it's making me crazy.

Well, *crazier*.

I pick up the bull skull waiting on the workbench, blowing away the fine bone dust that's settled into the cracks and crevices and heading over to the old half-broken mirror in the barn. It took a bit of time to get it sorted, but I think it'll be worth it. I slip it over my head, tugging on the straps to make sure it's tight.

Perfect fit.

Ripley's going to be ready this weekend, I can feel it. She's learned enough about the business over the last couple days, about how it all works, and now it's time to hone her skills. I don't usually use props, but the idea of her seeing me rushing toward her with this as my face? I get shivers just thinking about it.

Power surges through me as I imagine chasing her through the pitch black, feeling the earth bending beneath my feet with every stealthy step. I can hear her rapid breath. I can smell her sweat, her fear.

Her sweet pussy.

My cock stiffens as I allow myself to sink deeper into the fantasy.

For so many years, my existence has been simple: hunt, kill, repeat. Hunt, kill, repeat. Now, all of a sudden, this random woman is disrupting all of that, invading my home and my mind, but... for the first time it doesn't feel wrong.

I find myself wanting to nurture another human being, to watch them grow.

And what if, once she was ready, we worked as a team?

We'd be unstoppable.

I reach down, rubbing myself through my jeans as I gaze longingly beyond the mirror. I picture her on all fours, bloodied, bruised, and covered in mud from the hunt, howling like a beast while I fuck her.

I want to baptize her in darkness.

"Cool mask."

I nearly jump out of my skin as Ripley's voice slices through the stillness of the barn, turning to see her perfectly silhouetted by the harsh sunlight behind her.

How the hell didn't I hear the door?

"It's for your test," I reply, sliding it off and setting it carefully on the table with a frown. "It was supposed to be a surprise."

I don't think she's afraid of me anymore, not in the traditional sense, at least. There are fragments of the terrified woman she used to be, little pieces that come to the surface from time to time, but I've been seeing fewer and fewer with each passing day.

"Well, I won't tell if you won't."

A coy little smirk tugs at her lips, inviting my eyes to wander up and down her body. Over the last few days her skin has taken on a golden glow, the sweat on her body making it glisten in the sunlight. In direct contrast to her dark hair and electric blue eyes, it's damn near breathtaking.

Ripley licks her lips, slipping past me and leaning over to study the skull, gently tracing her fingers over the small imperfections in the bone. It's hard enough to focus when she's acting so playful, but at this point she's practically shoving her ass in my face.

"Do you use this a lot?"

Her shorts are so fucking tiny, I can see almost everything.

"This'll be the first time," I reply. "Wanted somethin' special for you."

"And the mirror?" She asks, her voice laced with a delicious malice. "Do you like to watch yourself while you work?"

"It's more that I want *them* to be able to see what I'm doing, even from behind. That way they get the full experience."

"Damn, you're a sick puppy."

"Takes one to know one, little rabbit."

Ripley glances back over her shoulder, smirking at me as a thick strand of dark glossy hair falls in her face. She's resting on her elbows, bent over in the *perfect* position for me to take her— and she knows it.

"I need something from you. It's kind of personal."

"Name it." I shrug. "The worst I can say is no."

She gnaws at her lip.

"Tampons."

I blink.

"What?"

"Tampons?" She looks at me like I'm stupid. "Please don't tell me you've never heard of—"

"Of course I've heard of 'em."

She turns around, leaning up against the table, the mask still in her hands.

"Well, I'm on my rag. I need some supplies."

The thought of her blood running down her thighs while I chase her, while I fuck her... while I devour her sweet pussy.

I'm moving the test up. It's gotta be tomorrow night.

"Supplies," I murmur.

But there wouldn't be any harm in having a taste of her right now.

"That's right. I'm not even picky about the brand... so long as it does the trick."

Her eyes float down to my hand as I adjust my cock in my jeans. Her breathing is shallow, patches of bright red spreading down her neck and chest like watercolor as a smile stretches across her face. She doesn't even need to say anything and I'm still drawn to her like a fucking magnet.

"Would you like me to beg you? Because I've been a very good girl lately, and I don't think you appreciate that as much as you should."

"You think you're a good girl, walking around in these tiny fuckin' shorts with nothing underneath," I growl. "Bending over right in front of me?"

I should shove something into that smart mouth to teach her a lesson.

"You seem to appreciate it," she purrs, not missing a beat. "Do you have a habit of grabbing your cock in front of women you barely know?"

Her tone is playful, but her eyes remind me of a shark's, pitch black and voracious.

"Oh, I know you, little rabbit... probably better than you think I do."

She draws herself up to her full height, taking a brazen step toward me while my cock strains even harder. The piercings make it extra sensitive, with each pulse adding to the building thrum in the pit of my stomach.

"Then you know what I want," she murmurs, her eyes like flames licking the back of my neck. "And you still won't give it to me."

I keep thinking back to the sound of her moans when I slid my fingers inside her; she was everything I needed in that moment, and when it was over, I found myself craving her presence.

"I told you, you need to learn how to beg."

I'm trying to stay strong, but there's no denying it: she makes me feel alive.

"See, I was hoping you'd break a few rules for me, cowboy."

Oh, she wants to be a fucking brat, does she?

I snatch her by the waist, pulling her close and relishing the little gasp of surprise that tumbles from her lips. I can smell the desperation on her.

"And what about what I want?" I chuckle. "So selfish, rabbit."

When I fuck her, I want to hear her scream. I want her to feel like her heart is about to burst through her chest, but for now I have to take things slow.

"Selfish is denying someone pleasure." Her jaw ticks, her gaze becoming defiant. "Did you know that a woman's sex drive is increased when she's menstruating?"

"So get yourself off."

"I *can't*." Ripley places her hand on my chest, leaning into me and licking her lips like a hungry predator. "You know what I *really* want."

She's playing games, trying to entice me into bending to her will.

"Do I?"

"Don't be stupid, Preacher. You had your hand down my pants the other day for a reason." She wrenches my t-shirt in her fist, snarling as she gets up onto her tiptoes. "And I know you want me just as much as I want you."

I spin her around, shoving her down against the table, and positioning her just right so that she's staring directly at her reflection in that dusty old mirror. Her dark hair is obscuring most of her face except her eyes, bright like burning embers.

"I knew you'd give in," she cackles,

"Oh, this isn't giving in." I grab her flimsy little shorts and tear them right down the fucking seam, exposing her supple ass and little pink pussy. "This is just a taste of what you'll be getting."

She was right about one thing, that's for damn sure:

I want this just as much as she does.

I slide my hand between her thighs, and I'm immediately greeted by a shocking amount of wetness. Ripley moans, wiggling her hips in the hopes that I'll play with her throbbing little bud, but I pull my hand away, almost drooling at the sight of her blood coating my fingers.

Lord, lead me not into temptation... or however that goes.

I turn my head, locking eyes with her in the mirror and lap up the smears of crimson staining my fingertips. Just the taste of her makes my heart race. She's sharp, and sweet, and the copper flavor on my tongue makes my eyes roll back. I smear the rest of the blood on my chin, relishing the quiet gasp she lets out as I press down a little harder with my other hand.

"Is that all you've got?" She rasps. "Why don't you use that belt and show me how tough you are?"

I unbuckle my belt, yanking her head up and sliding it around her neck like a leash.

"Is this what you want?"

"*God,* yes."

I reach into the back of my jeans and pull out my pistol, making sure I have a good grip on the makeshift-leash; her eyes are as big as saucers as I put the barrel in my mouth, lubing it up with my saliva, then I slip the gun between her thighs, gliding it against her swollen pussy lips.

"You're a greedy little whore, aren't you? Say *red* if you want me to stop."

Ripley wiggles her hips, letting out a dark chuckle.

"Green means go, cowboy."

Alright then.

I yank hard on the belt around her neck, forcing out a choked grunt. All it takes is the sound of her voice warbling to make my dick that much harder.

"So fucking pathetic. You wanna fuck my gun, don't you?"

She manages a grin, her eyes full of fire once more.

"Is that how you fuck? Too afraid to use your cock?"

I constrict the belt even more, choking her harder.

"Would you like to find out?"

"Please baby," she rasps. "Show me."

She thinks that's what I've been asking for, that she's really begging me for it now, but it's still not good enough.

"We'll see how well you can take this." I tease her with the tip of the gun, pushing it in ever so slightly— just enough to make her gasp. "And if you behave, I'll give you what you really want."

I push the barrel of the pistol the rest of the way inside her and she fucking *sings*, her voice shattering into a thousand tiny pieces. I thrust in and out, intently watching her as she watches *me* in the mirror.

She's so tight, it's hard to find a rhythm at first. I need her to relax, but she seems to get pleasure from the resistance.

From the pain.

I yank on the belt again, listening to her sputter. The sight of her beet-red face, her tears, and the spittle running down her chin only strengthens my resolve.

I'm going to absolutely destroy her.

"You're mine now. I'm going to fuck you, devour you, and make you scream my name."

"Yes!"

My thrusts grow more violent as she bounces on my gun, taking every single goddamn inch, all with a frenzied look in her eyes.

"Do you feel your heart beating faster? Adrenaline pumping... You're teetering right on the edge of bliss, but you know I could kill you with one rough tug on this belt, don't you?" I grin. "And you can't decide if that turns you on. Am I right?"

Ripley drags her nails along the table, leaving shallow marks in the wood as her hips work double-time to reach her peak. I press the gun downward, stroking her G-spot.

"Tell me you like the pain."

"Yes! I love it!"

Beads of sweat are forming all over her, covering her shoulders and the back of her neck. She's so close, I can practically taste it.

But just as she tips her head back, I pull the gun out, releasing the belt and leaving her empty.

A hollow scream of rage ricochets between the walls, like so many that have come before, yet different at the same time.

"You *fucker*!"

She spins around and I'm more than a little surprised by a particularly hard punch in the jaw. I thought the exhaustion would have gotten the better of her, but instead she seems like something dredged up from the pits of hell. It's like every horror buried deep within her is unleashed in a fury of rage each time I drag her kicking and screaming from her climax. I'll use that, unearth the demon that's been kept quiet, told to sit still and be good.

I bring the gun up to my lips, doing my best to stay calm when I see the streaks of red on the barrel. With my eyes firmly fixed on her, I run my tongue along its length, licking up every drop.

"Tomorrow night. I'm gonna hunt you, and I'm gonna make it hurt... just like you wanted."

I'll have her.

And I'll have her at her worst.

You Can't Masturbate to Jesus

RIPLEY

I feel like a caged animal, like the ones you see at the zoo pacing back and forth because they've been cooped up for too long. I went to sleep dreaming about him and woke up with my hand shoved down my sweats while I pathetically bucked against it.

And I *still* couldn't get off.

Preacher's kept me locked in my room all fucking day, only opening the door to drop off some food before he vanishes again. Everything in this room feels like it was pulled out of the most boring museum in the world, and the longer time ticks on, the more restless I become. The only few books I could find were about birdwatching, crocheting, or Jesus.

You can't masturbate to Jesus.

Well, I'm sure you *can*, but even I have my limits.

I sigh, striding toward the window, and spotting him out in the field, sipping a beer while he watches the sun setting in the distance. He's shirtless again, because of course he is.

"Fucking asshole," I grumble.

Remnants of golden light drip down his skin, making his whole body glow as I trace the thick ropes of muscle that run down his arms. The way his forearm flexes as he tips that beer to his lips... His thighs are my favorite, though. I don't know if I want to ride them or bite them.

I slide my fingers into my shorts, strumming my clit for the umpteenth time today. I've been sure to moan extra loudly when I hear him make his way upstairs, trying to get him to pay me a little visit.

I want to be hunted.

I want to be torn apart by those massive hands.

I want to be marked, bitten, bruised...

Scarred.

But he's got far more willpower than me, and so the door stayed shut.

Preacher slowly turns his head up toward the window, his big dark hat obscuring his face. All I can see are his plump lips as he raises his beer bottle, knocking back the last of it, but still I'm certain his eyes are locked right on me.

One more shot at enticement.

I let my free hand wander playfully beneath the hem of my t-shirt, teasing my nipple in exaggerated motions so that there's no question what's going on, even from a distance.

He tosses the bottle over the fence, turning his entire body to face me before reaching down and squeezing himself over his jeans.

Suddenly I've never been more focused in my life.

"Come on, baby," I mumble to myself. "Show it to me."

He unclasps his belt buckle, popping open the button on his pants, and I can already see my breath fogging up the window. This is pathetic. One surge of hormones and I'm no better than a desperate man at a strip club.

In fact, I might be worse, I'm practically drooling, watching him pull his zipper down.

But then— he puts his hand *inside* his fucking jeans? This asshole is playing keepaway with his cock.

I hate him right now, but I know I can break him.

I pull my t-shirt up, pressing my tits up against the window while I fuck myself with my fingers. I'll make myself come. I'll show him that I can do this all on my own and I don't need him *or* his dick for anything.

I slide a third finger inside, fucking myself hard as I pant like a dog, lubricated by my warm blood. I don't care how shameless this is, or how desperate I might look.

Preacher spits in his palm and *finally* pulls his dick out of his pants. Even from up here I can tell he's especially thick, and the thought of that alone might be enough to get me there.

I'm panting, hips bucking like a dog in heat as Preacher keeps up his languid strokes. Pleasure burns like starvation in my belly, painful, the ache so intense it's starting to consume me.

I catch myself moaning, but I don't stop, curling my fingers and hitting that spot which always makes my toes curl. He hit it with that gun yesterday, and I wonder if he'll do it again tonight once I've passed his little test.

I close my eyes, letting myself get lost in the rhythm, in pleasure, in the ripe and vivid fantasy of him pinning me to the bed and taking everything he wants. Flashes of lightning shoot through my nerves and my legs start to shake.

I'm gonna come.

Fucking finally.

I picture him chasing me through the woods, a knife in his hand, as he sings my name like a deadly melody. When he finally catches up to me, he slams me against a tree. In my mind I'm covered in dirt, blood, and sweat, and I swear I can feel him tear my leggings off of me and push himself inside with one brutal thrust. I can't stop. I'm dangling on the edge, grunting and trembling like the pathetic piece of shit I—

I whip around as the bedroom door slams open, ripping me from my well-earned climax. Preacher's leaning in the doorway, hat tipped low, a smirk on his face, and his cock very conspicuously *back* in his jeans.

They're buckled, too, like a damn chastity belt.

"That was quite the show."

I'm shaking with rage, another orgasm denied.

"I fucking *hate you*," I hiss through clenched teeth.

I'm starting to think he wants me to kill him before this test even begins.

Preacher slowly strides toward me, his hand resting lazily on his big gold belt buckle. I can see the obviously swollen shape through the dark denim, and resist the surprisingly powerful urge to drop to my knees.

"Look at how pathetic you are," he purrs, pushing me up against the window. "Fucking drooling for my cock."

He grabs my hand and stuffs my bloodied fingers between his lips, sucking them clean.

"Throw on some real clothes and meet me outside." He grins. "No panties."

I shiver, the last lingering hope that he's going to push me up against the window and fuck my brains out slipping away.

God forbid Mr. Control Freak break the rules.

As if reading my thoughts, Preacher pulls a knife out of his back pocket and brings it right up to my throat. He holds it there for a long time, olive eyes locked with mine as I feel the blade slowly dig deeper and deeper, my breath caught in my chest as it gets dangerously close to the point of no return. Then, like nothing happened, he hooks the blade underneath my little tracking collar, and in one quick slice it tumbles to the floor with a thunk.

I stand there, stunned.

"What are you doing?"

"No cheating," he purrs. "From either of us."

"That's a big risk, cowboy. I could run for help, I could even bring back some cops. They'd probably let me off easy for what I did, especially when they see what you've had going on out here."

His dark brows knit together, not in anger but more like some kind of intense focus, and for the first time I can see flecks of gold in his eyes, like the final little bursts of dying starlight.

"I'm sure you could, if you managed to escape me. After the test, that'll be the right you've earned, along with your freedom."

He's made it clear, after this there'll be no going back, regardless of how it ends.

"Or..." He tilts his head, playfully.

"Or?"

He smiles, a brand new intensity flashing across his face.

"Or you could choose to be reborn tonight."

Welcome Home
RIPLEY

I'm in no shape to be doing this, but I don't care. The only thing keeping me going right now is the potential I may get to murder someone tonight, and the more likely outcome of getting some good dick.

After all, isn't that what we all live for?

When Preacher laid out the few details of the test, he told me it wouldn't start until I reached the edge of the woods.

That's where he'll be waiting for me.

I fling the back door open and inhale deeply, the humidity immediately hitting me like a wall. In contrast to the disgusting heat, the sky has turned to stunning shades of intense copper, blue, and indigo, all perfectly swirled together– and topped off with billowy, lavender clouds.

It's been a long time since I've been able to appreciate a view like this. It would make one hell of a photo.

"Where's my phone?" I mutter, fumbling around in my pockets for a moment before the realization hits. "Probably smashed to shit in that stupid fucking car. Right."

Another thing I have no idea about anymore.

A whistle slices through the air, and I see Preacher standing near a big patch of forest in the distance, already all set up with his bull mask on. The horns stretch upward toward the painted sky, making his massive frame look even more imposing in the contrast.

"Damn, all of this for me? It's cruel to play with an unstable woman's hormones like this!"

He remains silent as I trudge towards him, and I'm feeling a little less sure of myself as I spot the coil of rope around his arm. Fear hums in my bones, but I reject the urge to run, embracing the feeling and taking everything I can from it.

"What's that for?" I ask, pointing to the rope. "You gonna do some tricks?"

Preacher still doesn't respond, instead reaching into his back pocket and brandishing the gun he fucked me with less than a day ago.

The air smells thick, like it could rain at any moment.

"You want me to shoot you?" I ask. "Because I'd be happy to, after the stunt you pulled today."

He places the weapon in my hands.

The light is getting low, and fast.

"There's one bullet hidden out in those woods. Good luck."

What the fuck?

"You're giving me an unloaded gun?! What the hell am I supposed to do with this?"

"You could throw it at me. Maybe you've got a good arm."

"Jesus fucking Christ you're an asshole."

Preacher looks up toward the sky, and I catch a glimpse of the butterfly tattoo on his neck.

"Look at that sunset. Absolutely beautiful."

He tilts his head to the side, one eye gleaming behind the mask.

"Better start running, rabbit."

All at once his demeanor seems to shift into something sinister, something to aspire to; tight muscles, heaving chest, veins popping out of his forearms, and wrapping around them like vines. I can feel my blood freeze in my veins.

He shifts his body again, turning to face me straight-on, and standing at his full height for the first time tonight. The second his two eyes meet mine I know it's time to run, and I'm off like a shot, sprinting into the dark woods with nothing but a pistol in my hand and the moonlight as my guide.

"Ten minutes!"

Preacher's voice echoes through the trees, emotionless yet full of a distinct violence. I don't know this terrain, I don't even know what direction I'm really running in. The only thing I can hear is my feet pounding against the dirt as the blood roars in my ears.

I'm rushing past trees and hopping over dead logs, my body aching with each step, still not fully recovered from the last few days, let alone the battering I took from the storm when I first landed on his doorstep.

I'm trying to keep myself from getting disoriented, but it's getting darker by the second, and my head is already spinning. He's counting on my lack of experience and lowered vision. I wouldn't be surprised if he got someone to make him a pair of fucking nightvision contacts or something, to go along with that mask.

Do they even make those? Or did I see it in a Mission Impossible movie?

In the middle of what must be the dumbest question I've ever asked myself, I feel the tip of my foot hook onto something and I stumble, landing flat on my face with a painful grunt.

Fuck.

I have to get up.

I have to keep running.

"Shit, shit, shit..."

I scramble to my feet, lurching forward and breaking out into another sprint like my life depends on it.

I mean, maybe it does. He keeps saying he doesn't kill women, but maybe that's just a line he uses. Maybe this whole thing has just been a ruse to kill me in the most fucked up way possible.

It doesn't matter though, I'd play this game the same either way. I'm supposed to think like prey, avoid him and survive. Should be simple, right?

Unfortunately, a part of my mind has been at war with my better instincts, and the thought of just letting him catch me and fuck me keeps running through my head. I have a feeling my punishment would be far greater if I just gave up, and yet...

I take a sharp right into a winding path through thick brush. I can just barely see the way forward, lit up with a sliver of inconsistent moonlight. It reminds me of the first night I wound up here, with nothing but the lightning to guide my way.

And it did guide me, right into the clutches and the mercy of a madman.

Suddenly I hear that familiarly sharp whistle from *much* too close behind me, and I panic, coming to a skidding halt as I slam my hands into a tree just fast enough to avoid a serious injury.

The revolver tumbles from my grip, landing in a pile of wet leaves.

I can't get enough air into my lungs.

All I see is darkness in every direction.

"Raaaaabbit!"

Oh, *fuck* that.

I scramble to scoop up the gun, and keep running through scorched lungs and burning muscles. I hear another whistle from another angle, and then the crack of a branch. The sound is all around me. Consuming. Crushing.

"Where are you?"

The internal conflict I was feeling earlier is completely gone now. I'm not going to make this easy for him. I'm going to show him just how strong I really am.

I'm going to be his equal.

Then, through the darkness and trees, I see something large and looming emerge.

Is that...?

A fucking cabin, the windows barely lit up from inside.

Tiny droplets of water start to splatter against my skin. The storm's rolling in again. Keep running, just keep running. All I have to do is get to the cabin, and—

My foot catches on a rock, and I don't manage to stifle my yelp as I go flying forward for the second time tonight, my voice echoing traitorously through the trees.

"You're making this so easy!" Preacher taunts.

I lay there for a moment, cheek pressed against the ground as I breathe. The smell of dirt and the sweetness of decaying foliage fill my lungs as I calm my heart rate, feeling the sharp pain from what's probably a broken rib.

How the fuck did he catch up to me? Am I running in circles?

Think like prey.

But that's just running and hiding, he'll be ready for that. More importantly, I get the feeling that's not the kind of prey he *really* likes to hunt. When he found me in the cellar, he was impressed that I fought back.

So... think like prey, in order to understand it?

Think like prey, but don't act like it.

I push myself to my feet, staggering toward the cabin as I hold my aching ribs. Each step makes me want to collapse, but I still need to figure out a plan of attack.

There has to be something in there that I can use, to stab him with, or...

He said there was a stray bullet hidden out here, right?

Would he be dumb enough to hide it here?

Or was the point even for me to find it?

I open the door, must and rotting wood immediately assaulting my senses. The place is barren, and I can't see anything useful in the makeshift kitchen but an old kettle sitting on the stove. Just beyond is a set of rickety stairs leading up to what looks like a half-attic.

Did he build some kind of beacon of hope for his victims? A place where they all end up, tailor made for him to finish them off?

That's sick.

And I kind of love it.

I make my way through the house, opening cupboards and cabinets and finding nothing but a couple of old butter knives and a bent fork.

"Fucking useless," I grumble.

There's nothing in the bathroom, nothing in the tiny living room...

"Looking more and more like it's just me and you, useless gun," I grumble, climbing the stairs to the attic.

A few steps up and I can immediately tell the boards are weak, threatening to give out beneath even the lightest step. I grip the railing, taking things one step at a time as I point the gun upward. I realized immediately when I walked through the cabin door that I don't actually know if he followed the rules, or if he's been cheating this entire time. I don't know if he actually gave me that ten minute head start because I didn't bother counting. Who knows, he may have even planted a second tracking device on me or something, cutting the first one off just to give me some false confidence.

None of that matters though, as long as I survive.

As long as I win.

I reach the top step, the dim light of a hanging bulb illuminating the tiny space, and the sight in front of me rips the air from my lungs.

Welcome home, little rabbit.

A message scrawled in blood.

Make It Hurt, Cowboy
PREACHER

I'm a better hunter when I'm riled up like this.

Everything is louder, more intense, more beautiful.

And I'm more deadly.

I can smell the earth, and feel the gentle rain pattering against my skin. It's warm and sweet, but it'll turn to thunder soon enough. The sun has fully set now, leaving only the moonlight to guide me. I won't even need it, though. I can tell you exactly how many trees you have to pass by to get to the edge of these woods.

I can also tell you that she's headed for the cabin just ahead. Hopefully, she finds the surprise I left for her.

I move carefully through the trees, the coiled rope still clutched in my hand as I hop over logs and brush. Right now, it's deathly quiet, and I'm a little surprised. I was anticipating another scream or a yelp, or for her to shoot out of the dark like a terrified deer. Maybe she's got it together more than I thought she did.

If she's smart, she'll go on the offensive once she's found a way to get her bearings, instead of trying to hide from me on my own property. She might even have a shot if she pulls herself together. I know she's powerful. Hell, I know she's ruthless enough to cut a man's tongue out.

"Raaaaabiiiit," I sing as I approach the cabin. "Come out, come out."

I love a woman with some fight in her, and I want to see exactly how much of it she's got.

I come to a stop at the front stoop, glancing around. No movement, no noise in the distance, just the sound of my own breath pushing against my mask. She's been here, though, that much is obvious.

I kick the door open, letting the loud bang echo through the little wooden rooms as I step inside. The sound of my spurs knocking ominously against the wood is enough to make *me* shiver, so I can only imagine what she's feeling right now.

She could do anything.

I haven't lasso'd someone or some*thing* in a few years now, but Ripley makes me want to dive back into my old bag of tricks and pull out some of the really sick shit I used to do when I first started down this path.

One time, I chased a guy all the way down to the water, let him get real close before I lasso'd him and took him out with a buck shot. The idea of giving him some hope, letting him think he was just a few heartbeats away from freedom... It was exhilarating. But over the years, everything that goes into my kills has become more routine, partially because of what my clients request, sure, but I'm getting older.

You tend to get stuck in your ways with age.

Thankfully, she's bringing back that old spark.

I move through the house quietly, avoiding all the creaky floorboards just like I used to when I was a boy. Raphael and I used to play hide and seek in this cabin, and ran around every square inch of it, or so we thought. My daddy built it with his bare hands, all the way down to digging out a little basement... and I didn't find out why until I cleaned it out after he'd died.

He killed a woman here, and left her in a shallow grave downstairs. I have no idea who she was, or when it happened, all I found of her was some red hair, bones and a pretty floral dress. I took what was left deep into these woods, and buried her far away from the evil that was done to her.

I never found another body, and I never figured out if it was only a one-time thing or something more. Maybe he realized killing wasn't as fun as what he was doing to all of us back at home. Either way, my rage toward my father only grew deeper.

I creep up the stairs, slowly and carefully crafting a slipknot in the rope without even taking my eyes off the top of the staircase. I can do this part in my sleep, easy as pie. I just hope I still remember how to lasso a moving target.

When I reach the landing I scan the room, the moonlight leaking in through the busted window making it all that much easier as it illuminates...

Nothing.

I take a step forward, muscles coiled and ready for a fight that doesn't come. Instead, all that greets me is my gun, sitting on the floor right below the message I scrawled for her.

"What kind of game are you playing—"

A harrowing roar fills the room like wildfire, and I feel something slam into the back of my neck, knocking me to my knees. The pain is intense, shooting all the way down my spine as my palms slam against the floor.

Ripley's throaty cackle makes the hair on my neck stand up, but I don't have any time to waste, leaping to my feet and whirling around ready to fight, only to be struck to the floor again. The mask takes most of the force this time, but whatever she's using is hard enough that it cracks the more brittle bones of the bull skull, and I'm still feeling a decent chunk of the impact.

A couple more like that and I might be in trouble.

Through the haze, Ripley finally comes into focus, all heaving breaths, matted hair, and fury. A glimmer of pride bursts through my pain, and I can't help but let out a chuckle as I dodge her next swing, making it back to my feet.

It's a fucking kettle.

I thought I threw that rusted piece of shit out ages ago, but obviously not. The way it's rattling around, sounds like she's filled it with rocks, too.

"Very clever, rabbit," I smirk. "But you'll need to hit harder than that."

Instead of taking the bait she begins to circle me, looking surprisingly calm as her dark hair obscures her face. All I see is one icy eye, looking like it could freeze me right in place.

She told me that for her, killing felt like being possessed, and right now? I believe it. She moves like water, unpredictable yet still confident, letting those years of suppressed animal instinct take over.

"What are you waiting for?" She growls. "I thought you said you were going to make it hurt, cowboy. All I see is you standing there like a bitch."

Her lip curls into a cocky little grin, and I wait for that inflated sense of confidence to kick in. It always happens, especially early on. I want her to think she's won, because that'll be the biggest weakness I can take advantage of.

I lunge for her, leaving just enough of an opening to ensure she'll take a chance, and of course she does. She bellows as she moves in with a powerful strike that lands right in the middle of the skull, ringing out with a sickening crack. I stumble back, raising my arms in faux-defeat as I slam into the wall.

"Come on!" She roars, striding toward me. "Can't fight back?!"

Add with a few more pained groans and I've got her right where I want her.

She lunges a final time, in what I'm sure would have been a devastating blow if it ever had any chance of landing. Instead, I move into it, kicking her legs out from underneath her, and watching as she tumbles to the ground with a surprised grunt. Her makeshift weapon rolls across the room, clattering against the back wall and scattering the packed stones and pebbles all over the floor.

I pin her to the ground, my hands wrapped firmly around her wrists before she even knows what's happened. The mask is cracked and crushed in places, but still only slightly obscures my vision. I can see her clearly: my perfect prey, struggling and growling as she tries to fight me with every shred of strength she has left.

The fear in her eyes makes my heart flutter.

Unfortunately, a knee to the gut cuts that feeling real fuckin' short, and I collapse on top of her, the two of us restarting our little tussle on the ground. Her strength surprised me, but I can already tell there's no way I can lose.

But then, she surprises me again; the rush I get when she pins me down is unlike any drink or drug I've ever had. She looks like a fucking animal, water dripping off of her hair and onto my naked torso, her thighs clamping down around my waist, squeezing hard like a vice. I can feel her pressed against my raging hard cock as she wraps her hand around my throat.

Then, she starts to move her hips, grinding against me, panting as she sinks her nails deep into my skin and drags them down my chest. I'm a little surprised she pulled the seduction card this early. Honestly, I thought she'd save it until she was a breath away from defeat. Still, I can't complain: a beautiful woman writhing on top of me while she glares into my eyes like she wants to slit my throat?

I think I'm in heaven.

"Did I win?" She drawls.

"We're still playing, little rabbit."

Her eyes darken, hooking into mine as she grinds down harder onto me, her maniacal giggles flooding the room like smoke.

"Are you sure about that?" Her voice sounds huskier than usual as she leans in close. "It looks like you might have lost."

My dick is so sensitive that I'm afraid to move. Nothing would ruin this moment more than coming in my goddamn pants while I'm trying to play tough. Ripley would never let me live it down.

A shock of lighting flashes outside the window, followed quickly by the deafening crack of thunder, and the rain begins to pound harder against the roof. It seems like mother nature is just as excited as we are.

Ripley peels off her shirt and tosses it aside, giving me a damn clean view of her tits. There are little scars spread across the two of them, like someone's burned her with cigarettes.

I grimace.

I wish we'd killed Gabriel together.

"Are you ready to give up?" She squeezes down on my throat again, purposefully pressing on my windpipe this time. "Because you can't seem to hide how much you want me, cowboy."

There's not an ounce of shame in her eyes as she starts to rock her hips back and forth, her pussy threatening to leave a damp spot on the front of my jeans, but I stay silent, not wanting to let her know how much she's affecting me. Unfortunately, with her hands wrapped so tightly around my neck, I *know* she can feel my pulse racing.

"Imagine if I was riding your cock like this," she moans. "Taking you *nice* and deep like a good little whore."

She releases my throat, wrapping her hands around the horns of the bull skull as she starts to buck her hips. Shit, it feels good. Too good. My breathing gets heavier and heavier as I struggle to maintain control.

But Ripley? She's riding me with total abandon, not a worry in the world.

"Don't you want me to?" Her voice is gentle and low in my ear. "Don't you want to feel how tight I am? How *wet* I am for you, cowboy?"

Searing heat fills my belly, and I clench my abs as tight as I can, but it's no use. I'm gonna come.

And she knows it.

"I can feel how close you are," she breathes, grinding down harder. "Just let me win and I'm yours."

I'm so screwed. My vision is going fuzzy at the edges and I'm sweating like a motherfucker under this mask. The friction is becoming too much to bear, and I can feel my balls start to tighten.

This woman is fucking relentless.

"I'll let you do anything to me. You can put it in my ass too, you fucking pervert." Her tits sway right in my face, the two of us completely covered in sweat. "I bet you'd love that. You know I'll be *screaming* for you, baby"

Well shit.

My climax feels like a burst of fireworks, my back arching as I cry out, but I barely get the time to enjoy myself before I hear a terrifying primal roar. Ripley rears back, wrenching at my mask violently until there's a brutal crack. I barely have time to register the snapped-off bull horn in her hand before she's wild-eyed and manic, driving it straight into my shoulder.

I hear my own howl of pain come out like it's part of the raging storm outside, a humiliating mix of rage and confusion. I got bested by my own goddamn dick.

"How did you like that shit, cowboy?"

In a flash, she's on her feet, rushing down the stairs, and then there's the sound of the cabin door slamming behind her.

And I'm left... Well, dumbfounded doesn't really begin to cover it. I stare at the ceiling with cloudy vision, and the blood roaring in my ears. My heart is beating so fast, my body ready to act, but my mind is struggling to process what the fuck just happened. Blood oozes from the wound, but luckily she only managed to get about an inch of the tip in. It hurts like a motherfucker though, and the ache I'm feeling is making me pretty certain she smashed right through a good chunk of bone, and into muscle.

It's hard not to feel a twinge of pride, even if that pride hurts like a son of a bitch.

"You might win this thing after all, little rabbit," I mutter, pushing myself up to my elbows.

"Come out, come out, Preacher!"

I snort, shaking my head as I struggle back to my feet.

"God, she's a pain in my ass."

But she's mine.

I let out a haggard breath, shuddering through the agony as I pull the broken horn from my shoulder. Blood dribbles down my arm, and I scoop it up with my fingers, smearing it across what remains of the skull.

And I breathe.

In.

And out.

In.

And out.

"What's going on in there? You scared, or are you already dead?"

I can't help but laugh as snatch up her discarded gun, staggering toward the staircase to check behind the bannister. Sure enough, it's still there: the single bullet I left for her, carefully tucked away.

"Just the opposite, sweetheart. I've never felt more alive."

The Hunt
RIPLEY

You know that scene in 28 Days Later where Cillian Murphy is covered in blood and running around the mansion like a man on a mission?

I'm not ashamed to say I fingered myself to it.

The rain is coming down in buckets now, and I'm soaked up to my knees, but I've got to keep going despite the mud threatening to suck me under.

"What did you do on Saturday, Ripley?" I grunt. "Oh, nothing! Just let a serial killer chase me through the woods!"

At first I thought about sticking around, taunting him into another fight, but then I realized... I don't have anything left to hit him with. I need to get back to the house, or at the very least the barn. I'll be able to grab a real weapon, get prepped for round two. All I have to do is wear him down, after all. Or maybe I'll have enough of a headstart to just make it off the property on my own two feet. My adrenaline is so high, I'd throw his big ass metal table at him if I could.

This whole thing's still a nightmare, but somehow... I just feel so *free*.

The loud pop that cuts through the rain reminds me of a car backfiring, startling me enough to dip behind the nearest tree. I can't immediately place what it was, but it doesn't take long to make the connection to the searing pain in my arm. I look down to discover the skin at the top of my shoulder is torn right open.

"You fucking *shot me*?! You goddamn psycho, what the fuck—"

I poke my head out, trying to figure out where the shot came from, but quickly realize it's almost pitch black save for the little bits of moonlight cutting through the trees. Then, in a flash of lightning, I see him. He's like a fucking phantom, appearing just for a moment as the rain bears down on him, battering his mangled skull mask.

Holy shit, he looks even more terrifying.

I count a heartbeat or two before lightning strikes again, and in those few moments he's already started charging.

I squeal, bolting in the opposite direction, my chest threatening to burst from adrenaline, blended with the thrill of the chase. Sure, I also feel like I've been run over about eighteen times at this point, but there's something about the smell of the dirt and the rain that keeps me going, filling me with a new energy. Somehow, it's like I'm experiencing everything, truly feeling it all, for the first time.

I duck behind another tree, listening hard for any hint or clue I could use to help stay one step ahead of him, but these woods are starting to play tricks on me again.

Was he the one who just made that branch snap?

Was that a whistle or just the wind?

My throat is dry, and my body's suddenly screaming for water. I try to catch some raindrops in my mouth, and failing that I turn to sucking in what little's gathered off of my skin in the hopes that it'll provide just enough hydration to tide me over.

If I know Preacher, it won't be long before he catches up to me.

Then, all of the old thoughts swarm their way past my new resolve. What's he going to do when he catches me? That knife he held against my throat in the barn felt like it was only a step away from something bigger, something deeper and more depraved than I've ever experienced.

Another whistle echoes through the night, and this time there's no mistaking the source. I'm off like a shot, my muscles burning with every twist and turn, the rain so thick I can barely see three steps in front of me. It's only a dozen feet or so before I hear a twig snap, far too close for comfort, but I don't have time to think before something heavy collides with me and I'm knocked to the ground. I let out a banshee-like screech as fear and anticipation mix in my veins, and the two of us roll to a halt on the ground.

There's a moment where it feels like he's about to say something, maybe gloat or threaten me like he loves to do so much, but I cut through the foreplay and sink my fingers deep into the wound in his shoulder. He howls, recoiling just enough to give me the space to clamor to my feet.

I run straight for some thick brush to try to get a bit of breathing room and gather my wits, but just as I start pushing through it I feel something light but rough slip over my body.

"What the fu—"

Suddenly, I'm yanked backward from the ankles, landing face first on the forest floor. My chin smashes against a mushy log and I let out a garbled noise as the wind gets knocked out of me for what feels like the hundredth time tonight.

Did he just lasso me?!

"What are you, a fucking Looney Toons character?!" I roar.

I feel his presence long before I see him, his boots squelching in the mud as he makes his way over slowly, looming like a bad omen. He grasps my hair, yanking my head backward and forcing my back to bow.

"I told you, you're *mine*," he growls.

I'm forced up onto my knees as he tears my leggings open in one fluid motion. My heart feels like it might give out from the adrenaline alone, and the pain in my shoulder temporarily overtakes my excitement about all of this. I have no idea what he's going to do next, and that thought is both terrifying and thrilling, like being on a rollercoaster just before the drop.

But I can do this.

I was born for this.

Preacher's hands glide up the back of my thighs, squeezing my ass. His touch is more tender than I expected, and I shiver. God, I need this like I need oxygen. I'm bruised and battered, scarred and bloodied, but I don't give a shit. All I need is for him to take me.

"I had you pegged, cowboy. I knew you'd give in."

Blood roars in my head and I can't hear anything else but the sound of the rain and Preacher's devilish groan as he glides his dick along my slick pussy lips. I can feel smooth little bumps on the underside of his cock, cooler than his scalding skin. I have no idea what they are, but it feels fucking amazing.

"That depends. Are you ready to beg yet?"

My back arches, giving him immediate access as I let out the most pathetic whimper I can muster. It feels like he's made of pure fire, and I'm planning to add as much oxygen to that blaze as it needs to burn the two of us to the ground.

Suddenly, the strange sensation of cool metal slides along my pussy lips, and I suck in a sharp gasp.

"Thought you'd be a big enough man to finally use your cock."

Preacher only laughs before thrusting the gun inside of me.

Slow.

Deep.

Savoring it.

"Ah, this? This is called warming you up, little rabbit." I feel something warm and slick on my asshole as he slowly pulls the gun out of my cunt. "And this? This is for stabbing me."

The cold tip of the pistol is pushed inside my ass and I cry, groaning as he works it in and out, moving deeper with each thrust. I said he could fuck my ass, but I guess I didn't specify with what.

The rain falls harder, the rich smell of petrichor overwhelming everything else, save for whatever's radiating off of *him*. I swear, I can smell his desire, so intense that it lingers on my tongue whenever I open my mouth to take a breath. I wish I could see what he looks like behind me, in that mask with all that muscle, while he uses me like his own personal fuckdoll. I think he could make me come without even touching my pussy at this point.

"You're still bleeding, too, aren't you? It's got you all *riled up*. It's why you haven't been able to keep your fucking hand out of your pants, huh? You filthy fuckin' whore."

I start to whimper, and immediately hate the sound. It's pathetic, powerless. It's not me, but at the same time... I need him. I want him. I can't think about anything *but* him, and then before I can even react, I hear the words come out of my mouth.

"Please." I gasp. "Please, Preacher, I need it. I need to be torn apart."

He pauses for a moment in silence, and then he pulls the gun out, leaving me feeling hollow before grasping my hips and pulling me toward him like I'm nothing but a toy. My mind is moving a thousand miles a second, with my body teetering right on the edge.

Maybe I'm getting the hang of this whole begging thing after all.

"You're dripping," he groans. "I bet you thought I wouldn't be able to control myself the second I got my hands on you, didn't you? Well, I wanted to *savor* this. It's been so long since I've been inside a sweet little cunt like yours."

He pushes the tip of his cock past my entrance, and my body coils like a spring. I'm filthy, terrified, and on the brink of collapse, but giving in to this desire that's been running through my veins feels like a kind of freedom. It hasn't been as long for me as it has for him, but if we're counting sex I actually *wanted?* Let's just say we'd both be in the running.

"Please, baby. You're the only one who can make me come, it's been fucking torture, I just—"

"How often have you thought about it?"

Every hour? Every minute?

"Every day."

He stills. Throbbing inside of me. I'm so turned on I could come right now.

"Keep talking."

"I want your cock shoved so far down my throat I choke on it. I want you to fuck my ass until I bleed. I want to ride you while I bite into a man's heart— oh *God!*"

"Now *that*, rabbit... is how you beg for me."

Preacher rewards me by forcing me into the dirt, filling me right to the brim. The full weight of his body is like a security blanket, and even though I know this is monstrous, and fucked up beyond belief, I've never felt stronger.

He wants *me*. He chose *me*.

And when he starts to thrust again? I think I've died and gone to heaven.

He pounds into me with a punishing force, and I take every inch like a good fucking girl. My whole body is on fire beneath layers of caked mud, leaves and dirt sticking to my bare skin, with each and every one of my cells primed for destruction by his hand.

He's taken me to the very brink of climax so many times, only to deny me, and I'm not letting it happen again. I dig my toes into the ground and start to snap my hips, matching each one of his brutal thrusts.

"Now that I've got a taste for you, I think I'll be having you every night." He nips at my earlobe as his hips snap harder. "You'll sleep in my bed. You'll ride my cock whenever I want, until we break that goddamn headboard."

He's fucking me so hard that my brain feels like scrambled eggs, and I think if he asked me for my name right now, I'd probably start meowing instead. It's truly incredible that all it takes is a man with a good dick who fucks *hard* to reduce my IQ to 6 in a matter of seconds.

"Is that what you want?" He asks. "Tell me."

I let out a muffled moan, only for him to punish me with a string of vicious thrusts.

"Use."

"Your."

"Words."

I'm going to come. I can feel it. I'm closer than I've ever been before, just one more push.

"Fuck! Yes! I want it! All of it!"

His teeth pierce the skin of my shoulder just as his cock slides up against my G-spot. For the first time in weeks, I'm falling apart, coming so hard the edges of my vision blur.

"PreacherI'mco—"

I can't even get the words out in the midst of his thrusts anymore, listening to his raspy moans as he starts to fall apart right along with me.

"Take every goddamn drop, rabbit." Another low growl rattles my bones, shaking me to my core. "I'm gonna fill you up every single night."

And then I'm coming all over again, or maybe it's just the same one going on and on and on, my body trembling as I let out strangled cries, my cunt spasming around him.

"Preacher..."

To my surprise, as his thrusts slow, he begins to stroke my hair.

The rain patters against the ground.

Against our skin.

And we breathe together.

Slowly.

Deeply.

"I'm here, rabbit." He kisses my temple. "You were perfect."

I've never craved physical connection after sex, mostly because that sex was against my will. The last thing I wanted was for Gabriel to fucking touch me. But now? This man's breath is warm, the weight of his body soothing. I just want him to hold me.

He presses soft kisses along the newly formed bite mark that he made, soothing it with his tongue the way an animal would.

He pulls out of me, and I'm left trembling.

Victorious.

Deeper, Little Rabbit

PREACHER

Bloodied gauze and sutures litter the bathroom floor as I gently wipe away the blood on Ripley's face. She's perched on the counter, right next to the sink, giving me a good look at the toll the night has taken on her naked body. Bruised knees, scrapes on her thighs, and...

"What are you looking at?"

I smile, gliding my hands up her bare legs. It's those eyes. They hook right into me, and suddenly I want to tell her every single secret I've buried over the years.

"I was thinking you've never looked more beautiful."

Her lips part and I brush my nose across her cheek, shuddering as her warm breath fans against my own skin. Her touch is like lightning, crawling down my spine and gathering there until I feel like I'm going to explode.

"You know what I was thinking?" She asks.

I dab my stab-wound with iodine; it looks worse than it actually is, and thankfully it seems like it'll heal up nicely. The fact that she got me right in the eye-socket of one of my skull tattoos is just the icing on the cake.

"Tell me."

"I was thinking that you still haven't kissed me, not really."

"I suppose that's true."

It's been a *damn* long time since I've kissed a woman, but honestly, I couldn't even remember the last time. That's how uneventful it was. Maybe sometime in my early 20s, before the business took over my whole life.

"Are you scared?"

She's got a sinister, hyena-like smile plastered across her face. The light is so low, almost sucking the color right out of her eyes until they're two black pools.

"Do *you* think I'm scared?"

"Not in general, no, but I think you might be afraid of intimacy."

That knot in my stomach pulls tighter. Intimacy means being known, it means ripping open the deepest and darkest parts of yourself and begging to be accepted.

"You do, huh?"

My tone is flat. Emotionless.

"Tell me I'm wrong."

She looks so confident, leaning forward and biting her lip.

"You're fuckin' annoying," I growl.

She breaks into laughter, covering her mouth with one hand, her cheeks bursting with red, like fresh blood scattered across snow.

"You think that's funny?"

"I know it is." Her words feel almost as brutal as that horn she stabbed me with. "You'll put your gun in my pussy, you'll chase me through the woods, but you won't fucking kiss me! You know what else I think?"

"I haven't the faintest goddamn idea, rabbit."

"I think you're afraid to be seen." She licks her lips. "But what you don't understand is I've already seen right through you."

"Are you sure about that?"

She watches me, her eyes dancing across my face like she can see right into my goddamn soul. I feel like a teenager, standing in front of a girl and not knowing what to do. I *want* to kiss her, and agonizing over something as goddamn juvenile and trivial as that has got me in a tailspin.

"I haven't run away yet, have I?" She reaches up, her fingers tenderly brushing against a cut on my cheek. "Now stop being such a little bitch and kiss me."

Her nails dig into the back of my neck, threatening to tear straight into my skin. It's not really a kiss so much as the two of us trying to devour each other, but I follow her lead, quickly learning what she likes: teeth, snarling, and the sound of my moans.

I tear my mouth from hers, my chest still tight with anxiety, struggling to swallow the urge to ask her if it was okay. One kiss and all of a sudden a shit-load of insecurity comes rushing in through the door.

But she just smiles up at me, her lips bitten-red, with a small smear of blood across them. I must have done that and didn't even notice. I flick out my tongue, lapping at her new wound and making her giggle.

"See, if you'd done *that* earlier, you probably would've had me begging a whole lot sooner."

"You're a goddamn brat, you know that?" She squeaks as I lift her up off the counter and carry her over to my big clawfoot tub. "But you've got me pegged."

The water is steaming, the smell of rich vanilla filling my nostrils as I gently set her down and help her in. Her legs are still trembling, so I hold her hand to keep her steady until she's safely submerged.

"Holy shit," Ripley lets out a relieved sigh, tipping her head to the ceiling. "This is *incredible*."

I pop the cork on a bottle of wine I had sitting off to the side, and pour two generous glasses, handing one over before stripping off my filthy jeans.

"Oh my god, are those piercings?"

Her eyes light right up at the sight, and I grin, climbing into the bathtub along with her.

"You like 'em?"

"I mean, I guess I felt them." She entwines her legs with mine as the water slowly strips away the events of the night, like waves against a shoreline. "It felt... really fucking good. When did you get them?"

"Long time ago, and it's a bit of a story, but that doesn't matter right now." I raise my drink. "It's time to congratulate my little rabbit. You were perfect tonight."

"Mmm. I've always loved validation," she purrs as we clink glasses. "So? What's the next step? I thought there was supposed to be a feast or something."

That's a thing I've learned about Ripley, she never lingers too long in the moment; she's always so focused on what's next. I appreciate the ambition, but sometimes you just want to revel in the now, basking in the fact that you chased a woman through the woods and fucked her senseless less than an hour ago.

"How about this weekend?" I ask, swirling my wine as I plan out a menu in my head.

"Sounds great."

This is the most comfortable I've seen her. She's relaxed, almost ethereal in her movements, gracefully examining her wine glass before setting it down to grab the soap. I watch as she lathers herself up, glowing golden and graceful in the candlelight, until she lifts one leg out of the water and lets out a loud snort.

"Somethin' wrong?"

She shrugs.

"Forgot to shave my legs."

Truthfully? I hadn't noticed. And even if I did, I wouldn't have given a shit.

But if she wants it gone...

Without a word I reach over to the small table next to the tub, grabbing my brush and small jar of shaving cream as I gently grasp her leg. She doesn't pull away, just watches me with a bemused look that quickly spreads into a smile.

"Are you serious?"

"About takin' care of you?" I ask as I dip the brush into some cream and begin to lather up her leg. "We're partners, right? Isn't that what partners do?"

I grab the straight razor, flipping it open and gliding it carefully along her skin.

"Never had a man do that before. It's kind of sexy."

I study her as I work, keeping my focus on the blade, but being sure to watch for her reactions out of the corner of my eye. In turn, Ripley's gaze is fixed on my hand as the razor glides effortlessly along the side of her leg.

"When's the last time someone took care of you?"

I work my way up to her knee before dipping the blade in the water and cleaning it off.

"Never."

I grunt softly as I switch to her other leg, lathering it up and getting to work. She didn't even miss a beat.

"Yeah, well I know the feeling. After my mama got sick, it was just me taking care of the three of us, so there wasn't a whole lotta pampering."

"Do you think that's why we're so fucked up?" She asks. "Because no one was there to help us?"

"Could be." I sigh, washing off the razor for another go. "But I don't really worry too much about all that. With so much fucked up shit happening to us, who knows what ingredients really make the difference in that soup."

Ripley grins, and I can see a new excitement flash in her eyes as I move up her thigh.

"Alright then, can I ask you another question?"

"Nothing's off limits anymore, little rabbit. Ask away."

She takes a moment to sip her wine.

"Okay then. I'm curious about what we are."

"That's not a question."

"Alright, fine. I live in your house, sleep in your bed, eat your food. We fuck, and you're apparently shaving my legs now..." She tilts her head. "So, what are we?"

Truthfully? I don't know. Are we student and teacher? Star crossed lovers with a murderous edge? All I'm sure of is if another man came near her, I'd tear his head right off his body.

I glide the blade along her inner-thigh, this time flicking it in such a way that it makes a shallow cut— close to her artery, but not quite.

"We're partners."

She hisses and I grab a cloth, wiping the excess soap and shaving cream away from the newly open wound, before dipping my head and gliding my tongue across it.

"Partners?"

The second the taste of copper hits my tongue, I groan and seal off the cut with my lips. Ripley lets out her own deep moan that makes my cock swell, but I take my time, sucking up every drop until there's only a thin line of red where I made the initial incision.

"I teach you how to be the perfect predator, and you teach me..."

Her chest heaves as she drinks me in, pinching and twisting her nipple gently.

"What can I teach you?" She asks, almost breathless.

"How to trust people. How to care for someone."

She smiles, those electric blue eyes digging straight into me.

"I'll try, but only if you promise to do the same."

I wish I knew what love felt like. I know the word, but the sensation escapes me.

Is it like that warmth I felt sitting on the counter watching my mother bake in the mornings? Is it the feeling I get when I'm riding one of the horses at dawn, one of the only times I ever truly feel free? Or is it something more obscure, like the crushing longing you sometimes feel when you're staring out into the empty sky at night?

I'm falling for Ripley, I'd have to be an idiot not to notice that.

But is it love?

I finish shaving her leg, and she watches with a patient curiosity as I twirl the razor between my fingers, still not quite sure what to say.

"C'mere. I want you closer."

She sets her glass down before slipping between my legs, the water threatening to spill over the tub.

"Close enough?"

I take in the cuts and marks on her face and neck, the bruises on her body, the stitched up gunshot wound on her arm; she's so beautifully fragile at this moment, and I'm seeing her now after all the layers of defensiveness got peeled away, bit by bit. Beneath it all, all the years of unhealed wounds buried away, is someone who's scared, and full of untapped rage. Anyone else would be terrified of her, and they'd be right to, but I think it's the thing that makes her shine.

"*Nobody* is ever gonna hurt you again."

I grasp her chin, running my thumb along her lips.

"I've heard that before," she murmurs. "How do I know you're telling the truth?"

I point the razor at a spot just beside my heart.

"I want your initial, right here." She's quiet, her gaze stormy as she eyes me with suspicion. "You want proof that I'm not lying to you, right? Carve yourself into my skin, and I'm yours. My body, my heart, my everything."

Ripley reaches down, wrapping her fingers around my straining cock before slowly easing herself onto it.

"Then I want something, too."

I rest one hand on her hip as she begins to rock back and forth, carefully taking the razor and brandishing it in front of me. When I meet her gaze, I don't see Ripley anymore. I see something mythical.

Medusa.

Lilith.

A beautiful Siren who lures men in with song, only to feast on their still beating hearts.

She brings the blade to my chest, choosing a blank spot with no ink, and presses down without remorse. I hiss as the pain shoots through me, but she only giggles, continuing to bounce on my cock as she digs herself into me.

The pain is delicious, even addictive.

"Deeper, little rabbit."

The smell of blood in the air only makes me harder.

"This is as much as I can take," she groans.

"No, cut me deeper," I growl, rolling my hips up to meet hers. "We need the skin to scar."

I grind my teeth as she runs it through again, breathing heavily through that searing pain.

"That's it, baby girl. You finish marking me up and then you can come on my cock."

I gently run my fingers down her spine, and relish the reaction as her whole body shivers. She sinks the blade in deeper, finishing off the *R* before dipping her head to lick the blood up. It doesn't take a goddamn rocket scientist to be able to tell that she's right on the edge.

I wrap my arm around the back of her neck and smash my mouth against hers in a violent kiss. All I taste is copper, basking in the intermingling intoxication of pain and pleasure as Ripley continues fucking me like a wild animal.

But I can't let her do all the work.

I lean over into the perfect spot between her neck and shoulder, biting down with a brutality that makes her cry out.

She's earned this.

"I'm coming," she whimpers. "*Fuck.* You feel so good."

"All over me, pretty girl. Let me fill you up."

She tumbles over the edge with a shuddering groan, but I'm only a few seconds behind, warmth exploding at the base of my spine as I pump her full of my cum. It's hard to catch my breath, and even harder to focus on anything but how good she feels. I'm perfectly locked in the moment, holding her close, breathing in deep as I play with the damp ends of her hair, feeling the sticky heat from the steam that clings to us.

All of that, and her heartbeat, almost in sync with my own.

And then it's all over, and Ripley's gazing up at me, her eyes filled with tears.

"Thank you," she murmurs.

I sit in stunned silence for a moment, unsure of what to do.

What to say.

"Of course, but... for what?"

She smiles, tears rolling down her cheeks.

"For everything."

That's My Girl

RIPLEY

I'm staring out the open window, watching the powder-blue curtains rustle gently in the morning breeze as my body starts to wake up. I let out a contented sigh, sliding my hand across the bed and feeling...

Nothing but cold, empty sheets.

"Preacher?"

I roll over to find his side of the bed vacant, the clock on the nightstand.

I frown.

7:00am.

Over the past week we've always been up around 4:30 to feed the dogs. I kept waiting for him to say we were going hunting, that I'd be reaping my rewards for all of my hard work, but then we'd wind up doing more fucking chores.

I cleaned up cow shit yesterday, out of the stables and off my shoes.

I sit up, letting out a big yawn before my eyes fall on Preacher's dresser. It's three drawers high of the darkest oak, carefully covered with a pristine white lace doily that his mother made during the last years of her life. But what's catching my attention now is brand new: a large white box with a big lavender ribbon tied around it sitting on top.

I toss the blankets aside and push myself out of bed, ignoring the sore ache in my joints as I spot a little cream colored card tucked beneath the ribbon. There's a single word scrawled on it in elegant handwriting:

Tonight.

A little thrill tickles at the back of my neck as I unwrap my gift, and I let out an involuntary whistle when I see the Prada emblem.

"Nice work, cowboy."

I've never worn Prada, or anything designer for that matter. My parents spent more time and money on their own appearance, selling real estate and running the local church in our town. All the other girls had cool clothes while I wore long wool skirts and dresses fit for a pioneer woman.

My father always said that modesty and submission were two of the most important qualities a woman could possess. Gabriel agreed with half of that.

If only they could see me now.

I slide the lid off, my breath catching in my chest at the sight of a wave of crimson silk that shimmers in the morning light.

"Holy shit."

It's stunning, almost iridescent, with a plunging neckline and two of the most delicate straps I've ever seen. I've never held something this expensive before, and I'm immediately afraid of ruining it, but when I press it against my body and look at my reflection in the mirror, all of that falls away. I feel like a fucking princess, even with my mussed up hair and bruises.

Down the hall I can hear the unmistakable sound of Preacher's heavy footsteps, followed by Hades and Charon's claws clicking against the wood. It's funny, that sort of sound used to scare the shit out of me before I got here. Now? It brings me home.

"You boys stay out here, and no fighting."

He's so gentle with them. In fact, he's gentle with all of the animals on the farm. Sometimes I catch him nuzzling up against the horses and cows when he thinks I'm not looking. There's a tenderness buried deep down inside of him that I don't think any other human's really been touched by.

The door swings open, with Preacher's massive body nearly filing the entire frame. He's in a blue plaid shirt that's just the tiniest bit too snug on him, black jeans that are faded around the knees, and his signature cowboy hat, sitting slightly askew as always.

"I know it ain't even on you yet, but I think I'd like it better on the bedroom floor."

I snort, looking back at my reflection. He didn't waste any time.

"How did you know my favorite color?"

"I didn't." Preacher wraps his arms around my waist, kissing me on the temple. "I spent five minutes scrolling through the website, took one look at that neckline, and thought, *my girl deserves to feel beautiful on her big night.*"

Anticipation thrums through my veins like wine as I tip my head back, greeted with his soft lips pressing into mine.

"And where exactly are we going?"

"Oh, little rabbit," he chuckles. "That'd spoil the surprise."

I HANG OVER THE RAILING LIKE A HUNGRY HYENA, GAZING DOWN ON A sea of potential prey, looking for the perfect target. The club was a few hours drive, and not somewhere I'd ever really choose to go on my own, but right now it's practically heaven. Everything smells like sweat and whiskey as the crowd throbs like a vein on the dance floor, strobe lights tearing across the room while the unrelenting and hypnotic bass has even *me* tapping my foot.

Gabriel used to bring me to clubs like this: private rooms, all the liquor and drugs you could want, and plenty of girls offered up on a silver platter to his creepy friends for the mountains of cash they'd bring in.

And of course, that included me.

"How do you do this when there are cameras everywhere?" I yell, raising my voice just enough to be heard over the pulse of the club.

Preacher scans the crowd one more time as he sips his whiskey.

"Carefully. But Raph helps with the details."

He looks good tonight, dressed head to toe in black, with a wide-brimmed hat dramatically covering half of his face. The only pops of color I can make out are in the brass toes of his boots, and the gold of his belt buckle.

"He helps? Is he hiding somewhere?"

"No, no, he just cases the joint beforehand. Looks up the tech, figures out how everything's wired. Look, see those cameras up there? They don't actually record anything." He slides one hand around my waist, pulling me closer to him. "Now, tell me—"

A wolf whistle cuts through our conversation and I look over to see a drunken frat boy in a dirty white t-shirt and a worn-out baseball cap stumbling toward us, a smirk plastered on his face.

"Thassa pretty dress," he slurs, somehow ignoring the 6'5" monster of a man holding me by the waist.

There's a part of me that wants to take my heels off and drive one straight through his eye socket, but Preacher was very clear on the importance of not making a scene. Still, I can feel his anger as he tightens his grip around me, staring the drunk down with daggers in his eyes. I'd pay good money to see him toss this dude right over the railing.

The drunk opens his mouth to speak again, but a woman in a pair of skin-tight blue jeans and a crop top strolls past, catching his eye just in time for him to spin around after her, stumbling along after her like he's being dragged by a leash.

"You think we should have picked him?" I ask, a little disappointed to watch him walk away to safety.

"Not an option, he's not on the list."

"List?"

"That's right." Preacher pulls out his phone, passing it to me. "You get to pick which of these men you want. My gift to you, rabbit."

I turn to him, brows furrowed in confusion.

"I thought I was choosing the victim."

"You are, but for now at least, it has to be from a limited pool. I can't be sure you won't pick someone who hasn't done a damn thing wrong." He shrugs, stone-faced but composed. "These two men fit the parameters the clients gave us, and they're both here tonight. Raph sent their photos and rap sheets over to me, and now, I'm leaving it up to you to pick our lucky winner."

I scroll through his phone, pouring over what looks to be a surprisingly detailed set of surveillance photos.

"Did your brother take these?"

Preacher nods.

"He finds out where they work, where they sleep, and their regular haunts. If we need more, and we almost always do, he hacks their phones, emails, all that shit. That way, we never miss."

It's starting to sound like I owe Raphael big time, because if Preacher didn't have his brother, I'm pretty sure he would have ended up imprisoned or dead long before we met.

I turn my attention back to the phone, studying the photos in more detail. One of the men has feathered blond hair and a bad 70s porn star mustache, while the other is clean shaven with dark, slicked-back hair, a long pointed nose, and wide-set eyes.

"Okay, so what did they do?"

"Well, Wes here..." he points at the blond man. "He broke into an elderly woman's home, bludgeoned her to death, made off with some cash and jewelry, and then framed an innocent man for the crime. That man is now serving a life sentence while this piece of shit burns through all her petty cash."

"And what about the brunet?"

"Jonathan's a real piece of work. Serial rapist. Just recently his DNA's been connected to several cases across Saskatoon and Moose Jaw. He subdues the male with a blow to the head, ties up the woman, and then waits for the guy to wake up. Makes him watch. Cops haven't done a damn thing because his daddy was tight with the Mayor."

"Was?"

"Daddy's dead. Suicide last year." Preacher leans in. "There's nobody to protect Jonathan anymore. Nobody to hide evidence, nobody to intimidate the people he hurt..."

I want them both, but weighing the options, we should probably go for the person who's more dangerous. It feels like this is Preacher's way of reining me in, refining me. He's got his ethics to worry about, whereas me? Not so much. After the hell I've been through, I think I'd kill anyone who so much as looked at me the wrong way.

I watch from the corner of my eye as the man who's become my teacher studies me, his eyes gliding up and down my body. It's never been clearer that he bought this dress with the explicit intent of ripping it right off me, a reward for us both once we've captured the insect in our web.

"It's Jonathan. There'll be time for Wes later."

"Good choice." He drains the rest of his drink. "Take some time to memorize his face, then see if you can pick him out on the dance floor. I'll be here if you need me, but I want you to handle this on your own if you can — and remember, you can take things slow. We've got all night."

I stare at the pictures on the screen for a while, burning the man's beady little eyes and sickeningly thin lips into my memory. I don't want to say he looks like a rapist, because a rapist can look like anyone, but Jonathan... well, it sure looks like the only time he's ever touched a woman would have to have been without their consent.

I sip my drink, scanning the crowd. The place is packed, and after a few minutes I start to wonder if I'll even be able to find him. Turns out there are a lot of rat-faced douchebags with slicked back hair that frequent this club. Maybe I shouldn't be surprised.

Just as I'm considering a new vantage point, a couple of men step away from the bar and I spot Dollar Tree Ted Bundy behind them. He's talking to a short, curvaceous redhead, and even from here I can tell that she seems... *less* than enthused. Her shoulders are tense, all the way up by her ears, her body half-turned away from him as she keeps trying to find a polite way to exit the conversation. All classic signs that she'd rather be anywhere else, but he's not listening.

He's found his next victim.

"You see him, don't you?" Preacher purrs.

I can feel his eyes on me, watching *me* as *I* watch my prey. He squeezes my ass and nips at my ear, but I can't lose focus now.

"She's looking around the bar looking for a way out, but there's no way he's going to let her go."

Preacher's warm, whiskey-laced breath fans across my skin like a soft mist of perfume.

"Remember, you're saving this woman from a terrible fate, and maybe a dozen more women besides. There's no reason to hesitate; guilt is a useless emotion when it comes to men like this."

I turn to him, feeling unsure and... almost juvenile. This is as natural to him as pouring a morning cup of coffee at this point, but my once-burning blood lust is quickly melting away into anxiety.

Can I do this?

I've killed out of rage, out of self preservation, but this? Cold and calculated?

Do I have that in me?

Preacher grabs my waist and pulls me toward him, obviously sensing my hesitation. The whiskey on his breath mixes with the leathery musk of his cologne, setting my heart aflutter as he brushes a strand of hair away from my face.

"Alright, let's talk it through. Tell me how you'll approach him, step by step."

"Me? Alone?"

"I told you, I'll be here if you need me, but this is your hunt. You're the spider weaving the web."

Preacher's grin is menacing, his eyes flooded with a twisted look that I've only ever recognized in the mirror, in my darkest moments.

I can feel the anticipation surging in, gripping at the back of my neck, and starting to replace all my anxiety and fear. After tonight, there'll be no turning back. That'll be me, for good.

"So?" He purrs, gently taking one of my hands and swaying us back and forth to the music. "What's your strategy?"

"I separate him from her, and anyone else he's with."

"Good girl." He trails his fingers up my bare arm. "Isolation is key. Next?"

"I turn on the charm. Flirt with him, compliment him, really lay it on *thick.*"

"But not too thick," he warns. "People like this? They like the chase. If you walk right into his open arms he'll get bored."

He pulls me into a deep and fiery kiss, and I can feel myself getting lost in it, tasting the smoky, expensive liquor he ordered. The moan he lets out as I bite into his lip is rich and velvety, like a drop of caramel on my tongue.

I've never been in love with anyone before.

Not really, anyway.

Gabriel was an escape plan gone horribly wrong.

But Preacher? Preacher is my salvation.

Even then, even knowing that...

"He's still at the bar," Preacher rumbles, turning his head and leaving me aching for more. "But he won't be there forever."

He's still talking to the same woman, and she's still trying to break away, but he's persistent, this time resting his hand firmly on her forearm. He's going to make his move, sooner than later.

"Once you've got him under your thumb, wait for the right opportunity, and slip some of this into his drink."

He pulls out a small baggie of white powder.

Pixie dust.

"You bring him out back, and we'll put him in the car." He gazes at me, a surprising softness brightening up his normally intense features. "Understand?"

"Yes."

"That's my girl." He presses one more gentle kiss against my lips. "Now *hunt*."

What's On the Menu
RIPLEY

I can feel Preacher's eyes on me as I slip through the crowd, but my focus is on Jonathan's target. She looks pretty pissed, finally reaching the end of her patience as she gives him a less than subtle shove backward. Even from my vantage point, I can see the tiny change in his expression. The fake smile falters, as a bit of artifice falls away; it's the same look Gabriel gave me time and time again when I 'stepped out of line.'

How dare you disrespect me.

All because a woman wants some fucking space.

But unlike my rotting ex-boytoy, Jonathan's a professional. He pulls back the intensity immediately, raising his hands defensively and laughing it all off as some misunderstanding.

"You know, all you had to say was no, sugar!" He calls out over the music.

The redhead stomps past me, bumping me right in the shoulder before the crowd of writhing bodies swallows her like a black hole. Maybe his act convinced her he's just some drunk asshole she can safely forget about the second she's out of sight, but I can see the venom in his gaze.

He's ready to strike— if not her, it'll be someone else.

I love that for me.

Jonathan shakes his head, turning back to the bartender and ordering another drink right as I slide into the newly vacant seat.

"She was something else, huh?"

He casts me a dismissive look before pulling out his phone.

"If you came to rip my head off about your friend, you can save it."

It's impossible not to smirk at his choice of words.

"You think I'm friends with that psycho? She slammed into me out there and didn't even apologize. Fucking rude."

Instantly, I can tell I've started to win him over. Guys like this are always so happy to be seen as the real victim.

"Tell me about it," he snorts. "She left me hanging after a single off-color joke."

The more I align myself with this asshole's worldview, the more he's going to trust me. It feels like shit, but I'll make up for it later when I show him what his own intestines look like.

"Jack and Coke. Twelve bucks."

The bartender slides a glass of dark liquid across the bar.

"Goddamn highway robbery," Jonathan mutters as he opens his wallet before letting out a groan. "Shit. I gotta go to the ATM."

There's a real chance he comes back, but I can't risk losing him this early, not when the compulsion to drink and dash is so strong.

"I got it." I pull a fresh fifty out of my clutch, sliding it to the bartender. "And I'll have what he's having."

Jonathan's smile sends a chill down my smile. He thinks he's reeling me in.

"You seem like you're having a rough night."

My tone is so honeyed it almost makes *me* nauseous, but he laps it up.

"Definitely not the night I was expecting," he chuckles, raising his glass. "Thanks for this, by the way."

Nice touch. If I squint, he almost seems human.

The bartender fixes me another, slipping me my change before moving off to deal with the rest of the crowd that's hovering around the bar.

"So, I guess the question is what *were* you expecting?" I ask, sipping my drink.

"I was *hoping* to meet a nice girl."

My heart starts to thump like a kick drum. I think I've got him.

"And she wasn't?" Some of the condensation from my glass drips onto my cleavage, and I giggle, blotting myself with the napkin the bartender gave me. "Sorry. Clumsy."

I take my time, dabbing at my chest with the napkin while Jonathan stares—well, not at *me* exactly.

"You know if you take a picture, it'll last longer," I purr.

His lips curl into a sly grin and he finally meets my gaze.

"I'm starting to think I met the right girl tonight. Jury's out on the nice part."

He's got about as much charisma as a pile of cow shit. Smells just as ripe, too.

"Well, what do you think? Am I gonna be a nice girl, or not?"

Before he can answer, his attention is pulled away as a woman in a tight black dress pushes past him, with barely more than the lightest touch. I'm not sure if it's just the contact, or that he's getting riled up by some imagined slight, but I can tell he wants to chase her. I can practically see it radiating off of him as he licks his lips.

That tongue might be the first thing I cut out.

Maybe I'll shove it up his ass so he can taste his own shit.

While he's distracted, I take my chance, reaching into my purse and stealthily tapping some pixie dust into his drink before giving it a quick stir. My adrenaline is through the roof and I have to remind myself to stay calm. If I freak out, he's going to know something's up, which is made all the worse when I realize the drink still looks slightly foggier than normal.

"So..." Jonathan turns his attention back to me as the woman in black vanishes around the corner. "You got a name?"

"Amber." My voice comes out real soft and smoky, even catching me off guard. "What about you?"

He wraps one hand around the glass and I can feel the beads of sweat trickling down my spine.

Drink it.

Drink it motherfucker.

"Jake," he replies, playfully swirling the drink.

He probably uses a fake name every time he goes out on the hunt; thinks it's enough to keep him from getting caught. I look over my shoulder, spotting Preacher lurking near the stairs as I take in the crowd, that big hat pulled down over his eyes.

My Grim Reaper.

"You lookin' for someone, gorgeous?" Jonathan purrs in my ear. "Because

I was about to ask if you wanted to come home with me, but I'd never want to impose..."

I can smell his cheap cologne, and feel his crusty, chapped lips against my skin. It's hard to suppress the urge to shudder, but I swallow the bile that's bubbling in the back of my throat and turn, ghosting my lips against his.

He might be a little too eager, because I need him to start sucking down that drink.

"Come on, Jake, put your hand between my legs." I resist the urge to vomit as I grasp his wrist, and place his hand on my thigh. "Don't you want to see what's underneath all of this?"

I can see the tent in his pants as he stares me down, but just before his hand can slip any higher up my leg, the sound of a piercing shriek drags everyone's attention to the back of the dance floor.

It's pretty easy to spot the source: an extremely intoxicated woman in a short blue dress is being hauled off of the redhead Jake was talking to. The frenzy of flailing fists quickly built up a little circle of onlookers, with only a couple actually trying to do anything about it.

Suddenly, I can feel my clutch buzzing, and I peek inside to see the burner Preacher gave me lighting up. I make sure Jonathan's distracted enough by the commotion, deciding it's safe enough to take a look. Preacher told me the phone was only for emergencies, so it's not really something I can ignore.

UNKNOWN NUMBER:

> You're compromised. Get out before the pigs show up.

I don't even get the chance to reply before I feel the arm around my waist, and Jonathan's crusty lips brush up against my ear.

"Did you really think you got away with it?" He asks, reaching into my bra and pulling out the baggie I stuffed in there. "You were so sloppy."

An icy chill rushes down my spine as he dangles it between his fingers.

"Tell me what this is."

This is just a speed bump.

I can spin this, I can still win.

"It's ecstasy," I beam, putting on my best dumb bimbo impression.

He drops the baggie on the counter and slides his drink toward me.

"Sure," he smiles, violence flashing in his eyes. "Prove it."

His lifeless, empty expression makes shiver.

I see Gabriel. I see my father. I see—

"I *said* prove it. If you're telling the truth, we can party. If not, you're gonna be telling the cops exactly what you tried to drug me with. Once you come down, of course."

"Okay! Jesus fucking Christ," I snap, snatching the drink off of the bar, and draining it in a few seconds. "You want me? I'm yours. Otherwise, I've got a whole bar to pick from."

This is a dangerous game. I don't fully know what he's capable of, or how quickly he might escalate, but it's too late to walk away now. According to Preacher, I have about five minutes before this shit fully kicks in, and only a few of the symptoms are gonna look like ecstasy.

I rest my hand on his pants, squeezing his cock hard enough to make him wince.

I've gotta move fast, because I'm sure as shit not leaving without my prey.

"So, did I pass your little test?"

He grabs what's left of my own, untainted drink, finishing it off with a reassured smirk.

"I'm parked out back."

"Perfect," I purr.

So is my man.

We slide off our stools, and Jonathan quickly starts leading me through the crowd of sweaty bodies. Only a minute or so in and I can already start to feel the effects of the pixie dust: cold sweats, clenched jaw, distorted vision... I feel like I'm walking through a dark tunnel, and all I can think about is finding the exit.

But I have a mission.

Sweat starts to pour down my face, or maybe it's been like that for a while now; the music is wrong, distorted, like someone's turning the volume up and down every couple seconds, feeding it through a shitty synthesizer they grabbed from a thrift shop.

I feel nauseous and my teeth won't stop chattering.

I feel every step I'm taking ripple through every cell in my body.

I feel like I'm trapped, walking three steps behind... me.

Jonathan pushes the back door open and I'm hit with a rush of warm summer air, momentarily snapping me back into a slightly more present state of mind, but I barely get to take a breath before he has me up against the wall, his mouth slamming into mine.

His kiss, if you can even call it that, is angry and demanding, and he bites down on my lip hard enough to make me bleed. I wince, trying to shove him off of me, but the pixie dust makes my limbs feel like they're made of concrete. I can taste the acid building up in the back of my throat, mixing with the thick film of Jack and Coke that's still lingering on my tongue.

He squeezes my hips, digging his nails into the fabric of my brand new dress, and pins me against the building with a strength I never would have guessed he possessed. My veins flood with ice-cold water, and a thousand racing thoughts come flying at me all at once.

This is not happening.

I should have kept my eye on him.

I was compromised.

Should have kept my phone on me.

I can still do this.

It's over.

Jonathan grasps me by the throat, slamming my head against the wall as he tears at my dress. Then I'm just... gone, watching it all happen from a distance.

Just like before.

"You're mine now, bitch." He squeezes harder, cutting off my air supply as I watch my body vainly try to claw at him. "We're gonna play a game, and these are the rules: you scream, you die, do you understand me?"

I watch as she nods my head for me, tears streaming down my face. I want her to scream Preacher's name, but that's not me anymore. It's not happening to me.

"Good girl, see how easy that was?" Jonathan snarls, reaching down to unbuckle his belt. "I think I'll have you right here—"

A tiny pained grunt is all that manages to escape his lips as Preacher's presence suddenly threatens to swallow the two of us whole. I watch as my head lifts, and she looks up—

No, *I* look up, expecting to see those beautiful, soulless eyes that are so like my own; this time, there's a hellfire burning inside.

"Jonathan Jackson, I believe I just severed your spinal cord." His deep, husky voice is cold and clinical, but there's a new edge to it I can't quite place. "That means you no longer have control over your legs, or most of your bodily functions for that matter... which means sadly, you probably won't be able to feel the rest of what's coming."

The muscles in Jonathan's face contort into a painful, torturous expression, sputtering and struggling to hold himself up against the wall as he crumbles. In the moments before he passes out from shock, he reminds me a lot of that Munsch painting, *The Scream*.

Preacher yanks him off of me and hauls him over his shoulder in one fluid motion, wasting no time at all.

"Follow me, rabbit."

I obey, walking behind him as he carries Jonathan over to the pickup, tossing him into the back like a ragdoll before turning back to face me.

He puts a hand on my cheek.

"Ripley? Are you okay?"

The sound of my name forces a straining, painful sob from my throat, and Preacher wraps me in his arms, gingerly stroking my hair.

"It's not your fault," he murmurs. "I should have been closer."

Angry tears rush down my cheeks.

He thought I could handle it.

He believed in me.

"I'm a failure."

Preacher slips a finger beneath my chin, tipping my head up.

"No, you're not. *I* failed tonight." He sighs. "This? It's on me, and I promise you I'm gonna make it right, little rabbit. You understand?"

He wipes away my tears, his face still twisted up in concern. Watching me. Waiting to see if I'm truly okay.

"Yes, sir."

But I'm not okay.

I need to hurt someone.

"That's my girl. Come on, let's go home."

Thankfully, that's exactly what's on the menu tonight.

Slaughterhouse Rules
PREACHER

I feel like shit.

Seeing him with Ripley up against that wall, trying to claw at her and take what he knew damn well wasn't his...

I wish I could have slit his throat and left him there, like abandoned trash in an alley, but I've got this whole thing about not leaving evidence behind. Raph's been giving me shit the entire ride home, waking up my phone every couple minutes with a new insult or accusation.

> **RAPH**
>
> You should have been there with her.
>
> **RAPH**
>
> You're lucky nobody blew your fucking cover.
>
> **RAPH**
>
> Even luckier the pigs didn't show up.

I got too confident in her untested abilities, too excited to watch her weave that web of hers, and it got out of control. Thankfully, I managed to get her some ipecac in time to get most of that nasty Pixie Dust shit out of her system. She puked her brains out for about half an hour, but her mind's clearer now.

But after all that, now she won't even look at me.

I pull up into the ranch, killing the engine and staring out at the barn in the distance. It's lonely in the dark, like an ominous beacon, just barely lit by my headlights as an eerie silence descends around us.

"You ready?"

Her jaw ticks, her fiery eyes and clenched fists giving away the rage that's been building inside her all night.

"Ripley." I rest my hand on her knee, giving it a gentle squeeze. "I need your head in the game. Are you up for this?"

"Yes," she rasps.

"How are you feeling?"

"Fine."

"Gonna need better than fine."

"I'm on top of the fucking world." She rips the seatbelt off, glaring at me. "Is that what you want to hear?"

I shrug.

"It'll do."

I hop out of the truck and she follows, watching me intently as I toss Jonathan's limp body over my shoulder and head for the barn. He blubbers and groans, his system still in shock as he struggles to adapt to his new reality. I glance over my shoulder to make sure she hasn't wandered off or passed out, but she's still just a few steps behind me, pushing her messy hair out of her face. Even covered in sweat, with mascara smeared on her cheeks, she's still a smoke show; kinda like Jessica Rabbit... if she were a rage-fuelled homicidal maniac.

I unlock the barn, and the two of us head inside, Ripley silently shutting the doors behind us.

"Wha'shappenin?" Jonathan slurs, his head wobbling around as I feel his heart rate start to spike.

I don't say a word, just carry him over to his hook. The sound it makes when it pierces through his shoulder sends a shiver down my spine, a beautiful accompaniment to his shrieking wails.

Once he's secure, I tear off his clothes, shredding them with my bare hands. His pale skin glows in the dim light. Tattoos decorate his chest and arms– shitty portraits of the Grim Reaper, guns, a maple leaf, and a lion's head. I poke at it with the tip of my blade. I like my prey to be as vulnerable as they've made their victims.

"You know, the lion typically symbolizes strength and protection...

courage too. None of those qualities seem to really line up with you, Jonathan." I lean in as close as I can, so close I can feel his sharp panicked breathing on my face. "You've avoided consequences for *far* too long. It's about time someone snuffed you out."

Out of the corner of my eye, I can almost see Ripley's anger possessing her, like a foreign entity pushing her to the brink.

This'll be my gift to her. The first of many.

I head over to the surgical table, my fingers dancing across the array of knives I laid out in preparation for tonight, each one with its own unique memory attached. I snatch up a particularly big one, with a brown leather handle, and flip it over in my hand.

"I shoved this up a guy's ass once, Johnny." I'm grinning from ear to ear, allowing myself a brief moment to reminisce. "Blade first, mind you. But don't you worry, it was his idea. That's the way he did it to the people he killed, after all."

Jonathan is doing his best to stay conscious, but he's struggling. Drops of dark crimson smack against the floor like the earliest stages of rain, and I can see the telltale signs as his body starts to go into shock. Pale skin, glistening with sweat, shivering... unlucky for him there's a hell of a lot more in store for him tonight.

All of this is just preparation, a preamble. I'm trusting Ripley to dole out the appropriate punishment for his sins. But first, and most importantly, she'll have to choose the music.

"Rabbit, c'mere." I pull out my phone, turning on the speakers in the barn with a couple button presses. "I need to show you something."

She doesn't say a word, just stares at Jonathan's limp body dangling from that hook as she makes her way over, more fury burning behind her eyes.

Her trauma runs deep, but I can relate. The relief I felt after I killed my daddy was palpable. After Raph and I buried him, I knelt in the dirt and wept. Finally, after *years* of torture, I'd found salvation. I was baptized in blood and reborn.

We'll get to the root of her pain eventually.

She deserves that same special kind of justice.

"Do you think I'm weak?" She rasps, taking her place at my side.

"There's nothing weak about you." I glide my thumb across her mouth before giving her a quick peck. "And everyone's gonna know it. We're gonna make you a god tonight."

I take her hand, leading her toward the table. She immediately reaches for a knife, but I grasp her wrist, clicking my tongue and shaking my head. It doesn't go over well, and she glowers at me.

"If I trust you, you have to trust me. That's how partnerships work, cowboy."

"I do trust you," I chuckle, handing her my phone. "But there's a certain set of rules we have to follow, like a ritual of sorts. First thing's first, you're going to set the mood."

She takes the phone, staring down at the open tracklist with a frown.

"Music?"

"It's important nobody hears him screaming if they happen to wander up the driveway. And just look at him, doesn't he strike you as a squealer?" I shake my head knowingly. "The squealers really do distract you, trust me. Really starts to grate on your nerves after a while."

She snorts as scrolls through my phone, but I can already see her mood lightening as she hems and haws over the song selection, ignoring Jonathan's choked sobs until she finally lands on her song.

Kokomo by the Beach Boys pours from the speakers and I nod my head.

"Classic." I gesture to the knife roll, pointing out a particularly large one with a drop-point blade. "You can pick anything. This one here's multipurpose though. Good for skinning."

Jonathan howls, the chain rattling as he swings his arms wildly, like he's trying to reach back and... Is he trying to pull the hook out? Poor guy must have failed basic physics, or he's just delusional. To be fair to him though, he has lost a lot of blood.

Ripley tries her best to ignore the noise, carefully looking at each knife one by one, but after a few more screams her eyes go wild, suddenly snatching the knife I suggested from the table and rushing for him. My jaw drops as I watch her swing her arm back and slash him straight across the belly, the beast of a woman getting up on her tiptoes and gripping his chin like a vice.

"What's the matter, Jonathan? Can't take it?"

Her jaw is clenched, and those eyes are fucking lethal.

"How do you two know my name?"

"We know everything about you. We know how many women you've raped, and we know your daddy covered it up." She smiles. "So many intimidated witnesses, Jonathan, was it just because you were family, or maybe it was something more. Did you do it together? Is that why he killed himself? Or did he really think you weren't that bad to begin with, that it was just some small time stuff. Maybe he couldn't live with the guilt when he figured out how much his son reveled in it."

"I don't know what the fuck you're talking about."

Ripley drives the knife into his other shoulder amidst his whines of agony.

"That's strange... because that's not the information I got. You're Jonathan Jackson, born October 17th, 1992 in Hamilton, Ontario, right? You're the guy who likes to rape women and make their partners watch, you pathetic piece of shit."

"I didn't rape anyone!" His eyes bounce over to me, pure desperation flashing across his face. "You gotta let me go, man! She's fucking crazy!"

I grab my cigarettes from my jeans pocket, lighting one and letting out a long exhale while the music continues to blare.

"I know. It's why I keep her around." I blow a smoke ring. "Fucks like an *animal*, too."

Ripley's mouth twists up into an even more menacing smile.

"You know what Jonathan, you should be more polite, because I just decided we're gonna fuck on top of your pathetic crumbled little corpse." She's practically spitting her words at him at this point. "I saw your rap sheet, I know how your daddy protected you. And you're trying to tell me you've never done any of it? Did you forget exactly what you tried to do to me less than an hour ago, you piece of shit?"

"You came on to me!" He screams, the veins in his forehead and neck popping in a grotesque fashion. "You fucking asked for it! I didn't do anything wrong!"

Ripley lets out a sound I've never heard her make before, like the mix between a war cry and a thunder clap, as she tears the knife from his shoulder and slashes him again, this time clean through his left nipple.

The cut is so deep I can see the muscle, but I don't have any time to admire her work, because she's already circling him, slashing at him here, there, and everywhere, her face twisted in a beautiful new kind of cruelty.

This is Ripley's reward, an opportunity to finally, and truly, become herself... and judging by the psychotic glimmer in her eye, she's enjoying every second of it. Sweat glistens on her forehead as she flashes me a delighted look, blood dripping down Jonathan's trembling body.

"You know what this is called?"

I gesture vaguely at his cut-up, heaving form.

"A rapist?" She asks, catching her heavy breath.

"F- Fuck you!" Jonathan manages to snarl.

It seems he's given up on the *'you got the wrong guy'* angle, but even as his strength fades to near-nothing, he can't seem to process that he's already dead; has been since he walked out of that club with my girl.

Ripley drives the blade deep into his side, her face twisting up into something demonic. She's beautiful when she lets loose, more than I could have imagined, and I can't wait to let her consume me like a brand new kind of sickness.

Something that makes even *my* blood run cold.

She pulls the blade out, holding it up to the dim light before licking it clean, like it's a popsicle on a hot summer's day.

"What were you going to say?" She asks, turning to face me.

"What?"

She grins, the crimson already staining her teeth.

"Did all the blood from that big brain of yours rush right down to your cock? You were going to tell me what something's called."

She's got me pegged, my dick is straining against the zipper so hard it feels like I could burst a seam, but I'm doing my best to keep cool.

"He's going into hypovolemic shock."

Ripley bites her lip, trailing the tip of the blade up her bare arm, and then over top of her shirt, ghosting those perky little nipples.

"And what exactly does that mean?"

Jonathan's still wailing his heart out, but I don't care. He can make all the noise he wants, it's not gonna make a lick of difference.

"It means his body is losing too much blood, so his heart can't pump properly. That's why he's..." I gesture at him again. "Like that."

She turns her back to me, giving me a good look at how the dress clings to her hips and thighs.

"Makes him look a bit like a painting, doesn't it? *The Agony of Mr. So and So.*"

I suck on my cigarette, imagining her covered in blood. Well, in more blood at least, with nothing but those heels on and my knife clutched in her fist.

"Fitting."

"Stop!" The dead man bellows. "God, please stop! You don't have to do this!"

Ripley's smile is as cold as it is haunting.

"You think anyone's going to feel sorry for you, you piece of shit? You think anyone's going to mourn you after tonight? You can't even say it out loud, can you?"

"I'm sorry!" He wheezes, some of his final shuddering breaths slipping out along with his words. "I'm sorry, okay? I did it, I fucking did it, just... let me go."

She smiles, running her hand tenderly across his cheek.

"There, now that wasn't so hard was it?"

She turns to me, gripping the knife tightly in her fist.

"Now teach me how to skin him. Alive."

Now, This is the Easy Part
RIPLEY

I feel like a God, finally embracing the anger I've buried so deep for so, so long.

At first, I was afraid it would cloud my judgment, but everything is crystal clear.

And I know exactly what I have to do.

"The thing about skinnin' someone?" Preacher comes up behind me, sliding a hand around my waist and kissing up and down my neck. "It's messy work. You don't wanna get your pretty dress dirty, do you?"

The soft sensation of his lips is only heightened by his rough stubble brushing up against me, spurring me on.

"Well, then you'd better take it off of me."

He slowly unzips the dress, sliding it off of my shoulders and taking my hand, helping me step out of it. I'm left in nothing but my heels and underwear, and he spins me around, gazing at me like an artist would a newly chiseled statue.

"Perfect, just perfect."

"Not quite. I hope you're willing to take your own advice."

I purr, popping open the buttons of his shirt.

"Tonight, I'll make an exception."

Preacher shivers as I unzip his jeans, reaching inside and wrapping my fingers around his cock. I watch those dark lashes flutter gently, the beginnings of a moan slipping from his lips, and I can't help myself, slamming my mouth into his.

"You people are fucking *sick*!" Jonathan manages to choke out.

"You focus on me," Preacher murmurs, resting one hand on my waist. "And I'll teach you everything you need to know."

He grabs a knife, placing it in my hand before leading me toward our victim. Up close, his skin reminds me of a dolphin's, slick and glistening as he takes his trembling breaths.

"Please!" Jonathan begs. "I'll give you money! I'll give you anything you want."

"The only thing we want is for your heart to stop beating, Johnny," Preacher chuckles. "And we'll get there, one way or another."

I can feel his cock throbbing against my ass as he gently guides my wrist, leaving the knife to hover just above Jonathan's heel.

"Now, sometimes I like to start by cutting right here." He dips his head, nipping at my earlobe. "The achilles tendon is the thickest one in the human body, which means it's a little tougher than usual. You have to use just the right amount of pressure."

Preacher smacks Jonathan's bare thigh.

"Count yourself lucky, pretty boy, you won't be feeling almost any of this, at least until we start peeling the skin off your back!"

The terrified howl the man lets out gives me goosebumps as Preacher guides my hand, the two of us making the first cut together. I smile as his achilles splits like a stick of butter beneath the blade.

I'm finally reaching my true potential.

Not a lot of people get to follow their passions, do they?

I've been so focused on getting this right that I'd completely forgotten about the music, that is, until I hear the scream of keyboards followed up with a thumping bassline.

Obsession by Animotion.

Another good choice.

Jonathan's pleas for mercy blend with the music as we work, and I'm relieved to realize that I'm not feeling any guilt. In its place, there's a beautiful anticipation, like I'm about to rip a cork out of a champagne bottle on New Year's Eve.

"Now, you wanna keep the pressure light, that way you're not tearing into the meat. The product needs to look clean; clients don't want the shit that looks like it's been chewed up, and I don't like spending extra time fixing mistakes when it's all over."

"I understand."

I lean back into Preacher's weight, trusting him to guide my hand while I do my best to memorize the exact method he uses to slip the knife beneath the skin. It's been a while since I've given something my complete and undivided attention, but I want to get this right.

I want to be perfect.

When he gestures for me to take over, I'm surprised by how easily I manage to detach the skin from the rest of the shimmering red muscle. It almost looks velvety, like it would be soft and luxurious to the touch.

"Atta girl," Preacher rumbles, kissing my temple. "Keep going."

Jonathan's pleas for mercy grow weaker and weaker until they're nearly swallowed up by the music. He's hanging limp now, barely moving, and the two of us ignore his little twitches and bursts of energy as Preacher guides me through the more complicated cuts. Once we're finished, our prey's pale skin hangs from his body like angel's wings.

"Now, this is the easy part. All we gotta do is make a couple of cuts like this..." He pulls the skin taut and slips the knife through it, the same way my mom used to cut wrapping paper. "And it comes right off. Easy."

We walk the large sheets over to the killing table, laying them out flat one by one.

"Now, we have one more thing to do."

Preacher dives into his knife roll, pulling out a long needle, tearing the cap off with his teeth, and spitting it onto the floor.

"What is it?"

"Adrenaline. You want him to be awake when you kill him, right? You just have to stick him with this."

I nod, taking the needle and sauntering toward my prey, swishing my hips as I walk.

But the closer I get, the more lifeless he looks.

"Is this even gonna do anything?" I ask. "He seems pretty dead."

"Trust me, little rabbit. He'll wake up."

I set my knife down on the ground, taking a deep breath before plunging the needle right into his chest. There's a beat or two where nothing happens, but just as I reach forward to check his pulse he begins to thrash and scream, his face twisted up in delicious agony.

"There he is!" Preacher snickers. "Welcome back, Johnny boy! We've missed you!"

"P— p—" He coughs, blood dripping from his lips. "Pl—"

"What was that?" I ask, retrieving the knife before dragging the tip across his belly. "Speak up, sweetheart."

He looks absolutely pathetic, tears rushing down his cheeks as he struggles to maintain a semblance of steady breathing, and if I had even an ounce of humanity still left inside me, maybe I would feel sorry for him.

Maybe.

But how many women has he left shattered? Blaming themselves? Wishing they'd never shown him an ounce of kindness?

The shock must be fucking with his ability to speak because all he manages to do is stammer, paler than a fucking ghost as he drips sweat and blood onto the floor.

And all over my new shoes.

I hate to sound like a yuppie, but that kind of pisses me off.

"You know, you should be thanking me. If we gave you to the cops, you'd spend the rest of your life getting shit-kicked in a maximum security prison. Did you know that rapists, wife beaters, and child molesters are the lowest rungs on the ladder in there? Or did your daddy not mention that before he went and left you all alone?"

I ready myself, placing one foot in front of the other, aiming right at his gut. He keeps stammering, struggling to speak, but before he can even make another concrete sound, the knife is in his belly, tearing through flesh, muscle, and organs with ease.

The familiar tingling sensation in my jaw returns with a vengeance, this time shooting all the way through the rest of my body. I can feel my cunt throb and ache with each twist of the knife, but all I can think about is Preacher.

I turn to him, pulling the knife out and licking it clean, my eyes rolling back as the beast inside of me claws its way to freedom. I'm starting to realize that he was right about the first time I killed. I was sloppy and enraged, not fully in control. This time, the quiet part of my anger has taken hold. The part of me that suffered in silence while the men in my life hurt me.

Gabriel.

My father.

That piece of me has been waiting for this kind of vengeance.

No more hiding.

Just before I can stab Jonathan a final time, I feel Preacher's hands wrap around my waist, stopping me in my tracks.

"You did good, rabbit, but let's finish this together. Just for fun, I can show you how to pull out his intestines."

Preacher plunges his hand inside the open wound, rooting around before dragging out what looks like a thick, glistening rope.

The scent of copper floods my nostrils and coats my tongue. I can almost taste it, like a dirty penny that's been left sitting in a puddle for months. It overpowers everything and almost makes me gag at first, but I can't help myself, reaching out and brushing my fingers against the intestines.

"Ripley."

His hand trails down my neck, smearing the sinner's blood across my chest and down my stomach as he lowers himself to his knees. Even the deep crease between his brows has disappeared as he gazes up at me.

"What are you doing?"

"Whatever you ask." He places a delicate kiss on my thigh. "Tonight, I serve only you."

Good Boy

PREACHER

"Serve me?" She asks. "What does that mean?"

I've only ever knelt before God.

But tonight, this is the church I worship in.

She's warm spring rain that makes everything blossom.

My Persephone.

I don't know when I got so damn poetic, but I'm *also* not sure when I started falling into love instead of only lust. Maybe it was during the chase, when she dug deep into the depths of her darkness and fought like hell.

I don't know much about the subject, but what I *do* know is that I would burn the world down for this woman. I've loved every second I've spent unraveling her.

I take her hand, pressing a sweet kiss to her knuckles.

"Break me, Ripley."

I feel so exposed like this, like I'm laying my soul bare for her. I want her to grasp the power that's rightfully hers, to hold it in her hands and use it to tear me apart.

"And show me how to please you."

She reaches down, plucking my hat off my head and placing it on her own with a sultry little smirk. It would be so easy to bend her to my will, but we've been playing that game for a while. I want her to unleash everything on me. I want to see what she does when she's given all that power.

186

I place my soiled palms on her scarred and freckled thighs, smearing dirt and blood over the marks that Gabriel left. Just seeing them sparks my rage, but I push it down, desperate to please her.

Ripley's eyes shine and she grins, baring her teeth as she takes a step backward. When I move to follow, she startles me with a quick strike across the face.

"I didn't say you could touch me."

Her voice is a snarl, the brutality radiating off of her.

I can't remember how long it's been since I gave in to the kind of anger she's grabbed hold of. For years, taking my past out on those sick sons of bitches was cathartic. I was creative, and passionate, but eventually I ran out of juice. Killing became as routine as taking a multivitamin in the morning.

Seeing Ripley like this makes me want that passion back.

She picks up a smaller hunting knife, one with a serrated blade and a thick leather handle, trailing it down her thigh and slicing ever so slightly into her soft, silky skin. Blood peaks from the edges of the wound, and she carefully dabs her fingers before bringing them up to pleasure herself.

"Do you know what I want, cowboy?"

She reminds me of a lightning strike, radiating raw and absolute power.

"Tell me."

"I want to watch the Devil crawl to me, do you think he can manage that?"

Condescension drips from her tongue as more blood starts to trickle down her thigh. She cut herself deeper than I thought; might need stitches by the time this is over.

But for now, it can wait.

"Yes, ma'am, I think he might."

Her mouth curls into a sinister smile as she shimmies out of her panties, tossing them across the barn.

"Then be a good boy and fetch."

I'm caught a little off guard, my dick throbbing at the very idea of being her pet.

"Did you hear me, dog?" She growls, fucking herself slowly with her fingers. "Or is watching me like this making you stupid?"

I swallow my pride, carefully turning around on all fours and crawling toward her discarded underwear. I've never felt more pathetic... or more turned on.

Little pebbles dig into my palms as I crawl, the humiliation adding to my discomfort, but all I can think about is the sweet reward at the end of this. I keep picturing her, and us, and the hell we'll unleash on every evil son of a bitch we get our claws into.

I reach the discarded lace, plucking it off the floor only for Ripley to click her tongue in disapproval.

"Bad boy, Preacher. Dogs use their teeth."

Is this the same woman who landed on my doorstep just a few weeks ago, battered and bruised and afraid? I dip my head, taking a couple tries before finally managing the task. The taste of her sweetness floods my mouth, and my whole body clenches as I make my way back to her.

"I bet you're *dying* to fuck me, aren't you?" She purrs, carefully grasping the blade of the knife and slowly sliding the hilt into her cunt. "Because this? It already feels amazing. Maybe I won't even need you after all."

A knot of excitement forms in my stomach as I slink toward her, drooling like a fucking animal over her underwear. I'd lick the mud off her shoes if she asked me to.

"You want a taste?"

I nod, and she removes the hilt from her pussy, offering it to me.

"Then bark."

I spit her panties onto the floor, cocking a brow.

"Are you ser—"

"I said *bark*, dog." She leans forward, wild and wicked, her messy dark hair obscuring her face. "Because I own you tonight, don't I? You're mine."

I push past the shame, all the prideful resistance I've built up over the years, and I fucking *bark*.

Once.

Twice.

Three times.

Ripley giggles with glee, covering her mouth as her eyes dance with delight.

"Wow, I didn't think you'd actually do it."

"I told you, tonight I'm serving you, rabbit."

"And you have, so now you get your reward."

She lets me clean the hilt of the knife with my tongue, playfully thrusting it in and out of my mouth like it's her cock. Everything about her makes me feel like I'm losing control, like a man crawling through the desert for weeks without a drop of water finding a fucking oasis.

"That's a good boy." She pulls it out of my mouth far too soon, hopping up onto the table and spreading her legs. "Now, make me come."

My heart hammers in my throat as my gaze fixes on that slick pussy smeared with blood. The taste of iron floods my mouth, her voice breaking as she starts to fuck my face. She's got one fist buried in my hair as I slide my tongue inside of her tight little cunt. I curl it upward, letting her juices dribble down my chin, like I'm eating a ripe piece of fruit.

Her taste, the way she clenches around me, the sounds she makes when she comes... there's not a song on earth sweeter than her. I could spend the rest of my life on my knees for her, and I'd die a happy man.

"Get off the table and bend over," I order, tearing my mouth away from her cunt.

I want to ruin her, just like I did in the woods. I want her begging me, pleading, but there's a sharpness to her look that makes me instantly shift my tactics back.

"Please?"

"What a good boy you are, using your manners," she purrs, sliding off the table and shoving her ass right in my face. "You must be desperate."

"You have no idea."

I spread her cheeks, my mouth watering at the sight; I've been wanting to get my tongue in there for quite some time now.

"Do you always stare at your dinner this long before you eat it?" She giggles. "Come on, cowboy. I said make me come."

I swirl my tongue around her asshole, savoring the moment. Never in my goddamn life did I think I'd find someone like Ripley Winter. She's my match in every way possible, and I'm going to spend the rest of my life being devoted to nurturing her demons, the same way I'd tend to flowers in a garden.

Because I know she'll do the same for me.

"I bet that pussy is nice and wet, isn't it?"

I pull away, only to slide two fingers inside her ass, stretching her wide but keeping my thrusts gentle as I listen to her sweet moans. The sweat on her skin, how her hips roll, the way she takes every fucking inch I give her... my love for this woman is growing stronger by the hour.

Her broken cries smash up against the walls of the barn before getting lost beneath a crash of drums and the whine of Clapton's guitar.

White Room by Cream.

I jump to my feet, grabbing a bottle of lube from the table before pouring some onto my palm and giving my dick a few gentle strokes.

"I was so close," she whines.

"Yeah?" I tease her asshole with the tip of my cock. "Keep touching yourself and I'll give you everything you want."

She does as she's told, her moans sounding as sweet as honey.

I can't wait any longer. I need her now.

I spread her cheeks and dribble a generous amount of lube onto her asshole, pushing it inside of her with my fingers. She slams a hand down on the table, clattering my set of knives all over.

"Fuck!"

"I know you can take my gun, and you proved you're more than prepared for that knife, but are you ready for my cock?"

She glances over her shoulder, her eyes gleaming as her lip curls into a smirk.

"Oh, how exciting, my dog is taking charge again."

I can't help but laugh, stroking her back as I admire her delicious curves. Yeah, I'd be this woman's dog for the rest of my life if she let me.

At least I'm well trained.

"You're gonna scream nice and loud for me, aren't you?"

I give her ass a rough slap, making her yelp.

"Did you hear what I said, rabbit?"

"Mmm, yes!"

I start to push my cock inside, immediately meeting resistance. She's almost *too* tight, and even though she's already moaning like a filthy slut, I can tell she's not fully relaxed.

I add more lube, spreading it around with the tip of my dick.

"Just relax, rabbit."

I rub her back and we breathe together, while the music continues to pound.

"I'll be gentle to start, but once I get goin', I'm gonna tear you apart." I lean over, grabbing a fistful of hair and carefully winding it around my knuckles. "But that's what you want, isn't it?"

She snarls as I push my cock back in, past the point of resistance, until she sings like a fuckin' canary. I start rocking my hips, reveling in the pleasure that's already beginning to spike. At this point it's not going to take much for me, but it's *her*, so I'm gonna hold on as long as it takes.

Our moans have grown so loud they're all but drowning out the music, and I yank harder on her hair as euphoria rushes through my veins.

"I'm close," she grunts, working her clit with frantic desperation.

I deliver another ruthless slam of my hips, feeling her ass flutter and clench around me. God, how is she getting tighter? I clench my stomach, praying that my body holds out long enough to get her over the edge before I do.

All I can hear are the obscene sounds of wetness, of skin against skin, of the complete and utter debauchery surrounding us as she chants my name over and over like an incantation. The taste of our sweat lingers in the air, beneath the unmistakable smell of gore.

Blood and death are scents I've grown used to... but buried underneath all of that here I'm sensing something new, something tangible and beautiful within all of this darkness, like a flower bursting through the cracks in the pavement.

Christ, what happened to me, am I waxing poetic during anal sex?

Ripley sounds like a wild animal, grunting and gasping for air in between random bouts of profanity. It's perfect, like a fucking symphony, and I want to hear every single note.

"I could fuck this tight little ass forever." I give her another rough smack, delighted by the way it jiggles. "In fact, I think I might. I think I'm gonna do whatever the fuck I want, whenever I want."

"It's yours, baby," she groans. "I'm yours."

She's shaking, her legs about to give out, and I have to grip her hips as tightly as I can to keep her in place, pinning her up against the table. We're woven together completely now, unable to tell where one of us ends and the other begins.

"And I'm yours," I growl. "Now let it all go for me."

There's no going back.

Not that there ever was.

Her scream rips through the air as she comes, my own climax not far behind as fire burns deep in my belly. It rushes through me, igniting my veins, and with one final thrust, I'm filling her ass to the brim. All of my fucking serotonin and dopamine fire at the same time, sending more and more warmth flooding through my body.

I'm falling to pieces, head tipped back toward the sky, eyelids fluttering.

And I just keep thrusting.

Harder.

Harder.

And even harder.

Until I simply physically can't anymore.

I pull out of her and spin her around in a fluid motion, grasping her face with both hands as her mouth crashes against mine.

It's the best kiss I've ever had.

She's the best thing I've ever had.

And I only want...

More.

More.

And even more.

Salvation

RIPLEY

There's a glass of wine in my hand, soft jazz flowing out of the speakers as I sit at the kitchen table, soaking in the last of the evening sun. I can't think of a single other time in my life where I've felt this comfortable.

The two of us have been on cloud nine since the events of last night. We took our sweet time, giddy in the afterglow of our shared kill, until Preacher finally decided we still had work to do and guided me through the disposal process. He even let me keep a few trophies.

Jonathan's heart is currently roasting in the oven, surrounded by rosemary, and covered in butter and a hell of a lot of spices. I have to admit, for my first time with prepared human meat, I'm kind of excited.

"When did you start eating them?" I ask, watching with an observant eye as he tosses some asparagus in the pan.

He tilts his head.

"Vegetables?"

"You know what I mean, smartass."

He chuckles, obviously tickled by his dumb joke.

"I'm not really sure. A few years ago, maybe? I got curious after cuttin' these fuckers up and... well, I wondered what all the fuss was about."

"Okay, sure, but like... what made you so curious in the first place? It's not really something people talk about doing very often."

"We tend to squash things that are considered taboo. To me, eating a human heart seemed like it wouldn't be any different than eating an animal's, so I wanted to find out if I was right."

"You know, there are different kinds of cannibalism? Some turn to it for survival, others engage in endocannibalism."

"Endocannibalism, huh?" He turns around, leaning up against the counter with a smile on his face. "Big word. Tell me more."

"Why?" I laugh, suddenly feeling shockingly self-conscious.

"Because I've always loved me a smart woman."

Loved.

I've spent so much time hating that word. It was spoken so casually to me, usually right before someone did something callous and cruel, or even more after. Now? It makes me feel...

I clear my throat, swirling my wine in the glass.

God, I don't even know.

"Anthropologists found that some cultures used it as a mourning ritual, or as a way to transfer spiritual power. It's fascinating when you start digging into it."

He raises a brow, smirking at me.

"Well now, just how many degrees you got, sweetheart?"

"Just high school, but that didn't help much. I did a lot of reading the last few years. It kept me... focused on other things."

He licks his lips, sauntering up and wrapping his arms around my waist while the veggies sizzle in the pan.

"Speaking of other things, you were incredible last night." His voice is all gravel with just a hint of honey. "How do you feel?"

It's surreal when I think back to the first dinner I had with him, how skittish and angry I was, how much I just wanted him to *let me go.* Yet with so much inside me screaming to turn and run, I still couldn't help but be drawn to him.

"Remember when you said that I would have to part with the truth in order to gain salvation?"

He nods, stroking my wine-flushed cheek with the back of his hand.

"Do you think you found it last night?"

There's always been a part of me that's felt disconnected from my own humanity. I understood it on a logical level: When I was supposed to be sad, when it was appropriate to offer sympathy, when to laugh, when to get angry... all through careful observation and rehearsal, but now...

"I think I found it with you."

Redness creeps into Preacher's cheeks as he brushes my hair behind my ear. He lets out a breath, and I swear I see him shudder.

"I got a hard time, uh..." He gnaws on his lip. "Tellin' people how I feel about them."

Sometimes his demeanor is so soft and caring I forget that we're not a regular couple. Luckily, all I have to do is think back less than 24 hours, to when he fucked my ass in front of a corpse to be reminded.

"Well, I suppose we have at least a couple things in common then."

His smile is surprisingly bashful, catching me off guard all over again.

"Look, I just want to..." He sighs, nodding to himself before starting up in earnest. "You're one of the most important people in my life, Ripley. I have a hard time picturing how things were before you got here now, and I— you— uh..."

The words seem to get tangled on his tongue, and after a moment of frustration, he's swallowed them.

But it's fine.

I know what he's saying, or what he's trying to say, because I feel it too.

We depend on each other. It's us against the world.

"I feel the same way."

His hot breath rushes against my ear as he kisses up and down my jaw.

"You know, I don't think I've ever loved anyone before."

I laugh, but my heart is racing as I let my body sink into him.

"Me neither."

It's such a foreign concept to me, and it always has been. I've needed people for protection, or guidance, or to keep a roof over my head, but if you asked if I loved them?

"I don't know what the hell I'm supposed to do," he whispers.

It's almost like a confession, shame dripping from his words.

"We can figure all that out together."

When he breaks away, his eyes are bright and sparkling, and... I guess now I know. It doesn't seem that difficult in hindsight.

With the meal finished, we each get a large portion of Jonathan's heart, stuffed with kale and dressed with some kind of sauce I couldn't quite place when I watched him prep.

"What does it taste like?" I ask, picking up my utensils like a kid prepping to try out a scary new meal.

Preacher cuts into his portion, popping a small piece into his mouth.

"Depends. Some cuts are gamey, and a little chewy, but something like this heart? It's not that much different from a real nice cut of steak."

"I've read multiple accounts over the years," I murmur, carefully skewering the meat with my fork. "Most people say it tastes like pork."

It's surprisingly tender, but not spongy like you'd expect from something that pumps blood all day long. Speaking of, I can't help but shiver with excitement when a little bit leaks out onto the plate with my first cut.

"They're not wrong, that's usually the result you'll get, but it all depends on how you cook it," Preacher replies, watching me while he finishes chewing his food.

He's waiting for me to take that first bite, fists clenched tightly around his knife and fork as they hover above the plate in quiet anticipation. It's like he's entirely forgotten about his own meal a single bite in.

I bet he's getting hard just watching this. He's such a freak, but he's *my* freak.

I slowly slice into the meat, immediately hit with the rich scent of garlic and onions as kale spills out onto the plate. I quickly scoop it up, packing as much as I can onto my fork.

"Bottom's up."

It's rich and buttery, the deliciously sinful flavor melting into my tongue; I think if I closed my eyes, I could still hear Jonathan's screams.

I haven't eaten this good in years.

"You like it?"

I nod to him as I take bite after bite, as if the speed I've been shoveling it into my mouth needs any further confirmation. Now I'm getting the sharpness of the kale, mixed with the salt and pepper seasoning.

Fuck.

"Incredible."

Except it comes out more like 'increbabble,' with my mouth completely full. Preacher doesn't seem to mind though, beaming as he reaches for his glass of wine.

"To you, my love. You did a hell of a job."

We clink glasses and I take a generous sip, the rich jammy flavor of the wine a perfect accompaniment to the last remnants of the meat dissolving on my tongue.

"So, who's next?" I ask, quickly skewering another piece.

Preacher chuckles at the question.

"For now? No one. There's a whole cooling off period where we lay low, and Raphael's gotta keep watch to see if any missing persons reports have been filed. If they have, he's gotta make sure they can't be traced back to us, and in a case like our good friend Jonathan... there's definitely going to be a report."

"He hacked the cameras though, right? So we're in the clear."

"Yup," Preacher sighs. "He did. But that doesn't account for random chance, or random people. Anyone could have been taking a selfie, or a video, or maybe someone just remembers one of our faces. Who knows, someone might even have seen him heading out the back with you in tow."

Shit, I didn't think about any of that. There's a lot more moving parts to murder than I anticipated, and I was so focused on my part that everything else became background noise.

"So how long do we have to wait then?"

I know I probably sound like a far-too-eager child right now, but doing what we did? It's addicting. I can see why so many of us go *way* overboard. The power, the thrill, the way it's already quieted the whispering in the back of my head...

I need more.

"A few weeks to start. That'll let us get a feel for things" He leans back. "And besides, it's not like we can just head out and pick some random sucker. Gotta stick to the list."

"The list that Raphael picks for you," I grumble. "You don't even get to decide who needs to die."

Preacher stiffens a little, his gaze growing more intense, and immediately I can tell I've taken a step or two across a line. And I get it, they have a system, but I'm needling at this because after that taste... I need more, and I need to get it my way. I'm not interested in advice from some jerkoff behind a laptop who's never even stuck a man with a knife before.

"I know you're antsy, rabbit, but we need to make sure we get the right people. It's always been this way, and it's how we stay under the radar. No reason to change it now."

"So what you're saying is I'm *never* getting a say in any of this?"

"No, that's not it at all, but you're still learning. You'll get there, but we're not there yet."

His tone is so icy I feel like it's more of a jog over that line I've taken at this point, so I figure why not go all the way.

"I passed your tests, I've done everything you ask me to—"

"And I'm asking you to hold your damn horses, Rip. The more people that go missing, the closer they're all laid out, the more the cops will start asking questions. We've got to act as a team, and *you* need to learn how to control yourself."

So much for a nice celebration.

Preacher promised me freedom. Salvation, he said, but salvation from what? I'm just under someone else's thumb again.

"I *can* control myself, despite what you might think. I've been controlling this anger for fucking years!"

"Ripley, I just want us to have a nice dinner."

"And I'm trying to tell you what I need."

"Then *tell me*," Preacher growls, practically spitting out the words. "Because I'm here, and I'm listening, but all I'm hearing are complaints about the rules that are literally keeping us alive."

I groan, gazing up at the ceiling, trying to pluck the right words from thin air. It's been a habit of mine since I was a kid; sometimes I would get so mad I couldn't think straight, and staring at the ceiling always helped.

"Rabbit, I..."

"It's actually really simple, Preacher. If you want me to be free, then you have to *let me* be free."

"I never said—" He rubs his eyes in exasperation. "I'm saying you need to be careful, that *we* need to be careful, and this is how we do that. You gotta remember what I told you happens if this whole thing goes tits-up."

"I understand the risks," I huff. "I'm not a child."

"Then quit acting like one!" He stabs at another chunk of meat. "Me and Raph, and now you, what we all got? It's a partnership, and partners—"

"If it's a partnership, then why do you let Raphael control everything?"

He stays silent, his jaw ticking as he tries to keep himself cool.

"You know what I think?" I lean forward, not willing to give even a single inch at this point. "I think you were serious when you said you wanted a pet. Maybe you wanted to keep me so you didn't feel so bad about Raph keeping you."

Normally, I wouldn't have said shit when it was clear he'd drawn a line in the sand. The old me would have swallowed it and silently choked, but the new me? She's smart, and she's a capable hunter; despite all the setbacks, we got our man.

"Rabbit, this is the way it's always been. You don't let a wild dog out without a leash before you've trained 'em. That's how it went for me, and it's how it's gonna go for you."

I could see the regret flash across his face the moment the words left his lips, but I'm not interested in an apology.

"Fuck you!" I spit, my rage flaring up inside me. "I escaped that fucking prison, and you just put me right back in a nother one?"

"That's not what I meant, Ripley. Raph said—"

"I don't give a fuck what Raph said! Jesus Christ, are you a fucking man or not? You're supposed to be a killer!"

"Will you stop interrupting me?!"

I straighten up in my chair as he slams his fist against the table, fully alert. His voice has never been more forceful, and I find my eyes bouncing to the steak knife set out beside my plate.

"Don't even think about it."

My whole body is primed for fight or flight, muscles coiled so tight they start to hurt, but I wait. I wait for him to reach across the table and hit me, to drag me upstairs by my hair and *teach me a lesson*.

But he doesn't do any of that, despite the white knuckles and clenched jaw.

He just... stares at me.

Breathing heavy.

And then evenly.

And I stare back.

And then, after an eternity of anxious silence, he speaks.

"I know you're eager, Rip, I know you want to get out there and really live in the brand new skin you've finally found yourself in." He takes a breath, steadying himself as his shoulders slump back to a more relaxed position. "But I don't want to see you get dragged off to fuckin' prison— or worse. I had to learn how to control these urges, and I can teach you that, but you have to be willing to work with me here."

I swallow hard, tears stinging my eyes. This fucker always goes for the heart.

"I understand what you're saying, but I've *been* controlling myself, Preacher. That's what my whole life has been about. Shutting up, keeping quiet..."

"Ripley, I'm not asking," he shakes his head, reaching across the table and holding out his hand.

Palm up.

An invitation.

"You're part of this team, and this family, as fucked up as it all might be, and I'm *telling* you that I love—"

Headlights flood the kitchen, accompanied by the unmistakable sound of tires against gravel.

"Goddammit, Raph," Preacher grumbles, shoving his chair away and striding toward the kitchen window.

I watch as he parts the curtain, full of irritation for the man who's interrupted what felt like a particularly well-rehearsed speech.

But then his whole body tenses.

"Stay here."

I frown, getting to my feet, more an act of instinct than rebellion.

"Preacher, what is it?"

He doesn't look back, his hand held still on the doorknob in coiled preparation.

"That out there in the driveway? It ain't Raph's truck."

Exquisite Monsters
PREACHER

Ripley's immediately on her feet, but I hold out a hand to stop her.

"I said stay."

"I'm not your fucking dogs," she growls.

"I know you're not, rabbit. Just let me handle this, alright? People might be looking for you."

I'm not taking any chances tonight. Yes, it was a risk to take Ripley in, and yes, I knew someone might be looking for her, but I made her a promise: nobody is ever going to hurt her again. There was always a high probability someone would come for her, one I was very prepared for when she first arrived, but that alertness ebbed away as the weeks grew on.

Love dulled the sharpest parts of me.

A soft knock at the door causes Hades and Charon to start growling, their ears snapping up, pointing forward and alert. I hold out a hand, signalling to them that it's okay as I stuff my revolver a little ways into my pants. Don't want them scaring the mystery guest away quite yet.

I pull my phone out and look at the ring camera on the doorbell. Raphael installed it a few years ago, but I don't find cause to use it too often, mostly because the only people on the farm are usually my family or my food.

The man at the door looks young, wearing a nondescript hoodie with his slicked back blond hair peeking out. Normally I'd tell him to fuck off and be done with it, but he keeps looking over his shoulder, like he's waiting for someone.

Or someone's waiting for him.

I sigh, making sure to keep myself between the dogs and the door. Even though I'd love to see it, the last thing I need is for them to tear a man to shreds, especially if he's got friends that'll hold a grudge.

He stumbles backward a little as I open the door, and he gets a look at the size of the dogs behind me. Fuck, he's practically a kid.

"Shh," I hiss, reaching down to calm Hades. "Can I help you?"

He's clearly terrified, so much so that I can smell it on him. When you've been killing as long as I have, you develop a sixth sense for this kind of thing. He might as well have the words *scared shitless* tattooed on his forehead. Walking prey.

"Um— I, uh— I'm—" He clears his throat. "I'm looking for someone."

"Well, you found someone."

I rest my hand on the revolver, staring him down. The amount he's sweating already makes me want to laugh, but it's even harder to keep a straight face when he pulls out his phone and flashes me a picture of Ripley.

"It's my sister, I'm looking for my sister. Have you seen her around here?"

She looks so different— I mean, just younger, but her eyes... They're practically fucking dead in this photo. Beautiful, sure, but there's nothing in there, just emptiness. She's about 20 in the picture, at most, and she's being flanked by two men, one with his arm around her. He has golden curls, and a tan one of those Jersey Shore fuckheads would envy. The other has dark hair, pale skin, and black eyes.

I'd bet my last dollar that I'm looking at Gabriel, and maybe the man he owed so much money to. The picture looks like it was taken during some kind of house party, but it's hard to tell when exactly. It's a little distorted, almost like someone zoomed in and took a photo of a Polaroid or something. Still, I manage to spot the telltale packs of cigarettes and crushed beer cans on the coffee table in front of them, along with all the rest of the expected paraphernalia.

It helps that they all look drugged out of their minds.

"She missin' or somethin'?"

"Yeah, for a while now." He tucks his phone back into his pocket. "We're all real worried about her back home."

He squeezes his eyes shut and sniffles, but it's a bad act.

No tears.

"Sorry to hear that. What's her name?"

"Christine."

My heart starts to race the same way it has so many times before. I could do it, pull the gun out and put a bullet right between his fucking eyes. If there's another guy, I'm sure I could stop him before he made it far. But something tells me he was sent here, and whoever sent him's gonna expect a report back.

The question is, how the *fuck* did he find us?

"You got a number I can call if I see her?"

He blinks.

"What?"

I chuckle, tilting my head. If Gabriel's friends sent this asshole, they should have picked a better liar because this dude is folding like a cheap suit. Still, I want to see just how far this thread goes.

"A number. Most folks have a phone number, email, social media... you got any of that?"

"Oh, right! Yeah." He digs in his pocket, pulling out a little black notepad and a pen.

Dead fucking giveaway.

"That's my cell." He tears off a piece of paper, handing it to me. "I'll be nearby, trying to get a room or somethin'."

"Nearest motel's about an hour away, south down the highway. Ain't nothin' 'round here anymore."

He puts his hands on his hips and nods, glancing around with a disgruntled sigh.

"An hour? Seriously?"

My eyes bounce to his car. Black. Maybe an undercover cruiser.

"Yep, this place is a ghost town. Has been for a while now."

"Shit, I had no idea."

That might just be the first honest thing he's said since he arrived.

"Well, good luck finding her. I'll give you a shout if I see anything."

"Thanks. I appreciate you taking the time to talk to me... oh hey, I just realized I never asked your name, Mr..."

"Ellis."

"Ellis," he murmurs with a gentle nod. "I'm Justin."

I stretch out my arm, just for shits and giggles.

"Nice to meet you Justin, and good luck finding her."

He takes my hand, giving it a firm shake.

"Thanks. So if you do see her—"

"I'll give you a call, like I said."

Justin nods, his shoulders slumping slightly as he heads back down the drive. Was he hoping I'd put up a fight? Clearly this didn't go down the way he thought it would, but I can't quite tell why. I wait until he's in his car and shut the door, being sure to lock it before heading back into the kitchen. Ripley's peering out the window, just barely holding the blinds apart with her fingers.

She looks scared.

"So I'm guessing you don't have a brother, right rabbit?"

The headlights flash on again, hitting the side of the house as she just barely manages to sidestep away from the window, her eyes fixed on me.

"Is that who he said he was?"

"Yep. Called you Christine. Not the most convincing guy I've ever met."

The car peels out of the driveway, the light slowly swallowed up by darkness as it trails away into the night.

"What did he look like? Was it Adonis?"

"Never met the man, but I don't think so. Guy seemed young, too young to be that deep into illicit shit."

I pull out my phone and show her the footage from the ring camera.

She's shaking.

"Before I ended up here, I got pulled over. During the storm. I think this is the cop—"

"Son of a bitch," I mutter. "You could have told me that."

"The car was fucking stolen, and everyone should think I'm dead! I didn't think it was important!"

My whole body starts to tingle, and I can feel the goosebumps rushing up and down my arms. My anger has always been quick, and all-consuming.

A gift from my father.

I can feel it gnashing at the back of my neck, screaming at me to lash out... to do *something* to show her how much she fucked up, how much danger she put us in by not telling me. I would have destroyed that fucking car if I knew, took it apart piece by piece and melted 'em down or some shit.

"Did you talk to him? Tell me exactly what you said that night."

"He pulled me over when I had Gabriel's body in the trunk, it's not like I could just try to outrun him."

I sigh, pinching the bridge of my nose.

"Did he take your ID? Get your name? I need to know everything, Ripley."

"No, he— He asked for my license and registration, and then before anything else could happen some fucking maniac flew past in his truck and nearly hit the guy. He dropped his flashlight and ran straight for his car to go after them." She tilts her head, her eyes suddenly going wide. "Oh fuck, I grabbed his flashlight. Do you think there's a tracking device in there or some shit?"

"Doubtful. What's more likely is that someone connected to Gabriel or his pals found another way to track you. Did you search the car before you fired it up and took off?"

My chest tightens with fear as she shakes her head. If you want to get away with murder, you have to be careful. It's why I repaint and detail my truck every few months to make it look like it's brand new. I never hunt in the same place twice in a six month period. I try to make sure that I'm as forgettable as possible. I don't make an impression when I'm out. I swoop in, capture my prey, and leave just as quickly as I arrived.

"Ripley—"

"Don't even start!" She spits. "My head wasn't exactly fucking *clear* at the time! But sure, next time I'll consult the serial killer manual!"

I need to be calm, to clear my goddamn head. We're no good to each other like this.

"Besides, why would the car matter? It probably got sucked up into that tornado!"

I sigh, slumping down into a chair. This is where my own fuck up comes into play.

"Not quite."

"What do you mean, not quite?"

"Because I dragged it out to the fuckin' woods and left it there."

"Are you kidding me?!"

"What did you want me to do with it?! You came roaring in here on the heels of that tornado, and—"

"And you're making that sound like a bad thing!" She growls.

Shit, I don't want to fight, but it's hard to keep myself in check.

"It's not a bad thing," I murmur. "Ripley, there's nothing I wouldn't do for you. You're the most exquisite monster I've ever met and I would burn *everything* down to keep you safe."

"You mean that?" Tears spill down her cheeks. "Please tell me you mean that."

To tell the truth, I'm not really sure what I'm *supposed* to do, or how to make this better. Years of isolation on the ranch have done jack shit for my social skills. I spend more time watching people than interacting with them, if you can even count what I do as interacting. Still, when I look at her, it all seems to come so naturally.

I gingerly wipe her tears away with my calloused thumb before pressing a kiss to her lips.

"Every damn word."

I HID THE CAR IN SOME BRUSH NEAR THE EDGE OF THE PROPERTY, somewhere if you weren't looking for it, you wouldn't ever know it was there. I was going to junk it and sell it for parts in a few weeks. There's this mean old motherfucker who works at an autobody shop about half an hour away from here. He'll buy almost anything, and anything he won't take gets spread out and ditched.

Flashlights in hand, Ripley and I root through the vehicle, trying to find anything that looks like it might be a tracking device.

In under an hour we've already torn apart the glove box, stripped the back seats, scoured the floor, and even torn the steering wheel off, but still nothing. I slit open the front seat, pulling out as much of the foam as I can to look for *anything* that could give me a clue as to how the fuck his cop found us.

We can't stop until we have results, or this thing is nothing but a metal frame.

"I'm starting to think we should have done this in the morning," I grumble.

Ripley snorts.

"Are you kidding me? You would have stayed up all night stewing about it."

I glance up, catching her bright blue eyes in a flash of blinding light.

"Could've had a real good angry fuck though."

She slits open the passenger seat with her knife, stripping the fabric and tossing it to the side.

"Who says we can't?"

I grin.

That's my girl.

I watch as she tears recklessly into the seat, going wild with her bare hands. I'll need to change that bandage again after this. She's still got a ways to go, healing-wise, and she's not making it easier by going so rough all the time. Every time I think about it, I've got to admit, cutting off your own finger is some serious dedication to the craft.

"Find anything?" She asks as she tosses some foam aside, digging in for more.

"No," I growl. "This is starting to feel like a dead end. Let's check the trunk."

"I thought you said you checked it when you found all of my shit."

"Sure, but I wasn't looking for a hidden tracking device, now was I?"

I pop open the trunk to find it practically empty, just as we left it. Everything that was in it we already moved or destroyed: the bloodied clothes, the knife, the zip ties... anything that could connect her to Gabriel's death or who she was.

Ripley lets out an irritated sigh as I shine the flashlight around the empty space.

"Okay, well it was worth a shot. I'll get under the—"

"No."

I scan the space, slowly dragging the light across the back of the trunk until I spot a small black tab sticking up from the very back corner. My gut told me there was a chance.

"And bingo was his name-o."

"What the fuck are you talking about?" Ripley asks, flashing the light back onto me.

I grin, pulling the tab with a grunt until the entire bottom comes loose. Buried in the darkness underneath is a large green duffel bag. Not exactly what I was expecting, but...

I open it up and my goddamn jaw almost hits the dirt.

"Holy shit," Ripley whispers.

Stacks upon stacks of cash.

This is what they're looking for. This is why they think she's still alive.

I start digging through it, and of course, at the very bottom of the bag, I find a fucking cellphone. Looks like one of those older Nokia bricks from the early 2000s.

It's dead, but it might not have been when I dragged the car over here in the first place.

"Fuck."

There's no doubt in my mind the cop would have been able to ping cell towers in the area, and triangulate her location. At the very least, he'd know to look in the only place with a living soul in a ten mile radius.

"What?" Ripley asks. "What is it?"

If he was using a police computer to search for this, if this is official business, we're up shit creek without a paddle. I have to hold out hope that he's doing all of this for someone else, and that it's all under the table.

"That's your tracking device, probably just took our cop friend a while to figure out the exact location. My guess is Gabriel was planning on having the cash, along with you, delivered as an apology before he got the hell out of dodge. The phone was an insurance policy to ensure it got where it was going."

Ripley stares at the duffel bag for a moment, and I can see the fury building behind her eyes. The next thing I know, she's kicking in the tail light with one foot, screaming at the top of her lungs.

"Fucking Gabriel! You stupid fuck!"

I let her rage, soaking it all in as she continues to kick at the car, making dent after dent in the fender, the trunk, and all over the back. When she's finally finished, she stumbles backward, her chest heaving and her cheeks aflame.

"Alright. Alright. So what do we do now?"

For the first time in my goddamn life, I have no fuckin' idea.

But I do know there are only two people in this world I can trust, and one of them is 10 seconds away from a full-on meltdown.

"It's time to call Raphael."

Hard Work and Boning

RIPLEY

Two hours later, and Raphael is pacing around the living room, tugging violently at his hair while the big grandfather clock in the corner ticks down the seconds, each click or chime seeming to push him one step closer to a complete breakdown.

"I'm going to jail," he mutters. "I'm going to jail, and I'm gonna get the shit kicked out of me because *you* couldn't keep your fucking dick in your pants!"

Raph thinks we're no better than animals; that we need to be controlled. Each of the rants he's gone on in the past twenty minutes ended with that punctuation. And sure, I know it's my fault, but I didn't fucking know about the bag, *or* the phone for that matter! Gabriel must have been planning the hand-off for weeks. I must have killed him just days before he was going to have me shipped off.

Maybe even the same day.

Preacher stares at his brother, his expression flat and unreadable, the fireplace crackling as the dogs follow suit, guarding the doorway and watching him like a ticking time bomb.

"Calm the fuck down," Preacher snarls. "We found the phone, now we need a solution. That's your job, isn't it? Solutions?"

"And the money?" Raphael asks, completely ignoring the question. "These bills could all be marked! Did you check?"

"Yes," Preacher sighs. "Unmarked. Untraceable, but that would only matter if we're planning on spending the money. Are you planning on *spending the illegal drug money,* little brother?"

He lets out a sigh, grinding his teeth.

"You should have killed her when you had the chance."

"Oh, please!" I laugh. "This little cop problem would still be yours to solve even if I was six feet under, you weasely little fuckrag! They'd just be looking for a dead body instead of a live one."

Raphael snarls, rolling his neck from side to side. The sound of his vertebrae popping makes my skin crawl, but I try to keep myself in line. He's been in a frenzy since he blew in here with his laptop; said he could extract whatever was on the phone, but instead, he's spent the last twenty minutes screaming at us.

"I should rip you a new asshole."

He hates me, and I hate him, and that's the way I like it, because It's simple. His anger gives me something tangible to take mine out on.

"You're too late, sweetheart," I purr. "Preacher already did that the other night."

"Can I kill her?" He asks. "Brother to brother, think of it as a gift to me for all my years of supporting you."

"You even breathe wrong around her and I'll hang you up in my barn, o' brother mine."

Raphael's jaw clenches, and he snatches his bag up from the coffee table, tossing it onto a nearby chair. The swift action makes Hades take a step forward and growl, but Preacher only has to whistle.

"Heel. You know Raph."

"Still, you should watch your temper, *Raph*," I tease. "You know violent outbursts tend to upset animals."

"Then how come you're so calm?" He grumbles under his breath, plunking himself down and pulling out his computer.

I kiss my middle finger and hold it out to him.

"That's for you, sweetheart. Happy birthday."

Preacher just snickers, pulling me close.

"I don't know why you two shitbirds seem to think this isn't a big deal."

"No one's sayin' it isn't, but I know how you get," Preacher rumbles, calm as ever. "You're already planning for a disaster, and you haven't even been here half an hour."

"Because this *is* a disaster, Preacher! A cop, who is clearly going to be coming back, basically went as far as to tell you he *knows* what he wants is here! Are you both fucking insane?!" He pauses, scrubbing his face with his palms. "You know what, don't even answer that. Ripley, be a doll for once in your life and pass me the cell phone."

"Sure, and how about you bend over so I can shove it right up your ass?"

I toss Raphael the phone and he immediately pries it open, pulling out the tiny SIM card from the back and sticking it into another device, one that he plugs straight into his computer.

"So what, does that chip track locations or something?" I ask. "How does plugging it back in help us?"

Raphael shakes his head, already tapping away at the keyboard.

"Only if the SIM is still in the phone. It has to ping off the cell towers—and anyway, unless it died before the storm, they already know it's here." He picks the phone up, looking at it like it's offended his entire bloodline. "God, this thing is ancient."

"Yeah, wait, why would he use such an old phone?" I ask.

"For a burner, it's great. All it does is take calls and texts. There's no cloud storage to worry about, no photos that could be used as evidence. It's hard to hack these things with software because there's no internet or data connection. Your ex was at least smart about one thing, I'll give him that much."

He keeps typing away, lost in his techy little world, and it's at that moment I realize that this is the first time he's actually spoken to me like a person. Suddenly I'm a lot more curious about Raphael. Specifically, how and why he decided to go into business with his brother, considering the fact that he's so repelled by the gruesome shit. Sure, money is the great motivator, but I wonder if there's something more to it than that.

"Okay, so what are you looking for on the card then?"

"Text messages, call logs, shit like that. I have a program that extracts them and spits them out into one big document. Makes it easier for me to sort through."

He flashes me the slightest ghost of a smile.

As a kid, I used to get called selfish and impolite because I never asked about people. I didn't really know how without it sounding manufactured, and I always thought that they would just *say* the shit that was on their minds, like I did.

"Where the hell did you learn all this stuff?"

Preacher isn't technologically savvy. He's got a phone and cameras hooked up around the property, but I'm sure Raphael did all that for him, and other than that? I don't think I've seen a single computer in his house. The guy owns a record player, and he still watches movies on VHS. It's hard to picture what made the two of them turn out so different.

"Our daddy had a computer in the basement of the church. At first I just used it to look at porn, as you do, but the more I snooped around, the more I realized how much... access he had. Banking information, email addresses, phone numbers, shit like that, and for pretty much the whole town. I started finding ways to dig up dirt on the good citizens of Babylon."

His ghost of a smile grows into a full-on cheshire grin as he works.

"Of course, that turned into hacking; the bullshit kind at first, you know, figuring out passwords or tricking your friend into handing you their messenger account or some bullshit like that, but before too long I was moving on to the real shit. Police computers, government computers... whatever I could get my hands on. Everyone's got a secret that they'd do anything to protect, and not everyone is who they say they are. You'd know all about that, wouldn't you, Ripley?"

"Don't try to profile me, you shit-sucker. I know exactly who I am, and I'm not trying to hide it."

And now we're back to where we started: he wants to piss me off and I want to punch him in the teeth. I think, deep down, he wishes he could enact the kind of justice his brother does, but the funny thing is Raphael's the one who does the real hunting... looking through police databases, court records, and dredging up people's dirtiest secrets. There's a lot of power in being the guy who rounds up sacrificial lambs for slaughter.

Before now, he had all the control, and by adding me into the mix, he's starting to lose some of it. It's not my intention to come between the man I love and his brother, but I'll be damned if I'm going to be pushed out of this business. I earned my place here after all, through hard work and a whole lot of boning.

"Are you two done squabblin'?" Preacher mutters, reaching down to give Charon a quick scratch behind his ears.

"No!"

Our reply comes in perfect unison, the two of us awkwardly letting things drift back into silence rather than acknowledge we may have more in common than we'd like to admit.

In the movies, they make it seem like this hacker stuff can be over and done within seconds, but that's far from the truth. By the time the half-hour of awkward silence is over, I've pretty much forgotten what we were even arguing about.

"Done!" Raph leans back in his chair, cracking his knuckles. "I've got everything that was on that fuckin' brick."

"And?" Preacher asks.

"Gimme a minute."

"You've had thirty."

"Perfection can't be rushed, dear brother."

Raphael pours over the information as we wait a little longer, listening to the *tick, tick, ticking* of the grandfather clock in the background. Now I know how that guy in The Tell-tale Heart felt, that shit would have driven me so crazy I'd have burned the house down.

But in contrast, Preacher seems all-too comfortable, leaning back and closing his eyes every few minutes, looking like he's always seconds away from a good nap. I wonder how he can be so calm about this while I'm feeling like I'm headed down an existential spiral.

Why was that cop looking for me? Is it a legitimate case, or did Adonis hire him? What—

"What was the cop's name?" Raphael asks. "The one who came here."

Preacher doesn't even open his eyes, digging into his jeans and tossing a piece of paper onto the table for Raph to snatch up.

"The number he gave you is registered to a Justin McKinney," he mutters. "What the fuck is an Provincial Officer from Alberta doing all the way out here... He's completely out of his jurisdiction."

"That's what we'd like to know," Preacher replies, opening one eye. "So, whaddya got?"

"Well, I can tell you officer McKinney here is under investigation for some *pretty illicit* activities."

"Such as?"

"Taking bribes from local biker gangs, and turning a blind eye to some serious shit. Right now, there's an internal investigation that connects him to three clubs in Edmonton, all involved in some level of sex trafficking. He's *supposed* to be on desk duty, definitely not out pulling over potential serial killers." Raphael looks up at me. "You must have been important to someone."

My stomach drops, the realization of my deepest fear turning my guts to jelly.

"The phone you found is a burner, but all the evidence shows that it belongs to your shitbag ex-boytoy. Almost all the texts are between him and some guy named Adonis. And like... seriously? That's his name?"

"Adonis Murphy," I sigh.

Raphael already seems to be a few steps ahead of me.

"President of the Disciples, yeah. But how did you get tied up in all of this?"

Adonis's favorite thing to do was to run his mouth, and talk about how tough and well-connected he was. I just assumed he was compensating for his limp little cock.

"Adonis had been saying he was gonna come kill Gabriel, and take everything he was owed, including me. We think Gabriel was planning to deliver me and the money to save his skin," I sigh. "He was planning to skip town. I had no idea at the time, but I killed him before he got the chance."

"And now Adonis wants what he thinks he's owed," Preacher mumbles.

"Well, that makes sense. These texts make it look like it was McKinney who was supposed to deliver you to some shithole in Swift Current. Gabriel had the whole thing set up; was gonna give the cop a shitload of money to do it."

My stomach sinks. I never liked the way Adonis looked at me when he would come over, his eyes always lingered too long. I even started dressing in baggier clothes when I knew he was coming around— well, as baggy as Gabriel would allow me. I just didn't want to be gawked at.

Preacher stands, leaning forward on the table.

"Okay, so we know what he wants, we know who he's working for, and we know he's coming back. I think that's enough for us to set a trap, and get this all sorted before *our* dirty little secret gets blown wide open."

He's right. If Adonis is the one after me, that means he's pulling strings with corrupt cops, which means the entire business is at stake. There's also no chance he'll just roll over on what he's owed. We could die, or we could go to prison, and I don't think that piece of shit really cares one way or the other.

"So what's the plan?"

"I call McKinney. I tell him I know he's lying about being your brother, and that we know all about his connections to the Disciples. We'll make him an offer he can't refuse, he'll think it's a trap and bring backup, and when they get here, we take 'em all out at once. It'll be easy enough to make it look like a gang war gone wrong in the middle of nowhere if we play our cards right."

"Adonis won't show up," I mutter. "He's too much of a coward."

Preacher's face breaks out into a big smile, and he turns to Raphael.

"You know what I'm thinking..."

"No," he snarls. "Absolutely fucking not. We keep this operation small—"

"Come on, Raph. Do your big brother a solid."

"I already drove *all the way* to this fucking slaughterhouse, dug up dirt on some corrupt pig, and saved both of your asses, and now you want me to call *her?!*"

"We could use the extra help. Extra protection, too."

Jesus Christ, this is ridiculous.

"If someone doesn't tell me what's going on, I'm gonna fucking scream."

Preacher is grinning from ear to ear, and Raph just puts his head in his hands and lets out a deep sigh.

"This asshole wants me to call my ex-wife."

Unholy Baptism
PREACHER

"Y"ou know there's a bedroom upstairs."

Raphael's lying on the couch, one hand behind his back while he scrolls through his phone. It didn't take him more than an hour to make himself at home.

"Nah, I don't want to be anywhere near what you two freaks do at night. Probably drink each other's blood, or use it as lube or some shit."

He makes an overdramatically disgusted face.

"Nasty."

"Your brother's a fucking cannibal cowboy, but drinking his girlfriend's blood is where you draw the line?"

Raphael tilts his head, that shithead smirk returning with a vengeance.

"You sound like you're a fucking teenager, I think it's the way you say *girlfriend*."

I gave Ripley a couple of Valium and sent her upstairs to take a bath, partially so that she could get her mind off of all this shit, but also to hopefully avoid her killing my brother in a fit of rage. Her head needs to be clear if we're going to put this plan into action, and *his* needs to be attached to his body.

"What are you trying to say, it's out of fashion to call someone your girlfriend these days?"

"Nah, it's just... You meet this woman and then a week later you decide you'll try your hand at love?" He chuckles to himself. "That's rich coming from you."

"What's that supposed to mean?"

"You're not capable of love, Preacher. Nobody who comes out of this fucked up family is. I thought that'd be obvious by now."

"Is that why you pushed Wren away?" I bite back.

"Fuck you."

"Don't dish it out if you can't take it, little brother."

"I said fuck off, Preacher. Leave it."

For a minute there I thought he might haul off and punch me in the face, but it never happens, and silence settles in the room as he glowers at his phone.

He just sits there.

Scrolling.

Scowling.

He never did tell me what happened between them. One day, they were married, and the next his wedding ring was gone. But he still thinks about her, I know he does. I remember he left his phone out on the kitchen table one night when he went to take a piss, and she was everywhere. Messages, photos he couldn't let go of, and he still had a picture of the two of them as his fucking wallpaper. I'd never seen my brother look so...

"She said I didn't know how to open up, said it was fucked up how I never talked about my feelings." He shrugs. "I don't know how to talk about what I don't have."

To her credit, she wasn't really wrong. The Blackthornes aren't good at heart to heart shit. We usually end up fighting it out, or in my case, coping in more disturbing ways.

I've gutted and skinned my father so many times in my mind it's become routine, like putting a new bandaid over a gaping wound over and over again, but every time I slip that knife into a guilty man's belly and watch the light leave my father's eyes, I feel like I get a little piece of myself back. I get to calm that angry little boy inside of me who only wanted justice.

Maybe that's what healing is.

"Maybe we can learn though, what love is, what it looks like. What it's supposed to feel like."

"But we'll never really know," he replies. "And just wanting it doesn't make it real."

"I said I'm trying to learn, I didn't say I was a fuckin' magician."

Raphael snorts.

"God, now I can't stop picturing it. You, in a stupid robe, and one of those dumbass hats too— actually, that's not far off from the dumbass hat you already wear."

"You wear hats too, asshole."

"Yeah, normal hats. I look better in them too," Raphael snickers.

I grumble, running my fingers through my hair and draining the last of my whiskey. I was only supposed to lay his bedding out for him and then crawl back upstairs, but something about his demeanor was bothering me. I can tell when Raph's hiding something. He always thinks he's real slick when he's got a secret, but simply put, my brother's the worst poker player I've ever met.

"She tore in here with that tornado and fucked everything up," he mutters. "And you just let it happen."

"She didn't fuck anything up."

"Are you serious?" He laughs. "Look at the shit I've gotta deal with now!"

"Look, I admit she's a little unstable, but—"

"I'm sorry, did you just admit I was right? Hang on, I want to savor this moment."

He closes his eyes and takes a deep, soothing breath, and I can't help but grin.

"Don't make me hit you, asshole."

The sound of the floorboards whining above shuts the two of us up, as Ripley closes the bathroom door upstairs and heads for the bedroom. I wait to hear the obvious sound of the door clicking into place before continuing, albeit with a lowered tone.

"Look, I know bringing her into the business was a risk, but I can mitigate it— hell, I already am."

Raphael raises a brow.

"You're... mitigating risk? Jesus, Preacher. Did you buy word-of-the-day toilet paper or something?"

"Raph, for once can you just—" I sigh, cooling myself down. "I know her. I know what she's capable of."

"Christ, maybe you are in love after all. Gotta be something that's made you so soft all of a sudden."

"And maybe that's not such a bad thing."

"Yeah? Talk to me in a few months once the shine wears off."

"Ain't gonna happen."

Raph chuckles assuredly to himself, but I know he's wrong. Ripley isn't just a casual fuck, she's someone who pried my ribcage open and clutched my heart in her hands. She's seen the bruises, the atrophy, and the rot that's growing within me and she's loved me anyway.

She's a brand new world for me to explore.

"Well, good talk I guess, but It's late, which means you need to get the fuck outta my face. I need some rest before I have to see Wren and her cloven hooves in the morning."

"You think she's grown horns now, too?"

"Probably," Raph snickers, reaching over to turn off the light on the side table.

I get to my feet, leaving him in the darkness as I make my way up the stairs. When I reach the landing, I spot the dogs snoozing in the hallway, guarding the bedroom. They don't move as I step over top of them, opening the door to the faint smell of lilacs, and her.

She's sprawled out on the bed with nothing but a sheet clinging to her waist, her damp hair surrounding her like an ominous aura. As I get closer, I realize just how exhausted she must have been; I watch the slow rise and fall of her breath, her lips barely parted as she sighs in her sleep. She looks so peaceful, nothing like the beast who slit a man's belly open in my barn last night.

Ripley lets out a soft sound as I climb into bed, and I slide an arm around her waist, moving in close. My mumbled name spills from her lips— honeyed, sweet, and just a little slurred.

I start to nip at her neck, working my way up to her earlobe, biting down gently and tugging playfully with my teeth. Her body's already starting to move with mine, and I'm certain that pretty soon the friction is going to be unbearable.

"More," she breathes.

I feel my heart jump in my chest.

"You awake?"

"Barely. Don't stop."

I was a little tentative before, but now I'm free to let my hand wander below the sheet that's bunched around her waist, teasing the soft hair that surrounds her sweet little cunt. Ripley's back arches, and she spreads her legs wider as if in response, but her eyes stay shut.

My fingers brush against her clit, stiff and slick with arousal as I start to work my way down her neck at the same time. Biting gently. Sucking. Never able to get enough of her. I can't help myself from giving her a particularly sharp bite as I slip a finger inside of her. Her rich moan sends a tingle all the way down my spine, and my cock is screaming at me to get things started, but I want more than just to fuck her.

I pull my fingers out of her sweet pussy and find them coated in a thin sheen of crimson. I lick them clean, iron cascading along my tongue.

"Fuck, rabbit."

Tasting her like this is a privilege.

I slide down her body until I'm nestled between her thighs. I can see the marks I've made over the past few weeks. Bites, bruises, and of course the surgical line from my straight razor that sliced her open. I run my fingertip over the faint red scar.

"You are *so* beautiful."

I place gentle kisses along her thigh, one for each bit of damage I've done, taking my time as goosebumps rise on her skin. I'm not sure how long I can last like this, but I never did get my dessert.

I spread her lips, feeling her clit throb gently between my fingers. I flick it with the tip of my tongue; feather-light strokes, just enough to keep her body clinging to that cliff's edge.

She's the perfect treat, both sweet and sharp, with her blood giving her just a little bit of extra bite. Ripley's introduced me to a hunger that only she can satiate.

Her body.

Her soul.

I groan, swirling my tongue around her entrance, lapping up as much of her as I can get until I start to explore further inside.

She lets out a whine, cupping her breasts as she grinds hard against my mouth, but I make sure to move with her, anticipating every peak and valley as I fuck her with my mouth. In and out, up and down, and everywhere in between. Her juices drip down my chin while I hump the mattress like a pathetic fucking dog.

She's turned me into something desperate.

I can still feel the sharp sting of humiliation as I crawled toward her with her panties between teeth, barking like a dog in that barn. I'd never been so turned on by someone else's power. In that moment, I knew I had created a fucking goddess.

Her pussy tightens around my tongue, beating like a heart. I hear fragments of my name desperately trying to claw their way out of her throat.

She's getting close.

And I need her.

Now.

I push the sheet aside, crawling over top of her and wrapping my fingers around my cock. I can feel it pulsing as I start to tease her, making certain my piercings bump playfully against her dripping cunt. I want this to be sweeter than before. Softer.

I want to show her how much I love her.

Ripley's lips part and I dip my head, capturing them in a tender kiss as I slowly push inside of her. This is what I've been missing out on my whole life.

"Good girl," I purr, grasping her wrists and pinning her to the mattress. "Fuck, it's like you were made for me."

I move slowly, gazing into her eyes and searching for the humanity I lost so long ago. I feel like I'm falling, shrouded in her warmth. Protected by it.

I would burn everything down to keep you safe.

My toes dig into the mattress as her cries grow higher and higher pitched. I don't give a *fuck* if my brother hears it or not. In fact, I think I want him to.

My spine feels like it's coiled like a spring. Tingles wrap around my hips, stretching down my legs. I'm so fucking close, chasing that high with each vicious thrust until her voice breaks, and suddenly...

"Come inside me, baby."

She sounds so gentle. Practically pleading.

"I'm gonna make you mine," I rasp.

My orgasm rips through me, its claws and teeth sinking into my back, tearing me to ribbons as I feel fireworks going off in every nerve.

In that moment, I see our future, clear as day.

Everything.

Adonis's body hanging from the hook in my barn.

The two of us bathed in blood.
Our unholy baptism beneath the moon.
And a golden ring on her finger.

Woman of the Hour

RIPLEY

"**R**aph, you want bacon and pancakes?"

Preacher's brother stumbles into the kitchen, all messy hair and puffy eyes, grunting as he wanders over to the coffee maker and helps himself.

I've been up for a while now, feeding the horses, moving the cattle, and cleaning out the stables with Preacher while Raphael slept in. It's a small blessing because I don't think I could listen to him yammer that early in the morning without wanting to take a shovel to his skull.

"So long as it's not human, I'll eat anything." He sighs, taking the first sip of his drink. "Coffee's good."

"I made it," I chirp, chopping up some melon.

"I take it back. Tastes like ass."

I point my knife at him.

"You wanna try that again, because it turns out I'm pretty damn good with this thing."

He snorts.

"I'm not scared of you, sweet thing."

"You two, cut it the hell out." Preacher flips the bacon in the pan, his face twisted up in irritation. "Raph, drink your coffee and shut the fuck up. Rabbit, finish up with that melon. Breakfast's almost ready, and I didn't sign up to be a goddamn babysitter."

Raph plunks himself down at the kitchen table like a pouty teenager, scrolling through his phone, but I can't help but notice he's still drinking his coffee. The petulant little prick can't even pretend he hates it with any conviction.

"Did she say how long before she gets here?" Preacher asks after a few moments.

"Nope. Just said it would be sometime before noon."

We set the food on the table and the three of us dig in, eating in total silence for a few minutes as I'm left wondering why nobody's bothering to tell me the details on Raphael's ex-wife.

"So... who is this woman?" I ask. "Feels like you guys won't even say her name. Are you scared of her or something?"

Preacher's lip curls into a smart-ass smirk.

"Raph is."

It's hard to imagine him being married, given how insufferable he is, but at least that part's believable.

"Jesus Christ, Preacher." He drags a forkful of pancake through the lake of syrup on his plate. "Look, I'm not scared of her, but even if I was, it doesn't matter. There's not gonna be any girl-on-girl commiseration, because you're not gonna say a damn word to her, we clear?"

Suddenly, I hear the roar of engines outside and Raphael smirks.

"Speak of the Devil, and she shall appear."

I move to the window, pushing the curtains aside as four people in helmets kill their engines and climb off their bikes. I watch intently as they walk toward the house, three of them dutifully following behind the other in lock-step, barely even reacting as Hades and Charon let out brief warning-barks as they trot out toward the door.

"Boys, heel," Preacher rumbles.

Three loud knocks shake the house as I follow behind him, excited to meet the woman who's got his brother so completely twisted up at just the mention of her.

Preacher opens the door just in time for me to catch the curtain of dark hair that falls over her face as she removes her helmet. She has a scar over her milky left eye, and an aquiline nose. The patch on her beaten leather vest says *FOUNDER*, but none of that is what really catches my attention.

It's something about the color of her right eye.

Still the same, piercing blue.

"Wren?"

Just like mine.

She stares right back, perplexed for a moment before her entire expression shifts.

"The fuck's goin' on?" Raphael asks, waltzing out of the kitchen. "You two know each other already?"

I turn, just about ready to shoot some barb back at him before suddenly I'm reeling, a brutal hit to the side of my head sending me stumbling backward. I'm on my ass before the commotion even starts, everyone shouting, the dogs growling and barking, but she follows me down, hitting me again.

"You bitch!"

And again.

"Wren, stop!"

I try to shield my face with my forearms, but only manage to let out a howl as she grabs my injured hand and digs her nails into the still healing wound.

"You fucking left me in that house to *rot*!"

She gets in close, striking me across the face hard enough to knock me flat, straddling me between her legs and prepping for another strike.

"That's enough!" Preacher bellows.

The next thing I know the two brothers are hauling her backward as she snarls, still raging like a beast.

"Calm the fuck down, Wren!" Raphael shouts, slamming her up against the wall. "The fuck's gotten into you?!"

It looks like her men had been surprisingly well behaved during our scuffle, but they're starting to look a little nervous, one of them slowly reaching for his gun as Preacher takes a step forward.

"I'd rethink that move, fellas. I promise you we don't want any trouble, but remember that you're in *my* home."

The men share a pensive look, but thankfully Wren gives them a signal to stand down before things get out of hand.

"You knew?" She pushes Raphael off of her, shoving him another time for good measure. "You knew she was fucking here for— god, how the fuck long has she even been here?"

"Wren, I had no idea you two even knew each other until five seconds ago. What the hell is going on?"

"That's my sister," she spits, pacing back and forth on the spot.

"Your— are you fucking kidding me?"

The last thing I saw when I left that house in the dead of night was Wren staring down from her bedroom window.

"You told me your last name was Monroe," Raphael mutters, sliding a hand through his hair. "This one's I.D. said Winter, so what the fuck's going on?"

I can feel myself almost crack up. *Some Like It Hot* was her favorite movie growing up.

"After our daddy went to prison, I wasn't going to be the daughter of a fucking pedophile. I'm not a victim." She turns to face me, her words full of venom. "But more importantly, I didn't want to be associated with *her*, or my cunt mother who *let him*—"

She starts to shake, her knuckles bone-white in her clenched fists. There are tears in her eyes, and I'm hit with a strange pang in my chest that begins to ache.

Is that guilt? It's been so long since I've felt anything like it.

Wren and I were never really close— we got along, sure, and she knew some of my dirty little secrets, but any chance of a sisterly bond was fractured early-on by our family's overabundance of secrets and lies.

"I created a whole new me: new name, new personality, new family. All you have to know is that Wren Winter is long dead."

Raphael grips his head with both hands, his mouth hung open in disbelief.

"I can't believe this is happening to me," he whispers, taking a step backward. "This explains so much, there's fucking two of you."

"Alright, that's enough," Preacher snarls. "If you ladies need to hash some shit out—"

"We can do that later," Wren snaps back, the leather of her jacket whining as she folds her arms over her chest. "Right now I want to know why the hell I'm here."

"You didn't tell her?"

Preacher's staring at his brother incredulously. I didn't think he could look more annoyed than he did a moment ago, but here we are.

"You want me to air all our dirty laundry over an unsecured line? I fucking told her she'd get everything she needed to know when she got here."

Preacher blows out a breath, tipping his head up toward the ceiling.

"Alright, you three in the kitchen. Wren, your boys can wait outside."

"My men should—"

"Your *men* will be just fine outside," Preacher growls. "You know we're not going to try anything, and they can come in when we're done."

She takes a moment, stuck halfway between frustration and smoldering rage, but manages to regain her composure.

"Fine, but you'd better have some damn good whiskey in that kitchen."

"Little early for that, isn't it?"

She flashes him a death glare and he raises his hands, chuckling softly.

The three of us follow him into the kitchen, sitting awkwardly at the table while he fills four mugs with piping hot coffee and a splash of whiskey each before taking a seat. He's all business, as though a cop on our trail is nothing more than an inconvenience, but something about his demeanor tells me this whole thing's made him more than a little unsettled.

I wrap my hands around the scalding mug, savoring the way the burning sensation takes my mind off the last few hectic minutes.

"Alright," Preacher murmurs, locking eyes with Wren from across the table. "You know this ranch has got a hell of a lot of secrets, ones that need protecting."

"You mean the cannibalism, or just the murder?" Wren asks dryly. "You can say it out loud, I'm not a fucking toddler."

"I just want to make sure you understand—"

Her chair grinds against the tile floor as she leans closer across the table, not shying away from his steely gaze for even a second.

"How much?" Her eyes flick to Raphael, giving him a look. "*Someone* was very vague about payment."

Preacher sighs.

"How's ten grand?"

"Ten?" She scoffs. "That's chump change, try again."

Raphael lets out a disgruntled groan, putting his head in his hands.

"Christ, Wren. Ten is—"

Her head whips in his direction.

"Excuse me, asshole. You're not the one I'm negotiating with right now, so unless you want to take charge and get absolutely fucking fleeced—"

"Hey, you know all the money goes through *me*, how about you show me some respect!"

"God, do you even listen to yourself? It was always money money money, and you're still just as obsessed with it as you were the day I walked out on your ass."

I might be wrong, but for the briefest of moments there's a look in his eye that says Raphael might not hate her *quite* as much as he likes to let on.

"Wren, be reasonable, you can't just—"

"Do you remember what you said back then? You kept telling me on the phone you wanted to make things right. Well guess what, it's time to make them right, and *pay me*."

"Ten grand is—"

"How's fifteen sound?"

Preacher's voice cuts straight through the argument, and I watch Raph deflate as Wren lets out the slightest snort.

"At least one of you is reasonable. I accept, obviously contingent on what exactly you're asking for not being fucking insane. Fair?"

He nods.

"Let's get down to it then. There's a cop on our ass, knows things he shouldn't, but not enough to really hurt us. Yet. Plan is to lure him out and take him, but he's got some hefty connections, and in case he decides to bring a few friends... well, there's power in numbers, ain't there?"

"Who's the cop?" Wren asks.

"Justin McKinney," Raphael replies, grabbing his phone and showing her a picture. You wouldn't know him, he—"

"I've tangled with him before," Wren replies curtly, not even looking his way.

"Tangled with him?" Raphael asks, shooting her a look of disbelief. "You fuck him?"

Wren's face twists up in disgust and her gaze grows steely.

"Did you somehow manage to get even more stupid after I left?"

"Alright, ignoring Raph's... colorful commentary, how do you know him?"

It's honestly a little funny watching Preacher try his best to keep shifting the conversation back to business; it seems like a near-impossible task with these two in the room. I can't imagine what the marriage was like.

"Nothing big. Picked up a couple of my men who were trafficking heroin from Calgary to Swift Current, something like two years ago if I remember right. They offered him a cut to keep his trap shut. Little surprised how quick he took it."

"Lines up with what we found," Raphael mutters. "Good to know he's consistent."

"And what about Adonis Murphy, you know him?" Preacher asks.

"The Biker? Gang banger, sex trafficker, dealer..." She frowns. "And he's dangerous as hell, too, why're you asking?"

"Because right now, that's who officer McKinney's playing fetch for."

"It's never simple with you Blackthorne boys, is it?" Wren chuckles, shaking her head as she leans back in her chair. "Let me make a call."

You're Here Now

RIPLEY

Preacher and Raphael are in the barn, prepping it for officer McKinney's arrival. The plan hasn't really changed: we pretend I'm Preacher's unwilling captive that he's prepared to trade, Wren waits in the wings to take out any backup, and when the cop lets down his guard, we strike. I want to be excited about this kill, to be feeling that familiar tingle that comes along with the thrill, but instead I only feel...

Dread.

I groan, taking a sip of my coffee as I watch the horses graze off in the field. I was never really a morning person growing up, didn't care about nature or the outdoors, too busy trying to figure out my own shit to realize there was a whole big world out there, but these days—

Behind me, the back door creaks, and I hear the sound of boots thumping against the porch. I keep my gaze fixed on the horses, trying my best to ignore her until she's so close that my skin bristles. She lights a cigarette, taking a long drag before passing it to me. I don't usually partake, but it would be rude not to accept a peace offering.

"You were the last person I expected to see when I walked in here," she murmurs, softly blowing delicate white ribbons of smoke from her mouth.

I hate this fucking guilt. I hate the way it gnaws and tears at you, piece by piece, because it's proof that you have some kind of moral compass.

Unfortunately, Wren was right. I *did* leave her with that monster. When you're in survival mode, all you can do is tell yourself to keep going; looking back is a death sentence.

"That makes two of us."

She sighs, tentatively placing a hand on my shoulder.

"I'm just here to say I'm sorry for punching you. I was surprised, that's all."

I shrug her arm off, a bit more aggressively than I intended, and reach up reflexively to feel my jaw. It's still pretty tender.

"It's fine. I've had worse."

"Gabriel?"

I nod, trying to ignore the shame clawing at the back of my neck.

"Jesus," she mutters, shaking her head. "I guess I was right about him, even at 13—"

"I don't need a fucking lecture."

"That's great because I'm not giving one," Wren grumbles, snatching back the cigarette. "But hey, if that's not a topic you're psyched for, can we talk about how you wound up with my ex-husband's freak of a brother instead."

I have an instinctive desire to set her straight, tell her she's wrong about him, but... Well, he does make stuff out of human skin. You don't really get freakier than that.

"Believe me, I don't know how I ended up here either."

I steal a glance as she taps the ash from her cigarette onto the railing, and it's immediately clear she's struggling to keep from hitting me all over again. Maybe it's time to be a little less difficult.

"Fine, don't tell me. I guess I shouldn't be surprised, you were always so secretive when we were kids. I felt like you were a ghost that just haunted the second floor." She lets out a breath. "Some nights, I could hear you crying up there."

I sigh, not sure I want to be doing this, but doing it all the same.

We each spent a lot of time alone in our own rooms, even from a young age when you might expect sisters to be bonding and spending time together. I didn't really think much of it at the time, but Papa was the one who always insisted that we sleep separately.

"Yeah. I'm sure you could. So when did he start with you?"

Her shoulders slump and her back rounds. I can see the lines of shame that have been carved into her ache as she takes in my words.

"The same fucking day you left." Her voice is shaky, but she's fighting to keep herself together as she speaks. "I tried to fight back, but he choked me until I was unconscious. I woke up with blood between my legs. At first, I thought I was dying or something, but he was just... rough. It went on like that all the way right up until the cops finally picked him up. Child porn charges. Never even found out who tipped them off, but I'm thankful."

I swallow the vomit in the back of my throat. I have so many questions for her, I don't know where to start.

"The day he got arrested, I ran out of that hell hole with everything I had shoved into a backpack. Later on I heard everyone who knew him was completely shocked. What a fucking joke."

"How old were you?"

"By then, twenty I think? I needed money, so I started working at a biker bar out in Cold Lake. Got close with the founder and some other members. I knew they were bad news, but I guess I got lucky. They took me under their wing and taught me everything I needed to know. It sounds crazy, but I built a whole new family; eventually started my own club, and, well, here we are."

Growing up, Wren was always the better out of the two of us. Kinder, more empathetic, more human. She was a sensitive kid, always so deeply moved by art, music, movies, all of it. I was jealous that I couldn't relate; I could never conceptualize that stuff the same way she could.

"So what happened with your face? You had two eyes when I left that house, unless my memory's failing me."

"I still *have* two eyes, bitch." She smirks, pointing at her milky-white eye. "One of them just doesn't work so well anymore. It's actually how Raph and I met."

My anger is quick to rise; I have half a mind to walk out to the barn and toss this hot coffee right in that asshole's face.

"Down, girl," Wren chuckles, clearly seeing the shift in my expression. "Although, it's nice to see you caring about something."

"You want me to relax after he did *that?*"

"*He* didn't do anything. Hell, it's not even that interesting a story. I was working a double, and there was this creepy dude at the end of the bar. Only words he spoke to me were '*another one,*' so, of course, I did what I was told and served him right up until last-call. Outside, when I was walking back to my car, he ambushed me. Hit me in the face with the bottle and tried to drag me back to his truck. I remember thinking that was it, but the next thing I knew I was down in the gravel, and he was next to me, life drained out of his eyes in a couple seconds flat. Someone had stabbed him in the back of the neck."

"Jesus, Raph killed him?"

"I guess he'd been watching us, and he decided to stick around in case the guy tried anything. Anyway, he took me home, patched me up, and as a thank you, I fucked him on my bathroom counter. It's not exactly a normal meet cute, but I guess it's kind of hard not to fall for a man after he saves your life."

"Normal's overrated."

Wren smiles at me. It's a little tense, and a lot awkward, but I'll take it.

"I'm sorry I left you there."

There was no going back once the abuse had started, but it doesn't make it any better. I drag in a breath, readying myself to complete the apology, but she cuts me off.

"You were dealing with your own shit, with Gabe and all that, right?"

"Yeah he... he broke me down. Not that I wasn't already broken, but I guess he saw something easy to manipulate, and jammed his hooks in me. He told me he had people outside the house watching, and if I ever left him, they'd find me, bring me back, and he'd torture me. Or kill me. Or any number of other things. I still don't know if that was a lie or not."

Abuse shrinks you, all the way down to a microscopic level. After a while, no matter where you are at the start, you begin to really, honestly, believe the things they say. Gabriel told me I was hideous, that I was nothing without him, and like clockwork I found myself echoing those thoughts whenever I looked in the mirror. But it wasn't just the fear. I stayed with him because I told myself that if I ever managed to be *perfect*, he'd stop, and he'd finally, truly, love me.

Every day he didn't, I could see more of the light leave my eyes.

"But you're here now, so... did you run?"

"Actually, I made his chest look like ground-fucking-hamburger." I shiver as that familiar tingle in my jaw returns. "And then I took his fucking tongue. Haven't heard any complaints since."

I don't know what I expected, maybe for her to be horrified? To be afraid of me? But she just nods, stonefaced.

"So I guess *that's* what you and Preacher have in common."

I know I'm supposed to be more careful than this, even with someone I called family, but the excitement of having another person who I can talk to, who might, I dunno, understand? It's overwhelming.

"What about you, Wren? Have you... killed anyone?"

She blinks, less dazed and more amused by my abruptness.

"No, not yet at least. I've shot some men in the shoulder, leg, a couple in the ass. I even stabbed a guy right through his hand once, but I've never taken the plunge. Never needed to, I guess." She takes a sip of her coffee, shifting nervously on the spot before she leans in toward me. "Hey so since we're doing this whole sisterly bonding thing again, can I ask you something?"

I nod. We never really got the chance to really *be* sisters when we were kids. I suppose now's the time to start.

"You said you enjoyed killing Gabriel, but... did you plan it?"

A smile comes to my lips, just from the memory.

"Planning it all out, running it through my head over and over and over, that was the only thing that kept me going. I'd lose entire days on it, and end up completely stuck in those thoughts, just like I did whenever I got obsessed with something when we were kids."

Wren turns her head, and I follow her gaze as she stares out at the horses, tracking a tawny colored foal clumsily galloping around her mother. I can't be certain, but I'm pretty sure she's the one Preacher named Buttons.

"They all look so free, don't they?"

I never knew horses played until I came out to sit on the porch one morning in the first couple weeks, and caught them in the act. I don't know why, but it moved me to tears.

"Yeah, they do."

We're both quiet for a while, each of us gazing out at the pasture as we sip our coffees, until she pipes up again.

"How the fuck did you end up here?"

"A tornado. Would you believe it?"

She chuckles, shaking her head.

"So you like it here? He's good to you?"

"Yeah." I nod. "Didn't at first. Thought he was an asshole, but… he saved me. I know that what we're doing is wrong, but—"

"The understatement of the fuckin' century," Wren snorts. "Do you even know how many people Preacher's killed? He tell you that?"

I shake my head, trying to mentally count how many body parts I've seen in that freezer.

"Not really. I know it's a lot, but—"

"It's dozens, Rip. Before I left Raph, I told him they had to tone it down, that Preacher's luck was gonna run out sooner rather than later. I just never thought I'd be around to see it."

That old nausea returns, the same way it always does when I think about what's coming. Unfortunately, that's been pretty much all I've been doing for the last day or so now: pulling pieces of my life off the shelf and analyzing them, trying to remember anything I can about Adonis that might help us. But I've come up empty. All I remember is how much he unnerved me, and how every atom in my being screamed to run whenever we were in the same room.

"Did you ever think about killing Papa?"

Wren's question comes out of nowhere, shocking me out from the midst of my spiral.

"Did you?"

I replied without even thinking, but it seems like she was expecting it, worrying her lip in consideration just like she used to do when we were kids. She used to chew off the dead skin until it bled, and mama would always grumble as she covered the bloody patches in olive oil.

"I guess I always dreamed about the house catching fire, and mama and I escaping while he burned to death inside. Or maybe one of those big semi trucks would hit him as he was driving home drunk from the bar." She shrugs. "But it seemed like no matter how hard I prayed, he just wouldn't fucking die."

"At least he's in jail."

She shakes her head, her eyes suddenly much more distant.

"He got a slap on the wrist for those child porn charges; I guess he managed to talk his way out of some serious jail time. I haven't seen or heard from him since, but he's out there somewhere."

"Does mama still talk to him?"

The thought makes my skin crawl, but I know from personal experience how easy it is to fall back into a terrible situation if it's all you know. Maybe she was able to finally find the strength to—

"Mama's dead, Ripley. Shot herself. On the day the cops showed up."

For a second, it feels like all the air gets sucked out of my lungs, but it's not from sadness, or grief. It's more of a shock than anything else.

Maybe I didn't love her enough.

Or at all.

"Shit."

Our mother was something untouchable, never showing us affection except for the briefest moments when she'd braid our hair in the morning before school. I don't know if her icy demeanor was malicious or simply a byproduct of having been married to my father, but I never heard the words *I love you* from either of them growing up.

Wren nods, and the two of us stand in silence for a minute or two, not quite sure what to say. The whole thing is so fucked up, just like us I suppose.

"I guess it's just you and me, then, huh?" I bump her on the shoulder. "So long as you're ready to stop hating me."

"I'm still mad at you, Rip. I mean how could I not be, have you ever even listened to yourself?" There's a moment there where I think it might be over, that she might just walk off for good, but then she chuckles, cracking me a warm smile. "But no, I never hated you. How could I? I don't think I ever really got to *know* you."

"I'm really sorry I left you," I murmur. "I just wasn't strong enough."

"I know, I know, it's fine, just... God this is so fucking awkward, can we just start over?" She sticks out her hand, tilting her head with a playful smirk. "Wren Monroe."

"Ripley... Blackthorne."

She raises a brow, her smile faltering ever so slightly.

"Blackthorne?"

I understand how awkward it probably sounds, but no matter how much I'd like it to mean more, it's not about any of that. Preacher took me in, helped me change myself from what I was into what I was always meant to be:

A hunter, and a killer.

And that's exactly what a Blackthorne is.

"Is that gonna be a problem?"

"No." She takes my hand, shaking it gently. "And I won't pry, but no matter what the name means to you, I need you to know one thing: Every Blackthorne I've ever met has been... obsessed with their work, over every other thing in their lives. Those boys can't spare an extra thought for anything or anyone that isn't on their list of future corpses."

"Is that why you left Raphael?"

She sighs, leaning against a porch post, letting her head fall lazily back into the wood with a light thunk.

"He was paranoid. Obsessive. I'm pretty sure you could classify what we had as a polygamist marriage considering how much time he spent with that fuckin' computer compared to me." I watch as a familiar sadness creeps into her eyes. "And yeah, I was lonely, but I loved him. I kept trying to make new connections with him, find another way to break through, but I don't think he ever really learned how to love. To him, it's about possession, nothing else. At the end he didn't even bat an eye when I packed my bags."

Wren's hollow laughter is enough to make even my heart break a little, but it's cut off by the sound of the back door swinging wide.

"We're gonna lure him to the church," Raphael announces, he and his brother stepping onto the porch as he taps a cigarette out of its pack. "Already got started setting everything up. Impressed?"

Wren's eyes rake up and down his lean frame, sizing up the man she used to know so well.

"The church? That shit's condemned, isn't it?"

"We decided it's best to keep him off the ranch, just in case he decides to bring in the cavalry," Preacher cuts in, snaking an arm around my waist. "They'll be making plans with the expectation this is where it's all going down, so the change of venue'll give us a little bit more room to blindside 'em. Unfortunately, it means we'll need you and those extra men you called to stand guard in unfamiliar territory."

Wren's spine straightens, obviously bristling at the change, and it doesn't take a rocket scientist to know why. The plan just keeps getting riskier and riskier by the minute, but I have to hope she's got at least a sliver of loyalty or compassion left for Raphael. She must, or she wouldn't have picked up the phone in the first place.

"If you think that I'm just gonna—"

"Oh, don't worry Wren, we're throwing in a little extra. Let's call it a fifty grand for your trouble." Preacher grins. "I figure that'll make up for the inconvenience? Raph's idea, by the way."

Raphael stammers, quickly running his hand through his hair as he stares at his feet, but Wren ignores him completely, clicking her tongue and extending her hand with a confident smirk.

"Looks like you've got yourself a deal, Blackthorne."

Roll Over

PREACHER

I haven't set foot in this place since I was a boy.

When folks started leaving Babylon in droves, daddy's church was the last thing to shut down, the stained glass windows now faded and dull from decades of neglect.

"You're going to tie me to *that?*"

Ripley gestures at the altar as we approach, making a big show of it.

"Well, we gotta make it look real, and if they've heard any stories about me I may as well play the part. He's gonna want proof of life, after all."

My bag sits near the altar, carefully tucked behind it and just out of view, filled with all the things we might need to take McKinney down, along with a brand new set of particularly hefty nails.

Tonight, this asshole's going to star in his very own horror movie.

I glance up at the giant wooden cross on the wall. My daddy carved himself from a piece of a tree that was struck by lightning, right outside this church. He said it was God's wrath, and he wanted to build something that would remind the congregation of what can happen to sinners and heathens at just a moment's notice.

Ripley climbs up on the altar, draping herself across it. Her dark hair pours down the back like a waterfall, the dim light making her look almost like the statue of a goddess, illuminated in silver with just a splash of color from the ancient stained glass.

My North Star.

I grab the rope and begin slowly coiling it around her, making sure it's snug enough against her body to fool our special guest. Everything is hanging on us tonight; so long as Adonis knows where she is, she's not safe.

We're not safe.

But I'll be damned if I'm packing up the ranch and running. It's my home, and I'll do everything in my power to protect the small semblance of peace I've made there.

I tie the first thick knot before pressing a kiss to Ripley's lips.

"When I get on the phone with that pig, I'm gonna need you to scream for me."

"Ooh, kinky," She grins. "So long as you do something for me in return."

First, I made her an animal, and then I got to watch her evolve into her true form. That's a gift that not many people get throughout the course of their lives, and for me it's the gift that keeps on giving.

"Anything," I rasp. "I'd do anything for you."

It's humid, and the sweat clinging to her skin gives her an ethereal glow as I glide my hands up her bare calves. Her nipples pebble beneath her short red dress, and I can tell by the involuntary arch of her back that she's already desperate for me to touch her, to tug and twist as she sits there, tied in place, getting wetter and wetter.

"Tell me what you're going to do to him."

I pace around the altar, watching her neck strain as she tries to track me.

"I make the call, and you scream like you've never screamed before; we make sure he thinks he's guaranteed to get what he wants, and then he comes to us. We give him a moment to think he's won, and when he lets his guard down, I'll take him out, ropes, drugs or otherwise. Then all we have to do is make him tell us everything we want to know."

"And then?"

"And then we offer up divine retribution, to anyone and everyone that has it coming."

My eyes flick over to the cross as Ripley giggles.

"Divine retribution," she murmurs. "I like the sound of that."

"Yeah?" I glide my finger along her soaked pussy lips. "It makes you wet, doesn't it?"

"Mmhmm." She moans. "I want to be the one to kill Adonis."

I slide a finger inside of her, groaning at the way she clenches around it.

"You will. I promise. We'll use his skull as a centerpiece at our dinner table."

I add another finger, playing with her slowly as I watch her eyes roll back. The sound of the rope straining against the table almost makes me chuckle. I already know how badly she wants me to throw caution to the wind and fuck her right here and now, but I'm having too much fun tormenting her.

Instead, I just curl my fingers, stroking her G-spot until she starts to shake on top of the altar.

"I want to bash that fucking cop's head in." Her moans float through the room like a spectre. "I want to see his brains splattered on the fucking wall. I want to beat him so badly he spits his teeth out onto the floor."

She cries out in frustration, not fully able to give in to her body's deepest desires, but I keep thrusting, stroking, and teasing her pussy until my fingers are soaked.

"I think we should give Adonis a little show once this is all over and done with." I work her clit with my thumb, grinning as my name comes out in a strangled keen. "Dangle what he can never have *right* in front of him."

I pull my fingers out of her, sucking them clean before I snatch up my knife and push the handle all the way inside of her.

Ripley's scream tears through the otherwise silent church as I fuck her:

Hard and deep.

In and out.

I hiss as the blade cuts into one of the rough callouses on my palm, a deep stinging sensation rippling up my forearm as it sinks into my flesh. But I don't stop, I welcome the pain instead, gripping the blade even harder. I want to take her to heaven just to pull her back down to hell, and I don't give a shit if I cut straight through bone to do it.

Her forehead is coated in an almost opalescent sheen of sweat, and her mouth is curling into a smile as she bucks her hips; her lips part, and her head tips back as she chants affirmations over and over again. I keep going, waiting until she begins to shake, before cruelly removing the source of her pleasure. Her howl of frustration fills the room and she thrashes against her restraints, her eyes a forest fire that burns right through me.

"I'm gonna kill you," she spits.

That's good. She can channel that. So long as she doesn't take a knife to my throat, we're fine.

"If you kill me, who would you have to play these little games with? Ain't no one who can drag you outta that shell like I can."

She's breathing through clenched teeth, and I already know what she's fantasizing about.

"Don't worry, little rabbit. You'll get everything you want and then some." I kiss her thigh. "But before that, I've gotta make a call."

She glares at me, her lips curling into a snarl as I dial his number, listening to it ring incessantly. After the 8th ring or so, I start to sweat. If he doesn't answer, all these goddamn theatrics were for nothing. Maybe they saw through us, maybe they're planning to hit us when we make our way back to the ranch. More importantly though, what the fuck am I gonna do with a woman tied to a table?

Besides fuck her, that is.

"Come on, you fuckin' pig," I grumble.

Finally, just before I'm going to end the call, I hear a click, followed quickly by some heavy panting.

"Who is this?"

I look at Ripley and arch a brow, and before I know it her harrowed and piercing screams are filling the church.

"You came by my property the other night, lookin' for your sister."

There's radio silence for a while on the other end of the line as he tries to get his lies straight.

"Ch— Christine. Yea—"

"Well guess how shocked I was to find out she ain't your sister, you fuckin' dipshit."

"Where is she?"

"She's been my dessert every night for the past few months. She's got a sweet, *tight* little cunt."

Ripley grins in between shrieks, clearly enjoying the little web we're weaving.

"And come on, McKinney. You don't think I know you're a fuckin' cop? I know everything about you, including the skeletons in your closet..."

"I don't know what you're talking about." His voice is shaking. *"She's my—"*

"Cut the shit, moron, and listen. I'm looking to expand operations. You know, get into sales. You understand what I'm telling you, McKinney?"

The silence on the other end threatens to choke me, but I do my best to let it linger.

"How much?"

"Atta boy, 20 grand and she's yours."

I can hear his breathing pick up on the other end of the line. We got him.

"You think I've got 20 grand just lying around? I need proof of life."

"What? Her screamin' ain't enough for you? Should I fuck her while you're on the line and you can listen to all the pretty sounds she makes?"

I end the call and Ripley stifles a giggle, reveling in the act as I open the camera app on my phone, signalling for her to get ready. She squirms against the ropes, faux-terror on her face as I glide the camera down her body, making sure to get a clear shot of her perky tits, and another all the way down her bloodied thighs.

I cut the video short, and send it to him along with a text.

ME

> I was gonna kill her, but I'm assuming she's someone your boss wants, and you were the good little lapdog who offered to fetch her, isn't that right?

The response isn't immediate, but it's quick. Quick enough that I'm not even sure he watched the whole video.

MCKINNEY

> I'm not a fucking lapdog.

ME

> Sure you are. You'll bark for anyone. So why don't you come over here and roll the fuck over?

For a minute or so there's nothing, and I catch myself starting to sweat all over again. Maybe I went a bit too far and he's just gonna ghost. Maybe he caught on that something's wrong. Was the video not convincing? Or maybe—

MCKINNEY

> Where are we meeting? I see her, alive, and then I'll get you your money.

I sigh, relieved, but also quite pleased with both our performances.

ME

It's the only church in Babylon. You can't miss it.

Wren, her men, and my brother are already in position, waiting in the rectory right next to the church. If he brings backup, they'll be the first ones to see it.

ME:

Make sure to come alone, or she dies, and you don't get to be employee of the month.

Hammers and Nails

RIPLEY

"It's too quiet," I grumble.

I don't know how long I've been tied to this altar, but it stopped being fun the moment Preacher's attention was drawn elsewhere. Where is this son of a bitch?

"You gotta be patient, for just a little longer now."

He says that, but he's been checking his phone at least twice a minute for the last half hour. Every creak of the old building spikes my adrenaline, and he's not doing much better, pacing back and forth, alternating between glancing at the door and staring at his boots. The ropes are starting to dig into my skin as I stare up at the rotting beams that are just barely holding this church together.

Where the fuck is this guy?

And then I hear it, the unmistakable sound of an engine rumbling.

Tires on gravel.

Preacher pulls his phone out of his pocket and starts texting madly.

"What is it?" I ask.

"He's here, and your sister said he's pulled up alone. I'm making sure her and her men stand down, and keep an eye out for the cavalry."

He turns to me.

"Looks like I'm going out to meet him."

Preacher slinks toward the church door, pushing it open and slipping outside with an agonizing creak. My cunt throbs in anticipation, at the thought of what's to come, and a lump grows at the base of my throat. I can't hear shit from all the way back here, despite being surrounded by nothing but old rotting oak and silence. Painfully ironic that my reward for all that waiting is even more waiting, but luckily this time it's not quite as agonizing.

A sense of calm washes over me when the church door groans as it swings open yet again, and the two men step inside. I catch sight of McKinney, just a few inches shorter than Preacher, and a hell of a lot less intimidating without the uniform on.

The second his eyes fall on me, he grins.

"Hiya, sweetheart. Remember me?"

My heart thunders, not from fear, but from a beautiful anticipation. I know Preacher's got a needle just waiting to be stuck into this prick's neck, but he's still a little bit too alert.

Time to put on a show.

"Please," I rasp as he gets closer, managing to squeeze out some crocodile tears. "You're a cop, right? You're supposed to be helping me! Please, you don't have to do this!"

"Yeah, I do." McKinney sighs, putting a hand on my cheek and doing an absolutely abysmal job at playing the good guy. "Don't worry, though, this'll all work out fine. I'll make sure to drop you off at a good home, a whole lot better than whatever shack or cage this guy had you—"

A few seconds of distraction was all it took for Preacher to get into position, driving the needle right into the side of McKinney's neck in one swift motion before putting him in a headlock. He yelps, sucking in a sharp gasp, and struggling against Preacher's strength as the two men stumble behind me, the church filling with the sound of boots on wood, and pained, haggard grunts. There's a moment where the fear returns and I start to picture all the worst possible outcomes: me, trading Gabriel for Adonis, Preacher and my sister dead... They're horrible thoughts that happily get quickly dashed away as Preacher drags him into my field of vision, both men red-faced and breathing hard.

But McKinney looks more than a little worse for the wear.

"Sorry, bud, looks like the plan is off. I think I'm a little too attached to her. But it's okay, I gave you something to calm you down so now we get to have a little chat. Nod your head if you understand."

He obeys, his eyes already glassy and fluttering like a moth's wings.

"Atta boy, you're doing great." Preacher tugs the needle out of his neck and tosses it on the ground. "Now, where's your boss? My friends and I want to have a little chat with him too."

"Swift Current."

His voice sounds robotic, almost lifeless, and he's already having trouble holding himself up. I can't tell if that's the circulation being cut off, or the drugs, but it feels like Preacher hit him with a stronger dose than usual. He's not wasting any time.

"His name's Adonis, right? Adonis Murphy?"

The cop nods, shuddering.

"Great, you're doing great. Now how much does he know about us? What was the plan?"

"I don't know."

"Oh, you were doing so well," Preacher snarls, tightening the headlock. "Don't fuck with me."

"I don't," McKinney slurs. "Never seen him face-to-face. Never even been on the property. Drops, or trade-offs. Only know Swift Current 'cause of a case file."

I can tell he's starting to fade, and Preacher can too. He's only got so long before the man's a slurring mess.

"Alright, alright. How about this, where do you meet when you're doing a drop?"

"Old gas station on highway one, just outside the city, but it changes. I get texts, always different numbers. Has phrases to let me know. Never sure but always ends... good."

He trails off, his head lolling off to one side.

"Fuckin' useless," Preacher snarls, releasing him and letting him tumble to the ground.

He checks for a pulse before heading back to the altar and untying me, hauling me to my feet and giving me a quick kiss.

"Is he dead?"

"No, of course not, that would spoil all our fun." He hoists the cop up off the floor, dragging him by the collar of his shirt like he's a misbehaving puppy. "We gotta get him up on that thing."

Preacher gets to work prying the oversized cross off the wall, and lays it out on the floor next to the altar. He carefully lifts McKinney up and splays him across it, stretching his arms out so that they're lined up just right while

I get to work on gathering our supplies: hammers, nails, and a little bit of rope.

I've never crucified someone before, but it's a surprisingly simple process. Step one: bind the good officer's feet and hands to the cross, making sure it's tight enough he won't fall off. Step two: hand your psycho boyfriend the hammer and nails. Step three: swoon as he shakes his head, giving you the warmest smile you've ever seen. He looks like he could be another one of those Angels etched into the windows of this building.

Preacher picks out a long, thick nail, already slightly rusted, but let's face it, the last thing McKinney should be worried about is whether or not he got his tetanus booster.

"We'll start with the wrists. You want to drive it through the soft tissue and into bone. That'll create a kind of anchor."

"I thought it went through his hands, like in the pictures."

"Lots of those paintings get it wrong. If you put the nail through the palm, the wrist dislocates because the ligaments are weaker. Right between the radius and the ulna? That's the sweet spot. It's how the Romans did it."

"Wow, aqueducts, gladiator fights, crucifixions... is there anything they couldn't do?"

"Survive," Preacher replies with a smirk.

It's a joke, but I can see trepidation flash in his eyes.

He's thinking the same thing I've been for the past couple hours.

Even Rome fell.

What's going to happen to us if this whole thing goes tits up?

"Press the nail against his wrist and I'll start hammering it in."

I obey, holding it carefully near the base as Preacher pounds on the head with a mallet, driving the metal right through the man's flesh. It's a little unstable at first, but once I hear that familiar crunch of bone I know we've hit the mark. The soft squelch as blood pours from the wound we've made is just a bonus.

It does finally get a real reaction out of McKinney, though, his strangled scream ripping through the building as he snaps back into consciousness.

"Probably should have stuck to desk duty, huh?" Preacher chuckles. "You're playing with the big kids, pretty boy, and unfortunately, *you* don't even know the rules."

I line up the second nail and he drives it straight through in one powerful strike, our victim letting out another piercing shriek. He's going into shock

— pale, clammy skin, shallow breathing, and his eyes already rolling back in his head. By the time we get the cross propped up, he might already be dead.

Preacher makes sure the nails are secured before he pushes himself to his feet.

"Help me lift him up."

"Yes sir."

Preacher grasps my face, pressing a delicate kiss to my lips.

"We make it through to the end of this, rabbit. You know that, right?"

"I know."

Sometimes when I look at him I think that maybe love *is* real, and not just some chemical concoction swirling in our veins. When I'm with him it feels like something tangible, that I can hold against my chest.

Either that or I'm really losing it.

We tip the cross, both of us grunting as we struggle a little with the combined weight of a soon-to-be dead man and his final resting place. It tears into the floor as we drag it across the church, leaving deep permanent gashes in the wood.

"Didn't the Romans make these fuckers carry their own crosses?" I grunt as we manage to make it to the wall, straining with all the effort. "Probably should have taken that lesson on."

He chuckles.

"Not sure. I definitely saw it in a movie though."

"The fuck kind of movies do you watch? Cathy's Crazy Crucifixion XXX?"

"Nah, you know, like Ben Hur."

"What the fuck is Ben Hur?" I ask as we— well, *he*— props the cross up against the wall with one final push.

"You don't know Ben Hur?"

I shake my head.

"Wow, you really know how to make a guy feel old," he grunts.

The sight of his heaving muscles beneath his thin white t-shirt gives me butterflies.

Our work of art is lit only by refracted moonlight, making the blood dripping onto the floor look closer to motor oil than what it really is.

"It's beautiful," I murmur.

"Mmm." Preacher pulls a knife out of his pocket, handing it to me. "Gonna look even prettier with you riding me while he bleeds out."

I stride toward our brand new art piece, grinning from ear to ear. He's barely conscious, blood oozing from the wounds in his wrists and ankles, and I can hear it dripping onto the floor like rain pattering against the roof.

I don't bother asking him if he has any last words. It wouldn't do him any good, and I wouldn't want to hear them anyway. Instead, I drive the knife right into his belly, twisting it and drinking in his scream as it echoes through the church.

"Hey, rabbit!" I turn around to see Preacher pulling his phone out of his pocket. "What if we made a little home movie, hmm? Just for us."

It's a fantastic idea, but just as soon as he's suggested it, I hear the scream of the emergency alert blare from the phone in his hand, followed quickly by Raphael bursting through the door in a panic.

"He dead yet?"

"Pretty much," Preacher calls back. "What's wrong?"

"Storm cellar. Now. Tornado's back, and it's close."

"You got the dogs?" Preacher asks, grabbing my hand and holding me back.

"Yeah, they're already down there, now come on."

"Great." He turns back to me, his eyes gleaming. "Chain the door shut when you leave, we'll join you when this is all done."

"No, seriously, this thing is—"

I grin

"You wouldn't get it Raph. We have work to finish."

Home Movies
PREACHER

I can hear the wind howling outside, rain pounding against the roof. My eyes flick toward the stained glass, and I can see the vague silhouettes of trees as they bend against the wind.

Ripley reaches up, cupping my face.

"Don't leave me hanging, cowboy."

I let out a low growl, my mouth crashing against hers in a feverish and fiery kiss as we devour one another, neither of us bothering to maintain any sense of control.

Once we're done here, I'll give McKinney's phone to Raph. Maybe there's something useful we can use to track down Adonis, along with what little we got out of him. I can't wait to watch the light leave that fucker's eyes.

I tear myself away from Ripley, relishing her bitten-red lips as I retrieve the discarded knife, placing it in her hand and gesturing at the cop.

"Time to put him out of his misery."

"You're recording?"

"Mmhmm. Ready when you are."

"Perfect." She shimmies out of her dress, her long hair tumbling down her past shoulders, just barely covering her tits. "Now get out of my shot."

I chuckle, bowing to her and taking a step back just as a bolt of lightning shoots through the sky outside, and a clap of thunder shakes the walls.

Mother nature has rolled out the red carpet for us, the brand new Gods of this place.

She drags the blade along McKinney's shirt, cutting it open to expose his naked belly, lily-white and practically begging for the tip of a knife. She stops just below his belly button before digging it in and gliding firmly upward like she's slicing through wrapping paper. He lets out a strangled, raspy death rattle as Ripley finishes her cut, pulling the knife out and tossing it aside before driving her hand right into the gaping wound she created.

Blood flows like wine, dripping down his body and onto her bare feet as she tears into him with a kind of madness I've never seen before. By the end she's pulling his large intestine right out, letting half of it splatter on the ground with a sound that reminds me of wet paper towel hitting the kitchen floor.

"You see this?" She snarls. "This is what you get when you fuck with me!"

It's like watching a natural disaster run its course. There's no method to it, only an unadulterated cruelty.

"Come to me."

The howling wind rattles the windows. Warning sirens scream in the distance, alerting us to run for safe haven, but she's just looking up at me, blood dripping from her fingertips while her face starts to twist into a sadistic grin.

Ripley's bloodied hand is stretched toward me like an offering, and I find myself dropping to my knees, letting her tower over me as she brushes her fingers against my lips, urging them to part. When I obey, I'm rewarded with the taste of copper and her silky, sinful voice.

"Clean me off."

I groan, sucking on her fingers as she pumps them slowly, in and out of my mouth. She's staring me down like I'm her last meal, and I'll gladly let her consume me.

"That's a good boy."

When she pulls her fingers out, I'm left feeling empty, a hunger burning inside of me that I don't think I've ever felt before.

"Take your pants off and lie down," she commands, her voice firm, and cool as steel.

A chill of excitement rushes down my spine.

I unbuckle my belt before pushing my jeans past my hips and kicking them to the side, watching Ripley's eyes as they fall on to my cock, throbbing and aching to be buried inside of her. I lick my lips and stride toward her, laying down in the blood that's pooled at her feet.

She quickly glances at the phone that I'd stacked up on a few Bibles, resting against one of the pews.

"You're sure this is getting everything?"

"Positive."

"Good." She straddles my face, sinking down onto me. "I hope you're hungry, cowboy."

"I'm fucking *starving*."

Ripley lets out a moan, grinding her pussy down onto my face, and I explore her with my tongue, dragging it all the way across her tight little asshole to her silky slit.

I wish Adonis could see what she looks like when she's completely in control. I wish I could watch him shiver at the power she holds in the palm of her hand, in her wickedness and vile truth.

A crash of thunder swallows up her cries, and suddenly I feel her mouth around my cock. She takes me all the way down her throat, her tongue gliding over my piercings as I moan into her pussy, feeling her juices drip down my chin as I devour her.

I reach down, smearing my hand in the pool of blood before reaching up and smacking her ass as hard as I can— all while I continue to voraciously eat her up.

A flash of lightning illuminates the windows, and I hear something close to a roar, almost like the building itself is trying to come to life in the storm. If my daddy could see what I was doing to his precious little sanctuary, he'd tell me I was the devil, that I brought evil to Babylon the day I crawled out of my mother's womb.

He'd do worse than kill me.

She claws at my thighs, snapping her hips harder and grinding down as much as she can without crushing my skull.

"Right there!" She groans. "Oh, fuck, make me come!"

She's in complete control, and as one last gift to me, she wraps her lips right back around my cock, taking me as deep as she can. The windows are starting to rattle as the storm envelops the church, but it's nothing compared to what's roaring inside of me.

It feels a little like leaving my body as she lets out that final blissful scream, and I just barely manage to register the sound of something shattering nearby. All of a sudden roaring winds are clawing their way inside the building, and I feel a blast of humid air as it all rushes by.

Ripley releases my cock, practically singing my name like a hymn as she rides out her climax, but just when she's at her peak I grasp her firmly by the hips, pushing her off of me before turning the tables and pinning her arms to the floor with one hand. Her cheeks are dusted pink, her eyes nearly black as she smiles up at me.

"I love you."

Warmth floods my chest and I slowly dip my head, brushing my lips against hers.

"I love you too."

Rain pours through the shattered window, and the wind becomes an animal unto itself, letting out an ominous bellow as it claws and scrapes at the building. It could tear this place apart and I wouldn't care, because right here, and right now, I know that Ripley and I are untouchable.

She wraps her legs around my waist as I thrust all the way inside of her, making her call out for just a moment before she regains control, biting down into my lip so fiercely that she punctures the skin. I groan, tearing my mouth away and lifting my head, tasting blood as I force her mouth open and spit on her tongue.

She swallows without hesitation.

"Fuck me harder," she gasps.

I obey, feeling heaven and hell collide inside of me with every thrust. She's not my protégée anymore, she's my Queen. She's proven that a thousand times over, and I would do *anything* to make her happy.

Our moans blend with the sound of the wind, becoming a macabre cacophony as yet another window shatters, this time even closer. Glass tinkles and cracks across the pews, but I just keep fucking her, digging my toes into the floorboards as I thrust harder and harder.

"I feel like we can beat this storm, rabbit. What do you think?"

Ripley lets out a sardonic laugh.

"I think it could kill us right now and I'd still die happy— *oh, fuck!* I'm gonna...!"

She winds her legs around my waist, taking me deeper until we've become a mess of frenzied licks, bites, and kisses, and I've lost all sense of time and space.

I'm floating. Flying.

And before I know it, my dick is pulsing, and I'm coming harder than I've ever come in my goddamn life.

There's another roar and crack, dull, and already fading into the background.

I think I feel glass prickling against my skin.

But it doesn't matter.

Because I have her.

And this.

Whatever it is.

I collapse on top of her, breathing deep as I bury my face in her neck.

In and out.

In and out.

Ripley's hands dance down my back and I let out a hiss when her fingers glide over a brand new gash with some glass still sticking out.

"Sorry. Looks like you took a bit of unexpected damage."

"S'okay," I mumble into her neck. "Not the worst pain I've felt."

The wind's died down, and we're engulfed in silence all over again.

Ripley strokes my cheek, licking blood off of her fingers, and at this point, I can't tell if it's mine, hers, or McKinney's. Just the sight of it staining her lips makes my heart beat faster, but before I can steal another kiss—

Another rumble, but this time from the ground.

And then the familiar sound of tires on gravel.

Doors slam in quick succession... I have no idea how many, but it's enough to make my gut twist into a painful knot as the two of us exchange a look.

"Get up and get dressed," I whisper. "Now."

And that's when I hear it.

Three loud, ominous knocks.

"Little pigs, little pigs... let me come in!"

And then, the gunfire erupts.

Ambushed

"I thought he said he was coming alone!"

"Yeah, and now I'm kicking myself for trusting a cop not to lie right to my goddamn face," Preacher snarls. "Come on, we gotta get downstairs."

"Downstairs?!" I yelp. "What the fuck are you talking about *downstairs*?! They're gonna kill my fucking sister!"

My head spins, my chest heaves, and it feels like I can't get enough air into my lungs. They're going to kick down that door and—

"Rip, baby, listen to me." Preacher grasps me by the shoulders, his eyes digging into mine like hooks. "I need your head in the game, do you understand me?. If we want to get out of this alive, I need you sharp."

Some*thing* rams against the door, nearly buckling it.

"GET THE TRUCK!" a voice booms over the gunfire. *"WE NEED TO GET THIS DONE QUICK!"*

I swallow the lump of dread forming in my throat and pull my shoulders back.

"Tell me what you need me to do."

His eyes sparkle and he presses a chaste kiss to my lips.

"That's my girl. Follow me."

He takes my hand, leading me past the pool of blood and McKinney's crucified corpse, to a door behind the altar and down into a dark basement.

"What is this, a goddamn bomb shelter?"

Preacher guides us through into the darkness, with nothing but the flashlight on his phone to light the way.

"Raph only chained the door to keep the tornado from knocking it in, it wouldn't have been a serious job; they're gonna be able to bring it down in a minute or two at most, even with the couple pews I managed to brace against it. There's a way out down here, but we have to gather some supplies first."

"Supplies?"

I hear a loud boom, and even more glass breaking upstairs.

Shit.

When we reach the bottom, Preacher immediately rushes for the corner of the room, motioning for me to follow him. Goosebumps rise on my skin, and I tilt my head up, trying to listen for the sound of footsteps. Someone could break that door down at any moment, if they haven't already, and we need to be prepared.

"Daddy always kept a stash of whiskey under here whenever my mama would try to pour his down the sink," Preacher pulls a few bottles out of a large wooden box, lifting them up and examining them under the glow of his phone light. "Seems like he left us a few."

Another grunt as he gets to his feet, and I count six bottles in total.

"Alright, so..."

"So we're making molotov cocktails."

I blink. It's not the worst idea in the world, but not exactly what I thought I'd be doing when I woke up today.

"Alright, sure, but how are we gonna even use them without getting shot?"

Preacher aims his light at another door in the corner.

"That leads to the back of the church, and the entrance is pretty hidden. We can ambush them from there."

"Preacher, we don't know how many of them are out there!"

His phone chimes and he pulls it out of his pocket.

"Text from Raph."

"And?"

"And they're up shit creek without a paddle."

"What about my sister's men?"

"He thinks maybe half of 'em are dead, but they got split up. We don't have a hell of a lot of time."

Preacher grabs another box, turning it over and dumping its contents onto the ground: soiled clothes, old vestments, and a couple of towels. I watch as he starts to tear them into smaller strips with his bare hands.

"You ever made a molotov cocktail?"

"Nope, but I'm a very motivated student."

He smiles, tossing me some strips of fabric before he starts soaking his own torn up cloth in alcohol.

"Think of it like a candle, where the cloth is the wick. Soak the wick, stuff it a little ways in the bottle, light it, and throw as hard and as far as you can. You got it?"

"Got it."

He grasps my shoulder.

"That's my girl."

Preacher places the bottles back into the small wooden box, and we head for the back door, both of us listening intently. I can't tell exactly where the gunfire is coming from anymore, but if someone *is* waiting for us outside, they're in for a rude awakening.

"On the count of three, okay? Once we get out there, we move till we find a target, then start throwing."

"And if we get shot?!" I hiss.

"We either risk dying out there, or dying in here. You decide."

I hear a loud crash upstairs as they finally breach the door, voices shouting overtop of each other as their footsteps clamor above us.

They're going to find us, it's only a matter of time.

"Let's go out swinging."

"Good choice."

Preacher grunts, leaning back and shoving the door open with his shoulder, and the two of us fly out of the back of the church, right into the blinding light of a truck's high-beams. I panic, my heartrate spiking into the stratosphere, certain we've just made our last mistake, but then... nothing happens. Once my eyes adjust, I realize there's nobody here. They must all be busy looking for us inside.

I stay close behind Preacher as the two of us creep around to the front of the building. We're met with even more glaring high-beams, positioned so I can't even tell who's shooting at who until I manage to spy my sister towering over a man across the lot, a crowbar clutched in her hand.

Preacher lets out a sharp whistle, and she turns, her shoulders slumping with relief when she sees us. I wave her over as he lights the wick of his first molotov and throws it straight at one of the trucks.

"Took you assholes long enough. Where the hell were you?"

"Getting supplies." I hand her a bottle. "Let's light these fuckers up."

She grins, snatching the lighter out of Preacher's hand and igniting the wick.

Her timing is perfect, tossing it straight at the front door of the church just as the men who had been searching for us returned empty handed. Glass shatters and flames erupt, the perfect accompaniment to the wailing of Adonis' men.

The sound of screams and bullets, the sight of flames licking the night sky, it all sends shivers down my spine. They're running around screeching like a bunch of goddamn panicked chickens with a fox in their coup.

Before they start to regroup, trying to figure out exactly how they got blindsided, we take the opportunity to push forward as a unit. We take cover behind a large statue out front and throw a couple more bottles as the flames around the vehicles grow larger. I have no idea how many of them there are, but I want to burn them all.

"What's the plan?!" Wren asks over the chaos.

"Raph said you lost a bunch of your men?"

She nods.

"They picked off two of 'em right at the start, before we had any clue what was happening. I think another two went down before you got out here. Maybe four or five left. They're with Raph, shooting it out with the rest of the gang that didn't head inside."

Preacher sighs, weighing the odds in his mind.

"Then we're not winning this. We meet up with the other group, kill as many of these fuckers as we can, and get the fuck out of here. If we can wreck the rest of their trucks there's no way they can follow us. Not quickly at least. We'll come up with more of a plan when we're somewhere safe."

It's a good plan, but I'm not leaving without Adonis. I want him hanging from that hook in Preacher's barn while we play with his insides.

A deep roar slices through the air and I turn just in time to see one of Adonis's men charging me from the side, clutching what looks like a nightstick in his hand. I take a step back and hurl a bottle as hard as I can, praying it lands *anywhere* near him.

Maybe it's my lucky day after all, because my makeshift weapon hits him clean in the chest, exploding into flame and forcing him to peel off to the side, dipping down and rolling in the dirt as his screams echo into the night sky.

Preacher glances around, eyes wide and frantic.

"Alright, then where's my brother?"

As if on cue, I see someone running toward us and immediately bend down to grab our last molotov.

"Don't you *dare* fucking throw that!" Raphael booms, nearly tripping over himself as he stumbles to his brother's side, blood dripping from his nose and mouth. "I didn't sign up to be barbecue today, even if that's what you sick fucks intended."

"Isn't that nice?" Wren sighs, the two of them covered in matching grime and bruises. "Even in a crisis, Captain Dipshit is still quipping."

"The longer we stand here and talk, the more we make ourselves targets for those assholes," Preacher snarls before his brother can snipe back. "We need more weapons. Where are they?"

"Back in the storm cellar," Wren replies. "There are still some AR-15s down there. Those assholes were right on the tail of that tornado, and pinned us out here pretty much the moment we came out."

"Okay, and Raph, what about the men you had with you?" Preacher asks.

"I told them to stay behind and keep shooting while I got some more ammo. They have about half Adonis's guys pinned for now. I think it's the only reason we're not all dead yet."

"Alright, so we have to assume it's just us until we make it back to them." Preacher nods to himself. "Let's make it quick."

We make a break for the storm cellar, with Preacher and Raphael leading the way. My legs burn, sweat pouring down my face from the heat as we pass the burning trucks, and all I can do is pray that I don't take a bullet to the back before we reach our destination.

Suddenly, I see the church doors burst open, and a hail of gunfire flies out.

"Rip, throw it!" Preacher bellows.

I panic, with no clue at all what he's talking about, sure we're about to get mowed down, but then I remember the molotov still clutched in my hand.

The last one.

I stop in my tracks, igniting the wick with a shaking hand and throwing it as hard as I can, bullets whizzing by close enough to sting. It misses the men entirely, but explodes into a fiery mess against the doorframe, splashing liquid-flame on few men brave enough to head outside. One goes down instantly in a mess of flailing limbs, but the other two flee back inside in a panic as flames begin to spread into the building and out along the grass.

Raph throws open the door to the storm cellar and we scramble inside, following Wren straight to two large duffel bags stashed on the shelves.

She unzips one of the bags, pulling out weapon after weapon, and I laugh shakily.

"What the fuck were you preparing for, the apocalypse?"

Wren doesn't say anything, her hands shaking as she opens the second bag and starts to pass out ammunition.

"You good?" Raphael asks.

She sniffles, wiping away the tears with her sleeve.

"Lost a lot of guys today. Nature of the business, but it still stings."

I want to reach over, to squeeze her hand and tell her it'll be okay, but I know that's not the truth.

And so does she.

Neither of us know if we're getting out of here alive.

"Alright, let's do this," Preacher growls.

I put my hand on Wren's shoulder, leaning in.

"Are you sure you're okay?"

She chuckles, tears still lingering in her eyes.

"Those men out there? They depended on me, and I let them die. I shoulda been better, that's all. I'll be fine."

I want to keep pressing, but Preacher steps in front of us, a strange mix of confidence and nerves.

"Ladies, we gotta go!"

Wren nods, and the group of us head for the entrance, Preacher peaking out first to ensure the coast is clear before the rest of us follow. It looks like we were quick enough to get out of there before Adonis's men regrouped. Flames continue to lick the air, and I can't help but notice most of the screams that were piercing the night have gone quiet, the only noise being infrequent gunshots from the other side of the building.

That means there are at least a few of Wren's men left, keeping the force split.

"Alright, here's the plan: kill anyone who's not on our side, regroup with the rest of Wren's people, and then we get the fuck outta here!"

I watch as Preacher takes the lead, alert and ready for anything. He moves like a goddamn soldier, the rest of us falling in line, moving carefully and laying down gunfire as some of Adonis's men come into view like we've been doing this forever. Sure, we're not that accurate, or maybe I should say *I'm* not that accurate, but it doesn't matter at this point, as long as it keeps them pushed back.

I will admit, the kick from the rifle has a sort of appeal to it, makes me feel powerful, in a different way from all the knives and ropes. Every burst of our collective gunfire slamming into metal, or wood, or anything really, it gives me new confidence.

For a few seconds, I feel like we might actually win this.

And then something sails through the air and hits the ground right next to my feet.

Small, metal.

My brain has trouble parsing what it even is.

Then the smoke begins to spew out, blanketing the area.

Fast. Far too fast.

Suddenly, our carefully composed group of soldiers are a coughing mess, stumbling forward to our goal, trying our best to keep shooting. My head is spinning, my ears ringing from gunfire. I'm not even sure if it's coming from us anymore, the combination of the smoke and the blinding lights making it impossible to tell what's going on.

Hell, I can barely see Preacher in front of me.

I lower my gun, trying to wipe away tears from the chemicals that are coating every inch of my lungs, the smoke seeming to follow as we run, like it's determined to trap us.

I should have known Adonis would pull some cowardly shit like this.

There's a sharp whistle through the smoke not too far ahead, and suddenly, my gun is wrenched from my grip.

Something hard hits me in the side of the head.

I collapse onto the ground.

All of my senses are tied up in pain, as something hits me again in the face, crushing the bridge of my nose as the choking chemical-scent keeps me struggling to even see straight.

"Ripley!"

I turn my head, desperate to find him, just as the smoke clears enough for me to see Preacher on his back.

He's being attacked, pinned to the ground as fists rain down on his head. He's not out yet, but he can't block every punch.

And he just keeps calling out for me.

I have to get to him, to get the two of us away from all of this.

I start to flail, not even knowing who or what I'm hitting, but it doesn't seem to matter, only making my attacker angrier. He hits me again, this time a strong hook right to the jaw.

And I'm screaming for Preacher, for my sister, for Raphael...

But everything sounds like it's under water, feels fuzzy and wrong.

Vision blurs.

And I slip away into darkness.

No One to Save Me
RIPLEY

I wake up cold, my wrists bound behind my back, tied so tight that the ropes are cutting off my circulation. I try to stand up, but my muscles are so weak I barely get halfway, everything made even worse by something heavy and metal attached to my ankle. And then I realize I can't see. They've got me in a goddamn blindfold.

"Fuck. Not again."

How is it possible that I get chained to a floor twice in less than a year?

I jam my eyes shut, trying to conjure up the last thing I can remember. If I can do that, I might be able to figure out where the fuck I am and how I got here.

The church.

The killing, and all that fire.

Preacher on the ground, getting the shit beaten out of him.

Screaming for me.

I think I woke up at one point in the back of a van, maybe heard a radio? But where the hell did they take me?

Bile rises up the back of my throat and I try to break down the reality of the situation.

No Preacher.

No Raphael.

No Wren.

No one to save me.

Just like when I was a little girl.

They say history repeats itself, but I didn't think it would be this goddamn brutal.

I slump on the ground, letting the grief overwhelm me, not in ripples but massive tidal waves, slamming against me over and over again. I scream until I'm hoarse, crying until there's nothing left.

I'll die thrashing. Fighting.

But I'll never beg.

Not even for death.

And then a voice cuts through my agonized sobs.

"Are you done? That was *really* annoying."

"Wren?"

"Yeah." She coughs. "Coming to you live from... hell, I guess."

"They took you too?"

"Yep. Looks like they got a 2 for 1 special out of us."

She gives a sardonic chuckle.

"Are you chained up too?"

"Well, if I wasn't, I'd be trying to fuckin' untie you, wouldn't I?"

I grunt, wiggling around as I try to figure out a way to sit up. It takes a minute, but eventually, I manage to heave my body upward and use my hands to weakly push myself into a sitting position.

"Try finding a wall. Hurts your back less if you've got something to lean on."

"I don't know where the wall is, Wren. I can't fucking see."

"Yeah, you just woke up, it'll take a minute for you to get your bearings."

I blink, breathing slowly as I try to center myself. I feel nauseous, and my head is pounding, but I'm not sure if that's from the gas or something else. Now that I think about it, the whole room smells like piss and unwashed bodies. That would make anyone want to vomit.

"I think they drugged me," I rasp.

"Yeah, me too. Probably so we couldn't figure out where they were taking us."

"What happened at the church?"

"Someone hit Preacher in the back of the head when we were stumbling around like idiots. They beat the shit out of Raphael with the butt of a shotgun."

"Did they make it?"

"I don't know," Wren mutters. "But we gotta figure a way out of this shit. I'm not dying here."

"Where the fuck are we, anyway? Did any of them say anything?"

"An old police station. I heard one of them talking about it when they were carrying us—"

The sound of footsteps echoing outside our cell makes me freeze, and I can hear Wren's chain drag along the floor, as she shifts away from the sound.

Keys jingle, and the door swings open, and moments later the blindfold is ripped from my face, and I'm hit with a bright beam of light.

I hiss, trying my best to turn away as my eyes struggle to adjust.

That's when I hear his stomach-churning chuckle.

"There she is."

Adonis lowers the light, towering over me in a black tank top and jeans, his pale arms covered in all the crude prison tattoos I remember. He used to intimidate me, but now he just looks like a shitty knockoff of Preacher, complete with a lit cigarette dangling preciously from the corner of his mouth. The only major change is a shock of white-blond hair. It was all black when I saw him last.

Maybe he dyed it to throw off the cops— you know, since some clever killer framed him and all.

"I told them to save some of this tight little pussy for me."

"Your breath smells like someone took a shit in your mouth."

He grabs me by the hair, yanking me to my feet and slamming me face-first against the wall so hard that I almost black out all over again. His flash-light falls to the ground, lighting up the space around me and as he yanks my head back, and in my dazed state I find my focus drifting. There are dull claw marks torn into the old brick, along with smeared patches of dried blood.

Suddenly, I know the smell I've been choking on is death.

"You think you're so fucking clever framing me for what *you* did to Gabriel." He spins me around, leaning in close and licking the side of my face. "I couldn't believe it when I heard, his quiet obedient little bitch actually did something for once in her life? Now I'm starting to wonder if it even *was* that you. Maybe you got those two fucks back at the church to do it, paid 'em with a quickie?"

I grit my teeth, swallowing all that rage.

"Doesn't matter I guess, they didn't put up much of a fight."

I can feel my stomach lurch. Preacher wouldn't go down that easily, it would take a tank and an army to kill that man.

"Nothing to say? I mean, I guess there's not much of a story to tell. After my boys beat the shit out of you all, we cleaned up the rest of those fucks with the guns real quick." He sneers. "If it helps you sleep at night, I want you to know those two you were with *absolutely* suffered. Left a couple of my best men and told them to make it as slow and painful as possible."

I can feel the tears coming.

I know Preacher is alive. *I know it*, but the last time I saw him, he...

I snap myself out of it, spitting blood right into Adonis' smirking face.

"You fucking cunt! You wanna know what happens to the bitches who fight back?"

He recoils, pulling his arm back and hitting me straight in the face.

Once.

Twice.

However many times it takes for me to barely be able to breathe, let alone see.

Don't react.

Don't give them anything.

"You fucking *whore!*"

He knees me in the gut, forcing me back to the ground, and my mind starts to wander, rattling off whatever facts it can relate to the current situation. There are four ways human beings respond to threats. Everyone knows about fight or flight, but some people freeze. Others fawn and appease to avoid getting hurt.

I did that for years with Gabriel.

I'll make the meal again.

I'll do it all right this time.

If I try hard enough, I'll finally be perfect.

Adonis wraps the chain around my neck while the sound of my sister screaming echoes in the distance like she's miles away. I can still feel everything, all the pain and the nausea, but it's like I'm experiencing it through a lens; like I'm floating above my own body watching him choke the life out of me. It's the only real defence I can muster, aside from digging my nails into my palms to keep from crying out as the tears fill my eyes.

"I had the RCMP on my ass because of you. They said they found a finger..."

He chuckles, grabbing my hand and twisting it until I finally let out a strangled, choking wail.

"I guess it was this one."

"Let her go!"

Wren lunges for him, but she clearly forgot about her chain, hitting its full length before being dragged back down to the filthy concrete.

"Shut the fuck up bitch, or I'll put a bullet through your head and let my boys take care of your corpse."

Adonis turns back to me, pure malice etched onto his face.

"I don't know if he ever told you, but Gabriel owed me. I guess he's finally paid up."

I'm pretty sure he keeps talking, something about all the torture he's going to put me through, about how I'm going to wish I was dead, but I'm already miles away, his voice fading into the background again. It's a tactic I picked up as a young girl, a fracturing of reality that allows me not to feel, or at least to feel less. The disgust, the blood pouring down my face, the pain that feels like a thousand bullets ripping through me... it all begins to numb into nothing.

And soon, I'm not even here.

I'm back at the ranch with Preacher, eating breakfast, and watching him read one of his old books of poetry, his brows knitting together as he nibbles on his bacon. The sun is pouring in from outside, the dogs laid lazily at our feet, as Adonis's skull sits in the middle of the kitchen table.

The perfect centerpiece.

I hold on to the image, to the pure, unadulterated joy it makes me feel.

To the hope that I'll be able to live to see him again.

"I thought about killing you, but that's too merciful," Adonis whispers, his words cutting their way through my fantasy. "Now I've got something much better in mind."

I close my eyes, keeping my focus on Preacher. On sunrises. On the way Wren and I laughed on the porch.

On the horses that galloped so freely.

I can be one of them today, even if it's just in my mind.

Adonis doesn't stop, but I take every hit, refusing to give him the reaction he's looking for, and after a few minutes, I'm back to barely noticing the pain. In the haze, my eyes fall on my sister, tears streaming down her face.

All I want is to hold her.

I've never wanted that before, and there's only one thing preventing it right now, one more thing I have to destroy to get what I want, and he's right in front of me.

Adonis gets to his feet, taking a long drag before blowing the smoke straight into my face. I don't even flinch, and he chuckles, shaking his head.

"You're mine now, bitch. I'm gonna teach you that, one way or another."

Show me Your Teeth
PREACHER

BLACKTHORNE RANCH

I wake up to ice-cold water hitting me in the face, sputtering as I jolt upright.

"Fuckin' *finally*," Raphael sighs, tossing the mug aside. "You were out so long I was starting to think you might be brain dead. More than usual, at least."

I'm in the living room. My living room. Why the fuck am I in the living room? Hades and Charon rush for me, both of them trying to climb up onto the couch at the same time.

"I'm here," I rasp. "I'm here."

I can still hear the flames crackling, and the last thing I remember she was screaming for me. Fighting for her life.

"How long was I out?"

"Two days," he replies. "I wasn't sure you were gonna make it."

"Two days?!"

Raphel reaches for my hand and I take it without hesitation, letting him pull me to my feet. He's not too much worse for wear, getting off with only a black eye, a split lip, and a big gash on his nose.

"Where is she?"

"They took her," he sighs. "Took Wren, too."

Anger singes the back of my throat, spreading through my body. I feel it all the way down in the tips of my fingers and toes. She fucking *needed me* and I couldn't do anything about it.

"I'm gonna fucking kill him," I snarl. "I'm gonna rip him apart piece by piece while he's still alive."

"I know." My brother squeezes my shoulder. "But we gotta find them first. We grabbed one of Adonis's men. He's in the barn, all tied up and waiting for you."

"How the hell did this happen, where are the rest of Wren's men?"

"Mostly dead." He gestures to a tall blond man sitting silently in my easy chair. "Far as we know only one of them made it, and we owe him big time."

"What's your name?" I ask.

"Gus, sir."

The patch on his vest reads *SGT. AT ARMS*. At least he's got some experience.

"Alright, Gus. Tell me what happened."

He stands, arms clasped behind his back like he's in some sort of military drill as he begins to recite the events that led us here.

"When things got bad, I broke away from the group to try and hit 'em from the side. Hid 'round the back of the church. Never really got the chance though; watched the rest of my friends get gunned down. When Adonis figured it was all over, he left two of his men behind. Told them to kill you two slow. Once the trucks and bikes drove away, I slipped back around and picked one off. Got the other real fucked up too, but your brother stopped me. Said we needed him alive to get the girls back."

Guilt gnaws at my insides.

For Ripley, for Wren, for the men she lost.

I can't help but think how close we were to killing the rest of those motherfuckers. There were only a handful of them left, and yet they completely overwhelmed us.

It's my fault. I let my guard down and got us into this shitstorm.

Now, I have to get us out.

"Alright, I'm gonna talk to this guy, but even if I manage to get what we want out of him, we'll be needing more men."

"I'm working on it," Gus replies. "Wren had just finished making nice with a gang in Moose Jaw called the Horsemen. Founder's got a sweet spot for her. Said he'd be willing to help when I called."

"When did you talk to him?"

"Late last night. Waiting for them to send me an address for a one on one."

"How long do we have to wait?"

He shrugs.

"I don't know. It's all on Titus's terms."

"We need a meeting tonight," I growl. "Tell them there won't be any Wren to save if they keep fucking around."

Raph pats me on the shoulder.

"Alright, great talk, but now I think it's time to worry about the thing we actually have control over. Adonis's goon hasn't made a peep, and I think that'll be a much more productive way for you to blow off some steam."

He's right. I need my safe haven: my tools, my music… I need to feel like myself again in order to find her.

"Lead the way."

Raphael tosses me my beaten leather jacket before I follow him out the door, leaving Gus behind to do the heavy lifting.

It's eerily quiet when we step inside the barn, only a single light on, poorly illuminating the man sitting slumped in the middle of the big open space.

"Damn, Gus really fucked him up, didn't he."

"Hey, I got a few good punches in," Raph retorts. "Hit him right in the kidneys, didn't I, fucko?"

Adonis's man is bound to a chair, wrapped up in a mess of ropes and chains that any other day I would call an embarrassing display. Right now though, I'm practically salivating at the opportunity for vengeance.

"My brother here tells me you're not much of a talker." I grin, glancing over at the knife roll resting on the table next to him. "That's why I'm here. I'm real good at getting piggies to squeal."

"Fuck you," he spits. "I'm not telling you shit."

"Look, I'm sure you've got some sort of code, or you've heard the same tired old threats about what happens if you roll over on your boss, but I promise you, Adonis's wrath is *nothing* compared to what I'm about to bring down."

I glance at my brother, motioning at him to follow me to a darkened corner of the barn.

"I'm gonna need your help on this one. I'm still a little out of it."

Raph grimaces, and I can tell he's not too keen on the idea of stepping into my shoes, however temporarily, but if we're gonna get this done, we need to work together.

"The sooner we do this, the sooner we get them back."

He takes a deep breath, tipping his head toward the ceiling.

"Fine. Just tell me what you need."

I pick up my phone that's resting right next to my knives.

"You got any requests?"

"Requests?"

"Can't torture without music."

"God, you really have seen Reservoir Dogs too many goddamn times," Raphael chuckles, before pausing and tilting his head like he's actually considering it. "Ah, fuck it. *White Rabbit* by Jefferson Airplane."

"Surprisingly good choice."

I stroll toward our victim and lean over, getting right up in his face. Despite his rebellious attitude, I can hear his hammering heart, and practically smell the fear wafting off of him. I like them like this: scared, vulnerable, all of their power stripped away. I bet this prick thought he hit the jackpot when he started rolling with Adonis.

"Tell me your name."

"Seriously? That's the best you got?"

With an attitude like that, it's looking like Adonis's little dog is going to lose a few teeth tonight. Maybe I'll use one of them for Ripley's engagement ring.

"Look, I'm sure you think you're doing the right thing, acting all brave in front of the scary torturer, right? Maybe you think Adonis is gonna reward you after he swoops in and saves your ass?" I sigh, cracking my neck. "I'm going to find out where you're keeping my girl, and there will be a fucking *reckoning*. Every single one of you pathetic vermin is going to pay for this, understand? It's just a matter of how much."

"Fuck you! You think I haven't been through this shit before? You're not getting a goddamn thing out of me, and when Adonis finds out what you've done you'll wish I had killed you both back at that church!"

I click my tongue and grab a set of pliers.

"Alright, sounds like you'll be paying up-front then. Raph? Grab his jaw, I want a good view, nice and wide."

Raphael wrenches his mouth open, gripping it tight as the man lets out a fearful groan.

"Every time you fail to answer my question, I'm gonna take one of your teeth. And don't worry, you won't lose them too quickly, I'm gonna take my time. Maybe, I'll mail them to your boss when we're done. Along with your eyeball... your fingers... your cock—"

He lets out a high-pitched squeal as I shove the pliers into his mouth, gripping one of his canines. I twist with just enough pressure to create the very tiniest of fractures while his tongue wiggles and pushes vainly against the tool.

Raphael grimaces while I work, keeping the man mostly still as his breathing grows more and more panicked, until finally the bone cracks.

"Forgot how stubborn these things are."

With a sharp tug I come away with the tooth, pristine and white aside from the splatter of blood. I chuckle, glancing at my brother over my shoulder. He looks like he's about to throw up as blood trickles from our victim's mouth like a small stream, but I figure I can make things worse.

I pop the tooth into my mouth like it's a Tic Tac, sucking the blood clean before spitting it back into this asshole's face.

"Jesus Christ, Preacher! What the fuck is wrong with you?!"

I flash my Raph a confused look.

"That's where you draw the line? Suckin' on a man's tooth? Do you even know what I'm doing here half the time?"

Raphael rolls his eyes, and I turn my attention back to our little guest. As much as I threatened to take things slow and savor his screams, we're working on borrowed time.

"Alright, now I hope you can see that I ain't gonna play nice, so we can either go another round, and then another, and then another, or..." I grin, flashing him my full smile. "You can give me what I want."

"Name's Ben," he gurgles, blood and saliva pooling between his lips.

"Good!" I laugh. "That's so good! Now we're getting somewhere, Ben!"

I hand the pliers over.

"Show Ben a good time."

He stares at them for a moment, like he's still contemplating whether or not he wants to go down this path, when he's already waist deep in the mud. But the thing is, I'm just the rabid dog he sends after the ones he really wants. He's always been the real hunter.

Metal grinds against bone as he braces his foot on Ben's leg and yanks on the tooth, tearing it out with a crackling pop.

"Where did your people take them?" He bellows. "Where the fuck are they?"

The music blares, Grace Slick's voice providing a hypnotic accompaniment to the scene as I step back and watch my baby brother fully immerse himself.

"Just say the words, Benny!"

All I hear from Ben is a violent hacking cough as Raph extracts another tooth with a sickening crunch. Fuck, he's choking on his own goddamn blood. I grab him by the hair, forcing his head down as more blood dribbles out of his mouth, soaking his chin.

Raphael moves to continue the torture, but I hold out an arm to stop him. Ben's jaw is slack and his eyes are starting to roll back. He doesn't have a hell of a lot of time left, and I'm afraid he's going to go into shock if we keep up this pace.

"Alright bud, this is your last chance. If you tell me where they are, I'll let you die with some goddamn dignity."

Ben stares up at me, only half-conscious at this point. I'm sure he doesn't believe me. Hell, I don't even know if I'd believe myself anymore.

"An o— an old j—" He coughs up more blood, along with a piece of his tooth that clatters onto the floor. "Jail."

"Where?" Raphael snarls through gritted teeth. "Don't fuck with me on this, Benny-boy."

"Swift Current." More coughing. Phlegm. Blood. "Adonis has been holding girls there for months."

I lean in, letting his blood stain my hand as I wipe his chin.

"You've been a very good lapdog, Benny, but I think your work here is done."

I grasp his head firmly with both hands, taking in a couple deep, steady breaths before snapping as hard as I can to the left. Everything is silent save for the quick sound of cracking bone, and the final notes of Raph's song hanging in the air.

He drops the pliers on the ground, looking dazed and more than a little confused, but we don't have the time to sit down and decompress.

"Can you find an abandoned jail with that info?"

He's staring at the corpse, his expression blank, and I have to snap my fingers to bring him back to me.

"Raph. Raph!"

He gasps, briefly locking eyes before looking away.

"Wh— uh, yeah. Yeah, I think so."

Just then, the door to the barn bursts open, and Gus stumbles inside, nearly out of breath but clearly excited.

"Whatcha got for us?"

"Moose Jaw. There's a gas station where we meet sometimes, one of Titus's Prospects will take us to him from there."

I nod, doing my best to keep myself calm and collected as my brain screams for more violence. For action. For retribution.

"When?"

The Horsemen
PREACHER

MOOSE JAW, SASKATCHEWAN

"This is a waste of fucking time," Raphael snarls.

The Horsemen's clubhouse is tucked into an industrial area in the middle of nowhere. It looks more like a military compound, actually, with a bar and a few other surrounding buildings stamped with their logo. The look hasn't filled my brother with confidence. The parking lot is littered with Harley Davidsons, and a couple of the bikes are still warm.

"Duly noted," Gus replies as we head for the front door. "But it's the best shot you've got right now."

"Duly— asshole, do you know who the fuck you're talking to?" Raphael snarls.

He was on-edge the entire drive, biting his nails while huffing and puffing about how we just need to find the jail and *bomb the shit out of it*.

"I'm pretty sure I'm talking to the guy who's the reason why I'm in this fuckin' mess in the first place."

"Me?!" Raphael snaps.

"Yes, you." Gus turns on a dime and shoves him back, anger etched into his features. "You can't stay away from her, can you? Can't let her live her goddamn life. You just had to call her up and drag us into all this chaos, and now my friends are fucking worm food."

"What, are you fuckin' in love with her or something?"

"Fellas!" I shout, stepping in between them before they bite each other's heads off. "You two lovebirds can fight about this later, once we get Ripley and Wren back. I'll referee the goddamn boxing match if you want, but until then..."

Gus raises his arms in exasperation, heading for the door while Raphael mopes beside me.

"I could have—"

I grab him by the arm and give it a twist, forcing him to look me in the eyes.

"I know, and I would have preferred not to owe some gang leader a favor, but at this point we gotta do what we gotta do. We don't have the goddamn firepower to go after Adonis by ourselves, and you know that. So you're going to play nice with the one and only man who can get us past those goddamn doors."

Raphael takes a deep breath and gives me a quick nod, but I can still see the gears in his head turning, trying to find a different way out of this. Unfortunately, I don't think there's another path that doesn't end with at least a few of us in a body bag.

And I don't plan on dying this week.

"Let's just get them back," he grumbles.

I clap him on the shoulder, forcing a smile as we follow Gus inside.

"Pretty wild that I'm the reasonable one this time."

"Fuckin' terrifying, more like."

There's a thousand different scenarios running through my head right now, but there's only one that keeps making its way back, haunting me as it worms its way to the top of my mind: that the future I'm trying to build won't exist after tonight.

The bar is bustling with people, drinks flowing freely while painfully loud music bursts through the ancient speakers. Some of the patrons look like club members based on their outfits alone, but others just look like regular blue collar folks, drinking, smoking, and playing pool. It's a smart strategy if the cops ever show up, but I have a feeling the Horsemen already do a good job keeping them out of here.

Gus leads us across the floor, past the bar, and toward a back room where a scrawny kid with acne scars on his face stands guard. I look him up and down, quickly spotting the gun on his hip and the *PROSPECT* patch on his vest, along with his massive inferiority complex.

"You Preacher?" He asks, his voice booming over the music as we approach.

"In the flesh."

"Titus is ready for you."

We're led into a small room with a comedically long table, occupied by men with ratty hair, leather vests, and a hell of a lot of tattoos. I take my hat off, nodding respectfully as Raphael's eyes dart nervously around the room.

"Phones," the Prospect demands, sticking out his hand.

"No fucking way," Raphael growls.

"You play by the rules or you get the fuck out."

The deep and rumbling voice echoes from the back of the room, and I look over to see a brick-wall of a man at the head of the table. He's got slicked back dark hair, bushy brows, and eyes as sharp as daggers. My gaze falls to the patch on his vest.

FOUNDER.

"Heard you boys have got yourselves in a bit of trouble."

"Yessir." Gus clears his throat. "It's like I told your men, Wren's been kidnapped, along with Preacher's old lady."

Titus sparks up a cigar, taking a long drag as the three of us hand our phones over, the silence hanging heavy in the room.

"There's a price for my help, you know."

"Really? 'Cause we thought you'd be doin' it out of the kindness of your heart." Raphael is practically spitting his words, barely holding on to his frustration, which was already one step away from the boiling point. "How about we can talk payment after you prove you can actually get shit done."

"You think you get to call the shots in my club?" Titus asks, two of his men getting to their feet, their hands already on their guns. "Because I don't think that's something you three can afford right now."

I let out a groan and step forward, setting my hat down on the table. Raphael's clearly too much of a loose canon to be negotiating any of this right now, so I guess that means it falls to me.

"He didn't mean anything by that. I'm sure Gus told you, there's a lot of shit goin' down. Our girls were taken by someone named Adonis Murphy. He's a big—"

"Yeah," Titus interrupts, a knowing grin on his lips. "We know Mr. Murphy."

"Great, then I'm sure you know how simple it would be to take him down after half his men got left dead in the dirt. I ain't interested in gaining territory or buttin' heads with anyone, all we want is the girls back. After that, we'll disappear from your life just as fast as we walked through that door."

Titus gives a quick nod, flicking his head toward Raphael.

"First, you call off your dog. If he looks at me sideways one more time, I'm gonna have my men take him out back and put him down."

Raph looks like he's going to retort, but I shoot him the deadliest look I can muster and luckily he gets the message, staring down at his shoes in silence.

"Atta boy." Titus takes a long drag from his cigar before motioning for us to sit. "Now, to business. One of our men broke ranks recently. Fucked off to The Disciples."

"Why'd he leave?"

"Who knows?" He sighs. "Maybe he thought he couldn't hack it here, maybe they had somethin' on him, I'm not really interested in motivation. When I woke up today, all I wanted was his head, but if you're telling me I get the opportunity to take The Disciples out in the process? Well that's a whole new barrel of fun."

I know what we're dealing with when it comes to a man like this: he's an arrogant, egotistical prick who doesn't give a shit about anyone outside of his club. Problem is, he's been doing this for a long time, and making it that far without getting a bullet in your head means you know more than a little about survival.

"Sounds like we have common ground."

Titus stares me down for a moment, like he's deeply considering a different course of action, before nodding to one of his men who takes out a pack of cigarettes and slides it down the table to me. I pluck one out, offering the pack to my brother who quickly grabs one and stuffs it behind his ear. It's a peace offering of sorts, and Titus gives a curt nod, seemingly satisfied with our reaction.

"My brother's found the jail they're holding the girls in, so—"

"Well, I actually found three of them. Had to go through the process of elimination in order to pinpoint the right one."

Raph reaches under the table, and in an instant, Titus's men are on their feet again, guns at the ready.

"Easy, gentlemen," Raphael chuckles, raising his hands. "It's just my bag, the one they had to search for us to even come in here. So, I'm going to reach in there, get my laptop, and show you what I've found."

Titus just keeps smoking, his hand resting on the pistol on the table next to him.

"What happened to all that talk about calling off guard dogs?" Raphael mutters, grinding the words out through clenched teeth.

Titus stares at the two of us, mulling things over as he puffs on his cigar, and I can feel the panic in me start to rise up again.

"Well now, it looks like we may have reached an impasse. It's too bad, I was really starting to like you two. Oh well."

His men level their guns, and I brace myself, ready for the worst.

But then Titus bursts out laughing.

"Down, boys! I'm only fucking with them."

Out of the corner of my eye I can see Gus's whole body relax, slumping back in his chair while Raph is practically chewing on his tongue to stop himself from saying something stupid. Instead, he just lets out a long, haggard breath before opening up his laptop, his fingers flying across the keys.

"Now, the prick we captured said the girls are being held at an abandoned jail in Swift Current. But he wasn't the sharpest tack, and there are a few places that have been shut down around there; at least three of them could be classified as 'jails.' One of them is gonna be re-opening as a prison, and another is scheduled to be torn down, which leaves this one."

He hits a key, pulling up a picture of an abandoned, crumbling building.

"This is Blackrock Correctional Facility. Abandoned five years ago when all the prisoners were transferred out after a fire, but the expected renovations never came. Government hasn't done a damn thing with it, and I can't find any records of future plans. My guess? It was just cheaper to let it rot. We find this jail, and we find the girls."

Titus sighs.

"Adonis has these big parties when he wants to get rid of them, usually ones he's done with or are too difficult. He bounces around to different places so frequently we can never really pinpoint him. We were still working on where he'd gone after he slipped through our fingers when we ran him out of Moose Jaw. Keeps trying to expand his territory, always touching things that don't belong to him."

"Tell me more about these parties."

He shrugs.

"Not much to tell. Lots of drugs, lots of booze... money exchanges hands and girls disappear. Now..." He leans forward, resting his palms flat on the table. "Let me ask you something. What makes you think you're even capable of going toe to toe with Adonis? Because the stories I've heard and the bruises on your face tell me you got your ass handed to you the last time you two tangled, pretty boy."

I don't take the bait, staying calm as I lean forward, only staring at him from across the table.

"Imagine something you're good at, something you do better than anyone else. Imagine something you can do without even *thinking* at this point. I don't know what the fuck that is for you, but for me, it's killing men like him. When I get my hands on him, I'm gonna pluck out his eyes and chew on 'em like grapes."

Titus blinks, silent only for a moment before he lets out a booming laugh.

"Well ho-lee-shit, Gus was right, you *are* crazy." He smirks, leaning back in his chair. "Okay, I'm sold. But now we get to work out what it's gonna cost you. How many of Wren's men are dead?"

"Everyone who went but me," Gus murmurs. "There's maybe half-a-dozen left, but they won't mobilize without her go-ahead."

"Well, would you look at that? Sounds like she'll *finally* owe me one."

Raph looks like he could explode at any moment, so I do my best to jump in and get this finished as fast as I possibly can.

"You'll let us stay here tonight, and tomorrow we go to that prison with everything we have. You'll get your man, you'll get your favor from Wren, and after that, you won't have to ever hear from us again."

"Mm, what else you got?" Titus asks, raising his brows.

"Jesus Christ, man," Raphael sighs.

"Jesus Christ nothin'. I told you I don't work for free, and last time I checked favors aren't worth a whole lot from folks who's rescuin' is part of the deal."

"Fine. You bring the men, and all the firepower you can muster, and I'll give you fifty grand, in cash."

Raphael looks like he wants to shoot me. Titus, on the other hand, looks absolutely ecstatic as he slams his hand down on the table.

"Make it 100K, and we've got ourselves a deal."

I can't stand this guy, but somehow I can't help but grin as I reach my hand out.

"Deal."

"See that? Now that's the kind of respect I deserve, and respect always gets repaid! Cheyenne! Molly! These fuckers drink free tonight!"

The Proposal
RIPLEY

I wake up to the sound of metal creaking, a massive silhouette filling the open door to our cell. It takes me a couple moments to get my bearings, blinking through the blurriness of sleep before I push myself back up against the wall, bracing for yet another assault. My mind starts to drift to the ranch again, to Preacher and endless sunsets, and watching the dogs play in the yard.

Anywhere but here.

"Relax, I'm not gonna hurt you."

Adonis's gravelly voice fills the room as he slips toward me like a snake.

"Funny how I'm struggling to believe that," I snarl.

I hear the flick of a lighter, my eyes going through that final little bit of adjustment as I watch the soft orange glow illuminate his face. After a puff or two, he crouches down in front of me and holds it out.

"What is this, a goddamn peace offering?" I hiss. "Get the fuck away from me."

I can't tell what's worse, the stench of menthol wafting from his cigarette, or his horrific breath it hasn't managed to cover up. He smells like he eats shit for breakfast, so I guess it's no wonder he has to buy women.

"You got a lotta nerve talkin' to me like that, angel."

"You said you wouldn't hurt me... so what do you want?"

"I wanna show you something. Upstairs."

My eyes flick to my sister, still asleep in the other corner.

"Are you gonna at least give me the chance to say goodbye to her?"

"What for?" Adonis snorts. "You ain't goin' anywhere."

He glances behind him.

"Her, though? Got *quite* a few men who would *love* to take a run at her."

I take the moment of distraction and go with it, spitting right in his face when he turns back around, knowing full well what the consequences might be. It lands on his cheek, and I wait for the strike or the screaming as it slides slowly down his face, but Adonis only stares at me, never breaking eye contact.

He finishes his smoke, tossing it to the ground, and I watch with coiled muscles while he fishes into his pocket for a tiny silver key. I could headbutt him, take it and free us, but of course I don't know how many men he has outside, or how much firepower he has.

He hauls me to my feet, wordlessly slapping a pair of cuffs on my wrists before dragging me toward the door. I could be watching the last grains of sand slip through my own personal hourglass, and just like so many times before, I have no control.

But all I can think is that I'm leaving Wren again.

Alone.

Scared.

In the dark.

A lump forms in my throat as the door clicks shut and Adonis locks it tight. Looks like two of his men were standing outside the whole time, permanent frown lines etched into their foreheads. They're big— maybe around Preacher's height, so it seems I made the right call on the no-head-butt plan.

Adonis leads me up the stairs, dragging me by the cuffs just quick enough to make me stumble a couple times in the low-light. When we reach yet another metal door, he knocks on it a couple times before a slat near the top slides open. There's some goon or other waiting outside, revealing the rest of the small jailhouse when he swings the door open, and confirming for about the hundredth time that even if I killed him in our cell, there was no way we were making it out of here.

This place looks like it hasn't been touched in years, but I can see the faintest echoes of what was once a busy jailhouse. A couple old uniforms and jackets still sit on the coat hangers, dusty phones where officers once took calls, a drunk tank off in the corner, and a few interrogation rooms with some less than savory sounds coming from behind closed doors.

"Some of the boys like to swing by for a couple of beers and a private room," Adonis chuckles, speaking for the first time since we came upstairs. "We keep the good girls up here, by the way. You know, the ones who don't cause any trouble."

I wonder how many don't make it.

How many bodies they've buried.

Adonis is sick, pathetic, and depraved. He's everything I loathe, but with escape out of the picture, maybe there's another option. If I get close enough, and I can get him to trust me, then...

Well, if Preacher can't save us, I have to find a way to do it myself.

My bare feet slap against the floor, sore and swollen as Adonis leads me down a long hall, his men close in tow. The lights are low, and even off completely in the spots with windows, probably on the off-chance someone swings by and alerts the cops... if anyone even comes out this way. No doubt Adonis has them in his fucking pocket already anyway if McKinney was any indication.

"This here is where the magic happens."

He pauses for dramatic effect, like he expects it to be some sort of grand revelation, but... I mean it's a fucking prison cafeteria. It even still has the yellow lines on the floor to tell prisoners where to file in to get their daily slop. He's turned the serving station into a bar, with bottles of half-empty whiskey lining the shelves, but it's not like that's made it any less depressing. The whole place reeks like unwashed bodies, cigarette smoke, and cheap liquor.

"Why did you bring me here?" I ask. "To taunt me?"

"I could have done that down in your cage. I'm showing you where you'll be working tomorrow night." He grins, flashing me a mouthful of rotting teeth. "If you accept my proposal, that is."

"Proposal?"

He reaches behind him, and my heart leaps into my throat when he whips out his pistol, aiming it directly at my forehead. That is, until I see the look in his eyes.

No commitment.

Just like Gabriel.

"You framed me," he snarls, but his face quickly relaxes back into his cocky smirk. "The head and tongue were a nice touch, I have to admit, and I was extremely impressed with your own little sacrifice."

He takes a step toward me, grabbing me by the jaw and forcing the pistol between my lips. The barrel tastes like sweat, and the blend of that with his own signature stench is enough to nearly make me vomit.

"You're resourceful, and you're vicious." He tilts his head. "But you also need to be controlled. Disciplined. So, you'll get to work for me for a while, and if you're a very, *very* good girl... I'll even let you recruit the new meat."

My stomach churns at the thought of being his lackey, a fuck-toy that he'll inevitably grow bored and discard. He will kill me, sooner or later. That much is clear.

Unless I kill him first.

He slowly slides the gun out of my mouth and I swallow hard.

"This place could use more of a feminine touch, don't you think?"

"Sure, whatever you say, *boss*, but what do I get out of it?"

"Your life..."

Adonis flashes me those rotting teeth again. He really loves that fucking move.

"And hey, maybe your sister's if someone doesn't snap her up tomorrow night." He shrugs. "Just depends on how generous I feel."

"Alright, it's a deal."

He narrows his eyes, and I can see his suspicion already start growing; not to mention how much work I'm going to have to do to get him to trust me. I'll need to get close to him, do everything he asks, and then once he's let his guard down, he's a dead man.

"You rolled over pretty easy."

"Look, I'm not going anywhere, and you've seen for yourself I'll do anything to survive."

He frowns, like his tiny little brain's working on overdrive just to grasp the concept, and I take the opportunity to start working my magic.

"You know, the man I was staying with?" I ask. "He taught me how to hunt."

"Hunt?"

"People, Adonis." I smile. "You've seen what I did to Gabriel— well, you saw the aftermath."

"Yeah, I fuckin' saw it," he growls. "You're a sick little puppy sometimes, Christine."

It's funny hearing that name now, knowing that he still sees me as that meek, terrified woman who took hit after hit and hid her bruises behind long sleeves and makeup. But he hasn't seen the woman I've blossomed into.

Not really.

Not yet.

"All I'm saying is you seem like a guy who likes to hold on to power. I can help with that, get rid of your enemies... and so can Wren."

"It's awful nice of you to advocate for your sister, but I'm only interested in you."

He needs to know that neither of us is a threat to him, and even though there's nothing but fury running through my veins, I'll be whoever I need to be to get that point across.

"Who've you got running that bar?"

"Dagger," he replies flatly, nodding towards a short man in the corner with a patchy beard. "But all he does is crack open beers. He's useless when it comes to anything else."

I do my best to move on, and not to emotionally eviscerate a grown man with such a stupid nickname.

"You said this place needed a feminine touch," I purr. "How about you let me and Wren handle the drinks. Your boys would probably like something stronger than beer, and I know your guests definitely will."

He raises a brow, his eyes brimming with suspicion again.

"I don't have a choice, Adonis. I either work for you, or you kill me, so consider this me acquiescing."

"The fuck's that mean?" He growls.

Everything I've learned from pretending to be a normal human goes into the smile: Demure, soft, and submissive, just the way he likes his girls. I know Adonis better than he thinks, and far better than he knows me.

"It means I'm surrendering. You won, Adonis. Enjoy it."

The Party
RIPLEY

The room is chaotic, the music blaring as dozens of drunk bikers guzzle their drinks, shouting and ogling the girls against the wall. The night hasn't even started yet, and I'm wondering just how much worse this is going to get.

The other girls are either dancing or serving drinks, each of them in nothing but a pair of underwear. They look just as miserable as I feel.

"*I have a plan*, she says, making us *fucking work for him*." Wren knocks back a shot of whiskey, shaking her head. "You're an idiot."

"I'm saving our lives, bitch," I hiss. "Unless you wanna be up on that wall with the rest of them. Now, keep your voice down and stop drinking the fucking booze."

"It's the only thing that makes me feel better," she sighs. "My goddamn back is killing me."

I'm hurting too, but all I can think about is getting out of here. Adonis said that our job is to run the bar tonight; *my job* is to make sure these assholes get nice and drunk. Preferably, it'll be to the point where they start to pass out, because It'll be a hell of a lot easier to do literally anything without a room full of horny assholes ready to jump us.

"Ladies."

I bristle at the word as I see one of Adonis's men leaning up against the bar. He's got long dark hair that's thinning at the sides, and faded acne scars on his cheeks. The patch on his vest reads *VICE PRESIDENT*. Wren gave me the rundown on some of these guys. They're big, they're mean, and they demand respect— even if they never give it to anyone else.

"Adonis wants another Jack and Coke. He's in a bad mood tonight, so make sure it's extra strong."

"Who pissed his cornflakes?" I ask.

The man scoffs, glancing over his shoulder.

"A couple of his men never came back after an assignment. Shit happens, right? I keep telling him it's no big deal, but..."

My heart starts to pound. It could be anything, but he might be talking about the men Adonis left at the church. Does that mean Preacher's alive? I know that'd definitely put him in a sour fucking mood.

"Some of the other boys are getting low, too, so you might wanna get on it."

And just like that, I'm snapped back to the reality of our situation, the very thought of going back out on the floor making me want to vomit.

My stomach churns as I finish making Adonis' fourth Jack and Coke of the night. The party hasn't even started, and these guys are already halfway to wasted, but unfortunately the man himself is holding his own.

"There she is," Adonis purrs, rattling his glass as I walk up to deliver his drink. "Been dry for a while, sweet thing."

I do my best not to make eye contact as I set his drink down in front of him, but I can already feel his hand gliding up my thigh.

"Do you need anything else?"

"Yeah, actually."

He gets to his feet, grabbing my wrist and dragging me toward the front of the room. My stomach bubbles, and my heart feels like it's lodged in my throat. Is he going to make an example out of me in front of all of his friends? Is he going to let them—

Fuck, I can't even think about it.

Just cooperate. Don't fight back, not yet.

"Gentlemen!" Adonis bellows. "I just need a few moments of your time to go over the rules for tonight."

I'm trying to stay calm, glancing over at my sister for some kind of reassurance, but I can't catch her eye. She's slipped out from behind the bar, quietly collecting empty bottles and glasses while the men are focused on Adonis.

"First off, this is a cash-only operation. No bartering. Once you've picked your girl, you pay up. Touching the merchandise *is* permitted— you want a sample? The rooms in the hallway are open. Any disputes will be settled by me."

"What about this one?" A burly biker grabs Wren's arm, pulling her into his lap. "She looks awful familiar."

The laughter rippling through the room makes my blood run cold.

"That right there is your bar-wench, and she ain't for sale."

My body slumps with relief. If she disappeared into one of those rooms, I'd probably never see her again.

"One wrong move and I go back on my word," Adonis purrs into my ear. "Don't fucking test me, bitch."

I swallow the urge to wrap my hands around his throat and *squeeze* as hard as I can. None of this works without the right opportunity. We just have to wait.

"Now someone turn the fuckin' music up!" Adonis roars. "Let's get this party started!"

The noise is so overwhelming I can barely think, and all I can do is watch as the men get to their feet and make their way over to the lineup of girls; none of them are shy about groping and grabbing whatever they want.

Adonis grasps my chin, literally grabbing my attention as he turns me to face him.

"I saved you," he growls. "So keep that in mind, and fix your goddamn attitude."

"You're right, thank you."

I can tell he doesn't trust me by the way his eyes dance around my face, like he's trying to see if I'm *really* thankful, and I feel myself starting to fall right back into the same habits I learned with Gabriel.

Smile.

Be soft and demure.

Don't give him a reason.

"Good, now get the fuck back to work."

I rush back to the bar, busying myself with some of the empty glasses Wren's brought back before I spot her opening a second big plastic bottle of whiskey, the first one still only half-empty.

"What are you doing? We already have one over here."

Her eyes dart around the room before she quickly digs something out of her waistband, tossing some baggies of white powder onto the counter.

"Lifted these off that prick who wanted to take me home with him. We put it in the liquor, and keep making drinks. If anyone gets suspicious we have that other one to show 'em."

"What is it?" I ask.

"Who gives a shit." Wren quickly empties everything into the bottle before securing the cap and giving it a good shake. "Now get rid of those bags."

I look around the kitchen, trying to find a hiding place less conspicuous than the trash sitting nearby. If we're not out of here tonight, tomorrow it'll be far too easy for them to trace this back to us.

My adrenaline is sky high as I watch the rest of the white powder dissolve into the liquor, and at the last second I spot a gap in the counter and quickly stuff the empty baggies into it.

This has to work.

"Evening, ladies!" A man calls, walking straight up to the bar. "I think I need another round!"

It takes me a moment, but I realize he's the same one who grabbed Wren, already having moved on to a young blonde girl that's practically glued to his arm. She keeps her eyes locked firmly on the floor, trembling like a leaf.

"What can I get you, sweetheart?" Wren asks.

"Jack and Coke. Strong as you can make it."

She fixes his drink with a sweet smile, sliding it across the counter.

"If you need more, you know where to find me."

He looks her up and down like a hungry dog.

"If you feel like joining us, let's just say I wouldn't mind some more company."

She lets out a flirtatious giggle.

"I'll consider it, baby."

"That's all I ask." He glances at me. "That and... bring your friend, too."

He strolls away, and Wren sighs as he disappears into the crowd.

"Fuck, I hope this works."

"You and me both."

There's another half-hour or so of drinks, drunks, and depression, the two of us straining to see the first signs of Wren's concoction taking effect, but time flies when you're having the worst night of your life.

"I don't see anyone passing out, Wren."

"Probably takes a while to kick in," she mumbles.

Maybe the shit she found in that guy's pockets was just bunk. Maybe he planted it there on purpose, and when he finds out what we've done, maybe—

But suddenly I'm not thinking about all the maybes anymore. Suddenly the only thing on my mind is the shattered glass, and the deafening sound exploding from outside. Suddenly there's the slimmest bit of room for hope.

Rescue Me
PREACHER

SWIFT CURRENT, SASKATCHEWAN

"How much further?" I ask, keeping my foot jammed on the gas as I nervously watch the last slivers of the sun slip beneath the horizon.

"About ten minutes," Raph mutters.

He's been staring at his phone the entire ride, like he's gonna find some sort of answer in it. I can see the anxiety swirling in him, and I wish there was something I could say to pull him out of his spiral, but I know he won't be okay until we find them.

Titus said he's certain that most of Adonis's men will be inside getting shitfaced while they bid on the girls, so that means all we have to do is surround the building, clear any guards, and make our way in. I can tell my brother isn't so keen on the plan; he's worried there could be casualties, very specific ones.

And if I'm being entirely honest, I am too.

Suddenly, the convoy of trucks and bikes veers off to the side of the road, and I have to jerk the wheel hard to keep in line behind them.

"What the fuck are they doing?" Raphael asks, leaning forward and bracing his hands on the dash. "What's going on?"

"No fuckin' idea. Maybe they saw something we didn't."

I follow them a little ways away from our initial planned spot, driving straight into a parking garage, and all the way up to the top floor before killing the engine and hopping out of the truck. Titus is already on his feet, his binoculars aimed straight down at our target.

"Looks like we might be fucked, cowboys." He hands them to me. "There's at least 10 of 'em outside."

"Shit."

The night vision takes a second to get used to, but once I've adjusted it's clear as day: I count 9 men outfront the jail, and another two pacing around the side. Some are alert, some smoking or shooting the shit, but all of them are between us and our mission.

"Lemme see." Raph snatches the binoculars from my hands, needing to fact-check us on yet another detail. "Well fuck, you weren't lying."

"Never do." Titus turns to me, arms crossed and face pensive. "So, what's the call, hotshots?"

There are around 20 of us, including myself, Raph, and Gus, and we armed ourselves to the teeth before we headed out. Titus had *everything*. AR-15s, AK-47s, glocks, grenades, even a fucking battering ram like the feds use.

But explosives and gunfire aren't the way to go here, not until we're sure we have full control over the situation. I don't want Adonis or his men seeing this coming, not until we're ready to breach those doors.

"I think we can take 'em."

Titus grins, his eyes shimmering even in the low-light of the parking garage.

"That's the shit I like to hear. So how do you wanna approach it?"

"I'm thinking we use the darkness to our advantage and pick 'em off in little batches."

"I like it. Once we're done, we can take out the bikes to create a distraction. Doubles as insurance that none of them sneak by and get to go for help."

He stares at me for a moment, his mouth curling into a cocky grin.

"Boys? Load up and follow our lead. We're going in quiet, but be ready for anything." He claps me on the shoulder, grinning from ear to ear. "Don't say I never did nothin' for ya."

"Don't worry," Raph grumbles behind me. "He won't."

"You're a funny motherfucker, Rufio."

"It's *Raphael*."

"'Course it is. Now let's head out before any more of 'em get added to the meat grinder."

My brother and I head back to the truck, and I load a big black duffel bag with everything we might need, from guns to ammo to a couple grenades. Of course, I can't forget my knife.

"You really like that thing, don't you?" Raph asks. "A little too much, I'd say."

I brought the one Ripley used to gut McKinney, already one of my favourites, but now... Figure there's a certain poetry to it.

"Second most reliable thing in my life so far," I reply, watching the moonlight glint off of the blade.

My brother glowers at me, his eyes stormy and intense.

"I find that insulting, just so you know, because I'm certain you're not about to say I'm number one."

"You know what mom used to tell us: if you don't have anything nice to say..."

"Shut the fuck up."

We make our way to the ground floor of the parking garage and start out on foot toward the jail. It's only a few blocks, but we make sure to stick to the darkness. Titus's men are surprisingly quiet and agile for a bunch of burly bikers, and I'm getting the feeling the training he puts them through is a little more intense than your average gang.

When we're only one block away, we loop around to the back of the building. While I'm waiting for the rest of the men to get in position, I spot some graffiti scrawled onto the old brick. A big ol' cock with *FUCK THE POLICE* underneath it.

Nice touch.

Everyone preps their weapons in silence, because in this kind of quiet, even a poorly timed whisper might as well sound like a gunshot. Titus looks to me, his gun at the ready, but then the barely audible music cranks up inside the building, suddenly loud enough that it might bring the whole goddamn thing down.

The Rolling Stones, *It's Only Rock N Roll*.

I share a glance with Titus, who grins.

"Well that's some fucking luck, huh, boys?"

He signals for us to fan out, creeping around the building and ready to strike. Some of Adonis's men are sipping beers, others are fucking around on their phones, and a few are even standing guard like good little dogs.

I spot one of the men wandering in my direction, his belt buckle jingling as he stops, whips out his cock, and starts pissing all over the pavement. He's whistling to himself, head tipped up toward the sky as I creep up behind him.

I clamp my hand over his mouth, smelling whiskey, piss, and cheap cologne.

My heart thunders. The anticipation hangs like humidity in the air as his body jumps and he starts to struggle, snarling, writhing, and thrashing against me. He's strong, but I'm a practiced hand at this, slashing his throat so deep I feel bone.

All he lets out is a muffled grunt before going limp.

"What the fuck?"

I turn, coming face to face with another one. Before he can make another sound, I lunge forward and grab him by the hair, shove the blade just below his chin. His eyes go wide, his lips parting just enough that I can see a glint of steel sticking up from underneath his tongue.

"Just tore right through all that soft tissue," I whisper, twisting the blade to cause just a little more agony. "Dead man walking."

He lets out a strangled, pathetic cry, that for a fraction of a second makes me think this whole plan has been fucked. But when I look up, all I see is man after man taking their targets down. Even Raph's staring at the knife in his hand, a corpse laying at his feet.

"Hey, you good?"

He stares at me, taking a few deep breaths just as I spot a mountain of a man turn the corner and start sprinting toward him. I tear my pistol out of my jeans, but Raph's faster, spinning around on the ball of his foot and shooting the fucker right in the heart.

"Nice shot—"

A loud explosion knocks both of us off our feet, and I scramble for my brother, trying my hardest to shield him from chunks of flying metal and rubber. It takes a while for the smoke to clear, but when it does I see Titus striding toward us, a bloodied knife still clutched in his hand.

"Sorry, boys! Didn't see you there!"

"You didn't see us?!" Raph yelps. "You almost blew us to smithereens, you asshole."

Titus shrugs, his chest heaving like he's just run a marathon as he helps me to my feet, before offering his arm to Raph.

"There's a back exit," he tells us, pulling my brother up like he barely weighs a pound. "Currently unguarded, after all our hard work, and there's no way they didn't hear that inside. They'll be sending people out front to check, so we're gonna make our way in the back."

Hope surges through me and I glance over at my brother who's staring at the building with a look of nothing but pure rage. Growing up, Raph was always the person who made all the plans, who calmed me down when I flew off the handle. I used to think we were so different, but when I look in his eyes now, I think I may be seeing what he first saw in me all those years ago.

"We're gonna get them back, right?"

I grasp his shoulder, pulling him in close.

"It's a promise."

Run, Rabbit

RIPLEY

"Get out there, now!" Adonis roars, doing his best to stir his men out of their dazed stupor "I don't give a shit who it is, no one comes at us on our own turf! I want their fuckin' heads!"

There's a brief moment of confused silence before the chaos erupts, Adonis's men scattering like leaves— well, more like stumbling, the effects of the drugs and booze finally hitting them.

Some of them head to previously assigned posts, some follow behind him toward the front entrance with their weapons at the ready, and others just panic, dashing here and there without thought to what they're actually trying to accomplish in their heads.

Wren, in sharp contrast, isn't wasting any time, grabbing my wrist and yanking me so hard it feels like she might pull my arm right out of its socket.

"Stay down," she hisses. "It's an ambush, no telling how long before the bullets start flying."

"Do you think it's—"

"I don't know," she whispers. "But we don't really have time to think about it. If it's them, or a rival gang, or even if it's the fucking army, it doesn't matter. We're sitting ducks if we stay here."

She's right. Even if they're here for us, there's a damn good chance we get caught in the crossfire, and I'm not about to take a bullet for being a fucking moron.

"Okay, then what the fuck do we do? The only two ways to go are straight toward all that chaos or back down into our cell."

As if on cue, the sound of an electric snap cuts through the air and the entire room goes pitch black. Someone hit the breakers.

"Come on, it won't get any better than this!"

I can't see anything more than a foot in front of my face, but Wren seems confident enough as she leads me by the arm, the two of us darting out from behind the bar and heading straight for a wall. I try to stay low, my heart in my throat as we follow the wall toward what I have to hope is the right door. All we need to do is get out of this fucking room; we get out of the crossfire, and we can lay low, just hold out until it's all over, or maybe make a break for it outside if we get lucky enough.

Or maybe, just maybe, I can pick a gun off a fresh corpse and head back in there to put Adonis down for good. The idea invades my mind like a virus, quickly taking over every other thought. I bet I could do it. Wouldn't even be that difficult... not in the dark like this. He'd never expect it.

"There, found the fucking door, now come on!"

We rush out of the room as quickly as we can, pushing past the panicked voices of Adonis's men, but just as we turn the corner my foot catches on something, or I guess it's someone, lying outside the doorway. I pause, barely able to see more than a vague outline of a man lying slumped over on the ground. Maybe one of Adonis' boys? But why is he—

Gunfire explodes just down one of the side hallways, and Wren yanks hard on my arm.

"Ripley, come on!"

"Wait, wait, we can probably..."

I crouch down and start searching the body. There's got to be a knife or a gun or something on this fucker. I'd even take a taser at this point. Anything to help us get out of here.

"We don't have time for this shit," Wren growls.

Just as she's about to yank me upright, the lights begin to flicker, weakly at first, followed quickly by the hum of a backup generator. In moments the hallway is illuminated, dimmer than before of course, but at least enough for me to quickly spot the two pistols he has jammed in his waistband.

That, and his cold, dead eyes.

I snatch them up, handing one to Wren before taking off down the hall.

"See? Have I ever steered you wrong?"

Every careful step down the hallway feels like an eternity as the sound of gunfire grows louder and louder, until we finally hit the lobby. I take a quick look around the corner and catch sight of at least three of Adonis's men, and a slew of others I don't recognize.

Before I get the chance to put any names to faces, a bullet sails by, just barely missing my arm as it buries itself in the wall behind us. My heart's pounding, and I can't stop shaking, completely unsure if it's fear, adrenaline, anticipation, or all three of them fighting for control of my body.

"The door's about twenty feet ahead," Wren hisses. "That was just a stray, wasn't meant for us. Stay low to the ground, and follow me."

"Jesus Christ, how many fucking gun fights have you been in?"

She smiles and cocks her pistol.

"Remember when I told you I never killed anyone? Didn't say anything about severe maimings."

I almost laugh, but the loud popping and snapping of gunfire thrusts me back into panic mode. I follow her lead, watching intently as she silently shows me how to take the safety off, and the two of us creep out slowly from behind the desk. Bullets keep flying, but nobody seems to take any notice of us. They're all too busy shooting at each other, and at this point I can't even tell who's who.

I guess it doesn't matter; everyone's just trying to save their own ass.

The two of us are moving as fast as we can, but there's only so much you can do when you're hunched over like a senior citizen, and that's before the bullets start to fly in our direction. We're forced to ditch the plan and head for cover again, my heart pounding, sweat pouring down my face as we hide in a nearby office.

"We'll wait for another break and run for it. It's gotta be just a few feet away now."

But at this point, I'm barely listening, because that's when I spot Adonis, crouched down and hiding behind the doorframe in another office across the hall. He's completely still, with a deep crease on his brow, like he's... listening for something?

Suddenly, the wood just above his head bursts into splinters and he retreats backward, giving me the clearest shot I can possibly imagine, straight through the office window.

"Come on!" Wren hisses. "What the hell are you doing?"

He hasn't even seen me. Not yet. He's too busy with whoever else is trying to blow his fucking head off. There's no way I'm giving up on this.

"He's right fucking there, Wren," I mutter, giving my head a quick shake toward the office as I line up my shot. She goes silent as she catches sight of him, giving me space as I level the gun, and take a deep, soothing breath. The sound is excruciating, but that's nothing compared to the feeling in my wrists as the recoil nearly knocks me to the ground.

And I miss.

Because of course I fucking miss, what was I thinking?

"Let's go!" Wren bellows, snatching my arm and pulling me to my feet as I come to my senses. "He might not have noticed with all the fucking shooting going on, but if we just sit here..."

"I know, I know, I just— fuck, why did I have to miss?!"

My legs feel like they're made of concrete, and my heart is beating so fast I think it might actually explode this time, but as we make our way past the offices and through the lobby, with all the bullets whizzing by, I just keep pushing. Keep dodging.

And then I can see the door.

Don't look back, just keep fucking running.

"We're almost—"

Wren's body crumples.

I stumble to a halt, spinning around and dropping to my knees.

Her shoulder is a mess of oozing red.

I don't even know if she was hit anywhere else, but she's barely moving.

"Wren... Oh shit, Wren. Just hang on I'll get you out of here—"

"You really thought I'd let you go that easily?"

My skin bristles at the raspy, whiskey-soaked voice that floats through the air behind me. My first instinct is to grab my sister. My second is to blow his fucking head off.

"Well, look at her," Adonis chuckles. "Little Wren, ain't she cute?"

With my back to him, I don't think he even realizes...

"Get the fuck back!" I bark.

I whip around to meet his gaze, raising the pistol as I do.

He looks... shocked, more than anything. His hair's disheveled, and there's a deep gash in his face, but the idea of me fighting back is the thing that's giving him pause, his gun only halfway drawn. The problem is he brought one of his men along with him, and it looks like he wasn't quite as slow.

"Aww, princess... you think we're afraid of you? Now be a good girl and put that down."

Breathe slow.

Smile sweetly.

And twist.

My shot's not perfect, hitting his goon right below his eye. I was aiming for the forehead, but it does the job well enough, blood spurting out like a geyser as the man drops to the ground. Adonis is taken completely by surprise, reaching for his gun before faltering, his face turning pale as his eyes flick to something behind me and back again.

And just like that, he's sprinting down the hallway, barely giving me the opportunity to empty the rest of the magazine before he's around the corner, just as another hail of gunfire erupts from behind me.

"Fuck this."

I whirl around, intent on protecting my sister in one final blaze of glory, but instead, there they are:

Preacher and Raph.

Armed to the teeth.

They rush up to us, Preacher scooping me into his arms while Raph crouches down beside Wren, tearing off part of his t-shirt to help staunch the bleeding.

"You came for us."

"Of course."

"I... I can't tell you how much—"

"I hate to cut this reunion short, but we gotta get the fuck out of here now. Wren's bleeding out."

Raphael grunts as he lifts her off the ground.

"How many men are left?" I ask.

"We took care of about 10 outside, plus some distinguished guests that decided to stay behind and fight," Preacher replies. "We've got people cleaning up the rest of them, come on—"

"No."

My rage has been coiling inside me like a spring, just waiting for the first opportunity to be unleashed, but if I wait any longer this might end up being the last.

"Ripley—"

"I'm not leaving until he's dead."

I take a step toward my sister. Still conscious, but barely, her eyelids fluttering as Raphael cradles her in his arms. She looks helpless, just like that little girl I left behind when I was 17.

"I love you," I whisper.

The brothers look at each other, as if they're silently deciding on a course of action, before Raph finally gives in, giving the two of us a curt nod before taking off toward the exit.

"There's another exit, the same one we came through. He probably headed out that way to avoid getting swept up by everyone swarming the front."

"I can catch up to him."

I'm filled with adrenaline and pure anger. This isn't over until I watch the light leave Adonis's eyes. But thankfully, the greatest hunter I've ever known seems to agree.

"He's got a minute on you, tops. The way I trained you? I'd be offended if you didn't have him gutted in the next 5."

Preacher places his knife carefully in my hand, closing my fingers around it as he holds me tight.

"And I'll be right behind you. Now hunt, little rabbit."

Hunt, Rabbit

RIPLEY

I'm barefoot, bloodied, and full of rage as my feet pound against the pavement. But Preacher was right, Adonis didn't get far. In fact, I was lucky enough to see him disappear into an old, boarded up building a block or so away, a couple seconds after I got outside. Sure, maybe I could have asked for one of Preacher's guns, and just shot him before he even made it inside, but it's time I really got my hands dirty again.

And just like the first time, I'm doing it alone.

As I get closer, the building starts to take shape in the low light of the street lamps. It looks like an old abandoned school house, and it even has a few tiny desks still sitting abandoned outside, most of them bent or broken, or faded from the rain. I make my way through the same door Adonis did, as quietly as I can manage, immediately appreciating the little bit of moonlight that's coming through the couple of windows that didn't get boarded up.

My chest heaves as my eyes adjust to the dark, and I continue to ignore the same message my brain has been screaming at me from the moment Preacher swooped in: just wait and hide, give up and let him take care of it. He'd do it in a heartbeat, if you asked him.

But he knows as well as I do that this hunt needs to be mine.

And so instead, I think like prey.

I ask myself, what would my prey do if I just threw caution into the wind.

"Hey Adonis!" I bellow, Preacher's knife clutched tightly in my white-knuckled grip. "Come out, come out, wherever you are!"

Of course, my taunt is met with a silence so crushing it hurts to breathe.

I stay still, straining to listen, my muscles coiled and my body primed and ready for my next kill. A reaction's not the point, after all, at least not a vocal one. He's in here, and now he knows I am too, and I've met very few men less patient than Adonis Murphy.

It's only a minute or two of waiting before I hear a floorboard creak above me, and it takes all of my willpower to keep from dashing straight for the stairs as my heart soars.

I glance around the room to find a single door slightly ajar, the floor in front of it showing the now-obvious signs of recent footprints. I make my way to it quickly, but silently, slipping my way up a flight of rickety stairs until I reach the top and am forced to pause.

A blackened hallway, lit only by a few cracks of moonlight pressing through the boarded up windows, and completely lined with doors on either side.

Shit.

Again, I ignore the instinct to run, and the far far too reasonable thought: who cares if he gets away?

Because I do.

I wouldn't be able to live with myself if I let him slip through my fingers.

Not when I'm this close.

So what would Preacher do in this situation?

How would he take advantage of his prey's natural response to being hunted?

He'd taunt him.

Emasculate him.

Then put him in a position where he thinks he has the upper hand.

I slink down the hall, whistling the melody to Kokomo, and taking a moment here and there to make my presence as obnoxiously obvious as possible.

"You know, Adonis, playtime works a lot better if you actually participate! Don't you want to play with me anymore?"

I hear something creak behind me, and give the slightest glance over my shoulder. I'm not afraid, I'm a fucking animal, and once I manage to sink my teeth into him, I'm going to tear him to pieces. I turn around casually, heading toward the only door the sound could have possibly come from, grasping the handle to the long-abandoned classroom.

I hear it click, grinding like old bones as I twist.

This is where he is.

Deep breath.

Knife ready.

I whip the door open, lunging inside to find—

Fucking nothing.

And then I'm extremely self conscious all over again. Everything I was sure of, all my plans and maneuvers suddenly second-guessed. I do a quick sweep of the room, taking care to keep my steps light as I explore every shadow. There's not much to see here though, just an old chalkboard with some faded handwriting, a couple chairs piled up in the middle of the room, and...

Is that blood?

I crouch down, gliding my finger through a little splash of crimson.

It's fresh, but I'm more taken by how easy it was to find. Obvious enough that it would be impossible to miss for someone actually looking. Hell, it's right in the middle of the room, and... right in the middle of one of the only beams of moonlight glowing through the cracks.

"Clever boy."

I hear the ringing in my ears before I even finish my roll to the side, making it to my feet just as an explosion of wood erupts behind me, moonlight pouring into the room from the newly-boardless window. Adonis and his menacing grin stand in front of me, his gun aimed right at my head.

Jesus, I literally brought a knife to a fucking gun fight.

"Not so tough now, are you bitch?" He takes a step forward, matching my movements as I pivot to the left. "No friends, no guard dog to help protect you... not even your half-dead sister. You're mine now, so do as you're told, and maybe you get to make it out of this alive."

"I'm not going back," I snarl.

I try to subtly put a bit of space between us, but every time I take even the slightest step, he follows suit.

"Then I guess I'll just have to kill you. Hell, maybe I'll fuck your corpse in front of your boyfriend, too."

What he doesn't know is that by now, Preacher's somewhere nearby, if not in the building already, but I'm not sure how much that'll matter if I can't figure my way out of this.

He cocks his gun, his eyes blazing with pure hatred, following me as I back myself toward a wall. I glance around, looking for anything I can use, but find absolutely nothing in the rickety old room save for broken chairs and creaky floorboards.

Wait...

I take a step to the left, and then another, and one further back.

He laughs.

"Just look at you, nowhere to run and you're still—"

Adonis's eyes go wide as his final step forward ends a little differently than he expected, the obviously rotten floorboard giving-way just a little under his weight, and I take the moment of panic to rush him. There's a look of pure confusion on his face as he stares down at me, dropping the gun and struggling to regain his footing, only to realize far too late that my blade's already halfway through his gut.

"See, that's something we agree on." I twist the knife, yanking it out and jamming it back in again, as deep as it'll go. "There's nowhere for you to fucking run, and nobody is going to come looking for a scum-fucking trafficker like you. By the end of all of this, your skull is going to be resting on my mantle, so why don't you just—"

My head erupts in a fiery halo of pain as Adonis smashes me in the skull, harder than I'd ever expect from a man with such a gaping stab-wound, knocking me to the floor before he stumbles out the doorway.

"Fuck!"

I scramble to my feet, ignoring the throbbing pain as best I can, but the violent spinning of the room makes it near-impossible to stay upright, let alone walk. By the time I manage to stumble to the door, Adonis is gone.

But luckily, he's left a little trail of bloodcrumbs for me.

I take off after him, my bare feet slapping against the floor as I push myself to my absolute limit, through burning muscles and searing pain. The little trickles of blood lead me down the hall, and through a side-door at the very end, down a fire escape to a small back exit, and out into a parking lot.

And there he is, lying flat on his face.

I approach him on wobbly, exhausted legs, barely registering the jagged gravel and little shards of broken glass along the way. All I care about is putting this dog out of his misery.

When I reach him, the extent of the damage I managed to inflict is crystal-clear.

He's trembling like a leaf, shivering in the cool air, a pool of blood pumping out from beneath him onto the gravel and dirt.

He's weakened.

Terrified.

Just like all the women he hurt.

I get on my hands and knees, slinking toward him slowly, like an animal. My jaw tingles, the scent of his blood hanging so thick in the air I can practically taste it.

"I think you're bleeding out, pretty boy." I grin, leaning in to make sure I'm the last thing he sees before he leaves this world. "You know, I get off killing men like you. There's just something about taking all that power away that makes me feel alive."

I flip him over, straddling him as I take his face in my hands, leaning in just like you would for a passionate kiss before sliding my thumbs over his eyes and pressing down. He starts to struggle, but I only push harder, until he lets out a scream that pierces the night. I can feel soft tissue give way under my thumbs as I scream right back in his face, giddy with the thought that his final few moments are being spent in pure agony.

Adonis keeps struggling despite it all, thrashing violently, beating back against me with his arms, his fists, his legs, but I hold steady. There's nothing he can do to take this moment from me.

Until I feel it pierce me in the side.

Something small, and sharp.

Burning.

And then I can't breathe.

I fall off of him onto the gravel, glancing down to see the shard of glass sticking out from between my ribs. Oozing blood.

"Oh…"

A low rumbling laugh echoes through the night, and I look over into two bloodied caverns where eyes used to be, his words a sputtering, wet mess of blood and spit.

"Looks like my skull might have some company on that mantle of yours."

I rip the shard out of me, screaming in his face as he laughs, and laughs, and laughs, going silent only when I bring it down on him with all that's left of my strength. And then I collapse, my body seizing up from the pain and the exhaustion, and everything else.

And that's when I hear Preacher shouting my name from across the lot.

I roll onto my side, barely able to breathe as I stare at Adonis's battered corpse, my vision already starting to blur.

But I can smell him, sin and spice, as his rough hand cups my cheek.

"You—" I choke. "Made it after all."

"I said I'd be right behind you, didn't I? You were just too quick for me, little rabbit."

"Preacher, I think—" I cough, more and more blood oozing from my lips. "I think this might be it."

He presses his forehead to mine, pulling me close as he puts pressure on my wound.

"You and I both know that ain't true. I need you beside me, because I ain't facing the rest of this life alone. I can't, not anymore."

His voice, usually so firm and controlled, is fraying at the edges, coming apart just like me.

And I find myself filled with guilt, for the man I have to leave behind.

And overwhelmed with grief, for the second life I never got to live.

"I'm so, so sorry."

"I won't let you go, rabbit."

He takes my hand, and I feel something cool against my finger.

"I'll tear you out of Hell myself if I have to."

We're Only Human
PREACHER

MOOSE JAW, SASKATCHEWAN

I've always been good at being patient.

Waiting for the right moment to strike.

Knowing when to back off before I pursue again.

But my nerves crackle and pop like fraying wires, my fingers tapping anxiously against the big wooden table.

Outside, they're drinking and mourning their dead.

Likely more of their own lives lost than they've seen in quite some time.

Titus has a private clinic out back behind his club. He pays a doctor in cash to keep his boys out of hospital records, which in turn keeps them out of prison. Mostly, the doctor patches up bullet wounds, but she said she had connections to some shelters, people who could look after the girls without the police getting directly involved.

I sigh, taking another pull from the whiskey bottle. It tastes like battery acid, and it stings like a motherfucker. I'm pretty sure they distill this shit themselves.

Raphael went to get an update on Ripley and Wren from one of the nurses while I stayed behind, trying to calm the perpetual anxious-gnawing at the back of my neck. If I lose her for good, I think I'll put a gun in my mouth; there's no point in living in this world if she's not right beside me.

It's hard to keep my mind from running out of control. Usually, in a crisis, I'm cool as a cucumber, easily seeing through the panic and the bullshit, but right now? All I want is to hold that woman in my arms again.

That ring is still on her finger, right where I left it when I found her lying in that parking lot, and when she wakes up, I intend to follow through on its implicit promise: a big wedding, a beautiful honeymoon... Somewhere gorgeous, like France or Greece.

The door creaks, catching my attention in time to see Titus lumber inside with a beer clutched in his fist. While the rest of his men are openly mourning their dead, he's been the same stoic leader since the moment I first walked in here.

I couldn't read him if I tried.

"Your girls cost us a lot tonight. Seven of my best."

"I'll pay you," I grumble, taking another swig of whiskey. "I'm good for it."

"Yeah, after seeing how hard you fought back there, I believe you."

Titus pulls up a chair, easing himself into it with a grunt. I was more than a little surprised when he said he was coming with us, and I half-expected him to just wait back with the trucks, but he's covered in dried blood and fresh bruises, just like the rest of us. He did more than his fair share of killing tonight.

"The boys and I were talkin' outside... we're going to take credit for the slaughter at the prison." He exhales. "Your brother gave us that cop's phone, so if we turn that in, they'll never touch us again."

I say nothing, just a quick nod to let him know I've heard him. Over the years, I've learned that silence is the key to getting anyone to tell you anything.

Well, maybe second to pulling their teeth out.

"He said that you two do *very* important work." Titus leans back in his chair. "That true?"

"Raph told you that?"

He's always been hell-bent on keeping things a secret. He never wanted outside help, always complaining about people who stick their noses where they don't belong. I think that's why he hated Ripley so much when she showed up.

We were safe.

Protected.

And she upended all of that.

"Yeah, apparently you get a little whiskey into that boy and his lips loosen up real quick. Or maybe this whole thing with Wren means he's not thinking clearly. Either way, he's spillin' a whole lot of secrets."

"Is that so?"

The events of the last few days will only make Raphael more protective of Wren. More possessive. He'll keep his distance if that's what she wants, but after all of this? He'll never stop keeping tabs on her.

"Straight from the horse's mouth." Titus chuckles, clearing his throat. "So, all that in mind, I'd like to propose a deal. We send you some names from time to time, you do your thing, and we take a *tiny* cut of the profits. Call it a... symbiotic relationship."

I raise a brow.

"Symbiotic, huh?"

"That's right. You like to cut bad men up into tiny pieces, and I like money."

"How much?"

"Let's say... ten percent?"

I'd be lying if I said I was happy, but I suppose it's a necessary evil. We knew going in how men like Titus operate: you ask them for a favor, and you're rarely let off scot-free even after the agreed upon payment.

"So, you're saying we'd work for you?"

"What I'm saying is we'd be a client, and clients don't have any say on how a business gets run." He sighs, taking a big sip of his whiskey. "Look, you got a real *I don't fuck with you, you don't fuck with me* vibe, and I respect that shit, but you know fifty grand ain't gonna bring my men back. They were family, you understand?"

"Sure." I shrug, barely paying him any mind. "So long as it's fine with the brains of the operation, it's fine with me."

Raph's not going to be happy about this, but I suppose he only has himself to blame. For me, as long as the cops stay the hell away from the ranch, I'll be happy. The business was Raphael's idea in the first place, after all. Said there was nothing more pathetic than a broke, unemployed serial killer.

Titus leans over, slapping me on the shoulder before raising his drink.

"That's what I like to hear. To new business ventures."

We clink glasses, draining what's left of our drinks just in time for Raphael to burst into the room, his eyes as wide as saucers.

"Doctor says she needs us."

I nod to Titus, who dismisses us both with a wave.

Raphael leads me out the back door, into the quiet warmth of the night. The sound of our boots crunching against the gravel punctuates the silence, accompanied by the slightest hint of crickets in the distance. He looks shaken, almost hollowed out from everything we've gone through, but there's a hope in his eyes that I'm more than ready to latch onto.

"You told Titus about the business."

He lets out a sigh, nodding his head.

"Apparently worrying makes me run my mouth. Stupid, huh?"

I shrug

"We're only human."

"Thing is, this shit's a lot for me to run on my own, and as much as I don't like him, I could use some help in the logistics department."

"So, you're finally willing to give up a little bit of control?"

"Look, you're the one who started us down this road when you brought Ripley into this damn mess." He groans, like the mere thought of his perfect little system being altered gives him physical pain. "But, if I'm connected to him, I can keep tabs on Wren a whole lot easier. He said he's gonna talk to her about his club absorbing hers, consolidating power and all that."

I smirk, saying nothing as Raphael stops at the door and presses a small white button. That's his smoking gun: if Wren weren't in the picture, he'd have told Titus to go fuck himself.

"Name?" A voice asks through the intercom.

"Raphael and Preacher. We're here for Ripley and Wren."

There's a loud buzzing noise and we make our way inside. It's definitely not what I expected from something so closely connected to Titus's dive of a bar. Everything is so damn clean that I almost feel guilty for tracking my dirty boots inside. The doctor's already waiting for us at the end of the hall. She's young, with dark hair, glasses, and a stethoscope right out of a TV show draped around her neck.

"How are they?"

She blows out an exhausted breath, running a hand through her hair. I can't tell if the expression on her face is bad news or if she's just completely burnt out from so many patients.

"Well, they're both damn lucky to be alive considering everything they've been through. I had to extract a bullet from one, and luckily we managed to avoid sepsis." She takes off her glasses, shaking her head. "The other patient's stab wound didn't do as much damage as it could have, though she may have trouble walking for a while. None of that's even considering their general condition. I don't know how much longer they would have lasted in that place."

The doctor leads us to a small room, gently ushering us inside. Ripley looks shockingly pale, hooked up to all kinds of tubes and IVs, and Wren lays in a bed opposite her, propped up on some pillows.

"They're both pretty loopy from the painkillers, but they'll be able to talk for a little while. Just try not to take it personally if one of them dozes off mid-conversation."

The doctor pats me on the shoulder, heading for the door as Raphael takes a seat next to Wren. I grab my own chair and carry it over Ripley's bed, intent to hunker down for the long haul. In all the chaos and confusion of the raid, I didn't get a chance to really see all the damage he'd done to her. She looks so small now, her skin mottled with dark purple-and-red bruises. There are stitches in her forehead, above her eye, and in her bottom lip, and my heart twists in my chest as I lean down to kiss her.

I don't just love her, I *need* her the way I need my heart to keep beating. Before her, I didn't have much to live for other than my dogs and the business, but now? I'm not leaving this room until she's cleared to come home.

I give her hand a squeeze, my heart skipping a few beats when I notice that her finger is barren. I glance around in a panic, but thankfully find her engagement ring sitting on the table next to her bed. I pick it up and gingerly slip it back on.

Still a perfect fit.

And then Ripley's eyelids flutter open with a smile.

"Welcome back, rabbit."

"Oh wow, am I in heaven?" She croaks, her voice barely above a whisper.

I shake my head, stroking her cheek gently as I struggle to find a spot *without* a bruise.

"Unfortunately, you're stuck down here with me."

"Oh, thank God," she sighs. "Pretty sure they wouldn't let me in, but I was scared for a second. They don't even let you kill people up there, you know."

I let out another laugh, kissing her knuckles. I may never forgive myself for not being there to protect her, but I'm content to spend the rest of my life making up for it.

They say it takes seven years for every cell in the human body to replace itself. In some ways it'll be like she never went through this brutality, but we all know scars like that don't really fade.

"I've been thinking... I wanna take you away for a while. Maybe Europe?"

Ripley smiles. It's pained, but it's real, her eyes sparkling with anticipation as she marvels at the ring on her finger.

"That sounds lovely, but there's something I want to do first."

"Of course. Anything."

She nods to herself, glancing over at Wren on the other side of the room.

"Find my father, Preacher. Help me do what I should have done all those years ago."

Set Me Free

RIPLEY

**TWO MONTHS LATER
THUNDER BAY, ONTARIO**

"Make sure it's nice and tight."

Preacher's deep baritone fills the room as I secure the man's wrist to the chair with a zip tie, glancing back over my shoulder and rolling my eyes.

"You still don't think I know what I'm doing?"

The setup was disgustingly easy: Raphael posted as a teenage girl online, they had a brief back and forth, and 'she' gave him an address for a meetup.

He agreed.

Not a great look for a guy who did a stint for child pornography.

Preacher kisses me on the cheek, his scruff scraping gently against my skin.

"I'm just making sure you're dotting your I's and crossing the T's."

My heart's been racing since the second he walked through that door and Preacher injected him, my jaw tingling in anticipation the entire time. Decades of pain and anger have led me to this moment. My father will *never* be able to put his hands on another child again.

I take a step back, smoothing out my long white lace skirt. My bouquet sits on the sofa, along with Preacher's suit jacket. We picked up our attire at a little vintage store we found on the road. Figured we'd have our own private ceremony before we hopped on a plane to Europe.

"Now, rabbit, the most important part."

I scroll through his phone, humming and hawing before finally landing on the *perfect* song.

Kokomo by the Beach Boys.

"Again?" Preacher chuckles. "You've picked this one before."

"Yeah, because it's fun! Besides, shouldn't a serial killer have a signature?"

"You might be on to something," He grins, flashing me his silver tooth. "Now, are you ready to do this?"

I draw in a deep breath to calm my nerves. The man tied to that chair looks nothing like I remember. His jet black hair has been replaced with thinning, wiry strands of silver, and the deep wrinkles in his face remind me of a wilting rose.

"I'm ready."

"That's my girl."

He pulls some smelling salts out of his pocket, wafting them under my father's nose until he comes-to with a violent gasp.

"Hi, Edgar," I purr, stepping forward to give him a good look at me. "It's been a while, hasn't it?"

His shuddering breath comes out in short wheezing rasps. Raphael mentioned his medical records say he's got emphysema, probably from years of sucking down a pack a day. Serves him right.

"Chris— Christine?"

"Wow, you remembered, even after all these years!"

I giggle, spinning around and showing off my dress.

"You like it? It's vintage. Chanel."

My father's eyes dart around the room, and back to me, caught somewhere between confusion and panic.

"What the fuck are you doing?" He hisses. "Let me go!"

"Oh, no," I laugh. "I can't do that. You're my wedding present! Isn't that right, baby?"

"That's right." Preacher hands me his knife, nearly giving my father a heart attack as he walks out from behind the chair. "She told me everything about you, Edgar, all the sick, demented little details about what you did to the two of them growing up—"

"I didn't do shit!"

"Liar!" I scream, storming toward him and striking him across the face. "That's all you ever did! It was all you were good at!"

His face is twisted up in frustration, the same way he always looked when he'd come home from the bar. He'd tear the house apart like an animal before he realized, like clockwork, that the thing he really wanted was already upstairs, with nowhere else to go.

"It's not true! I know I was harsh sometimes but I loved you girls!"

He's probably told himself so many lies over the years.

I was sick.

I couldn't help myself.

I was drunk.

"Yeah, I'll bet you did," I snarl, dragging the knife down his cheek until I draw blood.

The thing about men like him is that there's always a but, some situation or condition that explains away all the things they do; there's always someone or something else to blame.

"Christine, you're sick, I can tell. I was sick too, but I'm better now! We can get you help, it's not too late!"

Just the sound of my old name spilling from his lips makes me nauseous.

"Sick? Nah, I've never felt better. Besides, you laid the groundwork for all of this. It's time for you to see what you created."

I lick the blood on the blade clean, spitting it right back into his face, but he barely flinches.

"Please, Christine, it's like I said... I was sick back then. I didn't know what I was— I didn't know how badly I hurt you and your sister, but things have changed! I've gotten right with The Lord."

His voice is raspy, filled with desperation and a disgusting sort of hope.

"Spare me the sob story, old man, you've got one job tonight. Isn't that what you've always wanted, to see your little girl get married?"

I move to join Preacher near the window where the last of the sunlight is dripping in like golden honey. I drink him in: cold olive eyes, long dark hair, and that menacing grin which always gives me butterflies, and soon my father's desperate pleas become nothing more than background noise.

"Ripley Blackthorne, so long as I live, I'll spend every second of every day devoted to you, loving you, worshipping you, and keeping you safe. You're the other half of my pitch-black heart, and so long as I'm breathing, nobody will *ever* hurt you again."

He slips a ring onto my finger.

"With this, I give you my heart, my soul, and my body."

"Please, Christine!" My father wails, rudely interrupting our perfect little scene.

"Pipe down! This is my moment!"

"Don't worry about him. Focus on me."

I nod, slowly sliding the ring onto his finger with my heart in my throat.

"You saw potential in me, and embraced my darkness better than I could ever do myself. You're my everything, and I'll spend the rest of my life making sure that you know that."

I drag in a deep, shuddering breath, a little shocked that somehow this thing I've wanted more than anything else is turning out to be harder than cold-blooded murder.

"With this, I give you my heart, my soul, and my body."

I barely get the last word out before Preacher grasps my face, practically devouring me with a rough and passionate kiss.

"Christine," my father rasps. "Please."

I smile sheepishly, breaking away and turning my head to face him as Preacher gently nips at my ear.

"Don't worry, Papa, I haven't forgotten about you. In fact, we've got a surprise prepared, right, baby?"

"Do your thing, rabbit."

I walk toward the little table that Preacher's knives are laid out on, and grab a little vial filled with liquified Pixie Dust. I tower over my father, becoming that same imposing figure he was to me for so many years. All those times when I begged him to stop, pleaded with him through wide, tear-filled eyes... A father is supposed to fight the monsters under the bed, not be one of them.

I grab him by the hair and force the vial to his lips, making sure he chokes down every last drop before taking a step back, and watching as the concoction takes hold. It's agony to wait, but I crush my impulsivity, suffering through the few minutes it takes in silence until he's fully under, and staring straight ahead like a goddamn zombie.

Preacher said he made sure it was a strong enough dose, I just hope he was right.

"I want you to confess. And don't you *dare* spare me any details."

No more crying in the dark, wondering when the pain will stop.

I have to remind myself that I have control this time.

"All that weight you've been carrying around? All that guilt? It's time to let it go."

I stroke his hair, rocking his head back so he's forced to look me directly in the eyes.

"I don't— I can't—"

I smile down at him, shaking my head.

"I don't care."

I start to trace around his eye socket with my knife, barely grazing the skin. I wonder if I could pluck one out and put it in a jar.

He coughs, his body trembling as he fights the truth that continues to bubble up from inside him like lava. I can practically *see* his pulse hammering against his throat.

"Why did you do it, to us, to your daughters?"

"I couldn't control myself!" He begins to sob, horrified to hear the words coming out of his own mouth. "I didn't *want* to hurt you, but I—"

"But you did. You took our childhood— No, you took *everything* from us."

"I can get help, I can get more—"

"You're beyond that now," Preacher growls from behind me. "'God will repay each person according to what they have done.' That's Romans 2:6, I'm sure you know it pretty well if you've *gotten right with The Lord*."

I cut the zip ties on his wrist as Preacher turns the music up.

We're so in sync, he knows exactly what's coming next.

That's love, baby.

I place the knife in my father's hand, glad to be listening to his pathetic sniffles for the final time.

"I want you to put this to your throat."

He shakes his head, stammering as he struggles to get out the words.

I lean forward.

"You want to make me happy, don't you?"

"Of course," he nods, his grip on the knife tightening.

"It's fine, papa. I'll help you."

He stares at me, a blend of confusion, sadness, and anger smoldering in his eyes, and for a second I think he might lash out in one more act of violent domination... but then he raises the knife to his throat, and I know it's over.

My jaw tingles as I see the tiniest little glimpse of blood.

My breathing picks up.

My heart like thunder.

"Now keep still."

He barely moves as I cut deeper, and I'm leaning in so close I can feel his wheezing against my cheek. He might have slipped the knife right into my own neck if the drug hadn't taken such a firm hold.

"You are *nothing*," I whisper. "You were ruthless, you were cruel, and no matter what you say, I know that you never loved us."

I take his hand fully into mine, and help him slit his own throat so deep that I swear I can see his larynx. A deluge of blood pours out from the gaping wound we created together, father and daughter, and then his head tips back with a final, pathetic gurgle.

Eyes empty.

I let the knife fall to the floor, watching the blood flow like a river as tears rush down my face.

"Well done, little rabbit." Preacher's hand slips into mine, squeezing gently as he beams down on me. "Now how do you feel?"

I finally feel like I've taken my life back, the one that little girl lost so many years ago. There's no more fear. No more doubt. This is always who I was meant to be.

"Free."

When I was dying in that parking lot, Preacher made me a promise, told me he'd drag me out of hell. The thing is, he already had.

"You set me free."

Acknowledgments

This book was a long journey that had many incarnations along the way. Four drafts later, I finally landed on the story that was meant to be told, and I have a lot of people to thank for that. So, here we go:

My Wattpad OGs who read this story in its very first iteration. While this is much, much different than what I originally wrote all those years ago, I hope you enjoy it and thank you for always being in my corner.

My initial alpha readers for helping me work out the kinks in the first few chapters. You helped inspire me to keep molding this story into something beautiful, and I'm so thankful for your feedback on those very early drafts.

My beta readers: Donna, Becs, Tiffani, Kolina (my wife, my ride or die, and the loml), Rebeca, Beth, Netty, Courtney, Lizzy, and Katerina for reading some of the darkest things I've ever put down on paper. Your comments kept me going when I thought I was going to crash out editing this book, and I cannot thank you enough for bringing this manuscript to life.

To my husband/editor, who is *never* surprised at the manuscripts that cross his desk and always helps me fine-tune and make these books the best that they can be. Editing with you is a dream. You make me laugh, you teach me about grammar rules I definitely didn't pay attention to in school because I was writing Lord of the Rings fan fiction, and you're the reason I become a better writer with each book. I love you so much, thank you for being my creative partner in crime.

My mom and dad for always encouraging me to be creative. I know you don't read these books, but you *always* ask how authoring is going and you're always so proud when I give you the stats. Thank you for teaching me to always reach for the stars.

My street team, I love you all so much. You're my safe place to fall when things get tough, you make me fucking howl during bad days, and you always encourage each other.

To Joey, my PA, thank you for keeping me organized, Queen.

Sebastian Stan. I watched Fresh a *lot* while I was writing this book. Thanks for being *ridiculously* hot (seriously, incredible work), and the inspiration for Preacher Blackthorne.

About Thea Lawrence

Thea Lawrence is a PhD dropout turned romance author. After spending almost a decade in academia studying criminology, she decided to shift gears for her mental health.

A lifelong storyteller, Thea has been an actor, burlesque dancer, and a screenwriter for small, independent short films. When she's not crunching numbers and yelling at mortgage brokers during her 9-5, she loves to read smut, thirst over Bucky Barnes and Carmen Berzatto, and get lost in the writing process.

Thea currently lives in Ontario with her partner. Please buy more of her books so that she can pay off her student loans.

IG & Threads: @thealawrenceauthor

TikTok: @thealawrenceauthor and @thealawrencebooks

Website: thealawrenceromanceauthor.com

Patreon: patreon.com/thealawrence

You can also sign up for Thea's monthly newsletter (signup is also available on her website!) featuring sneak peeks at future books, advanced links to pre-orders, deleted scenes from previously published works, life updates, author spotlights, and more.

Also by Thea Lawrence

BLACKTHORNE RANCH

Ravenous

Reapers (Book II - Forthcoming)

THE EMERALD BAY SERIES

Swipe Right (Book I)

Crushing It (Book II)

Smoke Show (Book III - Forthcoming)

Fool's Gold (Book IV - Forthcoming)

THE REVOLVER DUET

Babydoll (Book I)

Dollhouse (Book III)

BLOOD & BULLETS

Heathens

www.ingramcontent.com/pod-product-compliance
Lightning Source LLC
Chambersburg PA
CBHW030533190726
48283CB00006B/1887